Praise for Lynne Connolly's
A Chance to Dream

"Lynne Connolly has crafted a historical romance that just oozes passion and intrigue. ...The story has drama and passion and intrigue and so many of the flavors that make historical romances marvelous. This is truly a magical, must have novel."

~ *Kimberley Spinney, Cata-Romance*

"This book is a must read, any historical romance fan will love this story. ...Full of passion, intrigue, plot and counter plot. I loved this book. I highly recommend it and have no hesitation in giving this book 5 roses. A thoroughly excellent read."

~ *Mary, A Romance Review*

"A Chance to Dream is another winning book! Ms. Connolly is in her element with her historical romances. The characters are expressive and feel real thus it was a pleasure reading this book."

~ *Susan T, Fallen Angels Reviews.*

"Lynne Connolly writes an incredible love story between two people who can't possibly be together I loved the way Ms. Connolly was able to weave another fantastic story with the right amount of sex and intrigue. I can't wait for the third book."

~ *Julianne, Twolips Reviews*

"Lynne Connolly has deftly weaved the two love story together. Lynne's TRIPLE COUNTESS series is looking to be another historical keeper not to be missed."

~ *J.T., Romance Junkies Reviewer*

A Chance to Dream

Lynne Connolly

A Samhain Publishing, Ltd. publication.

Samhain Publishing, Ltd.
577 Mulberry Street, Suite 1520
Macon, GA 31201
www.samhainpublishing.com

A Chance to Dream
Copyright © 2008 by Lynne Connolly
Print ISBN: 978-1-59998-520-6
Digital ISBN: 1-59998-683-3

Editing by Angela James
Cover by Anne Cain

First Samhain Publishing, Ltd. electronic publication: November 2007
First Samhain Publishing, Ltd. print publication: September 2008

Dedication

To Chris and Elspeth, who help me with much laughter and friendship.

Chapter One

April, 1754

Orlando Garland, seventh Earl of Blyth took his time studying the woman sitting on the hard chair on the other side of his desk. It was one of the few times it was acceptable to stare at someone so blatantly and he made the most of it, leaning back in his own comfortably upholstered chair to get a better view. What was it about this woman? The moment she had walked into his study, he felt the hair on the back of his neck prickle. There was something—something, though he had no idea what it was.

He suspected subterfuge the moment he saw her. Such elegant deportment didn't usually go with the plump, dowdy figure this lady presented to the world. Her hair, screwed up tightly into a bun at the back of her head, was a mousy brown, but despite the heavy, tinted spectacles perched on her nose he could see that her eyes were beautiful, almost violet. Her slim wrists belied her stout figure and her neck showed no extra folds of flesh. She had deliberately disguised herself.

It might just be an effort to make herself less attractive. Comeliness was not a welcome attribute for companion governesses in most households. Orlando glanced at the paper in front of him, noting her relative youth and lack of experience. He looked up, meeting her gaze directly, looking for any other signs of deception. "Have you worked as a governess at all, ma'am?"

She looked away and then lifted her head once more, meeting his regard with a spark of defiance. He liked that spark. It might prove useful for the position he had in mind for her. "I am considered too young by most prospective employers.

That is the reason I thought to apply for a position as a companion instead. It is only recently I have found myself in the position of having to look for work." She swallowed, the only sign she had given so far of nervousness.

Orlando sought to reassure her, wondering at the same time why it should be important to him to put her at her ease. "Your age will not be a problem here. I need someone about the same age as my sister, to share in her interests. Did Mrs. Thompson explain the nature of the post?" Not wanting to take any chances, he had sent his enquiry to the best—and most expensive—agency in London. He wondered if Mrs. Thompson had asked her about the efforts to disguise her appearance, or whether the practice was too commonplace to be remarked upon.

She bowed her head once. One small gloved hand clenched in the folds of her unbecoming gown. "I was told you wanted a companion for your lady sister."

Orlando pulled his mind back to the matter in hand. "Indeed I do. If I may, I will remind you of the circumstances. I am sure Mrs. Thompson was discreet when she explained the situation to you, and you may not be aware of the full story. It is essential you know the whole before you begin." He felt a pang of the sense of failure he always had when thinking of Perdita, but he took care nothing showed on his cool countenance. Picking up a quill pen from his desk, he put it in its proper place, in the pottery jar with the others. They formed a feathery bouquet on one side of him, the only flowers he allowed in this room. The rest of the house was dedicated to feminine delicacy, but here, and in his own bedroom, masculinity was allowed to declare itself.

He kept his account brief and to the point, firmly locking his sadness deep inside. That was too private to show to someone he had only just met. "My sister, Lady Perdita Garland, had a riding accident last year. Sadly, she broke both legs. She has not walked since." He paused, but refused to allow himself to dwell on that dreadful day. There was nothing to be gained by remembering it now. "According to her physician Dr. Sewell, her legs have healed completely, but she needs rest and will always be weak and in need of medical attention. I fear she has lost the confidence she once had in abundance. By providing her with a companion, she might be encouraged to take her place in society again." He wondered how much to tell this young woman; she might not stay more than a week, if he decided to take her on. He decided on the truth. After all, there was nothing shameful about it, and most of it was known, at least by his family. "Perdita is a lovely woman, but she is seven and twenty and she feels she is past the age of looking for a husband. Until recently I could only offer a modest dowry, and Perdita is a fastidious woman. No one has come up to her exacting standards." He hid his deepest sadness with a deliberate lack of emotion, something he had become used to doing over the years. "Now she doesn't go out at all. I would like that to change."

Orlando stared across the table. Something underneath her disguise called to him, made him wonder. There was an underlying grace she couldn't hide, despite the careful concealment, something about the way she disposed her hands upon her lap. He felt sure she was a beauty, disguising her natural assets to obtain a position. From the detailed account Mrs. Thompson had sent him, she was a clergyman's daughter from the North. She had worked as a teacher, but the school was closed now, and she needed another situation. Her references, such as they were, were excellent. "Do you feel up to the task, Miss—ah—" He consulted the paper on his desk, although he didn't really need to. "Miss Lambert?"

She coloured up slightly, for no reason he could discern. "I would like to try, my lord."

He shuffled the papers on his desk, straightening them between his hands and putting them down. "You will be required to make an appearance in the highest circles, should my sister decide to re-enter society. I trust you know how to conduct yourself?"

"Yes indeed, my lord. I was born into a good family but we found ourselves in straitened circumstances shortly after I left school."

He frowned. "Lambert is a familiar name. Have we met before?"

"No, my lord, I'm sure of it. I would have remembered." That charming tinge of colour crept into her porcelain pale cheeks once more.

Orlando suspected hidden depths. It boded well. If he was

11

interested, it was to be hoped Perdita would be, too. From a lively young lady his sister had turned into a listless stranger in the last year. Engaging a companion was the last of a series of strategies Orlando had tried to get her back on her feet. Even if she never did that, he wanted to see her the centre of a group of admiring beaux again.

"Then, Miss Lambert, let us be frank. You are not the first young woman I've employed to try to encourage my sister to return to society. I need someone to take a strong line with her, to fight her if need be. I am convinced that is the only way. I have tried kindness, persuasion, even bribes, but she doesn't respond. If I employ you, I would require a degree of frankness from you. While I don't expect you to break any confidences, I would appreciate regular reports on my sister's progress. Since I do not particularly wish for anyone else to know, this would involve personal contact." He took a breath and watched her closely. It was impossible to read her expression, serenely regarding him from those remarkable eyes. "In case that should cause you any alarm I should inform you I consider it bad form for a man to take advantage of his own servants."

"In any circumstances?"

Her comeback was so sharp he grinned, forgetting his dignity in his pleasure at her impertinence. "I'm only human, ma'am, but I do my best. However, I never use underhand methods, and I always honour my obligations."

Miss Lambert appeared unperturbed, not changing her calm expression one whit. "I do not judge until I meet the person involved, my lord. My—family has been subject to gossip, and I know how much rumours can exaggerate a basic fact."

He wondered what she meant by that intriguing comment. Strangely, Orlando had no doubts about allowing this young woman, for all her false padding, near his sister. There was a bone deep integrity about her that he trusted. He had always succeeded when he had trusted his instincts, invariably failed when he ignored them. He trusted them now. "What would you say to a week's trial, to be terminated without prejudice on either side? If Perdita dislikes the stance you take on my instruction, I promise to give you a good character to take with you. Unless, of course, you've transgressed in some way."

"It seems fair, my lord."

"Very well then." He stood and shook the heavy skirts of his formal coat into place. It was an automatic gesture, but with her interested gaze on him he became aware of the movement as he'd rarely been before. The coat was an expensive one, bought new that season but wasn't particularly unusual. The dark red was positively staid compared to some of the coats that he used in the evenings. Perhaps it wasn't the coat, but Orlando himself she stared at so fixedly. He was not accustomed to such a frank appraisal by a woman. He moved towards her.

She came to with a start. "I beg your pardon, my lord, my mind was elsewhere. I could start almost immediately, but I have relatives in London, with whom I am staying. May I have permission to visit them to let them know what has happened? I would hate them to worry."

"Yes, of course." He walked around the desk and was interested to see that his proximity didn't seem to bother her. A sign of good breeding, not to shrink back when a man came close, though the other companions he had engaged had shown a particular preference to withdraw at his approach. "May I take you to meet my sister?" He lifted his arm in an invitation for her to lay her hand on it. She did so and immediately removed it, then put it back.

Orlando stood silent, absorbing the unexpected sensation. Had she felt the jolt that had gone through his body at the touch of her hand on his coated and shirted arm? That was impossible, surely. How could a mere touch have such an effect? He looked away, gently urging her forward, trying to forget the shock. This was a perfectly ordinary young woman, and what was more, she would be an employee.

He found the jolt impossible to forget. As they climbed the stairs to the drawing room, his mind lingered on the strange shock he'd experienced. She was a small woman and one he found himself attracted to, despite the heavy spectacles and mousy hair, but it couldn't be that, surely? It had been too long since he'd given his last mistress her congé. Perhaps it was time he looked for another. That must be the reason for his visceral response to her touch.

Perdita would be in the drawing room at this time of day,

although the only visitor she received was her friend Judith Wayland. Orlando sighed when he remembered the lively social life his sister had enjoyed a bare year ago. Men lined up to offer for her this time last year, and during her "at home" days the house had rarely been quiet. Now it was so peaceful Orlando missed all the activity. It was like a deserted mansion, except for the lack of dust. The silence was uncanny sometimes. He could go out for his amusements, but Perdita refused to leave the house, even to take the air. He was more worried than he cared to admit. If this didn't work, this firmer line, he had no idea what he would do next to help his sister.

He turned to escort Miss Lambert into the drawing room and caught her looking at him. He stared back. She looked away. This was so unlike the prim, proper lady he had thought her that it gave him pause, but not enough to prevent him rapping lightly on the door and then pushing it open. In a statelier house, there would be a footman stationed outside the door to perform this role, but since no guest was allowed entrance any more Perdita had deemed it a waste of money. Despite his recent affluence, Orlando had become accustomed to counting the pennies, and to Perdita it was second nature although she was fond of cavilling at the economies they had been forced to use in the past.

As Orlando had expected, Lady Judith Wayland was keeping his sister company that afternoon. It appeared he had interrupted a comfortable gossip, for he heard a flurry of silken skirts when he opened the door. Despite her seclusion, Perdita seemed to know what was going on in the fashionable world outside her window. Lady Judith regularly relayed all the information she came across, and the papers were delivered daily, even the more disreputable ones. Perdita read them all. They looked up from their conversation, silver-gilt head and darker, golden one moving in harmony. Two sets of finely plucked eyebrows arched in surprise.

He stood to one side of Miss Lambert, so she could make her curtsey. "This is Miss Lambert, Perdita. Thompson's sent her. I hope she may prove of some use to you. She has permission to visit her family tonight, but she will be living here while she is with us." He felt rather than saw Lady Judith's fulminating stare at the newcomer so was not surprised to see it when he turned. He smiled guilelessly. "My dearest wish is to

14

see you return to society, Perdita, but if you will not, you will doubtless need some company."

Perdita smiled vaguely at Miss Lambert and immediately looked away, towards Lady Judith. "You always think of my comfort, brother." The two ladies exchanged a speaking glance. "Won't you stay and have some tea with us?"

"I fear I cannot. I'm expected elsewhere." He turned and bowed to Miss Lambert. "Ladies, I will leave you to become acquainted."

Lord Blyth left the room in a flourish of heavy silk and sheer male presence. Violetta felt her senses relax; they had somehow been surrounding him while he had been present. Her heritage, she supposed. It came of having a mother like hers, a woman who needed an intimate knowledge of men for her livelihood. Violetta schooled her face to what she hoped was an expression of a humble desire to please. It wasn't easy. Lord Blyth may have advocated the strong approach, but she wanted to assess Lady Perdita first, to plan her campaign.

"Miss Lambert," Lady Perdita said. She tapped her pale pink lips with her fan. "What is your first name?"

"Charlotte," Violetta replied without blinking or looking away. It was a name she had always liked and one that suited her disguise well.

"Charlotte. Very well. Have you had much experience at this work, Charlotte?"

"Not a great deal, my lady."

"I see." There was a pause, which Violetta was aware Lady Perdita deliberately allowed to lengthen. Of all things, she disliked the way Lady Perdita and her friend stared at her. The gazes seemed to violate her, where the frank gaze of his lordship had not bothered her at all. Violetta waited.

"You may sit down, Charlotte, in the chair beside me. We will discuss your duties." The cold, flat voice came as a relief.

"Yes, my lady." Violetta took the chair indicated, a hard chair next to the comfortable sofa on which Lady Perdita sat. She kept her regard steadily on the young woman while Lady Perdita examined her.

"If I could stand I think I might overtop you by an inch or

so," Lady Perdita said, tapping her fan against her hand. "Your dark hair is an excellent foil to my looks. I would call your skin olive, don't you agree?"

Violetta humbly agreed although she'd heard her skin described as "creamy" before. She knew she was striking, and had ample evidence of her attraction to the opposite sex, but she had no vanity. Violetta knew exactly how she looked. Another gift bestowed by her mother; the ability to see herself frankly. The knowledge had enabled her to disguise herself into a dowdy female, a disguise she felt uncomfortably sure had not entirely fooled his lordship.

"Do you need the spectacles all the time, Charlotte?"

"In general, my lady." Violetta met her ladyship's pale stare steadily. She had become good at untruths over the years, a skill forced upon her by necessity. It didn't make her enjoy it, though.

Lady Perdita waved her fan in a dismissive gesture. "Keep them. I'd rather you saw what you were doing when you hand me my tea. Your figure is a trifle full, don't you think?"

Violetta inwardly rejoiced. She had laced her stays loosely and stuffed a shift down the front to pad it even more, succeeding in giving the illusion of plumpness on her normally trim figure. However, her new mistress bade fair to outshine her even without the padding, wig, spectacles and dowdy clothes.

Lady Perdita was ethereally lovely. Her unpowdered hair was the fairest of blondes, gleaming pale gilt in the spring sunlight. Her eyes were a heavenly blue, lighter than her brother's but the shade suited her porcelain-pale complexion. She would have suitors at her feet if she decided to re-enter society, whether she walked or not.

Under the voluminous skirts of the ice-blue gown Lady Perdita wore, it was impossible for Violetta to see what damage the accident had done to her ladyship's legs. Lady Perdita had fallen from a bolting horse last summer. The breaks had been clean and they mended, but her ladyship refused to leave her chair. It might be a failure of confidence, but looking at her ladyship Violetta did not think that was a quality Lady Perdita lacked. Everything about her said elegance and poise.

"My figure has never been remarkable," Violetta ventured. Not to her, anyway.

"Gentlemen are such swine. They will go after anyone wearing a skirt," Lady Judith put in. "I've remarked it often." Her supercilious air seemed to Violetta, used to summing up people quickly, bone deep. Violetta mentally scolded herself for prejudice.

"Most gentlemen," Lady Perdita agreed. "My brother, however, is more perceptive. He used not to be, but I have great hopes he is more discriminating in his choice these days. It is why you must be here for him to notice you, dear Judith!" She patted her friend's hand, and they exchanged a fond look. Violetta began to understand.

Violetta knew a great deal about Lady Perdita and her family, having an intimate acquaintance with a close family member, but thought it more discreet to pretend ignorance. She also knew of Lady Judith.

Lady Perdita raised an eyebrow. "Where were you before?"

"Yorkshire," Violetta answered and immediately wished she had said Cumbria, because it was further away from London. "Yes, my lady, I know something of your family's history, but I don't listen to gossip."

The two ladies exchanged a speaking glance. "You won't last long in London if you don't listen to gossip," Lady Judith commented, a tone of acidity in her voice. "I would advise you, however, not to take part."

Violetta did her best to look shocked. "Of course not, my lady!"

"How much do you know of us?" Lady Perdita demanded.

"I know your mother is known as the Triple Countess, and you and Lord Blyth are her children by her second husband, the late Earl of Blyth." Violetta carefully filtered her extensive knowledge of the family as she spoke, repeating nothing that was not general knowledge. "Your mother lives with her third husband, Lord Taversall, and their family."

Lady Perdita nodded. "Very good. Our elder brother, the Earl of Rosington, is the most fortunate, his father having left him with a tidy fortune and no siblings." Lady Perdita's pretty mouth turned down. "Our revered mama is prolific, and has always done her duty by her husbands. I do not find it an incentive to marry. She was married to her first husband, an old man, for the money, she ran off with Blyth and lived to regret it and now she's so happy it is quite a sight to see."

Lady Perdita's bitterness astounded Violetta. It would have made her happy to have a brother or sister to share with, but as an only child she'd only had her mother to rely on. It had made them closer, but Violetta always had a feeling of isolation and a yearning for someone of her own, someone special.

She knew better than to hope that could be Lady Perdita. She was an employee here, made clear to her by every movement of the other two ladies towards her, even to the hard chair she sat in. Besides, she was wary of letting too much slip.

"I will have the housekeeper show you about," her ladyship said. "It is important you know your way around, because I will require you to fetch and carry for me."

Violetta murmured a reply in the affirmative.

"When we have company, you will stand by my chair and take no part in the conversation. I will require you to be at least presentable, but no more. I wish you to be devoted to me." Violetta listened to the requirements and tried to think humbly, but the more Lady Perdita spoke, the more her arrogance irritated Violetta. "Now I wish you to leave," the lady continued. "You will have the room close to mine so you will be ready for my call. Listen." She picked up a bell from the side table and shook it. A pleasant but penetrating tinkle. "When I ring, I expect you to attend me immediately."

"Yes, my lady." Violetta stood and kept her hands folded neatly before her, head down.

The door opened to admit a footman.

"Have Miss Lambert shown to the bedroom that has been prepared for my companion. She has permission to visit her family this evening." Lady Perdita turned to address Violetta. "Be back first thing in the morning. I will expect you to be ready to take up your duties."

Violetta curtsied and left the room to the sound of a giggle from Lady Judith. She had no doubt her slightly eccentric appearance would cause discussion as soon as she had gone. She followed the footman to the end of the corridor and through a small door to the backstairs. "We've been told you are to stay with us, Miss—"

"Lambert," Violetta supplied.

"Lambert. If you want anything, just shout down the stairs. I hope you don't mind me taking you this way. I thought you might like to know about these stairs, because you're near the end of the corridor." They climbed a flight of narrow, wooden stairs and he opened a door. They were back in the main house, on the second floor. "This is where the family bedrooms are, ma'am. His lordship's suite is across the staircase and yours is next to her ladyship's. I hope it suits."

Moving to a door, the footman opened it for her. The room contained everything necessary to her comfort; a bed with a light canopy, a washstand and a tall clothes press. A single candlestick stood on the plain nightstand that presumably contained a necessary in its lower cupboard. No carpet or rug covered the polished floorboards, and the shutters at the windows were bare, with no drapery to soften them. "This was her ladyship's dressing room, ma'am, but she had the sitting room on this floor converted for her use instead."

It was obvious the furniture had been moved in recently, as some of the pieces didn't quite fit in the places allotted to them and fresh scrapes marked the bare, planked floor. It was all simple, country stuff, probably brought down from a servant's bedroom. She tried not to be disappointed. Companions were sometimes treated as equals, but obviously not in this household.

Her cloak had been brought up and thrown on the bed. No chance of more than casual help from a maid, Violetta guessed, so she must learn to fend for herself. Even at school, she'd had fellow pupils to help her with her stays in the mornings. Remembering the girlish companionship with a pang of nostalgia, Violetta picked up the cloak and put it on, finding her bonnet hung on a peg screwed to the back of the door. At least there was a mirror, even if it was a trifle spotted. It looked as though it had been a grand piece once, but was in an outdated style, the frame elaborately carved in a dark, dull wood.

Outside, Violetta went down the main staircase, elegantly curving into the neat hall and left the house by the front door. She would do that until instructed otherwise. She made her way across the square where she hailed a hackney cab. Time to go home, to her other disguise.

Chapter Two

"La Perla Perfetta!" Violetta heard the announcement, felt rather than heard the anticipation in the room, the rustling of heavy silk, the low murmur. Putting her hand to her elaborate silk mask, she made sure it was firmly fixed in place. It had become a habit for gentlemen to try to remove it, but her mother forbade it. Flicking her fan open in a flurry of feathers and spangles, she put up her chin and entered the drawing room.

The murmurs rose appreciatively and she let them look. Used to the reaction she could arouse, she allowed herself to smile, but only a little. She knew she was a man of fashion's dream. Dressed in her customary pure white, her mask covering the top half of her face, her shining black hair drawn back into a simple style, she let them look.

The glitter of spangles, precious gems and candlelight reflected off the room's numerous gilded pier-glasses and demonstrated the success her mother, La Perla, had found amongst English society. The French gilded chairs and costly Aubusson carpet bore mute witness to her personal wealth.

Uncle Lucius—Lord Ripley—came forward to lead Violetta to her mother. La Perla sat in state, in the chair she preferred, set between the two large windows of the salon on the first floor. Only the highest, the most expensive courtesans were allowed into this room, and Violetta in her guise as La Perla Perfetta was one of them. Except that La Perla Perfetta was a virgin, and likely to remain so, if her mother had any say in the matter.

La Perla was magnificent in cobalt blue, her hair, still black with a very little help of walnut juice, her face carefully made up but in no way the white mask some society ladies preferred. La

Perla at fifty, was still lovely. She acknowledged her daughter's low bow with a gracious smile, motioning her to rise.

Violetta stood next to her mother's chair, watching the company. As usual, the cream of society had attended her mother's public salon. The only segment significantly absent was the ladies. Occasionally, with careful connivance, a respectable woman made a heavily disguised appearance here, but only in the rarest circumstances. The gowns were as expensive and brilliant as those worn in the Duchess of Queensberry's drawing room, the conversation as scintillating, for La Perla was the queen of the demi-monde, the ruling monarch of her world. And Violetta was her daughter, and her heiress.

Once Violetta had found it thrilling to appear so, especially after her sojourn in a stuffy finishing school in France. Now it was almost routine.

Lord Ripley, standing on the other side of La Perla's chair, cast Violetta a frowning glance. He knew then. La Perla must have told him. Violetta loved him as a father, but she dreaded his knowing what she had done. Perhaps her mother had done her a favour by telling him. At least she would not have to tell him herself.

She turned at a familiar voice. "La Perla Perfetta, you are such a welcome sight!" A man she knew well, dressed elaborately in dark purple with red trimmings. Wealthy, privileged, he took her hand and pressed a fervent kiss to her palm. A wet kiss Violetta longed to wipe off. "When will you relent and allow me to take care of you?"

The meaning was not equivocal. "I am still considering your generous offer, Lord Quenby." Violetta allowed her native tongue to suffuse her voice, lending it a heavy Italian accent. It was one more layer in her disguise.

"My daughter is a prize. She does not bestow her favours lightly, my lord," La Perla added, in an accent on which her daughter had modelled her own, but hers was natural. "You must be patient. She will make her decision soon. It is not your person, or yet your fortune that makes her hesitate, but her standards are of the highest. You must prove worthy of her."

This was the game they played, keeping the gentlemen coming and constantly attendant. Violetta had not yet taken one, though she was discreet about her refusal, unless the man in question proved importunate or ignorant, assuming she was his for the taking. She was not. However, Lord Quenby had shown admirable restraint and had never behaved in a less than gentlemanly manner to her. Some of the women in this room wielded a great deal of power and influence. Perhaps more so than their respectable equivalents, since they held their own fortunes, ran their lives as they saw fit, unlike a wife, who, when all was said and done, was wholly owned by her husband. It was generally assumed La Perla Perfetta would be one of the most important when she chose to take her place.

Violetta had tired of the game long ago, although it was impossible to allow it to drop. Soon she would leave it all behind. The sooner the better, she decided, except for one aspect. She would not be able to see her mother as much as she would like, and it would always have to be in secret.

She studied the elegant, attentive male by her side and wondered. Did she really want it, the respectability denied her as the daughter of the best courtesan in London, or was it a dream, something she would not want at all? It was the reason for the mask, a precaution she had accepted at first, but now sometimes regretted. She was not ashamed, she thought fiercely. She was proud of what her mother had wrought. All by herself, refusing to allow anyone, even Lord Ripley, to help her.

Violetta knew she could do worse than Quenby. He would initiate her into the world of intimacy with respect and consideration, she was sure. La Perla always left the decision up to her but so far, no man had appealed to her. Lord Quenby was kind, and Violetta was tiring of playing a part, always hiding behind a mask of one kind or another. If it had not been for her Aunt Virginia's concerns about Lady Perdita, she would never have considered another disguise. Or so she told herself, but when she thought of appearing in public as herself, terror gripped her in its paralyzing vice. She had never appeared in public as Violetta Palagio, except for one brief visit to her family in Italy after her father's death. She didn't know if she could sustain the illusion of being herself any more.

So she smiled at Lord Quenby, allowed him to monopolize her company, feed her titbits from the supper table, even, at the end of the evening, to steal a chaste, closed-mouth kiss. Perhaps it was time to give up her foolish dreams and become what her mother had been. Perhaps.

Having seen Quenby off the premises, Violetta lifted her skirts and climbed the marble stairs to the drawing room, empty now except for her mother, Lord Ripley and the servants, busy clearing away the results of the evening's revels. Very few gentlemen left alone, but they had all left. Even in the days of her active career, La Perla had rarely allowed guests to stay in this house. That way lay imprisonment and disgrace, the label of a house of ill repute, the life of a common prostitute. La Perla had never been a common prostitute.

By common consent, they moved to a smaller salon, one they had not used that night. La Perla leaned back in the comfortable sofa with a weary sigh and held out her hand. Lord Ripley immediately took it and sat next to her. Violetta, used to such sights, was not perturbed, but warmed by the sign of affection between her mother and the man she had always loved.

While not in the first flush of youth, or even the second, La Perla was still a lovely woman. Dressed simply but with a style that proclaimed a lifetime dedicated to the art of self-presentation, La Perla never used a clumsy move, never appeared in slovenly dress. The beauty that had captured a generation was still blazingly real. "My dear, tell us all about the experience. Has it changed your mind? Will you come home?" Her voice still held its Italian lilt, unlike Violetta's which had disappeared with the last guest.

Violetta ignored her mother's question for a moment. "I'm glad you're back, Uncle Lucius."

"Yes indeed, my dear, back from my duty visit. I brought my daughter to Town, but she knows better than to expect me to be at home too often." His deep voice rumbled, happily familiar.

"He will make his home here," La Perla said firmly.

"I always have." He turned back to his mistress. Their affection was immediately obvious; the intimate smile they exchanged expressed it all. The affair between the Marquess of Ripley and La Perla had always been a love affair. Looking at him again, the dark eyes and friendly, handsome smile, Violetta wondered for the umpteenth time if Ripley was her real father, but they never spoke of it, and her mother had never told her.

She was almost convinced of it now, but instead of the shame she should have felt, she felt only pleasure that this man, not the violent man her mother had been married to, had given her life.

Now he turned back to Violetta, seated in a deeply upholstered armchair opposite the sofa. "Tell us all about your day, my dear. Did you succeed in your plan? Please tell me you did not!"

Violetta smiled. The marquess had aged, true, but he still stood tall and strong. He was dressed formally, in full-dress coat and wig, but Violetta knew that under the fashionably queued, white-powdered confection, his short, dark hair was only grizzled at the temples and showed no sign of a receding hairline.

"I succeeded magnificently," Violetta announced. "I have the position of companion to Lady Perdita Garland."

"Oh, Violetta, how clever!" La Perla was charmed.

Violetta beamed. "I want to help the family all I can."

"I know that. It is a clever disguise, *cara*, the Charlotte Lambert one, but don't you think they will recognize you?"

"They won't." Violetta lifted her hands to her mask, pulling out the pins that secured it to her hair and loosening the strings. She removed it and dropped it on the small table beside her.

"So many disguises!" Lord Ripley murmured. "Your mama says you have a wig and spectacles in this part."

The wig was necessary. Violetta's hair was almost a trademark, as unlike the tresses of most English maidens as could be. The blue-black shade proclaimed her Mediterranean origins as clearly as if she had spoken Italian all the time. "The wig is excellent. You have some very clever people in your employ, Mama."

"I have drawn the best to me. I never fail to pay them their worth." It was a simple fact. La Perla reached a white hand to the coffeepot reposing on a table by her side and poured three strong black cupfuls, but added a quantity of cream and sugar to one of them. This she passed to the marquess, who took it with a smile. "I have need of good people to help me." The marquess touched her hand with his own, briefly, a gesture speaking of years of sympathy and comfort.

Violetta couldn't imagine how her mother's lover had coped with the men who had come into the house and left it again over the years. She never asked, and Ripley never volunteered the information, remaining always urbane and accepting of La Perla's necessary profession. It must have been hard for him to bear, though.

After escaping the clutches of a man who'd nearly killed her, La Perla had been determined not to allow any man control over her ever again. Violetta's memories of her life in Italy were vague, but the few, terrifying flashes never left her. It must have been so much worse for La Perla, who had, for the sake of her child and her family, withstood the abuse for seven years before leaving. Violetta knew why she had left, and deliberately blocked the scene from her mind most of the time. She did it again now.

Ripley was a constant in their lives, doing everything he could to dissuade La Perla from her choice of profession. He failed, but remained, watching and waiting for her, knowing she needed him. Violetta knew he had never been so happy as in the past five years, when La Perla closed her bedroom door to everyone except him. They were for all the world like a happily married couple. Except they had never been married to each other, and never would be.

She took a sip of the rich, dark brew. "You're right, Mama, Lady Perdita needs help. She is old for a single lady, but her brother is eager for her to take her place in society now he can suitably dower her. Aunt Virginia may not like it, but I'm there now, and I'll give her daughter all the help I can."

The marquess sat up a little straighter, his brow creased in a frown. "You've met Judith, haven't you?"

Violetta grinned. "Yes, I met your daughter, sir. She didn't recognize me." His daughter, so perhaps Violetta's half-sister. What a tangle!

"I can't approve of this." There was no sign of amusement on the marquess's face. "You are mad, girl! Did you help her, Donata?"

"Naturally. I did not wish it at first, but you would not know her, my dear, as Miss Lambert. Violetta sincerely wishes to help her godmother's daughter." La Perla frowned faintly, which was a serious expression for her. She tried to keep her face perfectly smooth at all times in the general way of things, a strong believer in the theory that using too much facial expression was eventually aging. It was not vanity that had inculcated these actions, as it might have been in a society matron. It was the deep vein of practicality that ran through La Perla as a streak of gold through rock. In her profession it was necessary to retain one's looks as long as possible. "I told Violetta about Lady Perdita, and I think her way of helping is ingenious. Virginia will not be pleased, though. I know Lord Blyth's reputation but he is above all things always in control of his emotions. A cold man, I do not believe Violetta stands in any danger in his household. Violetta is her own mistress, Lucius. She wishes to do this for Virginia, and we should not deter her." Violetta smiled gratefully at her mother, who flashed a grin back.

Lord Ripley glowered at her. "I don't know Blyth well, although I'll certainly do my best to remedy that. I know Judith has hopes in that direction."

"He seems very cold," Violetta ventured. "He's handsome enough, but there's no humanity there."

"There is. It's hidden deep. He wouldn't take money from his stepfather, all that he's achieved he's done himself. It must have taken a great deal of discipline and control. He refused to be sent abroad on the Grand Tour when his stepfather offered. He succeeded in restoring his family's fortunes, but at great personal cost. Perhaps it is he who needs the help, though I wouldn't suggest it." The marquess smiled at Violetta, a particularly warm, avuncular smile. "Violetta, my sweet, I knew you when you stood no higher than my knee. I've watched you turn into a lovely, poised young woman. I know I won't be able to dissuade you, but I have to ask you to think again. You have your own future to think of, one that is much brighter than we considered it three years ago." Two years ago, Violetta's father died in Italy. The disguises were no longer necessary, but it had been too late for La Perla, whose face, if not her real name, was known by the highest in English society. Violetta, however, had another chance at respectability.

"No, sir, I do not think this will affect my future. I want to help Aunt Virginia."

Ripley sighed. "You don't have to help her this way."

Violetta set her mouth into a stubborn line. "I have the choice, and this is what I want. Aunt Virginia has stayed with Mama, through all our times, good and bad. I would like to repay her somehow, and I know she is terribly worried about her daughter. Now I know why. I think Perdita Garland has been surrounded by people who have allowed her to have her own way for too long. She needs someone not afraid of her, someone to challenge her."

Her mother's expression cleared. "Very likely, my dear. Perhaps you have the right of it. Perhaps." She shook a warning finger at her daughter, when Violetta smiled in relief. "Though I shall keep you to your promise. If anyone sees even the slightest resemblance between you and La Perla Perfetta you will leave that house and come home."

Ripley handed his cup to La Perla to be refilled. "I wondered when you would meet my daughter. I hadn't planned for it to be like this. I am afraid they will recognize you, once you enter society as yourself. Your dreams will be at an end."

"People see what they want to see." She paused, not knowing what to say about Lady Judith, whose dislike of her had been palpable. "Your daughter seems charming, sir."

Lord Ripley grimaced. "Too high in the instep, just like her mother. She'll treat you like nothing." He paused, frowning.

Violetta knew there was something else, something he wasn't telling her. "What is it, Uncle Lucius?" Was he about to tell her, once and for all that Lady Judith was her sister and therefore she was his? She held her breath

"She can be more perceptive than you think. Be careful."

Violetta let her breath out in one long sigh. "They only saw a dowdy woman in thick spectacles. It was Mama who taught me people notice one distinctive thing about a person so I decided on thick spectacles."

"You could hardly have chosen a more unbecoming pair," her mother commented. "It will doubtless be what people remember about Miss Lambert. It is so sad, that no one will see my beautiful daughter as she should be!" Her voice held a yearning sadness, which moved Violetta as little else could.

"Mama, they will. When I enter society properly they will."

The marquess gave her an apologetic grin. "I would support you, but ten to one people will think it wrong."

Violetta shook her head at the marquess. "You have to keep your distance, or you will make them suspicious."

He shrugged. "It would be pleasant to look after someone. My wife and daughter have made it clear they don't wish my interference. I tried, but a man can only be turned away so many times before he refuses to come back. When the children were small I worked hard to be the father they needed, but my wife opposed me at every turn. Long before I renewed my friendship with your mother, she made my life untenable. Now, at least I have some happiness, thanks to Donata." He reached out once more and touched her hand. She smiled back. They could be an old married couple, Violetta thought fondly, except for a few details. Like his marriage and her career.

It passed Violetta's understanding, the level of the devotion between London's most notorious courtesan and one of its wealthiest peers. It was an open secret, that these days La Perla was exclusively for Lord Ripley. Hardly anyone asked her any more.

La Perla was at the top end of the market, but a whore was a whore and Violetta had long decided that life was not for her. Now, thanks to her mother's careful investments and her father's death, there was enough money for her to do as she wanted, and a family to support her. She hadn't done anything about it, except for a visit to her family in Italy, but she couldn't put her decision off for much longer. She could enter society as a respectable woman. No one would turn away from her in the street, no one would avoid her gaze at the opera, and no one would ever size her up as goods to be bought and sold. No one. Not even a cold, handsome man who regarded her without desire.

Violetta wrenched her thoughts away from Lord Blyth. The likelihood was that she would see him rarely in the weeks to come. "The earl's sister needs some encouragement to re-enter society. After her riding accident last year she has refused to see anyone except Lady Judith."

"I used to see a lot of Lady Perdita, before her accident," Lord Ripley put in. "Now Judith goes to her, rather than the other way about."

"She's very proud." Violetta didn't want to upset the marquess by talking out of turn. She hardly knew Lady Perdita at all.

"That might be an effort to distance herself from others. Does she seem well?"

"Aunt Virginia told me her doctor says she is fully healed, but she isn't walking." Briefly, Violetta let her mind dwell on the pain Lady Perdita must have endured. It was all very well for her brother and doctor to accuse her of malingering, but there was more than physical healing to be overcome.

"Judith says she is low," Ripley said.

"I will help her for now, and if it becomes too difficult, or I am in any danger of being recognized, I will return to you."

La Perla sighed heavily, the sigh of every long-suffering mother. "I will ask Virginia to visit, so she may accustom herself to your appearance there."

Violetta looked up and grinned girlishly. "I haven't told Aunt Virginia that I've actually gone ahead with it."

"You two are a fine pair!" The marquess stood. Violetta watched him cross the room to where the brandy decanter waited on a side table. He poured himself a glassful and drank it in one gulp before glaring balefully at Violetta and returning to the sofa, flicking his heavy coat skirts up carelessly before he sat down again. "This is foolish. You should stop this immediately, Violetta!"

Violetta smiled. "There may be a devil in us, Lord Ripley, but we are more alive than most of the women you know."

She wrenched a reluctant answer from him. "That must be why I've stayed with your mother for so long. I never know what she'll do next. Without me, she could find herself in a mess."

La Perla leaned across to lay her hand over his, tightly fisted on his knee. "You have cared for me well, *mon amour.*" It was hard to express emotion as frankly as she did, Violetta knew. It was one of her mother's breathtaking braveries in a life full of courage.

"I will take care," Violetta promised. "If you tell Aunt Virginia, that will be one less worry, Mama, but—" she paused, the mischievous grin back once more, "—I would dearly love to see how long it takes her to recognize me!"

The marquess groaned when La Perla clapped her hands together. "Then I shall not tell her! Let it serve her right for her shabby treatment of me at the opera the other night. She would not risk meeting with me in one of the trysting rooms. I shall make her pay!" The crow of laughter robbed her words of any maliciousness.

"This," the marquess declared with great decision, "is pure madness."

Chapter Three

"Miss Lambert."

Violetta lifted her head when she heard his voice. In the last three days, Lord Blyth had not been at home often, especially in the middle of the day. She found her marker and folded her book closed around it as he came into the room. "I'm sorry, I have startled you."

"Not at all, my lord." She got to her feet, but he waved her back down again.

"I wondered if we could have the first of our little talks." When she nodded, face as composed as she could make it, he sat down in the deep upholstered chair opposite her that matched her own. "How is my sister?"

Violetta bit her lip. "She is low in spirit, but I have found no way to get close to her yet. I have not suggested an outing. I'm sure she would reject it out of hand." She had not begun on her campaign, deeming it more advisable to study the lay of the land first.

He nodded. "Very wise. You don't want to build up her resistance to the suggestion. You know I have several carriages and they are all available for her use whenever she wishes it. Do you drive?"

Violetta bowed her head, avoiding the eyes that seemed to see right through her disguise. "I have learned, my lord, though my skill is not great. I have never driven in the town, only in the country, and never a fashionable vehicle."

"A country gig?"

"Something like that." Remembering the golden sunlight over her Uncle Lodovico's vineyards in Italy and the delightful

31

vehicle he'd put at her disposal, she lifted her head and dared to meet his cool gaze.

He regarded her with a thoughtful gleam in his eyes. "I may teach you. Would you like that?"

Her heart leapt, but she controlled the foolish feeling. "If it would help Lady Perdita, yes, my lord, I would."

"Would you do something for me?"

She was instantly on her guard. She had heard that kind of remark in her mother's house. Innocuous it was not. "If it is within my power, my lord."

"In private, will you call me sir, or even Blyth? All this 'my lord' wearies me. I have never stood on ceremony."

Violetta could not be sure but she thought she detected a gleam about him, something that was for her alone. She was imagining things. "I would be honoured, sir."

"I'll take you up one afternoon when Perdita has her rest. She never learned to drive properly, although she rides—rode— as though she was born on a horse. I would like to see if you have the skill to drive around town." A small smile touched one corner of his mouth. "It is a notion I had. If she sees you driving, she may wish to do so herself. Perdita has too little fresh air. She doesn't need to walk to be able to drive."

Violetta returned his smile, at once relaxed, now they were talking of his sister. "It is a good notion, sir. If she drives, she might meet an acquaintance."

His face was now entirely solemn. "It is, I think, what she fears, but in a fashionable phaeton, such as the one I sometimes drive, she would show to advantage. She has no need to get down, especially when in charge of a pair. I have two pairs presently in the stables. A spirited pair that I mostly use and a quieter pair for the days when I merely wish to drive somewhere. Perhaps, in time, we may persuade her to ride. Dr. Sewell has not mentioned it, but I think exercise will do Perdita good."

"I have thought so myself, my lord." Violetta folded her hands in her lap. "Dr. Sewell has not visited yet, but I understand he is to pay us a visit soon."

"Good. You should meet him." He stood as if to leave the room, but turned back on a thought. "We have extra guests for dinner tonight, one Perdita will be glad to see. My mother is coming, with her husband and my younger brother, Corin, Viscount Elston. He's heir to my stepfather, Lord Taversall."

"Then you would rather I ate from a tray in my room." Violetta prayed he would not want her presence.

He frowned. "Not at all. I wish you to be there."

Violetta swallowed. At last, she would get to test her disguise! She had been here three days and only seen Lady Perdita and Lady Judith every day. Why she enjoyed such mad challenges was a mystery to her, but she hoped her mother had not told Lady Taversall the secret. She knew Lady Taversall well enough to be sure the lady could keep her wits about her, but even if she did not, she would never admit the truth to her family.

Dressing for dinner later that afternoon Violetta knew an insane desire to make herself more attractive. The maid sent to help her dress was only allowed to assist her with lacing her outer garments. Violetta had recently learned the knack of lacing her own corset, so no one would guess her increased bulk was because of carefully positioned padding rather than her own gifts, and that her hair was not her own. She dusted powder over the dowdy wig, but allowed the soft golden brown colour to show through a little, in the tradition of a bluestocking who did not care about her appearance, which was the image she was trying to create.

There must be something of her mother in her as well as the deep violet eyes and the shining blue-black hair. A devilment, a desire to play a part and take others with her. Not as an actress would, but a real deception. It gave her a power over others, a delicious teasing contact that thrilled her while it appalled her sense of morals. Nevertheless, she was trying to do good here, so surely she could not be blamed for having a little fun.

The gown she wore was a sickly green colour with a plain green petticoat under it. The only decoration was some light embroidery on the robings at the front. It was hideous.

Violetta regarded her reflection in the mirror critically. This masquerade gave her a different satisfaction. A need to be someone else, to learn what others' experiences were like. She

33

wanted to be more than one person, hold more than one set of values and needs. She had spent her younger years in disguise, under a variety of names, in an effort to elude her father's searches, rarely in the same house as her mother until she had called a halt, after finishing school in France. Whatever would come, would come and they would face it together.

Only waiting until the maid had ensured her gown's lacing was secure, Violetta gave her a vague smile and drifted out of the room to Lady Perdita's. She entered on a scene deeply unlike the one in her room and recognized an undercurrent of panic. "Charlotte, come in. Do you think I will do?"

"Indeed, ma'am, you'll do very well." Seated before her dressing table, Lady Perdita made an ethereal picture in palest blue gauze overlaying a gown of heavenly blue and a heavily embroidered petticoat. Her skirts floated around her, completely concealing the useless legs. "You would captivate anyone."

Lady Perdita grimaced. "Unfortunately I won't need to do that. However, I appreciate the comment. Come here." Violetta obediently crossed the room to stand before her mistress. Her feet sank into the soft, rich carpet. "Why do you insist on playing down what good features you have?"

Violetta met her gaze frankly. "I have no good features."

"Your skin is good. Your eyes are lovely." This was the first time Lady Perdita had said anything complementary to Violetta. "That gown does you no favours. I have an appointment with the mantua-maker soon. You must order a gown or two."

Violetta bit back the response "Not on my salary," and remembered her dressing room at home, full of the gowns she had brought back from her recent prolonged stay in Italy with her father's family. After her father's death, she had gone to Italy, invited by the Palagios. She returned with a new resolve and trunks full of the latest styles from France and Italy. Buying Miss Lambert's dowdy gowns had proved an amusing exercise, but not one she cared to repeat. However, she agreed with Lady Perdita, bowing her head submissively, inwardly determined not to add to Miss Lambert's wardrobe.

"That will do." Lady Perdita flicked her hand in an irritated gesture and at once, her maid stepped back. "Fetch Perkins. I want to be sitting in the drawing room before they arrive."

Perkins, the footman assigned for Lady Perdita's personal

requirements, and another footman, were waiting outside, and came in the room immediately. They carried in an item that, from the glare Lady Perdita gave to it, could have been an instrument of torture, but was in fact an ordinary chair with two sturdy handles fixed to the outside.

Perkins carried her ladyship to the chair and seated her in it, and then the maid bunched the voluminous skirts so the men could get to the handles. Violetta watched Lady Perdita's mouth tighten and thin lines form around it, the only sign of her dislike or perhaps it was nervousness of the ordeal to come.

They formed a little procession, and followed the men outside and down the stairs. Lady Perdita didn't make a sound and her body sat rigidly upright in the chair. It was not something Violetta would have cared to try for herself, even if they did tilt the chair back a little when they descended the staircase.

They were the first to arrive in the drawing room. Violetta waited until they had settled her in a chair and left before she said anything. "It seems terribly uncomfortable." She watched Lady Perdita closely.

Lady Perdita busied herself with her fan, flicking it out and back. "I am always afraid they will tip me down the stairs."

"Perhaps it would be better if you made an effort to walk."

"Don't be foolish, girl! I doubt I'll ever walk again!"

"There is no reason why you should not."

"No?" With a sudden, shocking gesture, Lady Perdita lifted her skirts to just above her knees. Violetta stared.

Her silk stockings fastened just above her knees with pretty blue garters, but they didn't hide the legs beneath. They were thin to emaciation. The calf muscles looked wasted, the thighs flabby. Both legs were marked with ugly scars, legacies of the accident. This was what Lady Perdita dreaded, what she faced every morning.

"Looked your fill?" Lady Perdita's voice came sharp and shrill.

"No." Forgetting her veil of humility, Violetta went down on her knees in front of Lady Perdita and took one leg in her hands. She felt the muscle, wasted from months of disuse, and the firm bone beneath. Lady Perdita twitched the leg away. So she did have some movement, then. "You need to exercise." It looked to Violetta that once the muscles had been built up again Lady Perdita would be able to walk as well as anyone.

"And how am I to do that without walking? Don't talk nonsense!"

Violetta heard hope in the condemnation. "There are ways. We can stimulate the muscle. Here." She put her hand on the bottom of the foot. The shoes were unmarked underneath, as fresh as the day they were delivered from the cobbler's. "Push against my hand."

Lady Perdita gave a long-suffering sigh, but then Violetta felt it. A definite push, pressure against her hand. A surge of triumph welled inside her. "You wouldn't be able to do that if you were paralyzed. We can do this, I know we can." She dropped the foot and watched Lady Perdita place it carefully on the floor next to its mate. "You can control your feet. You can feel through them, you can push. How brave are you?"

"That is not your place to say, or to ask!" Lady Perdita looked astonished at the effrontery.

"Maybe not, but what have you to lose? We can exercise, we can try to improve the muscles until you're ready to stand." Violetta felt excitement surge within her. She could do this, she could help her ladyship to stand. However, she understood better than she had the previous week the pride the lady used to push people away, to stop the pity. She sat back on her heels. "If you agree, we can exercise every day. There's no need to tell anyone, even Lady Judith if you don't wish it. That way, if we fail no one else will know." She knelt on the floor and rearranged Lady Perdita's skirts. While she smoothed the shining satin and gauze, she continued, in an unthreatening tone she did her best to make soothing. "What harm is there in it? We can try."

"I can't." The whisper was low, hardly there at all.

"Why not? You aren't afraid, surely." Violetta smoothed the last wrinkle and got to her feet. "Lady Perdita, I'm sure it can be done, but if I'm wrong, we'll keep it between ourselves. Just some exercises."

She waited. She knew the power of not being the one to break an uncomfortable silence. Lady Perdita worried her lower lip between her teeth, staring up at Violetta. "Very well."

Violetta would have cried her triumph to the stars, had she been able to.

There was no time for more. The door opened to admit Lord Blyth and the three members of his family invited for dinner. Violetta hastily hurried behind Lady Perdita's chair. Her heart seemed to increase in intensity and a nervousness she had not felt since first stepping into this house threatened to overwhelm her. She was sure she had been mad to take this post, and mad to meet Lady Taversall without allowing her mother to warn her old friend first, but it was done now.

"Mama," Lady Perdita murmured.

Lady Taversall swept forward in a flurry of scented skirts. "My dear girl!" She bent and embraced her daughter, then frowned. "Still not walking, I see. Why is this? I had thought to see you at the Devonshire ball last week!"

Lord Blyth came to his sister's defence. "Dr. Sewell says rest is the best thing and she will walk when she is ready."

Violetta wondered at that advice. From what she had seen, it didn't take a genius to deduce that the muscles needed building up again. Perhaps it was a matter of poor advice. She would be sure to be there when the good doctor made his next visit on the morrow.

It seemed Lady Taversall thought the same thing for she turned back to her son with a frown marring her smooth forehead. "Nonsense!" She stood up and faced Violetta, who stood mutely behind Lady Perdita's chair. Violetta saw the words leave her. She stood, her mouth slightly agape, staring. It hadn't taken her long at all.

"Mama, this is the lady I have engaged to provide Perdita with some companionship while she is recovering." Lord Blyth came forward smoothly. The pause passed unnoticed by everyone but Violetta and Lady Taversall. Violetta, ready for the confrontation, stood still and blank faced. Only Perdita saw anything of Lady Taversall's expression. Before she remembered where she was and corrected it, it was frank astonishment.

Perdita stared, Violetta kept her face clear of expression. "Why, Mama, can it be that you know Miss Lambert?"

Lady Taversall blinked once, and looked down at her daughter. "No," she said evenly. "I merely thought she reminded me of someone I once knew. You're not related to the Palagios are you, Miss Lambert?"

A direct challenge. Violetta had to lie or reveal her secret. She felt the grim amusement, although she did not reveal it. "I have no idea, Lady Taversall. I have no influential relatives, or I would have prevailed on them to give me a season."

Lady Taversall gave her an infinitesimally small lift of one eyebrow in acknowledgement. "I see. Well, it seems you will have your season, Miss—er Lambert. One way or another."

"I can hardly wait."

This earned Violetta a sharp, suspicious look from Lord Blyth. With another quirk of an eyebrow Lady Taversall turned away and allowed the introductions to be made. Violetta was introduced to Lord Taversall, a tall, distinguished man, and his and Lady Taversall's son, Lord Elston, a natural charmer, from the way he bowed over her hand and let the contact last a fraction longer than was absolutely necessary.

During dinner she caught a few piercing glances from Lord Blyth's bright blue eyes, but she pretended not to notice. She could only hope he would forget any suspicions he might have about her, but she was beginning to know him a little better. She doubted he would forget.

Lady Taversall and Violetta studiously ignored each other through dinner, except to exchange the occasional polite comment. They behaved as strangers should until it was time for the ladies to leave the dining room for the drawing room. The hostess, Lady Perdita, motioning a footman to her and requesting the presence of her personal attendant, accomplished this. When he arrived, he lifted her and the gentlemen stood, just as though Lady Perdita had used her own limbs. The ladies followed the men out of the room, but as she would have turned and followed, Violetta felt a tug on her sleeve. She had expected it. Without a word she turned and followed Lady Taversall to one of the smaller family rooms on the first floor.

Lord Blyth's study was warmed by a small fire on this still chilly March evening. The fires lit the mahogany furniture to warmth. They did not need any extra light. Lady Taversall turned to Violetta, her face grim. "What are you doing here?"

Violetta didn't pretend to misunderstand. "Following my

dream, Aunt Virginia."

"Explain."

Violetta regarded her mother's dearest friend. Would this be a step too far? Now she had stepped into her world would Lady Taversall deny her and her mother? If that was so, Violetta thought with a slash of anger, she wasn't a friend worth having. "I know how worried you are about your daughter. There is time, before I make my debut, to help. And it gives me an opportunity to observe, before I must take part."

"You're mad, child! If anyone recognizes you, I cannot do anything for you!"

Violetta turned away and stared into the fire before lifting her head and staring at Lady Taversall with a defiant lift to her chin. "My mother is the bravest person I know. She has faced years of ignominy with the courage of a saint facing the stake. She gave up respectability. She is as well-born as you, Lady Taversall, she has as much right as you to happiness, but she can never go back. I can, but I mean to do this first."

"You think I don't know that?" Lady Taversall looked surprised more than anything else. "Your mother and I understand life isn't fair. We take what we have and make the most of it. It's all any of us can do. I don't deny your right to take what should be yours. What I am wondering is what you're doing here, why you've decided to take the risk. Be quick, girl, we'll be missed if we stay here much longer. Taversall already suspects the worst."

"Does he know you come to see us?"

Lady Taversall smiled. "Yes, he does, but he's never seen you or your mother, except at a distance. He knows her story, and yours. He's a wise man, Violetta, wiser than my other two husbands, and infinitely more dear. If it had not been for Daniel and then Orlando, I might have followed in your mother's footsteps. I was destitute when Blyth died. It would have been easy had I only daughters. But sons are not so fortunate. They are born into what they will always be. I could not betray them like that, so I was forced to keep to respectable poverty." She turned suddenly in a swish of expensive silk. "You terrify me, Violetta."

Under that piercing gaze Violetta was not so sure any more. She tried to explain. "I have my legacy from my father, and since my mother won't touch hers, I have hers too. I have more than many respectable girls. You have never wavered, you have always supported my mother. I know she found her years of—work—hard, although she tried not to show it. I know you could have been excoriated for being her friend. I want to pay you back in some way." She took a few steps away from the fire, to Lord Blyth's desk, picking up one of the quills, running the soft feather through her fingers. "I know why Lady Perdita hasn't walked, or I'm beginning to suspect it. I truly think I can help." She looked up, straight back at this lady she had known for most of her life, seeing the void that lay between them. "I want to be respectable, Aunt Virginia. I don't think I'll find a husband, but I can make a life for myself."

"You'll break your mother's heart if you're recognized, my girl. It will be the end of all her dreams for you. Italy isn't too far away for gossip from England to reach it." She spoke the words softly but they fell on Violetta worse than anything roared in anger could have done.

"I know." Her hands went to rub her arms as if she was cold, although the room was perfectly warm. "I knew as soon as I told her. But you know what she's like, Aunt Virginia. She insists I go ahead with my plan, now I've started." She paused, clutching her arms closely to her. "Lady Perdita needs help. She can walk, I know she can. I can help her."

"By being a friend? She has friends. One of them is your mother's lover's daughter."

"I have met Lady Judith. I didn't plan for that, but it wasn't too difficult." Violetta felt something unnameable closing around her. "No, Lady Taversall. I think your daughter can walk again, but she is being told the wrong things."

"You know better than Dr. Sewell?"

Violetta was taken with a mad urge to plead. She knew she wanted to help Perdita, she needed to help her, though she was far from understanding why. "I think, in this case, I might. Dr. Sewell has told her to rest. Aunt Virginia, she doesn't need rest. The breaks are healed, but her muscles are so wasted they need work. If she doesn't exercise, they will waste away and then she will never be able to walk again. Tonight I persuaded her to try. If I leave now, as I probably should, her legs will atrophy."

In the warmth of the firelight Lady Taversall's face paled.

"You're sure?"

Violetta shrugged. "Of course not. It's merely common sense. I won't do anything until I've spoken to the doctor."

"You were never without common sense." Lady Taversall stared into space. Violetta didn't interrupt her thoughts. Eventually she turned to Violetta again. "Very well. Do what you can. If you can help Perdita to walk again I will be more than grateful. However, if you're in any danger I want you to come to me or your mother at once."

"I don't need your gratitude. That's not why I'm doing it."

"I know."

The door opened to reveal Lord Blyth. His bright eyes took in the scene and then returned, and met Violetta's startled gaze. Before she could say anything Lady Taversall went forward. "I wanted to discuss Perdita's situation with Miss Lambert. I have heard some interesting things. I feel sure Miss Lambert can help her." She continued to speak, not allowing her son a word. "She seems a most competent young woman." She took Lord Blyth's arm, talking all the while. "Did you miss us? I thought you would be ensconced in the drawing room this age! When you and your brother get together we can't expect you to join the ladies much before ten. Have they set the card tables up?"

She heard Lord Blyth's answering murmur but by that time Lady Taversall had propelled him halfway up the corridor towards the drawing room. Violetta followed more slowly. It was true. Her own plans no longer mattered. She wanted to see Lady Perdita take her first steps. Then her schemes could take precedence. Not before.

Chapter Four

Violetta didn't want to go into the drawing room, but she was afraid she would be missed. Lady Perdita would be bound to ask for her. So instead, she went in and stood behind Lady Perdita's chair, trying to look like a servant.

It didn't work. When he saw her, Lord Blyth fixed her with a blatantly interested stare. He studied her until she looked away. She caught his small smile although she wished she had not.

She had only been here a few days, but already she was far too attracted to Lord Blyth. His reassurance not to take advantage of her because of her position in his household increased in worthlessness every day. Because she wanted him. She found herself wondering what it would be like to feel his hands on her, on her most intimate places, things she didn't know she knew, things that made her hot inside. Her background had given her access to information. She knew far more than any virgin had a right to, but before this the knowledge had been academic, for her at least. She had never wanted to do anything like that before. Now she did.

It was impossible. She could not, she would not allow him to see how she felt. If she did, he might react, dowdy disguise notwithstanding. When he looked at her sometimes she felt as though he could see through the padding, the wig, the spectacles, to the Violetta beneath. Ridiculous!

Violetta was glad when Lady Perdita excused herself and was carried upstairs for an early night. After she had seen the lady settled comfortably, her duties were over and she could retire, leaving Lord Blyth to see his family out.

When she came out of Lady Perdita's room he was waiting for her. Outside in the corridor. She didn't see him at first, not until she had got her door open. Then she heard a movement and spun around. "Who is it?"

"No, don't be afraid. It's only me. I wanted a quick word, that's all and I didn't want everyone to know." He came closer. "Can we go inside your room? I don't want Perdita hearing me. I promise to be good." He gave her a wry, one-sided smile.

"Y-yes." Asking a man into her bedroom now. Whatever next?

He followed her into the little room. In his evening clothes he looked out of place here, in this plain space. He stared around him. "I didn't know your chamber was so spartan. Who arranged it?"

"Lady Perdita gave the orders, but I think the housekeeper arranged it."

He nodded as though that explained something. "I'm sorry, I ordered the room furnished but didn't oversee the process. I'll see this is improved for you."

"It doesn't matter."

He spun round, the skirts of his evening coat swirling around him. "It matters to me!" His tone was vicious, but when he saw Violetta's instinctive withdrawal he took a deep breath and then smiled. "I'm sorry. I hate such pettiness. It's not you. I merely wanted to ask you if you were free tomorrow. And to thank you for what you've done for Perdita so far."

"I don't think I've done a great deal, not yet."

"Does that mean you will stay and help?" His look held a plea.

"Why should I not?"

He shrugged. "She's not an easy person. You're not the first companion I've engaged for her. She said she was displeased with you earlier this evening."

"She is proud."

"She is." He went to the door. "I'm glad you want to stay. Be assured of your welcome." He turned, his hand on the doorknob. "May I take you out driving in the morning? Early, before the fashionable world is awake?"

Violetta felt shy. She had never been out driving with a gentleman before. Not in this country, anyway. And never with someone she found so disturbingly attractive.

෬

Violetta tried to dress in her dowdiest clothes in the morning, but she had little choice. In her guise as country spinster she had been careful to buy dull colours in durable fabrics. Most of her wardrobe was second-hand, because it had the right air of shabbiness about it, but she'd had the clothes thoroughly laundered before she had worn them. Her French maid, Lisette, with Violetta since her days at the French finishing school, who seemed to have become more French since she set foot on English soil, had thrown up her hands and refused to touch them, but Violetta had insisted and they had been sent out to a laundry.

Now she had a plain gown of dark brown wool, which she wore over a flat hoop, the kind that had been the height of fashion a few years before. It was a warm day, even though it was only nine in the morning, and the gown was too heavy, but it was all she had that was suitable.

He was waiting for her in the hall, although she had half doubted he would be there. He gave her a charming smile and led her outside. He was dressed in brown too, but there the resemblance to her clothes ended. His coat was of fine, dull silk, lined in amber silk. His waistcoat matched the lining, and was embroidered in the same colour as his coat. The effect was one of quiet elegance. The only showy part was the gold braid around the brim of his cocked hat. Violetta, in her shabby, dowdy outfit, felt ashamed to be seen with him.

He helped her into the passenger seat of an elegant but modest phaeton, drawn by a pair of bays, then went around to the other side, taking the reins from the groom who stood patiently waiting.

The well-sprung vehicle sagged when he climbed into his place and then settled again. He glanced at her. "I'll drive to the park and then we'll see how you do. All right?"

She smiled. "I'll do my best. Which horses are these? The

sprightly ones or the others?"

He gave her a slow, wicked smile. "I'll let you find out."

By the time they got to the park she was almost sure this was the more docile pair. Almost. They were well-bred, of course, but they responded beautifully to his touch and showed no signs of skittishness.

They had left the groom behind, so they had to manoeuvre carefully to change places, for her to sit on the right. They managed it. He stood, and she slid along the seat behind him. It brought her too close to him, but the moment was over quickly. Before she could react he settled himself next to her and handed her the reins. "Let's see what you can do."

As soon as she touched the reins Violetta felt them, as though strings of flesh connected them, and not inanimate strips of leather. These horses were the best. Prime, fresh and sprightly.

She no longer felt uncomfortable, no longer felt aware of the man sitting silently next to her. She knew he watched her carefully, but it no longer mattered. She flicked the animals into a walk, marvelling at their matched steps. One, the lead horse on the left, pulled a little. Just a little. It was all it took. Its partner followed. Violetta knew if she hauled on the reins she could ruin their mouths, as well as precipitate a reaction she might not be able to cope with so she just pulled, very slightly. Then she remembered the fashionable way of holding the reins and she looped them up into one hand with a deft move.

Orlando watched, leaning back, giving the impression that he was at his ease. He rested one hand on his knee, ready to take control if she needed it. So far it was not. He watched her carefully, not allowing his concentration to waver. These were tricky animals, but so blissfully responsive he was prepared to put up with their skittishness.

Miss Lambert had a light hand with them. After she had negotiated the first few curves in the path successfully, Orlando knew he could trust her with the other team, the more docile ones. She could cope with them. Relaxing a little he studied her face with the heavy spectacles perched precariously at the end of her short nose. As if she realized he was staring, she wrinkled the nose, pushing up the spectacles. He found the unconscious gesture charming. Her eyes were a remarkable shade of violet, truly remarkable. The shade cast by her plain straw hat couldn't hide their vivid intensity. He wondered how many men she had fought off in her short career, to want to make herself so dowdy. If she had managed to fight them all off.

The surge of murderous anger took him by surprise. It had come with the mental picture of a man, any man, trying to force her into compliance. He'd seen it. Hell, he'd helped some of the unfortunates himself. Any halfway decent woman was in danger if she was alone and unprotected. He had never stooped to that kind of assault. He never would, but this young woman might not believe that. Which was a shame, because he liked her. She seemed to put all men into the same category, the way many spinsters did.

He didn't speak; it might have interrupted her concentration, and if he knew this pair she would need every ounce of it she could muster. She bit her lip once, the sharp white teeth sinking into the soft lower lip. Orlando felt a sudden urge to taste those lips. He grinned. After all his good intentions? No, he would not force her, but one day he might ask. She was no beauty, especially in the deliberately frumpy clothes she chose. She couldn't hide what she had. Orlando had seen it before, and it must cause her no end of trouble. An appeal, right to the basic animal instincts inside every male, like a primeval call, a promise. Some women exuded it, some tried to, and some manufactured it. This was it, whatever "it" was, in all its glory.

Orlando shifted when he felt a stirring far too urgent for the time of day and the public place they were in. He deliberately tried to move his mind away from inappropriate thoughts and back to the real reason they were here that day. He leaned forward and touched her gently on the arm. "I'm satisfied. Two circuits of the park is enough."

She didn't argue but returned the reins to him. He didn't bother to change seats, having only done it before out of a desire to give her the best chance possible. When he was back in control of the horses, she moved, but he stopped her. "I can manage them from here." He shot a grin at her. "I should have asked you to urge them into a gallop, but somehow I think that might have led to talk. However early in the day it is there is always someone around to gossip." Her little sigh surprised him, but he didn't pursue its meaning. "If you can control this pair you can control the others. I'll give orders they be available to you when you need them. Do you like this vehicle?"

"Yes, but I could not possibly deprive you of your transport."

"You can if you persuade my sister to drive out with you. Besides, I have another, a curricle. I'll inform Perdita you are quite capable of managing the grays. She won't believe you took the bays out without mishap!"

"This is the skittish pair, then, sir?"

"Yes. I wanted to test you properly. I'm sorry for it, but my sister is precious to me, and I wanted to be absolutely sure you could manage."

She didn't take offence. "It wasn't easy."

He chuckled. "It never is with these two. They make up for it. Thoroughbreds generally do, but these are exceptional. You did well, Miss Lambert. Thank you for putting up with my skittishness as well as the horses'."

It was her turn to chuckle. "Are you ever skittish?"

"Frequently." He turned his head to smile at her. Her cheeks were flushed with the breeze that had sprung up, giving her an air of recklessness he'd never noticed before. "Something else comes to mind. They say this will be a warm summer, though I haven't the faintest idea who they are or how they know. The point is, you would be a lot more comfortable without those extra layers of flannel, or whatever it is you're winding around your middle."

They were sitting close. He felt the seat beneath them jerk when she reacted. "How did you know?"

"You haven't an ounce of extra fat on your face or your arms, my dear girl. It just doesn't work. Have no fear, I won't force my unwelcome attentions on you. Neither, while you are in my employ, will I allow anyone else to do so."

She bowed her head, letting the straw hat slip forward over her forehead. "I'm sorry."

"Nothing to be sorry for." She sounded so vulnerable. He made his voice brisk when what he really wanted to do was haul her close and comfort her. "I suppose you've done it for the usual reasons?"

"Yes." The voice was a whisper.

"I won't ask further. I do know that governesses are considered fair game in the hunting set. Some of it, anyway. Not the set I run with." He glanced at her to see her lift her head and put her hand to her hat to straighten it. "If you feel safer with your padding, by all means keep it, but I thought I ought to tell you it won't do any good. A determined man doesn't care for a bit of plumpness. Some prefer it. You'd do a lot better to hint at a physical injury. Walk with a limp, maybe, and spin some tale of a withered leg."

"Not in your house," she commented, and he knew she was thinking of Perdita. As he was. As he had been for the past six months.

"If you succeed where others have failed and persuade Perdita to walk," he said lightly, "I will be exceedingly grateful. A substantial bonus and a glowing character at the very least."

She had recovered herself now, clasping her gloved hands tightly together in her brown clad lap. "Thank you, sir."

He cursed himself for reminding her of their relative status. He had been in a fair way to winning her friendship before he forgot himself in that remark. He would keep trying, he decided. There was something particularly interesting about Miss Charlotte Lambert, something he was not sure he knew about, but he wanted to find out.

୫

She was a fool. Violetta felt stupid. The man was an earl, he needed a well-born, well-dowered young lady, not her. The only thing he would ever consider her suitable for was the thing she had set her soul against having. She would not, she swore. Anyway, who would want her in this guise? She might not have fooled him with the stuffing, but she still had the spectacles, wig and the dowdy clothes.

She turned the handle to her bedroom door, planning to remove her hat and see if Lady Perdita was awake yet but she stopped, the door open, staring inside. This was not the room she had left a scant hour or so before. This must be a different room. She stepped back. No, it was the right one.

She heard his voice before she detected his presence. "Like it?"

He stood outside his sister's chamber, hands negligently thrust into his pockets, watching her with an amused smile.

"I—I don't know what to say. How did they do all this so quickly?" The room was transformed. The bed was replaced with a canopied one, light draperies tied back at the head. The rest of the furniture was now in a fashionable mahogany instead of the lumpy oak that had been bestowed on her at her arrival and there was more of it, a comfortable sofa at the base of the bed, a chest of drawers and a bookcase. Rugs covered the bare floorboards.

"Oh, they can be quick, given the right incentive." His smile was grimmer. "Perdita didn't know you'd been offered such scanty comfort, either. The parties have been dealt with."

She must have betrayed her dismay, for he walked forward and took her hand. "What is it? Did we do something wrong?"

"No, sir. Nothing."

"Tell me!"

His gentle urging had its effect. "I'm resented in the servants' hall. Governesses and the like often are. I'm afraid this will make it worse." She tugged to recover her hand from his grasp.

Instead, he turned it over, studying the palm as though he could read something there. "Then we'll have to treat you as family, won't we?" Before she guessed his intent he turned her hand again and lifted it to his lips, kissing the tips of her fingers. "I will not have anyone shown such discourtesy and spite in my household. I hope I made it clear. You must come to me if anyone makes matters difficult for you." He released her hand and walked away. "Enjoy your room, my dear."

"Thank you, my lord."

The room was lovely, but Violetta suspected she would pay for it in other ways. She generally tried to create as little disturbance as possible in the well-ordered household. She could put up with the occasional black look such as the one she received from Lady Perdita's maid when she knocked and entered Lady Perdita's room. "Good morning, my lady."

She heard a chink from the bed as Lady Perdita put down

her tea dish. "Good morning. I slept uncommonly well last night. Are we—" There was a significant pause. "Chivers, you may go. Come back when I ring to help me dress."

"Yes, my lady."

The door closed softly behind the maid and Violetta tried not to care about the look she'd received from the woman on her way out. It was difficult, she had never been able to ignore servants, caring too much about everyone's opinions of her. She went round to the front of the bed. The drapes were still partially closed, but were open around the bed head. Lady Perdita handed her the empty dish and Violetta replaced it on the tray standing on the nightstand. "I suggest we begin the exercises this morning. I've had some ideas, and I would like to research them later, if that is acceptable."

"Yes. Judith is to visit this afternoon, so you may go then. What had you in mind?"

The haughty look would have daunted Violetta a week ago, but now she knew the lady a little better. It was not disapproval but fear she saw in the heavenly blue eyes. "Perhaps you would allow me to rub your calves, try to stimulate the muscles a little. Then if you feel up to it, a little pressure."

"Pressure?"

"Yes, my lady. If you would roll onto your stomach, I'll show you what I mean." Violetta had come prepared. Dipping into her pocket she pulled out a small bottle of amber-coloured liquid.

"What's that?"

"Oil, my lady. Rose-scented oil." Violetta didn't mention she had most of her ideas from the stables, where horse liniment was commonly used with the animals. The oil she'd brought would decrease the friction and help to increase the heat. It might be better if she kept Lady Perdita in ignorance of the origin of many of her ideas. She might work them out for herself, but if the methods proved effective, perhaps she would not mind.

Violetta set to work. She had tucked her elbow ruffles out of the way, and continued to give her mistress a thorough massage. It seemed to meet with Lady Perdita's approval. She popped a clean towel under the limbs and rubbed up and down her legs, trying to improve the circulation, to bring some sensation back to the withered limbs. Her hands smoothed over the scars caused by the accident. They were ugly. Lady Perdita was fortunate only her legs were involved. If she were careful, no one need see them, not even the man she married, but the man Violetta would like to marry, the mythical man she had dreamt about all her life, wouldn't care for such superficialities.

The massage took place mostly in silence. Violetta kept up the motions until half an hour had passed then asked her ladyship to sit up.

"That was wonderfully stimulating," Lady Perdita remarked. She did look better. Her cheeks held some colour and her smile seemed the most natural Violetta had seen on her to date.

"I thought, my lady, you might be able to put increasing pressure on your feet." Violetta brought a footstool over to the bed and placed Lady Perdita's feet onto it. She lifted the lady's nightgown up over her knees. "If you put your feet flat on the stool and push, it will help to build up the muscles. If you do that several times a day, it might speed your recovery."

Lady Perdita sat and stared, making no effort. She gazed at her feet, then lifted her head. Violetta saw the terror behind the glazed look. She was trying to cover her fear up with her usual veneer of aristocratic disdain, but Violetta was determined not to allow her to push her away like that. She met the stare head on, when it was obvious Violetta was expected to drop her gaze in a submissive way. "Do it."

"How dare you speak to me in that way!"

Violetta didn't drop her gaze. "I dare because I want you to recover, and the only way you can do it is to work at it. If you don't want this, say so and I shall leave."

"You should treat me with proper respect. What will happen to you if I dismiss you without a character?"

Violetta knew just what would happen, and it wasn't what Lady Perdita expected. Her thoughts shot, unbidden, to Lady Perdita's brother. She felt a pang, and at that moment she knew who she would miss the most. Horror swept through her in a hot tide. How did that happen? How did the sight of him, his presence, give her so much pleasure she would miss it if it was no longer there? She must not allow that. She *must* not.

She turned back to the task. By the end of the day she

might well not be in this house. "I will treat you with respect, Lady Perdita. However, when we're like this, when we're private, it might be better to allow me to guide you. I will research this more, and see if I can find any way to help."

Lady Perdita looked at her legs again. "You have a point." The words were grudging, but they were there. "Do you think Dr. Sewell should have told me of this?"

"It's not for me to say."

"Why stop there? Say it."

"Yes, I think he should. I'm not an expert in such matters, and the techniques I'm using are common knowledge, not secrets. I have never had any experience, which is why I'm only suggesting things to you I know can do no harm."

Lady Perdita continued to stare at her legs. Then Violetta saw Lady Perdita press. Her heels whitened when she exerted pressure on them. She flattened her heels onto the stool and pushed. The strain was obvious. The lady took a rest and looked back at Violetta. "I will tell you something now. I do not expect this to go any further. Do I make myself clear?"

Violetta knew when to back down. "Yes, my lady. Perfectly clear."

Lady Perdita swallowed, a sign of her nervousness. "I do not like Dr. Sewell's examinations. I broke the long bones in my lower legs, but he prefers me to remove my petticoats and skirts. He doesn't like a maid present when he examines me."

Violetta shuddered. It sounded appalling. "But your bones are mended now. Does he need to look?"

"He says he does."

"I see." Violetta bit her lip in thought. "If you wish, I will make sure I'm always there when he comes. Will that help?"

"Yes!" The sound was so heartfelt Violetta knew Lady Perdita had been upset about this for some time.

"Did you not tell your brother? Or even Lady Judith?"

Lady Perdita shook her head, sending her loose, fair curls bouncing. "Orlando would have been very angry. He would cause a scandal and I can't bear for it to be made public. Judith is a dear friend, and she knows something is wrong. Sometimes she soothes me, but sometimes—" she broke off, biting her lip,

"—but she gossips. If I tell you and you spread it, it will be easier for me to deny your stories. Won't it?" Her lips compressed into a firm line.

"Yes, it will." Violetta had no intention of telling anyone, but Lady Perdita was right. Her word would not be taken above her mistress's. It was also true the gossip mongers and the anonymous writers of the scandal sheets would pounce on this particular morsel with the appetite of vultures. "I will not tell anyone, but you have that for extra security. No one would believe my word against yours." She wondered what Lady Perdita was about to say about Lady Judith. It wasn't the comment she finally made about gossiping, Violetta was sure.

"As for the other," Lady Perdita continued. "I will require your presence when the doctor calls. I believe you are right and we won't have to tolerate his presence much longer. I won't tell him about these exercises, and I won't expect you to, either."

"No, my lady. I will not. Does this mean you will consent to continue?"

Lady Perdita shrugged her delicate shoulders. "Well, as you say, it can't do any harm, can it?"

Chapter Five

Violetta's days took on a pattern. She would dress and go to help Lady Perdita with her exercises. After a few days they took the maid into their confidence, and she took over the leg massages, morning and night. Violetta would then go with Lady Perdita to the salon, where she would spend most of the rest of the day. Her mistress's afternoon nap gave Violetta an hour or two on her own. Then came dinner. There were rarely guests, and Lord Blyth was often absent, but it was noticeable that when he was present for dinner, Lady Judith often stayed, too.

Violetta was treated as a member of the family. Despite that, she never forgot her place in the household, never put herself forward, or drew attention to herself. It was a novel experience, to observe and remain in the background. She began to enjoy it, the observances and education. She took Lady Perdita out for an airing, but never at an hour when the fashionable world was out and about, and they never met anyone, never stopped to acknowledge a greeting.

When Lord Blyth's elder brother the Earl of Rosington came for dinner with his wife, they were accompanied by Lord Elston, the Triple Countess's third son. Violetta was interested to see Lady Rosington, who rarely appeared in public since her illness after the birth of her second son. Her ladyship was beautiful, a lovely golden vision and her manners were gracious, even to Violetta. Lady Judith was present, and monopolized Lord Blyth's company. After dinner, Violetta ensured Lady Rosington had a seat out of any draughts, and was surprised to find her efforts met with a small scowl. "I'm quite all right, my dear, really I am. Please don't fuss."

"I would hate you to be uncomfortable," Violetta ventured.

"So would I, so sit down and talk to me instead of fussing. Tell me about Perdita. She has confided some of her problems to me in the past and I would be glad to know how she is progressing."

Violetta sat down on the sofa next to her and was the blinking recipient of a dazzling smile. Lady Rosington told her; "Dr. Sewell tells me to do all sorts of things, but I've started to ignore them."

"Dr. Sewell is Lady Perdita's doctor, too." Violetta hesitated. There was no one within earshot. Lady Perdita and Lady Judith sat by the harpsichord, going through pieces to impress the gentlemen with when they arrived, heads close together, whispering and giggling.

Lady Rosington saw her hesitation. "If you tell me, it won't go any further. If it makes you feel any easier, I have my doubts about the good doctor. He wants me to rest, constantly." She paused and flushed, but didn't vouchsafe why.

"He's coming to examine Lady Perdita soon," Violetta responded, gliding through the slight awkwardness caused by the blush. "He seems to be giving her some dubious advice. He doesn't want her to exercise, although her legs are healed."

Lady Rosington frowned. "That can't be right. How can she learn to walk again if she doesn't exercise?"

Violetta leaned forward, lowered her voice. "I have persuaded her to try. It's going well, better than I could have hoped for. I don't propose to tell Dr. Sewell."

"Very wise, my dear. It makes me wonder if I really need him. I feel much better than I used to, almost back to my old self. He's the most fashionable doctor in London. Will you let me know if you need any help?"

The door opened to admit the gentlemen. Violetta looked up and just for a moment met the clear gaze of Lord Blyth. The room melted away, and for that moment out of time there was only the two of them.

Violetta looked away hastily. A foolish notion, not to be thought of. She had found a friend in his lordship; it would be a shame to spoil that. It could not continue much longer, she knew, but she was determined to see Lady Perdita back on her feet before she left. What had begun as an adventure, a learning experience, had continued for other reasons. A desire to do something, anything, to benefit someone else, and a growing reluctance to leave. The reason had nothing to do with Lady Perdita.

It was something to fight with all her heart.

Instead of turning to the harpsichord, where his sister and her best friend sat waiting for him, Lord Blyth came across the room and bowed over Lady Rosington's hand. "Miranda, you're looking well."

Miranda gave him her charming smile. "I feel much better, Orlando. I've been discussing health matters with your charming Miss Lambert."

He glanced at her and smiled. It seemed too intimate to Violetta. "She isn't my Miss Lambert, she's Perdita's." Violetta smiled back, although she'd had no intention of doing so. "I merely found her." His eyes seemed to tell her something else, something she must be imagining.

Violetta was annoyed with herself. How could she fall for such practised wiles? She had lived among rakes and Cyprians for a long time, she should be immune to such behaviour! Although she had given up the extra padding around her middle, she still wore the mousy wig and the spectacles, kept her clothes loose, and used no artificial enhancements on her face. Before she had come to this house she had been certain that was enough to pass muster as a dowdy companion, but Lord Blyth's perceptive gaze seemed to slice through it all. She looked away, down to her cloth-covered lap, hoping the heat she felt in her face wasn't showing in a blush.

"I am grateful for the position, my lord. I hope the results will be to your satisfaction. May I pour you some tea?"

"Yes please."

While he settled himself in a chair opposite the sofa, Violetta could turn away and pour the tea. When she took it across to him he looked at her again, but his gaze this time was friendly, no more. Violetta retook her seat, with a small sigh of relief.

"You are looking so much better, Miranda, that I dare ask you something."

Lady Rosington arched a delicate brown eyebrow. She was

fortunate, Violetta reflected, that her golden hair was darker on her face and she did not have the fair eyebrows and lashes that could be almost invisible. If Lady Perdita did not employ a subtle stain her eyelashes would be almost invisible. Violetta saw no sign of paint on Lady Rosington.

"I have to have a new coat made. I would greatly appreciate your opinion on it. Would you care to go with me on a shopping expedition?"

"What's this?" Lady Rosington's intimidating lord came over to join them. He stood beside his wife's chair in a protective gesture. "You're enticing my wife? Really, Blyth!" If it weren't for the slight smile in his gray eyes Violetta might have feared for Lord Blyth.

As it was, his lordship grinned at his brother, unintimidated. "Merely to ask her advice. I'll return her to you unscathed."

Seeing she was no longer needed, Violetta stood and went to the harpsichord, where she received a frosty glare from Lady Judith. "You may turn the pages for me," she announced. There was no escape.

Violetta stood and turned the pages for what seemed like an eternity. Lady Judith played competently, but no more than that, and the pieces she chose were well within her capabilities. She received polite applause but the only applause she acknowledged was Lord Blyth's, staring at him with a smile and a blush.

When Lady Judith rose from the instrument she did not recognize Violetta's help by so much as a glance. She went straight across the room, and sat next to Lord Blyth. After years of watching the best in the business, Violetta winced at the tactic. Such a direct approach did not only deter the pursued, but made the intention so obvious that rejection would humiliate the pursuer.

She turned away, but was confronted by Lord Elston. "Come and sit with me," he said, leading the way to a broad sofa. "We'll leave the would-be lovebirds in peace."

Violetta frowned at him. "Are they lovebirds, my lord?"

He grinned, unabashed. "One of them is trying to be. They're taking wagers in the clubs that she'll snag him before the year is out."

Before she could censor herself Violetta replied, "I'll take a guinea against."

Lord Elston tipped his head back and roared with laughter, effectively bringing all conversation to a halt. He immediately recalled himself and smiled apologetically. "Dreadfully sorry, everyone. Blyth, where did you discover this treasure? Are there any more?"

Lady Judith glared at Violetta when Lord Blyth smoothly got to his feet and crossed the room. "As far as I know there are no more. You'll have to ask her. But Miss Lambert is too valuable to us for me to allow her to leave." He bent and took Violetta's hand, drawing her to her feet. "Do you play?"

"A little," Violetta admitted. She did play. A little. She danced better than she played, but this was a family gathering and there would be no dancing. Still, the exercise kept her out of the conversation and allowed Lady Judith a free run at Lord Blyth. Violetta did not grudge her that, although from Lord Blyth's reaction to her Violetta doubted anything would come of it. Polite but distant would describe his manner reasonably accurately, while Lady Judith made her efforts too clear. Violetta watched her lean towards him, positively pushing her décolletage at him, but while he spoke to Lady Judith, he kept his gaze on Violetta's face. He leaned back and reached for his tea dish when Lady Judith wanted to move closer, ostensibly to whisper a secret in his ear. The lady could do with lessons from La Perla.

Violetta finished playing to a smattering of polite applause and then, tired of watching Lady Judith's efforts with Lord Blyth, bowed to Lady Perdita and received a nod of dismissal. She left the room, sighing with relief.

Orlando watched her go with mixed feelings. He was thinking about her far too much for his own peace of mind these days, but he had promised to keep away, and he knew she was good for Perdita. His sister seemed much more confident these days, and he was sure that was all she needed to regain her strength. Lady Judith offered to take her place at the harpsichord, and crossed the room. Orlando knew she was planning to impress him with her superior musicianship. He turned when his older brother addressed him. "I'm sure I've seen your Miss Lambert before."

Lord Elston leaned forward, speaking in a low tone so no one else would hear. "A good wig, but she missed something."

"A wig?" Orlando was startled. "How can you be sure?"

"Because there was a small strand of dark hair on her shoulder. Careless of her."

Orlando blinked at Elston and then turned back to Daniel. "Where have you seen her before?"

Rosington frowned. "Have you seen La Perla?"

"Who hasn't?" Realizing the implication of this, Orlando turned fully to his brother. "You've been to her salon?"

Daniel shrugged. "Merely curious. Besides, La Perla is off the market these days. Her salons are more and more intellectual gatherings. Very decorous affairs."

"With beautiful women for sale," Elston said. He exchanged a glance with Orlando. "What would Miranda think?"

Daniel looked towards his lovely wife. Orlando thought he saw regret or something similar in his brother's gray eyes. Daniel turned back. "She might be relieved." Neither of his brothers said anything, but Orlando knew they both had the same opinion. Miranda had been an invalid for too long. Daniel refused to put her in peril again, for Dr. Sewell had told them another child could kill her, but Orlando knew how much his brother cared for his wife. He couldn't imagine being in such a situation. He might not be as patient as Daniel had been. However, he had never been in love. He turned his mind back to the other subject of the conversation. "You think Miss Lambert looks like La Perla?"

"Yes. It's the eyes, I think, and the shape of her face, that point to the chin."

"Elfin," said Lord Elston. "Charming. But why should she wear a wig?"

"She wore padding to make herself look bigger, but I thought that was because she was trying to make herself unattractive. She told me she was a target for all the young men in her previous position. It sounded reasonable to me."

"Possibly." Lord Elston reached for his wine glass,

displaying the fine lace at the end of his sleeves. He studied the red liquid in his glass. "Why else would she do it?"

"To hide her true identity?" Daniel ventured. "La Perla has a daughter, the one she calls La Perla Perfetta. No one has seen the girl's face. But why would she want to do that?"

"I don't know," said Orlando grimly, "but I intend to find out."

∞

Before Violetta had time to ready herself for her morning visit to Lady Perdita's room, she had a summons to attend Lord Blyth downstairs in his study. Surprised, because his lordship rarely stirred from his chambers this early, she pinned her wig into place, gave her dowdy dark-green cloth gown a tug to settle its folds and hurried out of her room. Her heart beat a little faster as she approached the study, but she told herself it was merely the unexpectedness of the summons.

Deep inside her she knew it was not. She felt a lifting of her spirits every time she saw him, whether she welcomed it or not. It worried her.

She entered on her knock, and stood, hands folded together demurely before her, waiting for him to look up. He was dressed simply, dark hair tied back, pen in hand, seemingly concentrating on the papers laid before him on his desk. This was no bonheur du jour, a spindly elegant desk, but a heavy piece of furniture, containing a plethora of drawers and an expanse of leathered work surface. It was where, when his lordship was in London, necessary business was conducted.

He looked up and simply stared at Violetta. She stared back. His gaze was hard and deeply focused. He took his time. Not a word was spoken. Then he got to his feet.

Violetta could stand it no more. He came round the desk. She took a step back at the look on his face. She had never seen him so determined, so grim. All his usual humour was gone, replaced by something hard, something that made her afraid.

"Take it off."

"What?" The word was a question and an expression of disbelief. What did he want?

"The wig. Take it off."

He stopped a bare six inches away from her. She dared not disobey. Faced with this absolute determination, she knew he would rip it off rather than allow her to leave. Bending her head she took out the long, black-headed pins with shaking fingers. She didn't know what to do with them, so she kept them in her hand. Lifting her head she met his hard gaze and lifted the offending article away from her head. She tilted her chin.

Something else entered his eyes. Appreciation. She had seen it too often before to deny it. "Why did you do this?"

Violetta decided suddenly she would go the whole hog. She removed her spectacles and met his gaze fearlessly. They stared at each other for a fraught minute. Violetta let him look. "Would you have employed me looking like this? How could I be sure? And once employed, how would I prevent men laying hands on me?" She trembled with anger and the frustration that she hadn't seen this coming.

He swallowed, his throat moving soundlessly before he spoke. "Is that the only reason?"

She looked away, unable to lie to him at such close quarters. She felt ashamed of her actions. He had trusted her with his only sister, and she had entered his house under false pretences. She knew she was at fault.

He put his hand under her chin and turned her face back to his. The action was gentle, despite his agitation. "Tell me."

There was no escape. At the end of the day she might find herself out, back at her mother's house but this time with her reputation in shreds, but she had to tell him. She had come to like Lord Blyth and his sister, and hoped the service she was doing Lady Perdita was enough to make amends for her deception. It was not. She didn't flinch, but met his gaze. It was too close, too potent, but she could bear it. For now. After this he would turn away from her disgusted. Who would want her once they knew who she was, what she came from? "It's my mother. She's notorious, in her field."

"La Perla?"

The two words almost struck Violetta dumb. She found a

small breath, enough to say, "How could you know that?"

He reached out a hand, touched her hair, fastened in tight braids close to her head. "There is only one woman in London with hair and eyes like that, or so I thought. Only one woman with eyes so deep a violet that a man could drown in them, hair so black and glossy it reflects the sun. Now there's you. Where else could you have come from?" He put his hand over her hair, smoothed, and then dropped it back by his side as though the touch burned him.

Violetta dropped her glance. She couldn't meet that searing gaze any longer. She had wronged him. "I'm sorry. I didn't mean to cause any harm or anxiety."

"Then why in God's name do it?"

Tears came to her eyes. She blinked them away. She couldn't tell him of her mother's friendship with his mother. It would break the trust between Aunt Virginia and her family. "I wanted to be of some use to somebody."

His hand was still under her chin. He pushed it up when she would have turned away and he gazed at her. "What's your name? Your real name?"

"Violetta."

"Violetta." He repeated the name, breathing it gently. She felt the hot breath on her face. The finger supporting her chin urged her closer. She felt herself dropping into a void, out of which she had no way of climbing. His lips met hers, and she let herself go.

Just once. Just this once.

When she swayed she felt his arms sweep around her in support, firm against her back. She didn't fight him; she doubted she could. When she opened her mouth under the gentle pressure of his, his tongue tasted her lips, and then surged inside, taking possession with an urgency that made her tingle.

It felt right. It felt as though this was what should happen, this was the natural conclusion to everything she had done so far. Letting herself go, just this once, she felt bliss, joy she would never allow herself to feel again, but it didn't matter, because at the end of this day she would be back in her mother's house. Back where she started.

He didn't try to move his hands, held them still, supporting her while he plundered her mouth, took her soul. This was Violetta's first real kiss, the first she had let herself feel. Men had tried before, but either she had endured or had got away. This time she responded, lifting one arm to rest her hand at his waist, heavy with his plain cloth coat.

He took his time, once she made it clear she wouldn't fight him off. Drawing her closer so her head rested on his shoulder, he continued his exploration. Violetta felt herself drowning in his spell, sinking into sensuality. He lifted his head only to drop a series of small kisses on her face and return to her mouth. She submitted, and responded as he seemed to wish, touching her tongue to his, eventually accepting his invitation and entering his mouth, to explore it in her turn.

It seemed forever before he lifted away and regarded her through lids slumberous with desire. "Is this what you wanted? Is this all an attempt to trap me?"

The jolt in the vicinity of her heart was almost painful. Violetta wrenched herself away from his arms, strode to the door then turned back, her face set in a blank mask. She would leave this room with some dignity. She bent to pick up the hated wig. Only to meet his hand, also on the offending article. "What is it? What's wrong?"

"In answer to your question, *sir*," she spat out the last word, making it an insult. "No, it isn't what I wanted. No, it's not an attempt to trap you. I have no need of that."

Swiftly he moved to bar her exit, standing before the door. "Then why?"

"Perhaps I saw someone who needed help."

"You came here from Thompsons. You didn't know where you were going before you came here."

She stood before him, patently demanding to be let out, but he would not let her. "I knew. If Mrs. Thompson had offered me any other position I would have refused it."

"I want you."

"Why? Because you think I'm available?"

He shook his head. "When you came through that door on the first day I felt something. I was worried, considering how you looked that day. The padding, the wig, the spectacles. I

63

believed them all, but something told me it wasn't right, it wasn't you. I was right, wasn't I? You're lovely, Violetta, every man's dream." He reached out a hand, then dropped it back to his side.

"Which is why I wear the disguise," she pointed out, not impressed by his compliments. She'd heard too many of the same in her mother's salon to have her head turned that way. "I have chosen my path, and I intend to take it."

"Governess companion? When you could have so much more?"

Her ire rose within her like a living thing. "Are you offering?"

His smile was slow and sensuous. "I would love to. Would you accept?"

Yes, she wanted to say. *Yes, anything.* Something else rose within her, knowledge that such an arrangement could never be enough. Secure financially she did not need such inducements, but she knew, when the day of parting came, it would cause unimaginable heartbreak. For her. "I cannot." Reminding herself of her purpose here, she added, "I've promised to help Lady Perdita. She needs my help, you know that."

That seemed to move him. He frowned, and stood up straight, taking his back off the door. "In that you're right. I thought Perdita lost to me until you came, but even if she never walks again I think she will consent to take her place in society." He moved forward, and put his hands on her upper arms. She wanted to pull away, overwhelmed by his proximity to her, but stayed where she was, looking up into his face. "I owe you a great deal for that. But I won't give up. I can't remember feeling so strongly about any woman before. Desire, Violetta. I desire you. Your appearance makes no difference at all. Is that the only reason you dress in such a way? When I realized just how different you could look, I thought there must be something else, another reason for your disguise. I still think it."

Unable to bear it any more, unsure of her answer, Violetta pulled out of his arms and went to stand before the mirror, resetting the wig. She still held some of the pins in her hand, so she stuck them in, and accepted the ones he silently picked up off the carpet and gave to her. "I don't need the wig, the spectacles or the padding, but it helps immeasurably to fend off unwanted advances. I am what I am, a governess companion, and I have no wish to be anything else. Not yet."

He came up behind her, but did not touch her, just gazed at them both in the mirror. Violetta put the spectacles back on her nose. "Now I know what an exquisite creature lives behind the disguise, I won't give up."

She turned round, giving no ground, but her hooped skirts swung, forcing him to step back. "You mean to follow me and hound me? You mean to make me do what I have no wish to do?"

He smiled, sending waves of heat curling through her treacherous body. "No. I want you to desire it, too. I won't make you do anything you don't want to do. Neither will I betray your secret. I have seen enough of your work to trust you with my sister, although..." he frowned and glanced at her face, "...you are right in one respect. Had I known who your mother was when I interviewed you, I would not have engaged you."

Violetta felt vindicated. "You see? You know the demi-monde and you would have thought of me immediately. My colouring is more common in Italy, but not here. It is harder for me to hide in society here."

"You will have to hide your vitality as well, then." He moved to the door and put his hand on the knob. "It's what attracted me. Your vitality and your quick mind." He turned back, a new light in his eyes. "Are you ashamed of your mother?"

She shot pure blue fire at him from beneath her dark lashes. "No! Never that!"

She strode through the door when he opened it and went straight up to Lady Perdita's room.

Orlando watched her go, walking up the stairs with the unconscious grace that had first attracted him to her. He returned to his study, and closed the door quietly behind him. He could no longer concentrate on the estate work that had brought him to the study so early. He was deeply perturbed.

When she had taken off that wig, when he had seen her hair, and then her eyes without those dreadful spectacles, something inside him had clicked into place. At first it was a relief to find she was La Perla's daughter. That meant she could be had. And he wanted her, with a yearning he found almost shocking, something that threatened to overcome his senses, even his reason.

While not precisely a rake, Orlando had not been celibate either. He knew what he liked in a woman, and it wasn't generally Violetta's type. He preferred a generously built blonde for his dalliances. Elegant, unearthly beauty had never attracted him before, but in Violetta it was explosive, detonating a desire over which he had little control. Perhaps there was something about the family, something extra that made them special.

Going back to his desk, Orlando sighed and turned over the top sheet of paper, intending to concentrate on his work. Since this was an account of his investment portfolio, it needed all his attention, but he was unable to give it. Instead he sat staring into space, remembering the feel of her under his hands, the soft mouth under his, responding so sweetly to his kisses. He had always been blessed with the gift of concentration but this time when he tried all he could see was a pair of violet eyes he could get lost in for all time.

He had to have her. If he didn't he might go mad.

Chapter Six

When Dr. Sewell called to see his patient, the day after Violetta's confrontation with Lord Blyth in his study, Violetta was firmly in place, standing by the bed in Lady Perdita's room. The red-rimmed eyes and dark shadows caused by her sleepless night didn't show so much behind the tinted spectacles. She couldn't let Lady Perdita down now.

The doctor was a man in his early fifties, well-groomed as befitted one of London's most fashionable physicians, with a gleam in his pale blue eyes Violetta did not trust. It looked too feral to her. Her mother patronized a different doctor, but rarely needed one, so Violetta had never met this one before. Her instinctive reaction was dislike, though there was no ostensible reason she should feel so.

He greeted Lady Perdita with an avuncular smile, his gaze passing over the delicate lace confection she wore over her shift. Then he turned to Violetta, his expression frosty. "I don't think I've had the pleasure?"

Violetta had expected antipathy. "Miss Lambert, my new companion," Lady Perdita said, her voice tight and hard. "She has asked to remain during the examination."

The bewigged head turned from cold scrutiny of Violetta to Lady Perdita, the expression changing into warmth. "I don't think we need that, do we? You may leave, Miss Lambert."

"I'm sorry, sir, I have my orders from his lordship. I must remain." Violetta did her best to sound humble. The small falsehood came from a certainty Lord Blyth would want someone there and endorse her claim.

"I will explain to his lordship. You may go."

Violetta said nothing, but did not move. Not one fold of her full skirts twitched. The doctor swung to face her, his eyes blazing, his mouth set in a hard line. "Did you hear me?"

"I cannot. His lordship's orders were most specific. You must speak to him now if you don't wish me to be present." She did not meet that steely glare, not wishing to give him the advantage, but she didn't drop her head in any kind of submissive gesture either.

She felt his eyes pass over her, taking in the shapeless gown, the mousy hair, before he shrugged in a semblance of carelessness. "Very well." Despite the words and the gesture Violetta knew he cared very much, and wondered why it mattered.

When Lady Perdita nodded, Violetta came forward and helped her out of the lacy wrapper. She stood silently behind the chair and watched the gaze of the doctor. He was unable to hide the lasciviousness, a slavering greediness, a look Violetta had seen before in her mother's salon, but one he had no right turning on Lady Perdita. She was not for sale.

Dr. Sewell knelt at her feet and pushed up the shift, so it lay on her thighs. From that angle his view would be interesting, if he cared to look up. Violetta leaned forward and disposed the thin folds so they covered Lady Perdita better. As though it didn't matter, as though there wasn't some kind of duel going on, the doctor ignored Violetta's action, lifted one of her ladyship's feet and took the calf in his hand. It was noticeably better shaped than it had been before they had begun the exercises and massage. "What's this?" He probed and squeezed until Lady Perdita winced and took a sharp breath. "Have you been overtaxing your strength, my lady?"

He lifted his head to glare at Violetta, who steadfastly refused to meet his gaze. "Lady Perdita has been taking some mild exercise. It has not overtaxed her."

"Indeed," Lady Perdita put in, "I have found it stimulating. You told me the bones were healed, doctor. What harm can there be to try their strength?" Violetta saw her hand move, as though Lady Perdita would reach up to take her hand, but she waited, and saw the hand go back to rest in her lap.

Dr. Sewell kept hold of her leg, probing and kneading much harder than either Violetta or her maid had ever done. It must be hurting, but Violetta, from her vantage point behind the chair, saw Lady Perdita's jaw twitch as she set her face against showing any pain. She must have endured a great deal of pain. Setting the bones, Violetta had heard, was an agonizing process. Her admiration for her mistress rose an extra notch.

"If you put your weight on the legs before you are ready, if you overtax yourself, the bones will shatter like twigs!" The doctor's voice lifted in anger.

Violetta gasped. Surely that could not be true! Legs had been broken before. She knew of a girl at school with her who had a similar but not so serious injury. She had been back on her feet inside three months. There was something seriously wrong here.

The tears sprang to Lady Perdita's eyes. "I had hoped to walk again soon."

"Impossible!" The doctor got to his feet and dusted his hands off. Immediately, Violetta brought the lacy wrapper up and over her mistress, covering her from the predatory stare. "You must not continue my lady. It is important you rest and get your strength back."

"Of course." Lady Perdita sounded docile. Violetta could only hope she was not.

The doctor left without refreshment or what he termed his "delightful chat" with his patient, claiming another engagement. Violetta had the strong suspicion he left because of her. His lecture had been long and exhausting, even to Violetta. Lady Perdita was in no mood for her usual exercises or for anything but to return to bed.

Violetta rang for the maid, and helped to settle the largely silent lady back in bed. It was as well she was not called on to make much comment. She was too angry to speak.

Not waiting for her temper to dissipate Violetta hurried downstairs, to his lordship's study. She knocked and received the summons to enter. It was only after she closed the door she remembered, with a sharp sense of danger, what had happened here before.

It was of no account. This was far more important.

Lord Blyth looked up with a mild enquiry, his expression changing quickly to deep concern. He got to his feet. "Why whatever has happened? You look ready to explode! Come and sit down."

He helped her to a chair and Violetta took a seat gratefully. Now she was here she must order her thoughts. She took a few deep breaths. "I'm fine. Just very angry."

He turned from the sideboard, two glasses in his hand. He poured a small amount of brandy into each, and brought one to her before taking his customary seat behind his desk. Violetta took the glass with a small smile of thanks, but did not drink. She swirled the liquid around the glass, watching the facets reflect the amber liquid, watching it trickle in viscous trails down to the bottom again, readying her thoughts.

She looked up to see him watching her, a question in his eyes. She shook her head and emptied her glass, shuddering a little as the brandy left its trail of fire down her throat. Carefully she placed the glass on the desk before her and folded her hands in her lap. "Thank you. I needed a restorative." She tried to choose her words carefully, but she could think of very few ways to express what she had just witnessed. "Dr. Sewell is prurient."

He frowned, and leaned forward from his seat behind the desk, giving her all his attention. "Explain."

Violetta felt none of the thrill she usually felt when he moved close to her. Fury suffused her, leaving room for nothing else. "He wanted Lady Perdita in her shift, and he wanted her alone. He lifted the garment up far too high for his essential needs. He looked. I saw him look." Her mouth turned down in distaste. "You know I must have seen more in my life than most women my age." He nodded, not bothering to equivocate. "This was more like a voyeur, the sort of person who prefers to watch than participate. You understand?"

His mouth firmed. "Only too well."

"He told her not to continue with her exercises, said it's too soon to think of trying to walk again. He wants her docile and needing him." She paused, and the only sound in the room was low breathing. Hers, as she fought to control her temper and his, rising in anger. "I think you need to consult another physician, my lord. It's taking away all her confidence." She kept her sentences terse. She needed to, otherwise the tirade might lose her any advantage she had in getting to him first.

He tapped his teeth with the rim of his glass, took a sip. "I'll certainly do so. I'll inform Dr. Sewell his services are no longer required." He looked at Violetta sharply. "He will no doubt blame you for the change. Is that a problem?"

She shook her head. "No. My...family doesn't use him." She wanted to avoid any reference to her mother, not to remind him of her, but it was in vain.

She saw the understanding spark in his eyes. "Ah yes, your family. Have you a father?"

"Not any more." It was all of the truth she wanted to tell him at present.

"Which doctor does your mother use? Or is he a specialist?"

"In what way?" Realizing his meaning Violetta felt the hot blood surge under her skin. "No. There has never been any need for that. My mother might be notorious but she is neither a madam nor a prostitute."

"What would you call her, then?"

How had the conversation taken such a disastrous turn? Violetta couldn't remember. She sat straight and stiff in her chair. "I call her my mother. She has by necessity undertaken...things she wouldn't normally have considered, but she has made a success of it."

"Indeed she has." His voice was grim.

There was that edge of anger again. Violetta found it difficult to understand. Her anger had dissipated, once she had found a sympathetic audience, but now she was bewildered by his annoyance. "Why should my mother make you angry?"

He looked away. "I should say nothing."

"You've said too much already."

He shot a sharp glance at her. "No."

"Why not?"

He stood up from behind the desk and walked slowly to where she sat. She sat still, refusing to give ground. "Does my opinion mean that much to you?"

She met his gaze fearlessly. "You are my employer. It means something."

"I see." Without moving he watched her. His gaze passed over her face with a yearning she was afraid to interpret. She wanted him, but there was too much at stake. The kiss they had shared was nothing to a man like him, it may have been a way of controlling her. He sighed, a gentle outbreath she felt as a soft breeze on her cheek. "I have found you an exemplary employee, a bright, intelligent woman and even one I would like to call friend." There was a small, telling hesitation. "Perhaps more than that. I cannot imagine why anyone would thrust you into the world of the demi-monde. I can't see you there."

"Can't you?" She met his soft gaze with a harder one. He had been short of money himself. Surely it couldn't pass his understanding. He was being deliberately obtuse. "I have this Thursday afternoon and evening off. My mother is having a soiree, and I will be there. Why don't you come and see for yourself?"

"You take part?"

"In what?" She knew he had never been to her mother's house. She could only imagine what he thought. Her mother's was the only house of that type she had ever entered, but she had read and heard of the activities in the ones lower down the scale. She put up her chin. "Come and see, my lord."

To her surprise he smiled. "I think I will."

Too late she realized her challenge was one he could meet with no ill effects to himself. She could only hope that on her own ground she might have some advantage. She determined to make him understand, to show him his fears were groundless. Or perhaps she would not. It would be enjoyable to punish him a little, for the unspoken criticism of her mother.

He finished his brandy, lifting his arm and tossing the liquid down his throat with a gesture that seemed to indicate finality. Violetta rose to leave, but before she could go he laid a hand on her arm. "I didn't mean this meeting to end like this. I'm sorry. I merely find the thought of you in such a house uncomfortable. Please forgive me my naggy temper."

His smile was so winning she couldn't refuse him. She returned the smile. "It doesn't matter. I daresay we can live without your approval."

He grimaced. "I deserved that. Thank you for your help with Perdita. I'll be forever grateful to you for that."

She shrugged. "It could have been anyone."

"No." He sounded completely sure. "It could only have been you."

She felt uncomfortable, moved to shake off his arm when she saw his gaze become more intimate. "Lady Perdita merely needed someone to have faith in her abilities. I didn't realize it fully until I saw her with the doctor, but he must have been working for some time to diminish her in her own eyes."

"I should have done more."

She couldn't bear the note of regret she heard. "No, you could not have known what Dr. Sewell was doing. You did the best you could."

"Not enough."

He didn't seem to notice when she drew gently away and went to the door. On an impulse, she turned back. "I appreciate your faith in my abilities. Have the same faith in Lady Perdita. She will recover. I've made up my mind to it." With an impish smile she turned the knob and left the room.

Chapter Seven

They were to go shopping. Some time ago Lord Blyth had reupholstered the sedan chair in the hall in a cerulean blue, Lady Perdita's favourite colour, but she had never used it before today. Lady Judith arrived in good time to accompany them and the burly footmen his lordship had detailed to accompany them were ready and waiting.

Violetta was nervous. The mantua maker, Cerisot, knew her in another capacity—as La Perla Perfetta, one of the very few people who had seen the young lady without her mask or maquillage. Indeed, she had seen La Perla Perfetta without anything at all. Those sharp eyes wouldn't fail to detect the woman beneath the shapeless clothes, the mousy wig and the spectacles. Violetta had had no chance to warn the mantua maker that she was arriving, and could only trust in the quick thought that had helped to make Cerisot the most fashionable of all the fashionable mantua makers who thronged Bond Street.

Lady Perdita was lifted into the sedan chair and Violetta reminded herself of her duty. Despite or perhaps because of the heightened hauteur on her mistress's features Violetta understood that the lady was nervous and distressed. She let Lady Judith take charge, which she did with aplomb.

Lady Judith walked alongside the sedan, chattering all the way, not allowing Lady Perdita to reflect on her situation or order the footmen to return her to the house. Violetta admitted to herself that Lady Judith succeeded very well, even surprising a laugh out of her rigidly anxious companion. Violetta was free to watch the scene she loved so well.

It was why she loved London above all other cities. The bustle, the self-absorption of everyone in their business and the way people mixed so freely. Ragamuffins darted about the well dressed passers-by, some of them perhaps engaged in distraction for their colleagues, a chance to steal and cut purses. It wasn't unknown for hats and wigs to be snatched off heads and the thieves to get clean away. Violetta wondered what it would be like to be a street urchin. She often lost herself in dreams, imagining herself into someone else's shoes, trying to lose herself in someone else. She couldn't remember a time when she hadn't done that.

Violetta found she was invisible. She didn't look prosperous enough to be worth stealing from, and not attractive or well dressed enough to draw any interested looks. She loved it. Her distinctive hair, white clothes and eye colouring tended to draw attention in her other persona, but with this disguise she was no more notable than any other maid or companion in the street.

Bond Street was one of the most fashionable shopping streets in London, and therefore in the world. The street was full of people preparing for the coming season, dressed in the height of fashion, their dress inviting admiration and even adoration. Violetta thought some people were there not to shop, but to watch and she had to admit it was a fascinating sight. With more free time she would come here in this guise, just to observe.

The shop door was flung open when they approached, forewarned of their coming. The sedan chair was taken right inside the premises. Cerisot waited just inside the doors, and lost no time greeting her customer. "It is such a delight to see you here, my lady! Good morning, Lady Judith! Such a lovely day, too, to greet you!"

"Indeed." Violetta heard Lady Perdita's voice, small and tight. She felt nervous for her, and tried to understand how this bustle and haste must overwhelm Lady Perdita after a year's close seclusion. Perhaps a visit to the theatre might have been preferable, so at least her ladyship could observe from the seclusion of a box. It was too late to reconsider now.

Violetta moved forward in case her mistress should need her and it was then that Cerisot spotted her. She glanced up, looked down and then looked again, her dark eyes sharp with speculation. Violetta calmly met her gaze and then raised one eyebrow above the level of her spectacles. She kept her expression bland. An instant stretched to an eternity. Cerisot blinked and looked away and Violetta knew she was safe. "Do come this way, Lady Perdita, a room has been prepared for you."

Forewarned then. Violetta knew who had sent word, recognizing the hand of Lord Blyth in this. Of course he would not allow his sister to enter the lion's den without drugging the lion first. His protection was comprehensive, though not suffocating. He merely smoothed the way. Now it was up to her ladyship.

Lady Perdita was installed on a waiting armchair, and the footmen lifted her to carry her across the salon. The lady stared straight in front of her, ignoring the stares of the ill-bred, the glances flicked at her from the more knowing. It would be all round London by nightfall that Lady Perdita Garland had broken her self-imposed seclusion. Violetta knew they could expect a number of cards of invitation in the morning and wondered how Lady Perdita would react.

The room was small but well appointed, furnished with a couple of chairs, a table, a sofa and a long mirror, all in the first stare of fashion. Such items were expensive. Cerisot must be doing extremely well. With a bright smile to Lady Perdita and a puzzled glance at Violetta, Cerisot set to work.

She had prepared some drawings and gathered some prints from various publications. Her tape measure sat ready on the table together with a number of other items. "Lady Perdita, I am honoured you chose to visit me here. I trust your journey was uneventful?"

Lady Perdita smiled and replied in the affirmative. Violetta stood silently behind her mistress's chair and prepared to admire. Cerisot had the measure of her client, as she had of everyone. While Lady Judith exclaimed over the exquisite designs, she set to making Lady Perdita comfortable and assessing her needs. It was masterly. More than anything else it showed why Cerisot was the most sought after mantua maker in London. The designs were good, but the flattery and luxury must make the difference.

Violetta stayed on the alert, waiting for the sound of petulance in Lady Perdita's voice that she had come to recognize as a sign of tiredness. But it did not come. Until one moment. "Can you stand for a brief time?" Cerisot asked gently. "It would be better if I took the measurements with you upright, my lady. If you cannot, I am sure we will contrive, but the fit will be so much better!"

"No, I don't think so," said Lady Perdita. Her voice wavered.

Violetta decided it was time. She came round to stand in front of her mistress. "You have been held up in the last few days," she reminded her. When she had helped Lady Perdita from one chair to another she had been careful to hold her upright, just for a moment. "You have been leaning less on me recently. If I stand on one side and Lady Judith consents to stand on the other to support you, I'm sure it will be possible."

Lady Perdita stared at Violetta, horrorstruck, before the familiar arrogant mask settled over her features. "That will not be necessary. I'm sure Cerisot can manage without that."

Cerisot looked at Violetta, the first time their eyes had met. Lady Judith, missing the unspoken exchange, stepped forward. "Would you like to try, Perdita, my sweet? I won't let you down, I swear it, and if we keep the chair behind you it will give you somewhere to fall if you tire."

Lady Perdita gave in. "For a moment, then."

She stretched up her arms. While Lady Judith caught hold of one, Violetta bent and seized her mistress around the waist, but did not attempt to pull. With her face close to Lady Perdita, she murmured, "Ready?"

Lady Perdita nodded. This close Violetta saw the fear in her eyes, a fear she had not seen her without since she had first arrived at the house. She showed no sign of noticing, but tightened her hold.

Lady Perdita got to her feet without a sound, even though Violetta felt the effort she was making. She wore no hoops, since she spent most of her time sitting, but quilted petticoats that bulked up the thin body beneath to a semblance of the belled skirts currently in fashion. Looking at the mirror, Violetta saw the slight body tremble, and then felt the muscles tighten.

Her heart went out to the lady. For all her snappy temper,

arrogant air and haughty demeanour, Lady Perdita was a frightened woman. Afraid that her legs would break once more under the strain of holding up her body, afraid that she would appear clumsy and foolish in society, afraid she would be pointed out for all the wrong reasons. Violetta caught Lady Judith's triumphant gaze. "If we step back, my lady, and hold her ladyship carefully between us it should be possible for Cerisot to take her measurements. Madame Cerisot," she corrected hastily. Her status here wasn't such that she could use the name unadvisedly.

Lady Judith glanced at her, but apart from the heat rising to her cheeks, Violetta retained her calmness. When she stepped back, Lady Judith stepped in front of her, forcing her to let go. Lady Judith was a sturdy young woman, and Violetta had no fear she would drop Lady Perdita, or let her fall, unless she wished to. Considering her designs on Lord Blyth, Lady Judith needed Lady Perdita's approval.

Violetta caught herself on the thought. Even if it were true it wasn't her place to think so waspishly of the woman who had kept Lady Perdita company during her illness. The realization had grown on her that it gave Lady Judith enviable access to his lordship, but she told herself firmly that was nothing to do with the matter. Lady Judith probably sought out Lady Perdita for her own sake. In fact, now she came to think of it, Lady Judith took great pleasure in Lady Perdita's company. She watched the two ladies together, Lady Judith holding Lady Perdita around the waist in an almost possessive gesture. They looked like a couple.

Dear heaven!

The way Lady Judith touched Lady Perdita, so tenderly, the way she met her gaze so often. Violetta had put it down to a close friendship, but had not seen any more. It was not unusual for ladies to indulge in such friendships. It would not be her concern, if Lady Perdita assented. She watched. At a singularly intimate caress, when Lady Judith curled her arm around her friend's waist to pull her closer, Violetta saw Lady Perdita pull away, and cast her friend a doubtful look. Then all was well again and Cerisot continued in her work.

She watched her mistress for any sign of fatigue but there was none. Violetta was conscious of a feeling of pride. The exercises and massages were bearing fruit, whether the recipient of them realized it or not. She felt sure that success was just ahead of them. It was time to encourage Lady Perdita to take a few steps. Perhaps tomorrow. If she left it too long the lady might regret it or refuse to comply.

"Shall I go and fetch some refreshments?"

"Yes, do that, my dear," Cerisot replied, her mouth full of pins, her gaze distantly absent. Violetta left her unlacing Lady Perdita's gown to go and find a maid.

She returned to a scene of disaster. Lady Perdita was lying on the sofa, pale, with her eyes closed. Violetta put down the small tray of tea things and rushed forward to kneel by the side of the sofa. "What is it?"

Lady Perdita opened her eyes. To her surprise they were amused, laughing. "I did it! I stood all on my own for a full minute! Dear Judith thought I should rest after such exertion, and I do feel tired. I'll go home presently."

Her laughing countenance was so unlike her usual cold hauteur Violetta forgot herself, and gripped her hand tightly. "I knew you could do it! Slowly but surely, you are getting there."

"She only did it because I was here." Violetta could hardly believe Lady Judith had said such a thing, but when she looked up the triumph was unmistakable. "I shall come and encourage her every day. You'll be back on your feet in no time."

Violetta bit her lip and got to her feet. She was not sure the haste was advisable, but she could say nothing. She had not been present for the minute Lady Perdita had stayed on her feet. It had been Lady Judith's moment and Lady Judith was beaming triumphantly. "It won't be long before we can enter a ballroom together, dear Perdita. I long for the moment." As though Lady Judith had helped, had a significant part of the recovery. Violetta was not a saint. She resented the credit that Lady Judith fully intended to draw to herself. The possessive look, the way she blocked Violetta from coming any closer told its own story.

Cerisot, until now silent, made a small sound that drew attention to her. "If I may leave you ladies to your tea, I could inform Miss Lambert of our decisions about the clothes. Then she may assure the correct delivery of the items and not discommode her ladyship in any way."

Violetta bowed and followed Cerisot out of the small room and into another, on the other side of the large, central salon. As soon as the door closed Cerisot rounded on her. "You did not warn me, Miss Palagio. I could have given your game away in a moment." The heavy French accent, so noticeable in Cerisot's dealings with the ladies of the ton, had dropped away and now Cerisot spoke in the soft tones of the Devon countryside.

Violetta laughed, her expression light hearted. "It's no game. It started as one, but I am determined to see Lady Perdita on her feet before I leave her."

Cerisot threw up her hands. "Why on earth did you do this? And where did you get that dreadful gown?"

"Not from you." Violetta laughed again and pirouetted in front of the mirror, showing off the folds of the green gown. "Not my colour, is it?"

"Dear Lord, if you want to look dowdy. It's second hand, isn't it?" Cerisot reached out and shook out a corner of the offending gown, pulling it straight to see the worn lines left by over-pressing the pleats.

"If not third or fourth hand," Violetta agreed. "I got it from a shop on Ludgate Hill. I have three others."

Cerisot shuddered theatrically. "I hate to think there are such garments in existence."

"You haven't seen the brown one. That wouldn't suit anybody! I looked for an age before I found them!"

Cerisot regarded her with a mournful expression. "You are the most exquisite creature. Why should you want to do this? I brought you here to give you a severe scold, but I can see you're not a whit abashed. You don't care what I think."

"Oh no, of course I do! I'll come and see you soon for some new gowns. Some good ones."

Cerisot sniffed. "I don't make any other kind. What are you up to?"

Violetta smiled, feeling light-hearted. "I only took this position with Lady Perdita to see society without being seen, to get a taste of what I might have had."

Cerisot frowned. "To what aim?"

Violetta giggled. "I'm turning respectable." At the deepening of the frown, she explained. "My father died two years ago. There's no need for my mother or myself to hide any more. When I finished school I went to Tuscany, to the family estates and they welcomed me. I'm accepted as a Palagio, Cerisot. They gave me the legacy they said should have been my dowry and their blessing. Did Mama not tell you?"

Cerisot shook her head. "No. It can make little difference to her now."

Violetta's mood plummeted. That was true. It was too late for La Perla. Her mother had been delighted at the news of her abusive father's death, but she could not return to what she once had been. It was far too late for that. "You're right. The difference is for me. It means I don't have to hide any more. I'm planning to go to Italy."

"Will you join the fashionable world?"

Violetta laughed, an edge of bitterness in her tone. "I can't do that here, not immediately. If I'm recognized as La Perla's daughter I'll be ruined, and so will everyone who wants to associate with me. In Tuscany, I won't be forced to do anything I don't want to do, and I'll be another Palagio to add to the brood. I may even find a husband there, or I may return to England in the company of my family. I won't seem so unusual in their company."

"It sounds wonderful. But you have other plans, do you not?" Cerisot had seen the determination in Violetta's face.

Violetta shrugged. "I'm a little old to be a debutante. My only sorrow is that they won't accept Mama because of what she's done. They say she has put herself beyond the pale. She wants me to go to Italy, but I won't turn my back on her even if I do go."

"I should think not!" Cerisot regarded Violetta through narrowed eyes. "Though the sooner you get rid of that gown the better. Come to me when you can. I'll make time for you."

"Thank you."

They turned to leave but Cerisot turned back. "I know you won't take this amiss. Your mistress, Lady Perdita. Lady Judith is paying her a great deal of attention. Do you know what she is, what she does?"

Trust Cerisot to notice. "I was beginning to suspect

something. I don't know what Lady Perdita's desires are in the matter."

"Lady Judith prefers women to men. Any man she marries will have to share her with her women friends. Just make sure your mistress knows. I don't think she was very happy for a few moments in there."

Violetta nodded her assent and they returned. Crossing the salon, Violetta consciously took on the demeanour of the humble companion again. She did not find it difficult.

Preoccupied with her own thoughts Violetta followed the sedan chair out of the salon. Lady Judith kept Lady Perdita busy gossiping and Violetta was completely unaware until she collided with a large, solid male body. "Oof!"

Strong hands on her shoulders prevented her from tumbling. The sedan was some distance away now. Violetta looked up. "Uncle Lucius!" A deep blush suffused her cheeks at her error.

Thankful her mistress was out of earshot, she lowered her head at his warning "Shh!"

He put her back and regarded her. Out of the corner of her eye Violetta saw that Lady Judith had noticed the interlude, and had turned back. The sedan bearers had laid their burden on the floor. "Your mother is right," he remarked, staring at her. "You look terrible."

Violetta laughed. "I feel wonderful. I've been able to see without being seen."

Ripley frowned. "Don't stay too long. I thought you weren't staying more than a month?"

Violetta shrugged. "I want to help Lady Perdita. She needs someone on her side. I don't think she'll need me much longer."

He blew out a long breath of relief. "You're playing with fire, girl."

Violetta was tongue tied, wondering just how much she should tell him. Perhaps she should let the marquess and her mother know that Blyth knew her identity. It might just make them worry, though, and after all it was her problem, not theirs. She had a strong inclination to cope with her problems her way, not run for help the moment she met a snag.

"Father!"

The sound made Ripley start in surprise. He turned round and essayed a smile. "Judith, my dear, how pleasant to see you!"

Lady Judith regarded her father, her large blue eyes speculative. "You look very pleased with yourself, father." Her sharp glance went from Ripley to Violetta and back. With a start, Violetta realized what she was suspecting. Not the paternal relationship that was the reality, but something more intimate. She lowered her head in a submissive pose. "Lord Ripley and I had some previous acquaintance, my lady. He visited the house of my previous employer. He was surprised to see me in town." It was the best she could do at such short notice.

"Showing her about, Judith?" Ripley's voice gained a hard edge when he addressed his daughter. Violetta hated to hear it. "She's a remarkable young woman. Has a deal of learning in her head."

"Really?" Lady Judith's smile turned into a sneer. "I've never noticed it."

"Miss Lambert may not have been called upon to demonstrate her learning in her present position."

Violetta winced. Lord Ripley had just made clear his opinion on his daughter's intelligence, and that of her friend. He might be right. The problem had not taxed her, since her main consideration was with Lady Perdita's health, not the state of her mind. She frowned in abstraction. She hadn't thought of that before. Perhaps Lady Perdita might appreciate a little mental stimulation. She would have to discuss it with Lord Blyth.

From his vantage point across the street, Orlando watched the scene with more than a little interest. He had begun to cross the road to greet his sister, and congratulate her on her fortitude but as he had wavered he saw an old acquaintance approach the inhabitant of the sedan chair, and from her reaction, it was clear she had been welcomed.

He waited and saw Violetta and Lord Ripley. While aware of the connection between the two, it was interesting to see the ease they took in each other's company. Then Lady Judith joined them and Violetta had recalled her role as Miss Charlotte

Lambert. Her pose carefully resumed that of the humble companion, and Orlando watched Lord Ripley stiffen. He seemed more comfortable with Miss Lambert than he did with his daughter.

At the thought, Orlando straightened up. He studied the two females with sharpened interest, noting the similarities and differences. The ladies were of a height, slightly smaller than average. Lady Judith was built on generous lines but with her deliberately loose, ill-fitting clothing, Miss Lambert seemed to be similarly proportioned. That was an illusion, Orlando knew, but not the other. There was a similarity, something reminiscent of each other in them. He wondered. What if Lord Ripley's well-known devotion to La Perla was more than devotion to the mother? What if—what if Violetta was his?

This deserved investigation. Orlando turned away, no longer interested in making himself known to them, and sauntered up the street.

ജ

Having ensured that Lady Perdita didn't need her that evening, Violetta slipped out of the house and headed for her mother's establishment. There were some advantages to being a respectable servant. She needed no attendant, no one to accompany her. It was a fine evening, spring fast moving into summer, and she could enjoy the journey. It took her past no dangerous spots, and if she tired, she could hire a hackney. Money in her pocket, but not too much, dowdy appearance that didn't draw attention to herself.

Pondering her good fortune, feeling at peace with the world, Violetta didn't notice the steps behind her until someone touched her elbow. Turning her head sharply she saw her employer.

He didn't look happy, a forbidding frown creasing his brows. "You should take a maid with you."

"I'm only going to my mother's. It's not far."

"I know where you're going. I know it's broad daylight. I also know there's a man following you at a distance, waiting until you reach a quiet corner. No, don't look."

Violetta obeyed, looking at him instead. "I can take care of myself."

"Don't be foolish. The next time you leave the house, even to walk in the square, I want to know." He gave an exasperated sigh.

Violetta knew her protestation had been foolish. She was no match against a man with a knife, or even an unarmed man, but she had loved the quiet walks she took to her mother's house each Thursday. "I enjoy being on my own. Just to walk and watch."

"The attendant can follow you at a distance."

She bowed her head. "Then he'd know where I was going."

"Then call a hackney. I'll pay."

She knew he was right, but was loath to give her walks up. However, perhaps it was true. "I'm sorry. I didn't mean to give you any worries."

"No!" He sounded sharp. "Don't be sorry. I can understand some of your concerns. It would irk me almost beyond bearing to have to take a servant with me everywhere I went. If you prefer it, I'll walk behind you, or keep silent. I want to make sure you reach your mother's house safely, that is all."

"Thank you." Violetta was deeply touched by his understanding. "Perhaps if I lived in the country it might be possible."

"Have you ever lived in the country?"

She considered. "No. Only when I went to Italy to see my mother's people." She stopped on a gasp.

His look was perceptive. "I won't tell."

Violetta cursed her foolishness. She had let herself relax too much. Her mother's deepest secret was not known in London. She slanted a sideways look at him.

"Who are your mother's people?"

The last question she wanted to answer. She tried to shrug it off. "No one in particular. At least, no one special. I visited them two years ago. I was fortunate enough to have my own Grand Tour."

"Something few women can boast of."

Relieved, Violetta realized she had hit on a topic of

innocuous conversation. "I was very lucky. I went to France and Italy."

"Your mother's profession must be very lucrative." His bitten off curse made her smile. "I'm sorry. I shouldn't have mentioned it."

"Why not? I know what she is, what she was. She is still my mother."

His lips firmed to a thin line, but he said nothing because they were turning a corner into another street of prosperous houses. When it was clear there was nobody within earshot he continued. "I feel responsible for you, while you're in my house, under my protection. I think I may be taking too much on myself."

"What do you mean?" This speech left Violetta entirely perplexed. She smiled up at him, then turned to stroll along the street, enjoying the walk.

"I find it difficult to tolerate your living in such a house."

"What sort of house is that?"

"Do I have to say it?" His voice rose slightly. She knew the pause was while he regained control of himself. "Very well. A house of ill-repute. A house where demi-mondaines are found."

"And you don't see these women as anything but receptacles, do you?" The thought came to her, but as she said it Violetta realized this must be the truth. It was true of so many men. "The women I know have taken men as their lovers for money. It doesn't mean they didn't care, and it doesn't mean that they know nothing else. They have to have more than bedroom skills to attract and keep clever men. Equally, they have the right to refuse a man their bed, which is more than a prostitute does." She heard his sharply indrawn breath and smiled to herself. She had hit a nerve. "My mother's friends and colleagues are at least honest. I have met many women of fashion who have had more lovers than any of the women I know, but because they accept the occasional gift and not filthy lucre for their efforts, they consider themselves superior. None of the women I know commit adultery."

"Many of the men I know do. If it weren't for these women they might not."

Too late, Violetta remembered his history. His father had

ruined the inheritance by extravagant spending on women and gambling and by the time the present Lord Blyth had reached the age of five, he was fatherless and nearly penniless. "Forgive me. I spoke out of turn."

He stopped walking and turned to her with a frown. She turned to face him. "Now it's my turn to ask you what you mean."

She met his gaze fearlessly. She had thought it, she might as well say it. "My mother never had anything to do with your father. I know his history but I never met him."

"What about Lord Ripley and your mother? Isn't that a clear case of adultery?"

She bit her lip. "That's different. One day, perhaps, I'll tell you their story."

"Why not now?"

She turned away and resumed walking. He easily kept pace by her side. "I can tell you some of it. I don't know the whole myself." They walked for a while in silence. They were getting close now. Violetta knew she could spin the story out until they got there, so she wouldn't have to tell him anything else. He was altogether too perceptive.

She told him what she wanted him to know. "They met while his lordship was on the Grand Tour, when they were both young. They fell in love, but his lordship had married before he left. His family wanted the alliance and he accepted it. When he returned to England he tried to forget my mother and she him, but there came a time when she desperately needed his help. This did not include his taking her as a lover. He helped her without that. However, my mother decided to make her way in the world in the only way that was open to her."

"As a courtesan."

"Yes." If he had wanted to discommode her, he was foiled. She had heard that word, and worse, too often to be worried by the name. "They became lovers after that and have remained so ever since. They could almost be married."

"Except that he already had a bride."

"Yes." Violetta would not expand on that.

"And she had other lovers."

She shrugged. They had arrived at the house. "So she did." She gave him a bright smile. "I have to leave you here."

"I'll go back and change. I intend to make good your challenge."

Her heart sank. She wished he would not. However, if he insisted, then she would meet him. It was a matter of honour. "I shall see you later, then. See if you recognize me. I think we will all be wearing masks tonight."

"I'll know you."

A small plan began to form in Violetta's head. She smiled sweetly. "Very well, my lord. *Arrivederci.*"

He sketched a small bow. "*Addio.*"

He left. Violetta went into the house of ill-repute.

Chapter Eight

"It will do." Violetta studied her reflection and bit her lip nervously. She was too honest to deny the reason. To her knowledge Lord Blyth had never visited the salon, and now he was coming. One man tonight would know what lay behind the mask La Perla Perfetta always wore. "I wish I could be sure I'm doing the right thing."

Violetta's maid smiled and added a silver clip to Violetta's unpowdered hair. Black and glossy, it was the feature that prevented people from looking at her other features too deeply. It was coiled into an elaborate style, some of it pinned around her head, some flowing down her back. "Your mama has made sure the game will end without trouble."

The rest of her was white. White satin gown, robings and hem gleaming with brilliants, white half mask, slanting up above the eyes to distort the shape of the face, the eye holes cut on a slant. The mask was edged with brilliants at its upper edge. Violetta flicked back the triple lace ruffles at her sleeve and picked up her fan, a pretty lace affair. Her own grandmother wouldn't know her. Not tonight, at any rate. She turned to the door, her skirts shushing gently around her.

Quietly, just before she left, she murmured, "I'm not sure I want it to end without trouble."

Orlando paused just inside the doorway of the large, elegantly appointed salon. Another man walked past him, affording him a cursory nod of greeting.

Orlando had dressed in his best tonight. He wore dark blue with an ivory waistcoat and matching blue breeches, the coat heavily embroidered down the front and on the pocket flaps, the waistcoat a masterpiece of the embroiderer's art. A large sapphire rested on the second finger of his right hand. He was determined to make an impression tonight, and to give Violetta a kind of tribute. His kind of tribute.

He had never been here before. He felt uncomfortable, entering a room like this where desires were so blatant, so straightforward, and he wondered why he had come. If it had not been for that foolish challenge, instantly accepted, he would have stayed away.

The women at La Perla's were at the top of their profession but Orlando could only feel dull anger as he watched the practised flirting. Miss Lambert had no place here. He could not accept that she would be happy or that she could hold her own with such women. Or be expected to. Orlando suspected she had been trained, and the thought of her being used in such a way made him seethe.

He wasn't sure why. He was aware of the anger, but shied away from the reasons, or the possible reasons. Instead he moved into the room and went towards the figure that commanded all attention. It must be a masque, because every woman and some of the men sported masks of varying elaboration.

Blatantly gazing around, Orlando's attention sparked when he realized exactly what he was seeing. Every woman except La Perla wore white. Every woman sported a white mask, but they were all different. All of them wore a shiny, black wig. Except, he guessed, one woman.

She was fighting back. She would not let him have things all his own way. Good for her!

Well used to keeping his inner emotions private, Orlando showed nothing to the world. He crossed the room at his leisure and bowed before the woman seated between the windows in a gilt chair. She was almost regal in appearance. Appropriate, since this woman was the queen of the demi-monde.

She awarded him a gracious nod. "You are Lord Blyth, I believe." Her voice was deep and soft. Orlando caught echoes of it in her daughter's, but unlike Violetta's pure tones, La Perla's was laced with her origins, the accent a lilting Italian.

"I am, ma'am." He looked up and received a smile. It felt as though he had been awarded something special. This was the woman who trained sweet Violetta in the ways of sexual attraction.

La Perla was glorious. She must be fifty, or thereabouts, but her face was a work of art. Out of a smooth complexion gazed a pair of huge, violet eyes, topped by thin, arched black brows. He would have known that pointed chin anywhere, the full, rosebud lips and the high cheekbones. He had expected a lavish use of cosmetics, but he was surprised to find a light, artful touch, enhancing naturally piquant features instead of obscuring them into fashionable blandness. It would be a shame to conceal such an individual personality. Reluctantly Orlando was forced to admit he could see why La Perla had reigned for so long and so effectively. Her daughter was no doubt trained to take over, when the time came.

"I see you have heard of me."

"Who has not?" The stories of her were legion, and it was difficult to discern fact from fiction, they were so intertwined.

La Perla took her time. She studied Lord Blyth. He studied her in his turn until they caused a deadlock. Eventually the lady opened her lips. "You wish to court my daughter."

"I wish to see her," he corrected, "and make myself known to you and your friends."

"We know you, your lordship. We have seen you and wondered why you have not appeared before."

"I had no wish to be inopportune or gauche, ma'am."

The smile they exchanged was of total understanding. Now he could afford the wares, he would come. Two people who had faced financial ruin and survived smiled at each other guardedly, knowing, as others could not, just what that meant. Orlando recognized the bond, though he hated himself for recognizing it. He wanted to dislike her for dragging her daughter down to her own level, but he found, faced with her, that he couldn't. He hated himself for his weakness, too.

"Then please be welcome. Whether my daughter accepts you or not is her choice. She is old enough to make her own decisions." She lifted her gaze and scanned the room briefly. "However, we have a small amusement planned. You may make your choice, and converse with any of the young ladies present.

At midnight, they will unmask. Except one, of course. My daughter never unmasks in public. After that time, all the ladies here are forbidden to you if you have not won the contest."

"Forever?" He didn't care. There was only one woman he wanted.

La Perla shrugged, an elegant ripple of white shoulders under blue velvet. "It is up to them. Certainly for tonight. If you cannot identify her by midnight we demand a forfeit."

"Which would be?" Orlando wondered what he'd got himself into. He couldn't leave now. If he did, Violetta could find herself in the hands of any of the gentlemen present before the night was over.

"Something simple. One hundred guineas, to be paid to La Perla Perfetta." The lady stared at him, smiling sweetly. She could have been his maiden aunt.

Once that would have been a fortune to Orlando. Now it was the cost of an evening's entertainment. He smiled back, his expression turning elegantly bland, an expression his brothers had learned to mistrust. "Shall we say one thousand?"

Not a twitch marred the features before him. She regarded him in silence, then lifted her hand. "Very well, so be it. One thousand pounds."

"If we make it guineas, it might be more interesting."

"Are any of these gentlemen joining in?" La Perla looked around challengingly.

A few glanced at each other, and one stepped forward. "I'll take it, but only if I keep the lady I discover."

La Perla regarded him dispassionately. "For a night, perhaps, but the rest must be up to the lady. I don't run a bawdy house, gentlemen. The ladies here are my guests, not my employees. I will hold you gentlemen to the original stake only. One hundred guineas, to be paid to the lady. But this gentleman, who demands the ultimate prize, must pay more." La Perla lifted her gaze to glance around the room. She received a series of nods. Orlando watched closely. "I reserve the right to substitute another lady for my daughter." Orlando frowned and opened his mouth to protest, but she leaned forward and gently placed the closed sticks of her fan across it.

La Perla looked around again, taking in all the ladies present. Orlando watched her closely but she didn't hesitate anywhere until her attention returned to him. She studied him for a long moment, and Orlando saw, just for a fraction of time, the mother behind the courtesan, the concern. She was worried for her daughter. It went a long way towards reconciling Orlando. Had she allowed him to see her concern? "That no longer applies. La Perla Perfetta agrees to the challenge. Whoever successfully identifies her may keep her, for the price. However, she will not be unmasked except by her own will." Violetta's masks were cleverly designed and no one except the people who knew her best knew her eyes true shape and colour. She had masks with heavy artificial lashes, some with different shaped eye-holes, and a few with filters made of tinted mica. She would be wearing one of those tonight, Orlando felt sure.

Disappointment murmured through the room. La Perla smiled, serene once more and leaned back. "If that is acceptable, shall we begin?"

Orlando's stomach tightened. Did that mean that La Perla Perfetta would give herself to whoever identified her? It must. Her mother had appeared unwilling to allow this, but when she scanned the room her daughter must have given some sign of acceptance.

Someone moved. Orlando recognized Lord Ripley, garbed in splendid crimson, a startling splash against his mistress's midnight blue. He spoke softly. "Is this wise? The game is amusing, but La Perla Perfetta is a prize beyond price."

"Indeed she is, but she has indicated her assent to the game."

Ripley did not look around, but Orlando caught something, an instinctive movement. He followed the direction of the movement. Three women, all in white and masked, stood in that corner of the room. They stared back at him impassively.

La Perla lifted a hand and the quartet began to play a dance tune, a minuet. The floor cleared at the sound. Orlando crossed the room, squeezing past a few of the ladies with an apologetic smile, and bowed in front of one of the three women standing in the corner. "Would you honour me with this dance, ma'am?"

The lady smiled, her rouged lips curving seductively. "It

would be a pleasure, sir."

She was too old to be Violetta, and hadn't her sweetness. Still, Orlando enjoyed the dance. She had a grace that seemed to come naturally to her. As he guided her around the steps of the dance, he watched how she altered the steps and poses into a long flirtation. He was only allowed to take her hand occasionally, but a twist of the hand, a stroke of fingertips against his palm served to tantalize and tease. Well, two could play at that game. Orlando responded, allowing his fingers to curl around hers as though he was reluctant to release her. He let his gaze linger on her low cut bodice, as though enjoying the sight of her totally naked. A delicious game.

When the music stopped a slight pattering of applause surprised him. Ripley was leaning against the back of his mistress's chair, smiling warmly. Orlando placed the lady's hand on his arm and took her across to a vacant chair. "In the normal course of events," he murmured, "I would ask to spend more time with you. You will excuse me tonight?"

With a flutter of a fan she consented, keeping her voice hoarse and low. Orlando lifted an eyebrow and grinned at her. They were even trying to keep their voices close to Violetta's. However, he was not fooled. He went over to Ripley.

He knew the man but had no close acquaintance with him, despite the fast friendship between Perdita and Lady Judith. A generation lay between the men. Ripley nodded in greeting. "Any ideas yet, Blyth?"

Orlando regarded him closely. "No."

"Smitten by the thought of an expensive mistress?" Ripley grinned. "You can afford one now. Might as well indulge yourself."

"Something like that."

"You have an advantage."

"I'm paying for the privilege."

Ripley nodded and straightened up. "Refreshment, my love?"

"A small glass," La Perla replied, glancing up at her lover.

Ripley led the way to a sideboard, groaning under the weight of bottles and glasses. He picked out two and helped himself and Orlando to burgundy. He was totally at home here.

Orlando had never seen his lordship so at ease, so content. "Now," he said, handing Orlando his glass, "may I make something clear to you without you calling me out?"

"I'll reserve judgement." Orlando sipped cautiously. The burgundy was the best quality. He expected nothing less.

Ripley nodded and looked around, smiling, as though he was exchanging the time of day. "For various reasons, La Perla Perfetta is precious to me." Orlando raised an eyebrow, but said nothing. He had his suspicions. "If you want her and she wants you, there is no more to be said in the matter. She is her mother's daughter and she has made her desires known. However, hurt her, or treat her with less than kindness and I will call you out, scandal or no."

"I have no intention of hurting her. I have come to care for her. I owe her a debt, which only you, her mother and I know of."

"How much do you care?" The question sounded casual but was far from it.

Orlando chose his words meticulously. "She has done me a great service, but there's more than that. How much I don't yet know."

"You desire her."

Orlando sipped his wine, watching the figures gracefully disporting themselves before him in the dance. "Everyone does."

"They desire her because they don't know her. She's a mystery to them. You know her better than most. That is why I will hold you responsible if you hand her to one of these people tonight."

Orlando smiled. "Oh, I don't think there's any fear of that."

"There had better not be."

Orlando had the strong suspicion that La Perla would not give her prize away so lightly. His price might suffice, but one hundred guineas was a paltry sum for the woman who had tantalized the male population of London since her appearance in her mother's salon five years ago. His lips tightened in denial. No, he would not allow such a thing. It must not be.

"How long have you been with La Perla?"

"Most of my life." The reply came instantly, as though

Ripley no longer had to think about it. "I would have married her, but I was already married when I first met her."

Orlando felt an unexpected pang of sympathy for the unfortunate Lady Ripley. "Doesn't sound as though your wife had a chance."

Ripley turned to face him, face grim. "She had her chance. Believe me she did. I came back to La Perla only after my wife sent me away. It was not pique or temper that did it. It was her rejection of me, pure and simple."

"Still." Orlando took another sip. "You could not marry a courtesan at any time."

Ripley bit his lip. Orlando knew the older man had stopped a response that might have been unwise. He decided to further his acquaintance with the older man. It might help him discover more about Violetta and her mother. He knew there was more to it than an Italian woman of remarkable beauty taking London by storm. Where had she been until then? Why had she not appeared anywhere else before?

Orlando bowed to a young lady who curtsied to him. A golden strand of hair lay on one shoulder, loosened from under the black wig. Orlando let his gaze wander the room. Perhaps La Perla was known under another name. He knew more than the rest of London except, perhaps, Ripley. He knew La Perla Perfetta's real first name, if it was her real name.

He knew it was. She had told him without thinking, then looked regretful, as though she would take it back. Violetta.

"I would have defied convention for her," Ripley said softly. "There has only ever been one woman for me. The pity is I discovered her too late."

"What is it about these women?" Orlando wondered.

"Who knows? They are lovely, intelligent and accomplished, but then so are a lot of women." Ripley put his empty glass down. "Excuse me."

He picked up a full glass of white wine. Beads of moisture ran down the outside of the glass. Chilled to perfection, Orlando guessed. Nothing was stinted here. He wondered how much money La Perla and her daughter had salted away. Not much, he guessed. Now the mother was off the market it might be the time for the daughter to earn her living.

On her back.

What a tangle! Orlando bowed to a young lady and solicited a dance. While he knew this one wasn't Violetta, he could watch the rest of the room from the floor. This lady had an extravagant mask made out of white feathers. That, and the decoration of her gown showed her theme was the white peacock. It was exquisite, but the way the gown was looped up out of the way made Orlando realize it had been made for a taller woman than this petite beauty. Her waist was so tiny he could span it easily with his hands, should she let him. He had no doubt she would. Her fan looked as though it was made of white peacock feathers, and if that was so, it must have cost a pretty penny. Orlando grinned. He would never get out of the habit of pricing things. He should have been born a merchant. "Something amuses you, my lord?"

He gave her a sweet smile. "Nothing, dear lady. 'Tis the pleasure of your company makes me smile."

The lady dimpled prettily. She couldn't be more than seventeen. Orlando was struck by the varying ages of the women in the room, as varied as the gentlemen present. The only similarity between the men was their ability to pay. The women were from a variety of backgrounds, but all had the ability to please a man. Some liked young flesh.

He smiled at her. "What is your particular talent, my dear?"

She moved closer in the dance. "I can take all of a man in my mouth, and hum while I'm doing it."

Definitely not Violetta. A novelty welcomed by many but a pretty young girl with one particular talent would not last long in these circles. Such talents could be bought in any of the bawdy houses lining the Covent Garden Piazza.

There he was again. Money. He bowed to the young lady and immediately lost interest in her.

He had an hour to accomplish his goal, for his sake and for Violetta's. Some of the men here would only take her over his dead body. He knew for a fact that old Lord Cheshunt was riddled with pox; certain death for anyone who entertained him. He was also filthy rich, with the emphasis on the filthy.

Orlando circulated the room, exchanging a few words here and there, as though he was searching for the one. The ladies were all lovely. Not all were beautiful, but all had something. Grace, elegance, a luscious figure, sometimes all three. None of them could compare to a black haired fairy with deep blue eyes. He guessed that Violetta's wardrobe had been emptied for the occasion, since several women were dressed in gowns that looked to have been altered or pinned. He touched several of them casually, something society women would never allow.

As the evening progressed and the drink flowed, gazes and invitations became more blatant. La Perla stayed seated for the most part, only consenting to take one dance with Lord Ripley. Orlando was standing next to a full bosomed beauty at the time, casually conversing. "She doesn't see anyone but him any more," the lady commented. "She must be costing him a fortune."

"He isn't short of a few pence," Orlando said absently, watching La Perla, understanding where her daughter had found her instinctive grace.

"He doesn't look at anyone but her. I've heard he doesn't even sleep with his wife any more."

It was something Orlando suspected, but had not voiced. To hear it articulated aloud jolted him. The man loved his mistress. It was evident in his care of her, in his every look, although there was no embarrassing display between them. They could never marry, never form a true partnership. Deep sadness filled him, for everyone involved, even Lady Judith, whose attentions to him were becoming more marked every day. Orlando was finding her an increasing menace, but it didn't prevent him sympathizing with her family situation.

With a slight effort he brought the picture of Lady Ripley to mind. A tall, elegant woman, generously made. The words that came instantly to Orlando's mind were formidable, cold and formal.

Not a woman one would want to be shackled to for life. From what Ripley had said he had been married to her very young. Orlando shuddered.

He turned to more amusing pursuits. This was not the only salon open to visitors tonight. He went through to the smaller room. As he expected it was exquisitely appointed in the French style, with lots of gilt and light, clear colours. He liked it, graceful and elegant, a fitting setting for its owner.

Moving forward, Orlando greeted some of the people playing cards at the tables set up for the purpose. He knew, from the guineas and counters in front of some of the participants, that play on some tables was deep, but the atmosphere was not the concentrated oblivion of the dedicated card player. This was merely rich people amusing themselves. A sideline to the main event. There were no estates at stake here, no last minute efforts to turn fortunes.

"Thinking of something?"

He turned to see the dark eyes of Ripley gazing into his. He inclined his head. "Yes, and thanking heaven I didn't have to try to restore my fortune that way. I tried, but money follows money. I lost too much, then won, then left. I don't play for high stakes any more."

"You can afford to now."

"Yes."

There was a short, companionable silence. "I saw you once," Ripley continued. "Upstairs at the Cocoa-Tree late one night. You were losing. The way you held the cards, the way all the colour had gone from your face told me that."

"I remember." It was engraved on his memory for all time. The night he thought he'd lost everything. In half an hour he had recouped his losses, but won nothing. "After that, I left the table and didn't game again until I could afford it."

"Very wise." They contemplated the room again.

Orlando wandered around the room, but was careful not to interfere with the concentration of the more serious players. Men had been called out for less. At one table a group of ladies and gentlemen was playing for small stakes, enjoying the company. At his approach, one of the ladies turned and smiled a welcome. None of them was Violetta. Orlando sat down.

"My first spring ball of the year."

"They say the summer will be exceptionally warm this year."

"Warm enough to encourage the ladies to wear a little less?" one of the gentlemen ventured. He received a roguish smile for his pains. "Perhaps even to discard their stays?"

A chorus of derisory laughs greeted this sally. All female. The males' interest had sharpened. One or two looked slack mouthed, the way a man in heat could look sometimes. Orlando watched the women play them like anglers with small fish. "No stays!" one of them exclaimed forcefully. "That would set the fashionables on edge. Perhaps we should appear in public like that."

"Oh dear me, no!" another cried. She flourished her fan before her face, glittering brilliants in the candlelight. "They might try to vie with us and then, you know, imagine the sight!"

A chorus of light laughter followed. "They are fortunate," a young voice said from the edge of the group. Not Violetta. "They can afford to let themselves go to seed. We cannot."

There was a brief silence, but a sharp voice cut in. "It may be true of the lower sections of our little community, but not of us. Ladies, we are the best. We are here because we are the best. We can entertain, amuse and divert, but we can also question and challenge. Pity the respectable woman, forbidden to enter these doors!"

The short silence that followed this expressed sympathy rather than animosity. "I will convey your sympathies to them," Orlando said smoothly. "I'm sure they will be most amused."

"Lord Blyth, even you cannot achieve such a feat," said a girl, her green eyes alight with laughter behind her half mask.

"I know it. Ranked against respectable woman, every man must quail."

The girl deployed her fan, gently wafting it before her face, disturbing the lace covering her bosom. A clever ploy. She saw Orlando look and her smile became more intense. "I cannot imagine why you gentlemen waste time with your wives when we are here for your every need. The poor ladies must have their own amusements, you know."

Orlando got to his feet and managed a charming smile. "Of course. I do hope you will excuse me. I was distracted from my task by your delightful company, but there is a stake and I trust you will pardon me. Hopefully we can resume our acquaintance at another time." He shot a look at the green-eyed beauty who nodded in acceptance and he moved away.

He hated it. All of it. At that moment he would have left this house, thrown the thousand guineas in La Perla's face and left. Except that, if he left, Violetta would be at the mercy of someone else. He could not allow that.

A society that considered marriage a business arrangement was not for him. He had always nurtured a hope, deep down in his darkest soul that he would find a mate. Someone to love, someone who was his, and only his. At the least he wanted a companion and partner, a woman to share with. At best, a love he knew he would never find. He'd seen his elder brother fall in love with his wife, only to suffer when his wife gave birth to his sons, births that nearly cost her life. Now Daniel wouldn't touch his wife. He burned for her. Orlando saw it every moment he spent with them and he ached for them both. Still, his romantic soul told him it was worth it, that they had known some measure of happiness before disaster struck them. He had discussed Daniel's problem with Corin, his younger brother, but no plan had occurred to them yet.

A world that condoned adultery, even encouraged it, was a sad state of affairs. Orlando had to admit his hands were not completely clean. Until a few years ago he had not been able to afford to buy his amusements, and seducing young virgins was out of the question, although he knew men who made a pastime of doing just that. Widows and wives whose husbands were out busy with their own amusements had provided some experience for him.

Now it was different. His years of poverty, existing on the charity of his mother's third husband, had taught him the value of observation, of thought before action, but it had been a hard journey and not easily learned.

It lacked half an hour to midnight. Orlando, his choice made, danced with one young lady and then drifted from room to room, ostensibly studying the company, but in reality waiting.

At ten minutes to midnight Orlando went back to the salon, and waited for La Perla to orchestrate the next act.

"Lord Blyth!" La Perla had hardly raised her voice, but at her tones the quartet abruptly ceased its playing and everyone stopped, turning to the lady expectantly.

Orlando gave her a cool smile and walked unhurriedly to her side. He stood by the gilt chair, and waited. The room filled slowly, as the occupants of the other rooms drifted in, all facing the chair. The scene resembled a royal audience, Orlando thought wryly. With himself as supplicant.

"The unmasking!" La Perla exclaimed. Several hands went up to the strings of masks. "However, first we have some unfinished business. Will my daughter be richer for one thousand guineas, or will she take this charming gentleman?" Orlando didn't like the implications of that, or the publicness of the announcement. "We shall see. Have you made your choice, Lord Blyth?" She turned her head to fix him with a steely glare.

"I have." Orlando met the expression, waiting for a fraught moment. La Perla was not the only one who knew how to build anticipation. While he waited he noticed something deep in her eyes. Fear, perhaps, or worry. Something he didn't expect to see in this woman of the world. He turned back to the room. "I have gifted the lady of my choice. She will find, pinned to her sleeve, my sapphire cravat pin. It has my monogram on the reverse."

All the women turned their heads to examine their sleeves, a number of gentlemen joining them. There was a general disturbance, a breaking of the tension that Orlando and La Perla had built up.

There was a movement at the back of the room and the company parted to allow the lady through. She stood before Orlando and her mother, her face, what could be seen of it, still and serene. She wore an artfully uptilted mask, edged with brilliants, and a gown decorated heavily with brilliants and lace. "I found this earlier. I removed it, because I didn't wish it to tear the silk." Her accent was tinted with Italian, but she was the lady he'd chosen. Her words were steady, and strangely flat, as though she was hiding emotion.

She held out her hand. In it was Orlando's cravat pin.

The room exploded into applause and delighted laughter. All except four people. Orlando stared at La Perla Perfetta, no trace of a smile, and she stared back, impassively. La Perla visibly swallowed and Ripley placed a gentle hand on her shoulder.

La Perla cleared her throat. "I could not have wished for it, but I cannot be entirely sorry. Well done, my lord. You have won the prize. By her own wish, my daughter is now yours."

Orlando held his arm out. Silently, La Perla Perfetta came to stand by his side and placed her hand on it. They had not taken their gazes away from each other, for all the world as though they were deep in love.

Orlando heard a murmur, deep and low. "Take care of her."

"I will," he promised Lord Ripley.

He took her out of the room.

Chapter Nine

Orlando let Violetta take him upstairs and upstairs again to a floor where he knew the public wasn't normally granted access. She said nothing, but he felt the hand on his arm tremble and knew she was nervous. It was to be expected. So was he.

He said nothing until she closed the door of her bedchamber behind her and stood to face him. "This is new to me," she confessed, her voice low. "You'll have to tell me what to do. It's a lowering thing for someone in this house to have to admit."

"Not for you." He didn't move to take her in his arms, but rather, moved away. He had to get himself under control if he were to keep to his resolve, reached a couple of hours earlier downstairs. "Have you, then, decided to enter the Muslin Company?"

She shrugged, but there was no elegance in the gesture. Rather, it was an uncomfortable action, that of a young girl not sure of her own mind. "No. I can't bring myself to do that."

He folded his arms. "Why not?" He tried to make it a polite query, but it was not. On the answer to this question lay the future of this night, and perhaps many nights to come. If she wanted to make her own way, take a lover, then it might as well be him. The decision held much melancholy for him, as well as happiness. He could not deny that he wanted her, with a strength of feeling that surprised him, but this way he would condemn her to years of lovers, like her mother.

"I don't want it. I don't want to be the cause of dissension between man and wife. I don't want to rely on a man for my livelihood." She stumbled on the last word. Orlando looked up, at her face, still covered by the mask except for her ruby lips, unrouged but more inviting than any others he'd seen tonight.

"Then why do what you did tonight?"

The eyes behind the mask glittered. "You challenged me. You know you did. Was I to take it lying down?" She bit her lip.

Orlando grinned. "If and when we make love, I sincerely hope so. However, that is not the case." He paused. "Take it off."

"Oh!" Her hands fluttered to her bosom. "Yes—yes if you wish it."

"The mask, fool!" his voice grated. "I want to see you face to face."

"Oh." Her hands rose to the ties of her mask, but she fumbled.

With a sound of exasperation, Orlando strode across the room to stand behind her. "Keep still." He undid the ties and found the pins firmly fastening the mask to her hair, drawing them all out. There were six. He refrained from uncoiling her hair, but now, so close, he smelt the fresh scent, and felt a sudden need to undo the elaborate coils and bury his hands in the thick, shining mass. He breathed deeply and stood back. "There."

She turned, the mask in her hands. They stared at each other and Orlando came to a realization. Her gaze was strangely blurred. She was drunk, or not far off it. "Well? Do you like what you see?"

"I've always liked it. Even under a mousy wig and spectacles." He made no move towards her. She stayed where she was. Without her mask she was breathtaking, enchanting. The brilliants on her gown twinkled whenever she moved, so that Orlando found himself waiting for her next breath, to see the bows on her bodice shine. "You must know you're lovely. Especially dressed like that."

"Like what?" Her chin went up a little, as though she was challenging him to say "wanton".

She was not wanton. "Exquisite. Delicate. As you should be dressed." He frowned. "Do you intend to continue to wear those appalling gowns in my house? I would much rather see you in something like this."

She arched her brows. "Do you want me back? Attending to Lady Perdita in the daytime and in your bed at night? Is that it?" He watched her take a step so she stood wide-stanced under the expansive skirts of her gown. He was sure now. She was unsteady.

Reluctantly, drawn by the thought she had put in his mind, Orlando shook his head. "That's what I want to talk to you about. Come and sit down."

He held out his hand. She put her own in it. She still trembled. Ignoring it, he took her to the daybed at the foot of the large, elaborately draped four-poster bed. At least, with her back to the bed, she might be less nervous, but the daybed itself was an invitation to dally. Violetta would look wonderful against that pale lavender silk, naked and welcoming. He felt a stirring below and sternly suppressed the image from his mind. He kept hold of her hand. He turned it in his, and stared at it, frowning, like a gypsy fortune teller seeing a life within.

"Violetta, I'll try to explain something. It's difficult, because it's something I feel rather than something I know, but I'll do my best." He paused, gathering his thoughts. "First of all, I want to assure you that nothing will happen in this bedroom tonight that you do not want. I'll not force you, or try to seduce you against your better judgement. I promise."

Her shocked surprise could almost be felt. "Why? You won me, in a fair competition."

"There was nothing fair about it. No one has eyes like yours. Even behind that mask, I couldn't mistake them. I knew you as soon as I saw you. I put my marker on you early on, you know."

"No one has looked at me as closely as you do." She paused. "I haven't allowed it. I would have won the game had you not been here. I felt you put the pin on me and I took it off to prolong the game. If anyone had seen that sapphire on an all white dress, the game would have been up there and then."

Her soft voice came steadier now. Orlando hoped his assurance had helped her to come to terms with this. He meant it, every word. "If and when we come together, I want it to be on the bedrock of friendship." He lifted his head and met her gaze. "I don't want a mistress, a woman I only think of for one thing. I saw them tonight. For all the sophistication, they were all behaving like ravening animals." He grinned. "Don't misunderstand me. It's the same in polite society, and at least your mother's salon has the saving grace of honesty. I think it's more honest to pay for sex than to try to buy someone, body and soul."

"Yes."

Her quiet assent told him she understood. Not just superficially, but completely. "More than anything else I want a friendship with you, Violetta. I don't want to sound maudlin, but I've never had a female friend before. I find I can talk to you, and you understand. As though there was a link between us."

"Yes."

"It's precious to me, because I've never known it before." He grinned. "If you hadn't agreed to that silly stake, you'd be a thousand guineas the richer, you know."

"You would have reneged?"

"I had every intention of doing so. I owe you much for the way you've helped Perdita. I know she isn't easy, but you did what was needed. You bullied her into taking an interest. It's not just that. I want to know you'll be secure. Friends do that for each other. They share."

"A thousand guineas?"

"It's enough to buy you a comfortable annuity. Then you can make your own decisions. I won't miss it. May I still give it to you?"

"No."

"Why not? A gift, free and clear, in gratitude for helping my sister? Surely you can accept that?"

She shook her head. A small curl was dislodged from the elaborate coiffure, and fell onto her shoulder. She didn't seem to notice, but Orlando did. He swallowed a fresh wave of desire. "I don't need it. Did you think we were penniless? My lord, my mother comes from an intensely practical race. Ever since she began her career, she has salted away half her earnings. Investments have increased it. I have no need of your money."

This shook Orlando. In his experience, courtesans spent money like water, and he'd seen nothing to disturb that conclusion since he had stepped into this house. "A clever woman."

"Indeed she is. She knows what I plan to do, and approves of it. I was never meant to follow in her footsteps, you know. She is very upset about tonight, but she knows better than to interfere with my decisions."

He stared at her. "Upset? I thought this was her triumph?"

"Lord no!" For the first time the tragic look disappeared to be replaced by a mischievous grin. "She doesn't want me to do this."

"Then why did you?"

"A moment of madness," she said shortly. "That is all." She glanced away and then back to him, a new determination in her eyes. "And perhaps I wanted you too."

He couldn't help it. He drew her to him, and slipped his arm around her. "Do you?"

"I did. Now I'm not so sure." She didn't resist, but rested her head on his shoulder. "I like the idea of being friends. I've never had a male friend before, not really."

She felt good to him, the weight on his shoulder perfect. "I want the friendship more than the loving. At least, I thought so a moment ago. I want it to last. Tell me your plans, Violetta. Tell me what you want to do with your life." He knew that sober she would never be telling him these things, but drunk, or rather, a little the worse for alcohol, her tongue was looser.

She spoke softly, but he heard her perfectly well. "I want to be my own woman. I have enough money to set up for myself. I'm going...away soon, and when I come back, if I do, I want a small house, perhaps on the other side of Tottenham Court Road. Harley Street or somewhere like that."

Another role, he thought, wondering why she felt the need to take on other parts, other roles. He suspected it went very deep. Perhaps she wasn't aware of the need, but he had noted the way she immersed herself into whatever character she was playing, an actress taking on a part, trying to convince others and perhaps herself, too. "You want to shut yourself away?" He moved his hand gently on her shoulder.

"No. I want to be respectable."

She had difficulty with the last word. Orlando ignored it for the present. "Why would you want that?"

She jerked away and sat up straight. Eyes blazing, she

faced him, every word crystal clear. "I don't want men to look at me the way they look at my mother—with calculation, wondering how much she would cost. I don't want women to move their skirts when I pass by them, I don't want them to stare at me and look away when I try to meet their eyes. My mother is worth more than that and so am I."

Much struck by her statement, he agreed without pause. "Much more."

He watched the fire fade from her eyes and was a little sorry. She looked magnificent like that. Perhaps he could make her angry again. Not tonight, though. He had something entirely different planned for tonight. "I'm sorry, but you did ask."

He wanted to pull her back into his arms. She felt good there, but he had promised he wouldn't force her to do anything she didn't want to do. "You want respectability. Quiet obscurity." He smiled. "You think you have any chance of having that, looking as you do?"

"I'm a little different, that's all."

"You're remarkable." She opened her mouth to reply, but closed it again. "I've never seen eyes your colour before. I never even imagined such a shade existed. Your hair gleams blue sometimes, and sometimes red. You're the epitome of elegant, assured, graceful—"

She gave a sudden laugh. "Assured? I'm a turmoil of confusion inside. I never know who I am, what I'm doing. No, not assured. Never that."

"You look it."

"Would you like some brandy?" She stood up in a sudden, jerky movement that was untypical of her.

It was on the tip of his tongue to refuse, but he guessed she needed the respite. Her response to his compliments surprised him. He had thought her impervious to them.

She brought back two glasses of brandy, one larger than the other.

Orlando didn't want the brandy, but he took the glass and sipped, watching her carefully. In her state he didn't want her drinking any more, especially strong spirits. She sat down again, but a little further away from him. She eyed him, her face shuttered once more.

He took another sip. "I'll go if you like."

"You don't have to. You won me." She sounded like a sulky girl.

"No. I won the right to your company for one night. It's my right to leave, if I wish."

"You'll have to go through the company downstairs, or through the kitchen. Either way, people will know."

"So I have to stay a little longer, if I'm to preserve my reputation as a demon lover."

The muscles on her jaw relaxed. "Are you a demon lover?" The untouched brandy in her glass tilted when she relaxed her hand.

He sipped, tranquil. "So I've been told."

She laughed. He smiled, and they were back to where they were before the compliments. The brandy in her glass tilted so alarmingly he leaned forward and took it from her. She stared at him, as though she had forgotten its existence. "How much have you had to drink tonight?"

She considered, frowning. "I had some brandy before I went downstairs. Then I had some champagne, then some white wine." She lifted her head and stared at him, blinking owlishly. "Do you think I'm drunk?"

"No. Just well-to-go, that's all. But it might be as well if you didn't have any more."

"You sound like Uncle Lucius."

With a slight shock he realized she must mean Lord Ripley. "I'm not Ripley." He glanced around the room and saw what he was looking for. Getting to his feet he crossed to the small table and poured her a large glass of plain water, sniffing it first just to make sure it wasn't gin. Coming back to her he handed her the glass. "You'll feel better in the morning if you drink some water now."

She took the glass, frowning. "I'm not drunk." But she raised the glass to her lips and obediently swallowed most of the contents, handing him the remains afterwards to put on the small table at his side. "I wonder what makes a demon lover?"

Orlando blinked at her sudden change of subject, but quickly recovered himself. "Don't you know?" He saw something in her eyes then. Surprise, perhaps, or speculation. It was gone in an instant.

She shrugged again. "Maybe."

"If you want to, you can find out for yourself." He felt the tension rise inside him, but quelled it ruthlessly. He still wanted her badly, but he wasn't about to ruin everything for a night's fleeting pleasure. Keeping his voice low and unthreatening, he leaned back against the end of the daybed, stretched his legs out before him. "This isn't an advance, I swear it, but may I remove this coat? I would be more comfortable."

"Yes, of course."

She watched him put his glass down, stand up and remove his elaborate coat with its stiffened skirts. He laid the coat across the back of the chair that stood before her dressing table, interested to note that few bottles and brushes adorned its surface, but a large dressing case, glittering with silver and crystal stood next to it. He went back to the sofa and sat down again, in precisely the same place. If he moved closer, she would notice, he was sure. He had an unreasonable urge to see her come to him.

"Thank you. That feels much better. It will be summer soon and this coat is far too hot for such weather."

"What are your plans? Will you take Lady Perdita to the country?"

He glanced at her. She was tense again. "If you will consent to come."

"That depends."

"On what?"

She looked away. "If you still want me. Most men wouldn't want a woman like me dancing attendance on their sisters. I expected, once you—after tonight, you would want me to leave your household."

"What a fool I would be to do that!" She turned her head and stared at him in surprise. He met her gaze steadily. "You've made a real difference to Perdita. If I sent you away now, I think she would return to the apathy in which you found her. And without you, I would never have known how Dr. Sewell was keeping her in his orbit. I have suspicions about that man, and it occurred to me the other day that he attends my sister-in-law, also. She has a condition, but now I wonder if it's as serious as the doctor claims."

"What will you do?" She lifted a frill of lace from her petticoat and began to worry it between her fingers.

"What can I do? If I voice my suspicions I could be wrong. I don't want to come between husband and wife."

There was a short silence, but it was of the companionable kind. "You could try separating them."

"Miranda and Daniel?"

"No. Lady Rosington and the doctor."

He thought, then gave a crow of laughter. "Violetta, I think you have something there. Let me think on it. What a clever woman you are!"

She smiled at him, enjoying the compliment where the others had made her uneasy. "Merely an onlooker. Sometimes they see more clearly."

"More than that." He saw a slight stiffening of her jaw, as though she had suppressed a yawn. "Are you tired?"

"Of course not." She sat up straighter.

"Yes you are. You've had a long day, and here I am trying to make it longer." He paused. "I have a proposition."

"What would that be?" From her slanted eyes, Orlando knew she was suspecting the worst.

He proceeded to try to reassure her. "Don't worry. It seems that I'm trapped here for a while. Either that, or I traduce your reputation by leaving early. They will say you couldn't keep me entertained, won't they?" She nodded. "So why don't we go to bed?" He saw the stiffening he expected. He was ready for it. "Not like that. I said that when you come to me I want you wholeheartedly willing, and I meant it. I won't take you drunk, or even well-to-go. However, my dear, we're stuck here for the night and there's no sense us staying awake. I want you bright eyed in the morning, ready to resume your duties. Shall I take the daybed?"

She blushed delightfully. Orlando watched her, enjoying the sight. "Are you game?"

"Yes." She got to her feet with that unconscious grace he enjoyed so much in her and walked over to him. "For sleeping.

You may share the bed, Lord knows it's big enough for four." He chuckled, and she glared at him. "You know what I mean!"

"Yes, I do. My lamentable wandering mind." Reaching out, he began to undo her gown where it was hooked to the stomacher, trying to keep his touch practical, not lingering on that soft ivory skin he was uncovering. He wanted to know what it tasted like, quite badly by the time he had finished the long row of hooks on each side of the stomacher. "We'll get you out of your corset, then I'll leave you alone." Oh God, what had he done now? Could he do this, wanting her as he did? He would have to. Orlando set his will to it.

She submitted, allowing him to unhook her. When the gown was undone she shrugged her shoulders, and peeled it off, allowing it to fall to the floor. The stomacher followed it. He glanced at the gorgeous items lying on the carpet, rather than at the pale, pearly skin she'd just carelessly exposed. "I have a maid here," she pointed out. "That is one reason why we should share a bed."

He laughed outright, a sharp bark of tension. "Am I right in thinking this house isn't used for assignation?"

"Certainly not! My mother could be imprisoned for that." As though it was the most natural thing in the world, Violetta turned round to give him access to her stay laces. It was such a natural feeling he nearly fumbled them, nearly lost all control when he touched the soft skin of her shoulders. Violetta continued to chatter. "If people make appointments in our house, they must go elsewhere. In the past, she has occasionally lent a room, but no more." He disliked hearing about this. She didn't belong in this world. He wished her out of it for good.

"There." Deliberately, he stepped back and began on his own attire. She put her hands to her corset and let it drop, but didn't turn back to him. She undid her petticoats and side hoops herself, loosening the cord and letting the garments fall. Then she turned to her stockings. Orlando's greedy gaze followed her, never taking his attention away from her.

By now Orlando was down to his breeches and shirt. He watched her undo her garters and roll down the fine silk stockings, wishing with all his heart that she would allow him to do it, wishing he was somewhere else, anywhere else, wishing he hadn't made her such a foolish promise. Tonight would be sheer torture.

She turned and caught him watching. They exchanged a smile. "You can't blame a man for looking."

"I suppose not. You'd better take your shirt off. When the maid comes in the morning she'll expect to see some flesh."

"A perquisite of service here?" Nothing loath, he undid the ties at the neck, and drew the garment off over his head. "Satisfied?"

"Are you wearing underwear?"

Grinning, he removed his breeches, taking his time, now he knew she was watching. Perhaps he could torture her a little. Moving away from her he went around the room extinguishing all the candles except the one by the bed, pinching them neatly between finger and thumb.

He turned back to her. His drawers were reasonably roomy, but there was no hiding his state of arousal. With a deep blush she determinedly lifted her gaze to his face. He chuckled. "I didn't say I don't want you, just that I would behave myself. I've never allowed any one part of my anatomy to rule the rest of me. Come, Violetta, come to bed." He liked the sound of that. When he held out his hand she only hesitated slightly before she took it. It felt good, her hand trustingly in his, willing to do this with him.

He led her to the bed, feeling like a bridegroom. A strange thing in such an establishment, when he had made her that promise, but this was, after all, the first time they would sleep together. He sent up a prayer that it wouldn't be the last, that next time he would feel free to follow his desires. Drawing back the covers, he helped her in, then covered her and walked round to the other side. He got in and turned to her, lifting himself on one elbow. It was a large bed. There was no need to touch, but he couldn't resist. "Would a good night kiss be in order?"

"I think so." She freed her arms from the sheet and curled them around his shoulders.

He gave her a gentle kiss, but he felt it through his entire body. When he kissed her it was as though he had come home, met another part of himself. A feeling he could never remember experiencing before. He didn't dare touch her any more. He wouldn't let go, promise or no promise.

He left her slowly and sank into the soft mattress by her side, drawing the sheet up and allowing it to fold in deep creases between them. "Good night."

"Good night." He heard the yawn, and smiled into the darkness, feeling her settle and quickly fall into deep slumber.

Orlando didn't sleep that night, but watched over her. When dawn sent tentative threads of light through the shutters he got up, dressed silently and left.

Chapter Ten

"You're late."

Swallowing her resentment of the sharp words, Violetta stood before Lady Perdita and bobbed a curtsey. "I beg your pardon, ma'am. Did you need me for anything in particular?"

Lady Perdita glared at her, frowning. "Yes. I've almost decided to attend a public event of some description. I can't decide what would be best." She waved at a chair opposite her own.

Violetta sat down and picked up the small stack of gilt-edged invitations from a side table. "Don't you think a private affair might be best for a first appearance?"

"I don't know." Perdita frowned in thought.

At the gentle tap on the door, Violetta rose. Lady Judith swept in, resplendent in emerald green and pearls. "Good morning, Perdita! Such a lovely day! Will you come into the garden?" She bent down and kissed Lady Perdita fondly on both cheeks and then on the mouth. Lady Judith didn't spare a glance for Violetta.

Lady Perdita flinched away. "You look lovely, Judith," she said hastily. "Come and sit down and help us to decide."

"Us?" Lady Judith made a great show of looking around her and spying Violetta. She spared her a small, frosty smile. "Ah yes, Miss Lambert. What is it you wish to decide, Perdita dear?" Her caressing tone was the same as always, neither more nor less.

Violetta went into the dressing room and found a light shawl, all that Lady Perdita would need on this mild spring day. She draped it around Lady Perdita's shoulders and went to find a footman.

The ladies were soon settled in seats in the surprisingly commodious garden at the back of the house. Roses were beginning to blossom on the bushes near them, endowing their rich scent to the air. A tray containing a lemonade jug and glasses stood by. Correctly interpreting that she was to act the part of maid, Violetta poured two glasses and stood back. "Sit down, Charlotte," ordered her mistress. "I wish you to help us to decide."

Violetta sat and picked up the cards. She suspected Lady Perdita was using her to avoid intimacy with her friend. It was increasingly difficult for her. Lady Judith's attentions were becoming more marked with every visit. Knowing that Lady Perdita was standing by herself, that she would re-enter society, had made Lady Judith more proprietorial, not less.

Violetta learned much about the great hostesses in society, many of whom were worse than her mother for the number of lovers they took, and their fidelity or otherwise. She had heard of them before, only not in as much detail. Lady Judith was in possession of a great deal of knowledge not available to the general public. She must spend much of her time with her ear firmly to the ground. Or the nearest door. Counting up the tally of La Perla's lovers, the total was paltry next to some of the lists Lady Judith came up with. The knowledge only increased Violetta's feeling that something had gone awry with her life.

"A charming sight!" Violetta started more than she should have at the sound of his lordship's voice, only to receive a sharp stare from Lady Judith. When her ladyship turned to Lord Blyth, her face was a picture of flattered welcome.

"It was such a pleasant afternoon, my lord, that I prevailed upon dear Perdita to come into the garden for some air. The sunshine is not yet so great it will harm the complexion, and in any case, her ladyship's delightful new *bergère* hat will protect her from the worst of it."

"Indeed it will." Violetta caught his sharp glance. "But what is this, Miss Lambert? Have you no hat?"

"I forgot it," she murmured. In the fuss to get Lady Perdita outside and comfortably settled she had indeed forgotten her own needs.

"Allow me." Lord Blyth strode back to the house, only to

return in a very few minutes with a fetching chipstraw hat, and a glass. He placed the hat on Violetta's head, leaving her to adjust the ribbons, and poured two glasses of lemonade, handing one to Violetta with a smile. She returned the smile. An unspoken message passed between them, a look of conspiracy. They shared a secret now. Several secrets.

Violetta had woken up in the middle of the night in his arms, somehow finding her way into them. It had felt good, and she had allowed herself a few moments of drowsy contentment before moving away from him. He let her go.

It had been sweet, and so innocent.

Lady Judith shot a sharp look at Violetta who hastily turned to the cards. "Should you like to attend a recital, my lady?"

"How about the opera?"

The lazy tones had Perdita staring at her brother. "We thought somewhere private."

"We have a box. You don't have to allow anyone in you don't want to and you can spend most of the performance sitting down. What do you think?"

Lady Perdita nibbled her lower lip in thought. "It might do. I only need to be lifted in and then out at the end. Yes, thank you, Orlando, it's a good thought."

"You won't need Miss Lambert with you if I come," Lady Judith remarked. It seemed casual, but Violetta knew it was not.

"Oh, it is pleasant to have someone to fetch and carry for us," Lady Perdita protested. "I think Miss Lambert should come." She raked a glance over Violetta's dowdy gown. "She won't take the shine out of either of us, will you, Miss Lambert?" The question was a tease, but Violetta felt a pang. Like most women, she would have liked to have made a splash at a public event. She knew she could do so, and had done in the past, as La Perla Perfetta, but she could not afford to as Miss Lambert. Nor as herself.

He was looking at her, she knew it although she did not turn her head to meet his sympathetic gaze. It would only add fuel to Lady Judith's fire.

"You will come with us, Lord Blyth?" Lady Judith

prompted, slanting a look at him from beneath her lashes.

"It would hardly be the act of a gentleman to offer you the box and then abandon you," he replied with a smile. "Of course I will come, if you're sure I won't frighten your cicisbeos away."

For answer Lady Judith leaned over and struck him lightly with her fan, giving him a good view of her cleavage, had he chosen to take it. "My lord! Such a shocking thing to say!"

He laughed. "Your court of admirers may be put off to find me constantly in your company, as I seem to be of late."

"They should understand that Lady Perdita is my dearest friend and needs my support!" she declared roundly. She spread her fan and began to waft it before her face, which was a trifle flushed.

"I would hate to deter anyone," he murmured and got to his feet. "Miss Lambert—would you care for a gentle stroll around the gardens to allow Lady Judith to...ah...cool down a little?"

With a startled look at Lady Perdita, who nodded her consent, Violetta got to her feet and laid her hand on his lordship's arm. They moved off into the rose garden. "That was wicked of you," she murmured. "You know she has eyes for you!"

"More than eyes, I fear," he replied. "Her father made gentle enquiries last night. He wanted to know what my intentions were towards his daughter. It seems she's been indicating to anyone who will listen that my interest in her is more than particular."

Violetta lowered her voice. "I think her interest is more in Lady Perdita."

He shot her a startled look, and quickened his pace. "Tell me."

"I have no proof, just suspicions."

"I would like to hear your suspicions. If you're right it won't go any further."

Violetta sighed and stared at the springing grass by her feet. Then she lifted her gaze to his face. His dear face. "Lady Judith is telling everyone she has hopes of you, but I'm not sure it's you she's really interested in. She is increasingly possessive of Lady Perdita, standing guard when we go out, not allowing people near her." She paused, but didn't drop her gaze. They were out of earshot now. "Lady Judith touches her too much, more than she needs to. I would say nothing, but I think Lady Perdita is uncomfortable with it."

His lips firmed. "You mean if she was happy you wouldn't have told me?"

"Precisely."

He stared at her, but she didn't look away. Eventually he sighed. "You have a point. I won't argue with you about that, particularly because you say Perdita doesn't like it."

He turned and led the way further into the garden, deep in thought. Eventually he turned back to her, stopping her walking. "I need your help in this. For the time being, try not to leave her alone, solely in Lady Judith's company. Perdita has spent some time on her own, and she may not be as confident as she once was. Tell me if it gets worse. Be her friend, Violetta."

"Of course."

"Violetta," he murmured. "Violetta, Violetta." His gaze softened, became for her alone. She saw the thrall fall over him, like a veil of intimacy and she knew he was remembering last night.

"Sir!" she hissed.

"There's no one to hear. I want to ask another favour of you." She turned back to him, one eyebrow raised. "I would appreciate it if you could act as a chaperon for me, too, when Lady Judith is present. I have the greatest fear she will try to trap me into marriage and I prefer to make my own choice."

"Have you anyone in mind?" As soon as she said it she wished she had not.

He paused. "Not really." They continued to stroll.

Violetta desperately searched for something to say. "This is a very large garden for a London house."

"Some of them are deceptively large," he answered her, "but I like gardens, so I made sure I had a large one."

"How can you do that?"

He turned to her, smiling. "You haven't guessed? You didn't ask anyone?"

"Ask them what?" She was completely bewildered.

"No. You haven't. My dear, you know that my father left me destitute. Haven't you ever wondered how I brought us about so quickly?"

She smiled back. "Yes, I've wondered, but it's none of my business."

"Allow me to tell you." They walked for a moment in silence, taking a few corners. Violetta realized they were now out of the sight of the ladies, past the rose garden and heading for a pretty summer house. She didn't care. "When my father died he left me a hundred guineas in cash and a few run down and mortgaged estates." Walking in this beautiful garden, so carefully maintained, Violetta found it hard to believe. "My stepfather took care of my education and living expenses, but there was little he could do to restore my estates because he had his own to look after. Besides, I didn't want him to. The task was mine, as the holder of the title and the mortgaged lands. I asked for the hundred guineas to be invested for Perdita's portion." He smiled at her, his gaze remarkably serene when he discussed what must have been a distressing time for him.

"Deep down, Violetta, underneath all this folderol I have the heart of a farmer. It was always my ambition to bring the estates back to what they should be. But I needed money for that, to replenish livestock, bring in good breeders, invest in good seed." He paused and gave a self-conscious laugh. "I had my title, and I used that for all it was worth. They can't arrest peers for debt, you know. But I knew it wouldn't do, to put myself so deeply into hock, and so I dreamed up a scheme." He stopped and faced her, looking back at the neat house beyond. She kept her attention on him.

"There was once a very large house on this site, Garland House. It was one of the run-down properties I inherited, but it was the only one not in the entail. My father used it in preference to all the others, and kept it mercifully free of mortgages. I have no doubt that if he had lived longer he would have sold it or gambled it away. However, he did not and it came to me. I stripped it of all its assets and sold most of them. Then I went into partnership with a gentleman in the City. He provided the capital, I provided the land. We demolished the house and built several streets of smaller ones. Three in all."

He grinned at her in sheer delight. She couldn't help returning his joy. "You did it on your own."

"Yes, I did!" He circled her waist with his hands and swung her into the air, before depositing her a few inches closer to him. "I have two rich brothers, but I didn't want their help. With the money I bought more land, built more houses. People in London are clamouring for decent housing. Since the Fire there have never been enough, and more people are coming here to live all the time."

"You're a property speculator!" She gazed up at him in delight, proud of him for finding such a clever way out of his problems.

"I am." Without warning he lifted his hand and framed her face before taking her mouth in a deep and passionate kiss.

Her arms went around him without thought. He drew her closer, caressing her through her stays, responding to her unspoken invitation. His tongue caressed her lips and he moved away to whisper, "Open for me, sweet," his breath hot against her mouth. She obeyed, wanting him as much as he wanted her. He pressed himself to her, all the way down, and sealed his lips to hers once more, taking her with a thoroughness she had never dreamed of before.

It seemed to go on forever, but in reality it couldn't have been so long. Only sheltered by an ornamental tree, they could have been seen by anyone coming that way. It was when her befuddled brain reminded her that Violetta pulled away. He did not let her go, but watched her face. "I wanted to do that last night, but I didn't dare. You were so tempting, so sweet, but I couldn't take advantage of you. I want you sober and willing, when I finally make love to you."

She ignored the "when". She didn't want to break the mood. "You won the wager, fair and square."

He smiled gently and lifted one hand to trace the shape of her mouth. "Not so fair. I've spent a month studying you. I know how you move, the shape of you and even how you smell."

"How do I smell?"

"Absolutely wonderful." Before she realized his intent he kissed her again.

If he continued like this she would never be able to resist

him. His tongue plundered and caressed, holding a promise she knew he had every intention of fulfilling. If she allowed it. She responded eagerly, no longer able to hide her desire for him.

She wanted him. Oh yes, she wanted him and every moment they were entwined like this she wanted him more. She hadn't thought it possible to feel so much. With his hands on her, caressing her, holding her close, his tongue discovering her mouth in such intimate detail she felt naked.

This time it was Blyth who called a halt. He lifted his head and leaned against the trunk of the tree behind him, letting his head fall back so he was staring up into the green branches above. "This won't do." He gave a short laugh. "Anyone could see us."

Carefully and with obvious reluctance he released her. Violetta stepped away, just as reluctantly.

"I'm sorry," he said. "I truly didn't plan this."

Violetta smoothed her shaking hands over her gown. "I should think not!"

"Last night I kept an iron control over myself. I longed to do more than sleep, but I knew I should not. Today, here, I let my baser nature slip."

"Is it your baser nature?"

He laughed again and looked at her. She caught her breath; his eyes burned. "I don't know. I know I want you and it rages at me sometimes, but I know you deserve more. Physical passion is a wonderful thing, but not enough. Not for you."

She took a deep breath. "Is that all it is? Physical passion?"

"Truly?" He didn't look away. "I have no idea. The physical side seems to be dominating at present." He came away from the tree and shoved his hands in his breeches' pockets. "I've never felt it quite so strongly before."

"I feel it too." Her voice came out hoarsely. She cleared her throat.

"We'll see." Abruptly he turned and began to walk back in the direction they had come.

Violetta followed, and soon caught him up. He shot her a sideways glance. "I needed a moment. I'm sorry."

"Don't be."

They walked in silence and soon came upon the ladies who exclaimed at their absence, Lady Judith rapping him on the arm with her fan. "You should not abandon your sister in such a way, sir!" The roguish glance she threw him said something else.

Violetta avoided his gaze but picked up her glass and drank deeply of the cooling lemonade. She needed it.

∞

The days passed. A new doctor arrived and congratulated Violetta on the exercises and massage, which had become a regular part of Lady Perdita's day. "It's just what she needs at this stage of her recovery," he told her in a quick conference outside Lady Perdita's room after his first visit. "Push her a little bit harder every day, but not so much that she fails. The canes are a good idea."

Violetta thanked him and saw him out, afterwards returning to Lady Perdita's room. She stood by the window, leaning heavily on two stout canes. "I crossed the room five times," she said to Violetta, her note of triumph warming and rewarding. "What did the doctor say?"

"He said we're doing the right things. You must exercise until your legs are strong. He says the bones have mended well, and you need not fear any further damage." She crossed the room to her mistress, although she didn't touch her. She knew now Lady Perdita's fierce sense of independence, and could only guess how her recent helplessness had angered and frustrated her.

Tendrils of hair clung damply to Lady Perdita's forehead, demonstrating how much effort that short walk had cost her. "I need to be back in my chair. Judith's calling soon."

Violetta watched Lady Perdita go to the chair and sink into it with a sigh of relief. She took the canes and put them in their usual place behind the curtains at the head of the draped bed. "Why don't you tell Lady Judith about your exercises?"

Lady Perdita turned and gave her a wicked grin. "I want to surprise her. I want to surprise them all. Only you and the maid know, and now the doctor. Judith only knows that I can stand for a brief minute without help. When I can walk really well, I'll shock them all silly!"

Violetta laughed with her, feeling like a schoolgirl sharing a guilty secret. Lady Perdita's fear of walking had turned into this desire for secrecy, one Violetta was delighted to share with her. In private she was much less arrogant. Violetta suspected the hand of Lady Judith in this. Since Lady Perdita had not seen anyone else for the past year it was not surprising that some of Lady Judith's superior air had rubbed off on her. Violetta guessed it had helped her, when her pride had been damaged. She would lose it as fast as she had gained it. "I'll arrange some refreshments," she said, and left the room.

She went downstairs and towards the kitchen door, meaning to call down the stairs, but before she reached it an arm snaked out from the open bookroom door, pulling her inside.

Hard against his lordship's chest. "Got you!" he snarled, mock fierce, and bent his head to kiss her. Violetta relaxed into his embrace, but only for a moment. Pulling back, she stared up into his face. "We'll be caught! It's a wonder no servant has seen us before now!"

"Would it matter?" He kissed her again, softly this time.

"Not for you. We might have been seen already. Still, I am your servant."

He frowned at her, brows beetling. "No. You're not my servant, Violetta, though it puzzles me to know just what you are, and the moment you tell me to stop, I will." He broke the aristocratic hauteur with an impish grin. "Though it would cost me much."

It would cost her, too. She welcomed his kisses. Violetta had known many men in her short life, some of them her mother's keepers, but never before had she found male advances so difficult to resist. He insisted he was her friend, and she knew he was but she wanted more. Was it so sinful? Couldn't she have just a little taste of love? Something inside her knew this was her chance, this was the man. The only one who would touch her in quite this way. She had no idea if he felt the same way, but it didn't matter. He wasn't for her. This was all she could ever have of him.

The doorbell rang and they broke apart when a maid came

clattering up the backstairs to answer the door. With a quick pat to her head, to make sure her wig was still firmly in place Violetta stepped out and continued to the kitchen.

Lady Judith's voice echoed through the hall, stridently jolly. "Lord Blyth, what a surprise to see you! Are you not heading for the clubs and coffee houses? I thought every man of fashion would be there at this time of day! Can it be—" She broke off, though Violetta didn't need to see her to see the raised fan, the coy look.

Having issued her orders, Violetta turned round and waited at the foot of the stairs, knowing his lordship didn't want to be left alone with this predatory female. Lady Judith cast her an exasperated look and then ignored her, turning back to Lord Blyth with a smile. "Will you join us for tea?"

"Not today, I regret. As you guessed, I do have an appointment." Seizing his hat and gloves from the footman who had come up to the hall, Lord Blyth bowed to her and left. Lady Judith turned to Violetta with a frown and a sigh. "He's in such a hurry these days! Has he a particular reason?" She made a sound between her teeth. "Why am I asking you? I must be going mad." With a swirl of peach skirts, she swept up the stairs.

Violetta stared after her before following. She sincerely hoped that when Orlando did marry, as one day he must, it would not be to this proud, stupid woman. Her heart sank at the reminder, but she knew it must come. They would part soon, but try as she might she could not be anything but deeply unhappy at the prospect.

Chapter Eleven

Violetta grimaced at her reflection in the mirror. Dressing for the opera. She had been before, in her role as La Perla Perfetta, but never as Charlotte Lambert. This time her stays were deliberately loose, her gown that bilious green one she was so proud of discovering. The wig was fastened in its usual tight knot, no curls to soften the severe lines and her lace was but one ruffle at her elbow, cheap thin stuff instead of the gorgeous Brussels and Méchlin that adorned her white gowns, now laundered and resting in lavender at her mother's house. She tucked a fichu into the neckline, covering any hint of a swelling breast. No elaborate jewels swung from her ears, nothing precious circled her throat. Her shoes were plain leather and worn. Just the effect she wanted to produce.

So why was she feeling miserable? Violetta picked up the spectacles from the dressing table and slid them onto her face. Because she wanted to be pretty for him, that was why. That one night he had seen her as La Perla Perfetta had remained with her. He had wanted her, and burned for her, as it was right he should, as she burned for him. When she looked like this she wondered why he bothered to give her a second glance.

She stared at her reflection in the mirror then laughed at herself and deliberately turned and left the room. Miss Lambert would remain in character this evening. At least, in this guise, she knew just who she was supposed to be.

Lord Blyth waited in the salon downstairs when Lady Perdita sent word she would join them at the dining table. When Charlotte would have gone up to her, Lord Blyth caught her hand in his and said, "No. She was always like this, primping to the last moment. It's a good sign, not a bad one. Come and eat."

Sure enough, Lady Perdita joined them shortly after they sat down, being carefully lowered to her place by a footman. Lady Judith was with her, but since this was a family affair (as she archly told them) the inequality of the sexes did not matter. "Unless," she added, "we may count Miss Lambert as an honorary male." The laughing look she sent to Lord Blyth invited his complicity in her conceit, but he merely gave her a cold smile and got on with his dinner.

The taunts hurt Violetta, much as she would have liked to deny it. For her pride's sake, no one else need know that. She put her public mask of serenity firmly into place, as hard and rigid as any of the elegant confections she wore as La Perla Perfetta, and pushed another forkful of fricasseed chicken into her mouth. Lord Blyth had a good cook but the food tasted like ashes to Violetta. She wished Lady Perdita would support her against Lady Judith's taunts, but it seemed not. The lady's gratitude was obviously only to be expressed in private.

After dinner Lord Blyth, with an apologetic, secret smile to Violetta, escorted Lady Judith from the room and to the waiting carriage. Violetta had to wait until the others were seated before she could take her place next to Lady Perdita, and her green skirts were badly crushed under the pressure of Lady Perdita's wide hoops and full, celestial blue skirts. Lady Perdita's agonizing over her toilet had borne great results. She was elegant and poised; everything Charlotte was not.

The journey to the opera house was uncomfortable, at least for Violetta. The evenings were lengthening, so dusk had barely begun to dim the light when they entered the great opera house. Lady Perdita silently allowed a footman to lift her and carry her in, after Violetta had disposed her skirts so they had the least chance of creasing. They were patronizing the Theatre Royal in Covent Garden tonight, where a performance of one of Mr. Handel's works was to take place. "*Imeneo*," Lady Perdita said thoughtfully, tapping her closed fan against her lips. "Some pretty tunes in that."

The boxes were only half full, but most of the fashionable world would arrive later. The great auditorium was lit by a huge chandelier, which must have taken at least three men to lower for the candles to be lit each evening. Separate lights glowed in all the occupied boxes, but they could be extinguished at the owner's whim. Very few did, for above all, this was a place to see and be seen. Lady Perdita was lifted into her seat at the front of the box and Violetta moved forward to help her arrange her skirts in a becoming manner. The expensive satin flowed around her, gleaming in a liquid way under the warm glow of candlelight. As Violetta expected, Lady Judith settled herself next to Lord Blyth. Violetta moved to the back of the box, next to the footman commanded to stay in case anyone should need anything.

Then she saw them. Almost immediately across the expanse of the theatre, her mother's box. It was one Violetta had graced as La Perla Perfetta, but until she sat down she had not realized they were so unfortunately placed. The lights in the box were on. Someone was expected tonight. Her heart sank.

Violetta hardly noticed the performance begin. Her attention was riveted on the box, waiting. Perhaps her mother had rented the box out. She charged a small fortune for the use of it, and even more if she attended to give a *cachet* to whoever had rented it. The box was as notorious as La Perla herself. No respectable person would dream of renting it.

Violetta was not the only person to notice where they were situated. "Perhaps you should obtain another box next season," Lady Judith suggested.

Lord Blyth stretched his arm lazily along the seat. "I don't know. I rather enjoy the view. This box has a premium attached to it." He turned his face innocently to his companion's. "One has such a clear view of the stage from here."

She met his gaze. "I feel sure your wife will not approve."

"Ah but you see," came the soft rejoinder, "I'm not married."

Lady Judith smiled and turned her attention pointedly to the stage.

Someone entered the box opposite. It was the worst. It was Violetta's mother and four other ladies. Violetta knew all of them.

They made a fuss arranging themselves in their seats. The gentleman whose good fortune it was to accompany them enjoyed himself hugely, touching a white arm here, settling a gauzy scarf there. Violetta was not sure which lady he was playing for, but it wasn't her mother, for in a few moments Lord Ripley entered the box. He glanced around, and then over to where Lord Blyth's party sat. He stiffened, so slightly that anyone watching wouldn't have noticed, and then looked away. It would not have been appropriate for him to acknowledge any respectable women present, much less his daughter. He moved to the back of the box, directly behind La Perla's chair.

Violetta tore her gaze away and deliberately took in the rest of the company. She recognized many of the audience by sight, but she had only spoken to the male half. There was a face she thought she recognized. Yes, she was sure of it. Under an elaborate headdress of nodding plumes, she saw Lady Ripley.

Lady Ripley was tall, elegant and considered herself a great beauty. To Violetta's discerning eye, she missed it by a whisker. Her skin was flawed, although it could not be seen at this distance under all the make-up she wore, and her eyes were too small. Violetta knew her history and was not surprised to see a young man at her side, assiduously attending to her needs. Husband and wife ignored each other through the evening, but since this was hardly a new start it didn't create a sensation. The Ripleys were not the only couple who met rarely and went their own ways. It was a sad comment on a society that considered marriage a business contract and nothing more, but only outsiders like Violetta seemed to notice.

Violetta was glad Lord Ripley had found a measure of happiness with her mother. She knew her mother was as devoted to him as he was to her, but in the past she'd had her living to earn and had been forced into pragmatism. Usually a courtesan was owned by one man at a time, but anyone who wanted to enjoy La Perla's favours had to endure the knowledge that Lord Ripley was a constant in her life. Such was La Perla's fame and skill that most had put up with it.

Her mother was an expert. She never once looked in the direction of Lord Blyth's box. Unfortunately this gave the ladies an opportunity to study the occupants of the box opposite at their leisure. Lady Perdita spread her fan and traced the pattern with a gentle finger. "It passes my understanding how women like that can enter the same establishment as respectable females."

Violetta glanced up at the raucous crowd in the gods. Many of those women would consider themselves respectable, superior to her mother and her kind. They dressed in filthy clothes, had no idea how to behave in good company, might not be able to read, but they were better. Better because they were married to the man they spent their nights with. Better because they wheedled and persuaded their money out of their men instead of making an honest bargain.

Violetta turned back to the stage, but she couldn't work up any interest for the opera. It was a particularly busy night and no one was taking much notice of the musicians. At least they would be paid for their efforts.

Her glance strayed back to the box, and the increasingly cruel comments of the ladies would not be shut out. "How do they do it?"

"What?"

"Take a man a night."

Lady Perdita pursed her pretty lips. "I don't think single ladies should know much about that, Judith."

"Oh stuff!" Lady Judith waved her fan in the general direction of the box. "Whatever their airs and pretensions, they're common doxies."

Violetta bit her lower lip to stop the tears. It was not the first time she had heard that. It was not the first time she had wept over it, either. She had rarely felt so miserable, forced to sit and listen.

"They dress rather well, though."

"They have to." Lady Judith sounded almost vehement. "It's their livelihood." She shot a poisonous glance over to the box, where the occupants seemed to be enjoying themselves. She did not acknowledge her father. "I would hate to be forced to dress provocatively every day, instead of in something of my own choice."

"And to be forced to take whomever offers."

"I think you may be labouring under a slight misapprehension, my dear," Lord Blyth put in smoothly. "Those ladies are at the top of their profession. They are in a position to choose their partners."

"They'll die of an unmentionable disease." Lady Judith

131

certainly knew a lot about that particular profession. Then Violetta remembered that she seemed to know a lot about musicians, too, from her conversation of the day before. Shopkeepers also seemed to be an area of study for her, from what she remembered of the visit to Cerisot's. Lady Judith must be a natural scholar, Violetta concluded acidly. Lady Judith leaned closer to her friend. "I did hear tell that before she died, Katherine Taylor's nose was eaten up by disease."

A delicious shudder passed through Lady Perdita. Violetta hated to spoil their fun by reminding them that Miss Taylor had died from the ague. It had been a time of sadness, when the lively, beautiful girl had died so young.

"Do you know any of the women?" Lady Perdita asked.

All of them, thought Violetta.

"The old one in the middle is La Perla. It is said she has gone into retirement now, but she continues to take my father away from my mother's bed." Violetta felt mildly shocked that Lady Judith should put it so crudely. She suspected Lord Ripley would not have accompanied La Perla tonight, had he known his daughter would be in the opposite box, having more delicacy of feeling than Lady Judith.

"He must be very rich to be able to afford two such expensive women."

"For shame, Perdita! You are speaking of my father!"

"I only speak as you do, and only *en famille.*" Lady Perdita laughed. Violetta couldn't remember when she had last heard her mistress laugh. She didn't think it was only the conversation, but the knowledge that her confidence was returning, that she belonged once more. Violetta realized with a pang that she would not be needed much longer.

It was what she had wanted, to see Lady Perdita on her feet again and then to shake the dust off her own feet and start her new life, free from fear. Or at least, that's what she told herself. Now she was reluctant to go, and although she didn't like it, she knew why. She watched the cause of her discomfort. Their affair had not passed beyond kisses, and perhaps it was wiser if it did not, but she would miss him.

Lady Judith leaned forward, and spoke behind her fan. "I have heard that La Perla Perfetta, the daughter, is to enter the demi-monde. It is clear she has taken lovers before, of course, but she is to enter publicly, as the woman to take her mother's place."

"Really?" came the excited whisper. "Which gentleman is to take her?"

"She's been taken," someone replied. Violetta felt rather than saw Lord Blyth stiffen. There seemed to be a rope, taut between them, joining them.

Then it fell away when Lady Judith said, "I didn't hear that. I did hear there was a contest between several gentlemen. One thousand guineas was paid for her!"

Not if she could help it, Violetta reflected. She had lost that money when he recognized her and she lost her reputation to him. Now it was assumed that La Perla Perfetta had entered her mother's world. Violetta wondered what she would find when she returned to her mother's house. Before now, it was assumed that although she may have taken a few lovers, she was not wholly in her mother's world. Now, after the display last week, she was.

Lady Perdita laughed. "How can a woman sell herself for such a paltry sum?"

"Once," his lordship reminded her, "I only had a hundred guineas to my name. A thousand guineas is a great deal of money for one night of pleasure."

"One night?" Lady Judith turned a beady, inquisitive eye upon his lordship. "You were there?"

He didn't admit it, or deny it. "It was all round the clubs and coffee houses the next day."

"I thought you went to hear the latest stock prices, and the political news?" Lady Perdita teased.

He smiled at his sister. "One can't talk finance and politics all the time. There has to be some light relief." If truth be told, it was mostly light relief, leavened by the serious matters. Violetta heard the gentlemen chatting in her mother's salon and doubted it was any different in the coffee houses.

He had not succeeded in turning the subject. The ladies continued to discuss the occupants of the box opposite. Violetta caught a small movement from behind Lady Judith's head. His hand, motioning a message to her. She hoped it was comfort.

That was what she needed.

It seemed an eternity to the interval, but it could not have been very long. Violetta stood up to attend to Lady Perdita. From across the way a pair of violet eyes looked up. Mother and daughter let their gazes meet, and then looked away. In that brief exchange La Perla had made her displeasure known; Violetta was demeaning herself by serving another woman. She excused herself and went to find an empty retiring room.

By dint of a coin pressed into the hand of a willing attendant Violetta gained the use of a small room, at the other end of the corridor to the box. The room was tiny, containing a chamber pot, a spotted mirror and a small sofa. Not large enough for a comfortable assignation, but that was not why she wanted it.

A few moments that seemed more precious than anything else at that moment. Time to reconcile herself to the forthcoming entertainment.

She was not to have her few minutes. Without warning the door opened to admit Lord Blyth. He didn't hesitate, but took the two strides that brought him to her and wrapped his arms about her. Violetta had no chance to protest. It seemed pointless, so she took advantage of the comfort offered and found a place on his chest that was not scratchy with gold embroidery or lumpy with buttons. He chuckled, the sound rumbling though his chest. "I should wear more comfortable clothes, should I not? Hold tight."

She did so, and was surprised when he sank down on the sofa, settling her on his lap. "Hardly room for me on this thing," he commented, sounding very matter of fact. There was a pause while she fought back her tears. She had promised herself years ago she wouldn't weep, but she couldn't help leaning her head on his shoulder, blessedly free of embroidery or buttons.

"I'm sorry." His voice turned sombre. "I should have thought it through properly. I'd forgotten who owned the box opposite mine."

"Forgotten? I thought you paid a premium for it!" She sat up on his lap and glared at him, tears forgotten.

He reached out and drew off her spectacles, meeting her gaze. "I planned an outing for Perdita, not for me, and it completely slipped my mind. It's unforgivable, I know, but can you possibly forgive me?"

Violetta remembered a vision of sitting in her mother's box and being ogled by a group of young men in the box across the way. "You hired that box so you could watch us."

"Not you. Them."

She shook her head slightly. "I'm one of them. I've been one of them for a long time."

His hand moved up her gown to her shoulder. "You're you." The gentle pressure on her shoulder urged her closer. Nothing loath, she complied and sank into his kiss.

Warm and soft, comforting, but with an aftertaste of passion. She leaned into it, unable to resist. He supported her easily, spread his legs to give her a comfortable seat and held her around her back with one strong arm. The other he used to caress her, softly stroking her back in a soothing rather than stimulating gesture. Violetta felt wanted, no longer useless and foolish. She kissed him back.

He lifted his head and gazed down at her. "You fit very well there, you know that? Shall I take you home?"

"What?"

He chuckled again. "Because you're uncomfortable, not because of what you're thinking. Although, should you offer, I don't think you'll find me averse to the suggestion."

She laughed at him. "I'm too touchy aren't I?"

He lifted his hand to caress her cheek. "No. It was entirely my fault. If I'd told you in time you could have contacted your mother, or excused yourself from the opera. It's ruined your evening, hasn't it?"

"I didn't expect to enjoy it. I wanted to make sure Lady Perdita was all right."

"She's surrounded by admirers. In her element. It's as if she's never been away."

Violetta snuggled in. Just a few moments, she told herself. "We shouldn't be doing this."

"No, we shouldn't. I'll send for the carriage and take you home."

That was unwise. "Much as I'd love your company, it's not a good idea. I'm only the companion." She paused. "You won't

135

need me for much longer, will you?"

"Perdita isn't on her feet yet."

He did not know how far they had come. Violetta wouldn't spoil Perdita's surprise. "She is where you wanted her to be. Back in society. It will come. Take her away to the country this summer and all will be well, I'm sure."

"I won't let you go until she's on her feet."

"Or until I'm in your bed." She could have bitten her tongue out. She knew she should not have said that.

Before she could apologize he interrupted her. "That can happen at any time, but I want you to want me, to come to me of your own free will. Not seduced, not drunk, not bought and paid for." He bent his head and just caressed her lips with his.

"You mean I have to make the first move?"

"Not necessarily. I won't lie. I want you very much, Violetta. When I'm with you I have to touch you and kiss you. I have—" He flushed, and looked away.

"I know." There was very little reason why she should not. Only her reticence. Although she had the chance to enter society, she didn't look to marry. Any husband she might attract would have to know about her mother. She would make it a condition, and the Italian aristocrat, most of whom could out-stare and out-ancestor an English duke, wouldn't accept that.

"Very well." She lifted her hand and cupped his cheek. He turned his head and pressed a fervent kiss into the palm. She smiled. "Send for the carriage for me, but don't come with me. That would be showing me too much particularity."

He laughed, his mouth still against her palm, his breath hot. "At the risk of being too forward, ma'am, have you some time in the morning for me?"

"I—I'm not sure."

He moved his mouth away. "I'd like your opinion on something. Will you be ready to drive out at about eleven?"

"Yes. I do have an errand of my own. Lady Perdita has already given me an hour off in the afternoon."

"Everything well, I hope?"

"Yes. I have to go to Cerisot's as La Perla Perfetta. There's a gown waiting to be fitted. I could easily have gone another time, but Lady Perdita has her rest then, so she said I could go."

"We'll be done long before then."

She rested against him. "Very well."

"Thank you."

By mutual consent they rose, and Lord Blyth went to order the carriage.

℘

Having obtained the necessary permission from Lady Perdita, Violetta stood in the entrance hall at a quarter to eleven the next morning, wearing only a light shawl over her drab brown gown against the moderate weather the day offered. Her undecorated straw was pinned firmly to her head. Her gloves were well worn and definitely not made to measure.

Despite all this she felt better than she had last night. When she entered Lady Perdita's room that morning she even received an enquiry about her health. That was so unlike Lady Perdita that Violetta found herself stammering her thanks.

Today Lady Perdita was on her feet, leaning on one cane. "We should think of an event I can attend. If you have the invitations sent up to me I'll go through them while you are away. I'll want you later on, so don't take all day."

"I appreciate you giving me the time off," Violetta said, head down.

"No matter. Judith is coming, and no doubt Orlando will look in. They can help me."

Thus was she dismissed, but she didn't care.

Now, waiting for Lord Blyth, her light-hearted mood refused to dissipate.

He didn't keep her waiting long. He came out of the library dressed for the outdoors, and smiled in greeting. "Shall we go?"

"Yes. Are you going to tell me where we're going?"

His smile broadened into a grin. "No. It's not far. I've had the curricle drawn up." He glanced at her. "I'll drive."

"Of course, sir," she said with a glint of a smile.

She followed him outside and allowed him to help her into the curricle. The tiger swung up behind and when Lord Blyth had settled himself they left.

He had a single horse harnessed, a sprightly black he had no trouble controlling. Violetta had to admit he drove to a pin. Her driving skills were adequate, no more. He drove without effort, taking time to nod to a few acquaintances, one of whom stopped dead and fumbled for his quizzing glass. "I do wish you had worn something more becoming," he complained. "My reputation is suffering."

"You know I can't," she replied, mindful of the tiger behind them.

He sighed heavily. "I know. I must hope my reputation is good enough to survive."

She laughed. "Better me than La Perla Perfetta."

He shot a glance at her, mischief in his gaze. "I think my reputation might be enhanced if it were known I could keep her by my side. Miss Lambert, I'm shocked! What would you know of such things?"

"Very little." She bowed her head to hide her smile.

Instead of driving towards one of the fashionable parts of the city, Lord Blyth went in what was known by the polite world as "the wrong direction" up Oxford Street. He crossed Tottenham Court Road, something that filled Violetta's heart with dread, because it was one of the main thoroughfares out of London, filled with private and public vehicles. At least it wasn't a hanging day. The traffic in the vicinity of Tyburn was murderous on hanging days.

Having crossed the road they passed into a quieter area. A respectable residential area, plain fronted houses lining the long street. His lordship brought the curricle to a halt.

"Come." He waited for the tiger to come round to the front, tossed the reins to him and leapt down, walking around to hand Violetta down to the freshly laid pavement, a wonder in itself since so many streets in London had none.

At the end of the street Violetta could see green fields, and signs of activity. He followed her gaze. "They're still building. Shall we?"

She looked doubtfully at him. "I asked for your opinion,

don't forget. This street is mine—at least it's mostly mine. I want to know what you think of the houses."

She laid her hand on his arm and allowed him to unlock the front door and lead her in.

She looked around the hall, clean black and white tiles on the floor and a strong scent of freshly cut wood and paint. He sniffed, and wrinkled his nose. "It's been finished for weeks and it still smells."

"It needs a good airing," she said absently. She opened the nearest door.

A charming room, empty of any furnishings, painted plain white, waiting for its first owner to imprint her personality on it. "This would make a wonderful morning room."

"Wouldn't it?" He came into the room after her, his voice echoing off the bare walls.

"I've never been in a new house before." She looked around her at the bare walls, the sparkling clean windows. There was not a flaw anywhere.

"I've been in a few in recent years. Including my own. There is a certain charm in a new house. It's a blank canvas. Shall we?" He indicated the open door and she gladly followed him to continue her explorations.

She liked the house very much. The kitchens and servant's quarters were neat and furnished with the latest in cooking equipment, all shiny and unused. The rooms were well proportioned but not too large, all painted white, no nail marks on the walls where pictures had been, no old curtain rails or dents on the polished floors where heavy furniture had rested. Nothing save clean floors and walls and shining, uncurtained windows.

A fresh start. Something Violetta longed for. No reputation, no name, no distinctive looks. Nothing to mark her out.

Violetta entered the last room, a small room on the second floor. Above them were the servant's bedrooms, but time was getting on and she would have to leave to go to her mother's soon, to effect her transformation into La Perla Perfetta. She had seen enough. "I think it's an excellent house. It's well proportioned, airy, and quiet, considering how close to the main road it is."

"You like it."

"Very much."

He held out the key. "It's yours."

She whirled away from him, recoiling in an instant, hands gripping the stuff of her gown. "What do you mean?"

"I would like you to have it."

"Why?" She felt desperate, and couldn't work out why, her mind in turmoil. Trapped somehow. Suddenly the realization came to her. She was alone in a house with a man. All the warnings her mother had impressed on her returned now. La Perla was a courtesan, but she was also Italian, a race very protective of their children.

Lord Blyth wouldn't do this to her, surely he wouldn't do such a thing! The move was cold, calculated, just the sort of thing a man would do to a prospective mistress. She couldn't reconcile it to the man who stood before her, the key forgotten in his hand, a puzzled frown drawing his brows down. "What is it? What's wrong?"

"Why do you want to give me this house?" she choked out.

"I—" He paused, studying her closely. Whatever he was going to say remained unsaid. He changed his mind. "Why do you think?"

She edged towards the door. "Because you want to buy me."

Anger rose in his eyes. The blue became a spark of fire. "Buy you? Are you a slave, then?"

"My mother has been one. When you're born into slavery, you are automatically a slave. I should have known!" She turned angrily away from him and dashed the tears from her eyes.

"Should have known what?"

"All this! It's been a ploy, hasn't it?"

"Has it?" His fury not abated he turned on her. "I introduced you to my household to seduce you, did I?"

"Not entirely," she admitted, "but when you saw me you decided to do it."

He turned his shoulder. "Did I? You did your best to put me off. Is that why you wore that padding, those spectacles?

You're afraid of yourself!"

"So you chase everything in a skirt, do you? You want a courtesan, a mistress, someone you have power over?"

"Dear God, what did I do to deserve this?"

She was crying now, unable to stop herself. "I may take you up on your offer, but I may take offers from any number of gentlemen first! Dear Lord, don't you know that when a man wants to make a courtesan his mistress he gives her a *house!*"

He stared at her, dumbstruck, his mouth slightly open, anything but the epitome of sophisticated aristocracy. She glared at him, tears pouring down her face unchecked. She fought for her voice. "I'll wait in the curricle. I hope you'll be good enough to take me to my mother's." She walked away, her shoes striking hollowly on the floor. She wanted to stop somewhere, to wipe her tears but she knew he would hear her falter, and perhaps come after her. She wanted the last word. She fished out her handkerchief and paused before the front door, wiping it hastily across her face. It was all she had time for before she wrenched open the door and hurried out to the curricle.

Orlando stared after her, listening to the retreating footsteps. Even they sounded angry. He strode to the window and stared out at the expanse of green that would make someone a fine garden someday. Not Violetta, though. His anger was as much at himself as her. He should have made his gift clear from the outset. This house was to be her bonus, the bonus Perdita had reminded him about that morning. "You promised," she had said. "I won't need her much longer and she deserves a parting gift."

"You're still not walking," he had reminded her.

She had given him an arch look. "I'll wager it won't be long."

He had wondered at that, but had decided she would tell him in her own time.

Now he had wanted to make Violetta happy and had forgotten the realities of her life. It was true. The first thing a courtesan did with a new lover—or perhaps the second, if she decided to give him a free taste of the goods—was to sign a contract with him, for a house, or the use of one, and an annuity. Jewels were very pleasant, but their resale value didn't do them justice. Fine clothes were the same. How could he have been so stupid?

He held himself rigid, afraid that if he moved he might smash a window or something else equally foolish. The scene just enacted must remain private. She had not trusted him. She hadn't waited for an explanation, or asked him what he meant by it. That hurt him.

Slowly he turned and left the room, closing the door very carefully behind him. He took his time descending the stairs, polished shiny but left uncarpeted, hearing his footsteps as though they belonged to someone else.

She was sitting in the curricle, bolt upright, staring ahead. He took the reins and waited for the vehicle to dip, indicating the tiger had taken his place. Without looking at her he drove off and left her at the end of the street where her mother lived. She would not want him to stop outside the door. His one attempt at explanation met with a short "Not now," and after one glance at her rigid face he decided she was right. He wasn't giving in, but he wouldn't press the matter now. She wasn't in a mood to listen.

After a curt "Good day," she walked away. He didn't stop to watch her, as he might ordinarily have done. He drove off, to an appointment he had with his brother's wife, to take her shopping to try to cheer her up.

Was he cursed to be surrounded by dissatisfied, angry women?

Chapter Twelve

Violetta went straight upstairs and indulged in a hearty burst of tears before going outside her door and calling for her maid. The girl came quickly, and the customary conversion from Charlotte Lambert to La Perla Perfetta took place in just over half an hour. Violetta held her arms up when required, tipped her head back for her hair to be brushed out and re-dressed, and drank the tea which was brought up. One look at her mistress's face in the mirror convinced the girl speech was not necessary today. Until La Perla swept into the room it could almost be called peaceful.

La Perla made sure the maid had gone before she met the hard, set face of her daughter in the mirror. "Well?"

"I have an appointment at Cerisot's. Lady Perdita kindly gave me a few hours off."

La Perla made a "*tsk*!" noise and dragged a chair up to sit next to her daughter. "You come in, not a word to anyone, and storm up here as though the hounds of hell were after you? *Dio*! Do you think I am foolish? Have you quarrelled with him?"

"Who?" she asked, deliberately obtuse.

"Do not be stupid with me, child! Your lover, who else?"

She knew there was no help for it. Violetta turned in her chair. "He tried to give me a house."

"So he should! What is that to the matter?" La Perla reached out and took her daughter's hands. "Is he good to you? Tell me, and if he is not we will show him what we can do!"

"No—no. He is good to me." Violetta could not, after her mother's sorrow at her fall, tell her she was mistaken. It would be cruel to reverse her opinion now she had come to accept it.

143

La Perla had always told her daughter she must make her own decisions. An unwavering realist, she had accepted her own fate and never complained, teaching her daughter to do likewise.

"Then why should he not give you a house? Was it a poor one?"

"No." Violetta looked down at her lap. Her white taffeta petticoat gleamed under her hands, taunting her with its pristine perfection. "It was a good house." She looked up at her mother's face, taut with concern. "I think I was foolish."

Her mother patted her hand. "You did not wish him to perceive you in such a way."

"It puts me in my place, Mama. If I accept it, I will be there when he wants me, at his whim. I couldn't bear to think of that."

A spasm passed over La Perla's face, instantly suppressed. "The first time, it hurts. I think you should go to Italy and take your rightful place immediately. This life is not for you, *cara*. I have always known. If you had wished for it, I would not have stood in your way, but you are not happy with it."

Violetta shook her head, too distressed to think straight. "I won't go to Italy and disown you. I would be all alone, with people who hate you."

La Perla's hand was firm in hers. "No, you are wrong. They do not hate me. How do you think I got to England when I fled? Your uncle, your father's brother, helped me to escape with you. Without him we would have been caught. When he discovered how I made my living, he made me promise not to bring the family name into it, and explained that I could no longer be welcome at home, but he helped me all he could. It would not be right for me to return. They do not know who I have become. I have accepted that. That is all."

"They wanted me to say you were dead. I won't do that, Mama!"

La Perla shook her head, setting her curls dancing. "One day you must leave me. Be careful with this lover, and if you do not wish for him, come to me. I do not need anyone to support me any more, and neither do you."

"Yes, Mama." Despite her depression, Violetta felt the comfort warm her. She could never abandon her mother, always so careful of her, so loving. She had felt ashamed of her feeling of shame when anyone had spoken of her mother. The other night at the theatre had been humiliating in more ways than one. She had been aware of her shame, and felt deeply guilty for that.

"You will go to Cerisot, and have your fitting. You will enjoy it, and you will return to me soon, I think?" La Perla got to her feet and shook her skirts into place.

"I can't come back today." Violetta glanced in the mirror, checking her appearance before she left the room. "I'm on duty later."

"Pah! The lady will not need you much longer. You know it is not that I meant. You will return soon and we will plan your future. Yes?"

Violetta got to her feet and gave her mother a hug. She was almost the same height as her mother, both small, but never overlooked. When she shook out her skirts it was an unconscious similarity. "I will. Thank you, Mama."

"Think nothing of it. Come and have something to eat before you go. There is something laid out in the dining room."

Violetta went downstairs and found, despite her distress, she was hungry. Lord Ripley was there, and took some food with them. Violetta was used to his presence but she kept shooting glances at him until he turned to her and demanded, "Is something wrong?"

"No, no of course not. Should there be?" She flushed and looked down. With a grunt he returned his attention to his plate. Both knew what Violetta thought, though neither had ever spoken of it. Violetta didn't dare. She knew Ripley met her mother shortly after her marriage to the Conte d'Oro. He fell in love with her on sight, although he returned to England to try to make a success of his marriage, so there was a long gap before they met again.

The times were right. The new Contessa d'Oro had fallen pregnant almost immediately and gave birth to her only child six months after Lord Ripley returned to England. Violetta knew they had been in love for most of their lives. She knew Ripley fathered a family here in England, but she could see no resemblance between herself and Lady Judith. When she realized she would be close to Judith, she had taken the opportunity to study her, but she saw nothing. It didn't follow that they weren't half siblings, although knowing Lady Judith better now, she hoped there was no connection between them. The arrogance, the assumption of superiority all belonged to Lady Ripley, not her father.

She would have loved Ripley for a father, even though that would mean her actual, if not technical, bastardy, since her father's family had accepted her without question. Perhaps they knew something she did not, or perhaps, in the light of her mother's recent revelations about the family, they wanted to make amends, but either way, she would have given a great deal to be sure.

It was entirely possible that her mother didn't know who the father of her child was. The thought filled Violetta with a nameless fear. She told herself it didn't matter. Her mother loved her. Lord Ripley cared for her. She had enough money to ensure an independent future. That was all that mattered, surely?

If it were only her physical well being that mattered it would be fine, but it wasn't. Her soul needed to belong, to find a place it could call home. She had felt it all her life, before her mother had told her what her real name was, and where she came from, when she was masquerading as an English gentleman's daughter at the school in France, swamped under silken layers of marquesses and comtesses. That was where she had first taken on the name of Charlotte Lambert, although the wig and spectacles were later additions.

Now she would have given her modest fortune to know who she was, whose daughter she was, what her place was in the world. Something.

৪০

Violetta could not shake off her melancholy, nor the residue of her anger. Cerisot found her far from the cheerful customer she was used to. "Mad'moiselle, you are not attending!" she said for the seventh time that afternoon. "Would you like floss or spangles on this?"

Violetta regarded her reflection in the long pier glass. The gown was finished, but Madame had suggested a delicate application of some kind of decoration around the hem of the skirt. She picked a finish at random. "Spangles. Just a few."

Cerisot nodded and began to unpin the gown. "You've lost weight. I'm going to have to take it in. I hope your employers haven't been working you too hard."

"No." It wasn't that, though Violetta knew something had inhibited her usually hearty appetite. She didn't want to examine the reasons. It was all too raw, too painful.

After Cerisot had helped her into the plainer, but still white, gown she arrived in, Violetta adjusted the plain white half mask over her face. It was in almost every respect the same as many women wore to keep the dust off their complexions in the street, but it was white, where the usual colour was black. White was an extravagant, wasteful colour and the reason why Violetta insisted that most of La Perla Perfetta's gowns were easily laundered. Her mother employed a laundry-maid to keep her linens and La Perla Perfetta's gowns clean and what could not be washed was treated with fuller's earth.

The weather was warm, and Violetta had brought only a light shawl to drape over the gown. White of course, with white embroidery. She was heartily sick of white. Even Miss Lambert's gowns became a welcome change. There was little in her wardrobe that wasn't white.

Violetta arranged her white hat, pulled on her gloves and left the shop, her maid trailing behind her.

Only to collide with a solid male body. She sprang back. "Good Lord!" rumbled a voice she knew. The owner of the voice bowed slightly. "Miss—ah you are La Perla Perfetta, are you not?"

Violetta made her voice lower, huskier and added the Italian accent she customarily used almost without thinking about it. "Indeed, my lord. Good day."

"One moment, if you please!"

She turned back to him, surprised and a little worried. Had he recognized her? His dark eyes stared into hers, altogether too perceptive for her liking. "Does your mother hold an open evening soon?"

"I believe so, sir." Never had Violetta felt guilty about her mother's evenings before. However, he might want to come for the conversation. Only her self-restraint prevented her snort of derision finding its way to the surface. The conversation was good, the play was deep, but Lord Rosington had never been known to seek out either. Nor, she had to admit, had he sought out the demi-monde before. It might be his first time. She hoped so, for his poor wife's sake, but unlike his brother Lord Blyth, Lord Rosington had never been under any financial constraint. He could afford an expensive mistress if he wished for one. Such arrangements could be very discreet, the mistress not even a professional woman.

Violetta told herself it was none of her business. Then she saw a closed carriage turn the corner of Bond Street. She had come to know the crest of the Blyths very well by now, on an armament above the door of the town house, decorations on some of the other items in the house. Two swans as supporters, very distinctive. The carriage bore the crest on its highly polished black doors.

It might be Lady Perdita in the carriage, but she doubted it. Lady Perdita had declared her intention of resting that afternoon, preparatory to attending a small soirée that evening. Nothing like the great balls and routs she planned to attend later in the year, or the house parties she wanted to go to that summer, but a good start. So it was probably Lord Blyth in the carriage. And he knew who she was.

Without thinking further, Violetta put her hand on Lord Rosington's arm and leaned up to press her lips on his cheek in a brief salute. The carriage swept past. She caught sight of some sort of commotion inside, and Lord Blyth, leaning over a blonde woman she couldn't quite see. Lord Rosington remained ignorant of the occurrence, his back turned to the road.

Violetta gave him a bright smile. "I shall look forward to seeing you, my lord." With one last glance she left him and walked away, her maid trotting after her.

ଌ

Violetta knew she would not get away unscathed with her behaviour, but she was unsure how Lord Blyth would react.

Later that afternoon, back in the costume of Miss Lambert, she returned to the house for dinner. She did not want to face him, but she was no coward, and it was better got over with quickly.

Lady Judith waited with Lady Perdita in the salon. Violetta bowed to them and sat behind Lady Perdita. The ladies chatted, totally ignoring her until the door opened to admit Lord Blyth, dressed for the evening in dark red velvet.

He glanced at Violetta once, his gaze hard, and she knew his reaction. He was furious. She felt a tremor of regret, and perhaps fear, but quelled it firmly and followed behind with Lady Perdita. It was only the four for dinner. Lady Judith made a comment about Miss Lambert. "It seems Miss Lambert is the honorary man this evening. Do you mind, Miss Lambert?"

"Not at all." Violetta would not feed Lady Judith's malice by showing any reaction to her. The taunt was becoming a favourite one with Lady Judith. She'd heard it twice since that fateful evening at the opera, and suspected Judith repeated it because she knew it upset her. Her resentment rose when Lord Blyth did not come to her defence, as he might ordinarily have done.

What did she expect? Her action with Rosington had been impulsive, a defiance born of the fiasco earlier that day. She didn't regret it. It was only a light kiss, after all.

Violetta knew her thoughts to be disingenuous. She kissed Lord Rosington in the persona of La Perla Perfetta, and however innocent the gesture, it carried implications for all who saw it. She hoped it would have no repercussions for his lordship, but Lord Blyth deserved it. If she were to be a courtesan, it would be on her own terms. Not his. That afternoon, she had staked her claim, as far as her world was concerned.

She wondered if Lord Blyth knew it. After that one glance at her, simmering with rage held firmly under the surface, he ignored her and devoted all his attention to his sister and her friend. Lady Judith was in her element, teasing and flirting. Violetta was struck yet again by the similarities between the polite world and the demi-monde. A different set of women, that was all, with different expectations. The same men.

Was it really worth it, this striving for respectability? Men still looked at her mother with open desire, still made her offers despite her declared intention to retire. They made offers to

Violetta, offers that never included marriage, but frequently included houses. They took for granted that she would be expensive.

Not expensive enough. Violetta wanted more. She wanted it all. If she couldn't have that, she would go her own way and do without men in her life.

Looking at Lord Blyth at the other end of the table, his long fingers curled around a glass of red wine, she could almost regret her decision. His pose was studied, his smile practised and polished. Then she heard something that brought her a measure of relief.

"You are escorting us tonight, are you not?"

"Of course." Lady Perdita and her friend were attending a small soirée, one that Violetta hoped would ease her mistress back into her old life. "I've ordered Perkins in his best livery to turn out for you."

"He may seat me and return later." So Lady Perdita wasn't going to walk tonight. She was so good she hardly needed the cane any more. Lady Perdita put down her fork and turned to her brother with an eagerness she rarely showed in public. "What are your plans for the summer, Orlando?"

He took his time answering her, smiling slightly. "I hadn't decided yet. Later, we've been invited to stay with Daniel and his family. We must look in at the Court, and I would like to spend more time there. Why do you ask?"

"Lady Judith has asked us if we would like to visit her at her home in a week or so. Lady Ripley has planned the most delightful party!"

He regarded her, twirling his half empty glass absently. Not a drop spilled over the rim. "I can't see any reason why you should not."

"Would you come?"

He turned to face Lady Judith, his most charming smile in place, but Violetta didn't miss the flash of anger he turned on her on his way past. No one else seemed to notice. "Would you like me to? Aren't you afraid I'll cause havoc amongst your friends?"

"Why no, my lord, of course not! We would be honoured to have you!"

She said it too hastily, too eagerly, but it was doubtful that anyone but Lord Blyth and Violetta noticed. "I would be honoured to come, in that case."

Violetta knew he was doing it to annoy her, and she felt childishly pleased. At least she had some effect on him. He was not indifferent to her.

"Will your father be there?" he enquired mildly, but by the way he kept his gaze carefully away from her, Violetta knew that the comment was for her, rather than for her ladyship. Judith's face stiffened. "I have no idea. He tends to go his own way. He even had the effrontery to seek me out at Lady Masham's last night, but I was very cool to him. Very cool. Society cannot say there is a breach between us, but I will not encourage him."

"I'm sorry to hear that. I thought the decision was your parents' alone."

She didn't notice the reproof, or chose to ignore it. "My father distressed my mama by his recent appearance at the opera. He claims it was an accident, but he should have listened more attentively when my mama told him she would attend." She sniffed. "Respectable women have little chance next to those creatures."

Violetta lowered her head and attacked her food. If this was revenge, it was effective, but she thought it unkind of him to take advantage of information she had given him in a weak moment. She would know better next time.

Relieved that he planned to accompany the ladies, Violetta excused herself and went up to her room. She could spend the time reading.

Reading had always been a solace to her. Violetta read anything, from complex text books to the most scandalous novels, finding something of interest in every one. It seemed a long time since she had an evening at leisure with her books.

Wanting to make herself comfortable, Violetta changed into a loose sacque gown of antiquated style. Modern sacques were tailored to the waist at the back, but this one had its back pleats sewn down to the shoulders only. It meant she could remove her stays and relax, but would be decent if Lady Perdita should require her presence on her return. She settled down with an old favourite, *Robinson Crusoe.*

In the meantime, Lord Blyth, in full, hot formal attire, was sitting in an elegant salon fending off the attentions of the numerous young ladies who seemed to insist on his opinion about anything. It was a relief to see his brother Corin present, not just for the support of another male, but because he badly needed to discuss the matter of Daniel with him, which had suddenly, given the events of earlier in the day, become urgent.

He managed to convey to Corin his need of a private word and after two of the most tedious hours of his life, obtained his sister's permission to leave. "I shall be quite comfortable," she told him loftily. The few gentlemen present all congregated around her chair. Most gratifying, and delightful to see her back at her old flirtations. Or it would have been delightful, had Orlando been in a mood to be delighted.

No longer worried about her re-entry into society, Orlando and Corin took their leave, although the arch comments about their future destination made Orlando grit his teeth in annoyance.

"I'm in no mood for socializing tonight," Orlando remarked. "Will you walk with me?"

"Willingly. I'm for White's afterwards. I've no mind for female company after tonight."

Orlando slanted a look at him. Corin's face was as smooth and untroubled as always, but Orlando felt there was something new about his brother. A restlessness, perhaps. "What made you go there in the first place?"

"Perdita, of course. Mama couldn't attend, so she sent me."

Orlando made an exasperated noise between his teeth. "I might have known. I'm quite capable of caring for my own sister."

Corin stuck his hands in the capacious pockets of his dark green dress coat. "My sister too."

"Haven't you enough of your own?"

Corin grinned, his teeth a white flash in the moonlight. "Oh yes, but Perdita is my big sister. I've been worried about her. I couldn't tell you before because Mama insisted we make as little fuss as possible. When we knew she wouldn't die after the accident, that is." Orlando remembered the terror of that time, when Perdita was brought into the house lying on a door, used as an impromptu stretcher. She was white, and bleeding, and the extent of her injuries was far from certain. He had been so terrified of losing his only sister that all the blood had drained from him. He never wanted to feel like that again. "A bad time," Corin said softly, "but she looks well on the road to recovery now."

Their footsteps echoed up the empty street. They were nearly home. Orlando slowed. "I have to speak to you about Daniel."

"Daniel?" Corin didn't hide his surprise. Obviously he expected to discuss Perdita.

"I saw him today with La Perla Perfetta. You know who she is?"

"Aye. La Perla's daughter." His eyes narrowed in speculation and Orlando knew his brother well enough to realize he'd recalled the time Daniel connected La Perla Perfetta with Miss Lambert. But he said nothing about that. Not yet, at any rate. "A pretty piece. I've thought of making an offer for her myself."

"No, you won't."

Corin turned in some astonishment and too late Orlando realized he'd revealed too much with his vehement words. "Want her yourself, do you? Is that it?"

It wasn't worth trying to deny it. He'd wanted her—quite badly—for some time now. "Not just that. If you wanted her, I'd say 'let the best man win,' but not Daniel. Miranda saw them together today. I took her shopping, but that was all abandoned when she saw them. It's obvious she still loves him very much."

"Oh Lord." Corin frowned. "Daniel's only a man. He's been impeccably behaved for years now. He must be feeling the need of a little—feminine company."

"If any woman graces his bed, it should be Miranda."

"She can't, you know that."

"She might be able to." Swiftly Orlando outlined the situation with Dr. Sewell and his sister. He concluded; "I think he was holding Perdita's recovery back deliberately. When he pays his next visit I intend to tell him what I think of his methods. He's Miranda's doctor, too. What if he were doing the same there?"

Corin gave a long, low whistle. "My word, yes. And I always wondered."

"What?"

"Well—it's obvious that Daniel and Miranda are still in love. There's more than one way to skin a cat."

Orlando grinned briefly. "Precisely. We need a plan, something to get Miranda and Daniel away from Dr. Sewell and thrown into each other's company without the distractions of society."

Speaking in low voices, there in the street before Orlando's house, the brothers concocted a plan. Once Orlando recalled the derelict inn he owned in Melton Mowbray, it didn't take long. Corin finished with a low crow of laughter. "That will do splendidly. White's tomorrow night, then?"

"White's it is."

Corin waved an airy goodbye and strolled away while Orlando went in.

Chapter Thirteen

Orlando stood in the hall, breathing deeply. He felt he'd stepped through to another world. All his resentment and anger returned in force, as though he left it behind, only to pick it up again on his return. He glanced upstairs. He would not ask where Violetta was, but would find her himself. No sense rousing the household.

Having searched the first floor, closing the doors behind him with an exaggerated carefulness that amply demonstrated his attempt at self-control, Orlando went upstairs to his own room and removed his evening coat and formal wig. He put the wig on the stand put ready on his dressing table, a puff of rice powder rising from it when he twitched it into place. The coat and wig might look magnificent, but the weather was far too hot today for velvet and powder. He wanted to confront Miss Lambert—Violetta—with no encumbrances. He stopped only to brush out his dark hair and fasten it with a black ribbon at the nape of his neck, the way he wore it during the day. No sense in scaring her with an unkempt appearance, so unlike him she might think something was seriously wrong, perhaps with Perdita. Instead, tonight he wanted to clear the air. He'd reached the end of his patience, and something had to happen, though he was not clear what it would be.

She was not downstairs. There was always the possibility that she had returned to her mother's house, but he thought that unlikely. She was not someone who would renege on her responsibilities when matters became difficult. He was so sure of it he knew he would find her in her room. She wasn't anywhere else.

He knocked, purposely quiet so she had no warning who it was. It could be a maid with some tea. When he heard the command to "Enter!" he went in. That was the end of his consideration for her. Or so he told himself.

She looked up, eyes wide and startled. He caught his breath. Her loose gown, flowing about her slim body wasn't her usual drab colour but a rich, dark blue. The fine fabric did nothing to hide the luscious contours underneath. "Your spectacles are going under your wig," he pointed out.

Lifting her hand, Violetta pulled off the wig. Her hair, fastened in a thick braid, tumbled over her shoulder. The spectacles came off with the wig to lie forgotten at her feet. She sat bolt upright, a book face down by her side. She must have been reading when he came in and shoved the wig and spectacles on at his knock. She looked like a queen.

No. A deceiving whore. "You will not take my brother as your lover." He hadn't meant to be quite so straightforward, but there it was.

"I will take whom I wish." Her voice was modulated, carefully controlled. It made him angrier than before.

"Not my brother. Did nothing I told you find a home?" He stepped into the room, moved closer to her. "Or don't you care?"

If she found his presence intimidating she showed no sign of it. She sat up straighter. "In what way should I care?"

"That he and his wife are—experiencing difficulties." He was still speaking quietly, although it was becoming more of an effort.

"You think I can't help?"

"Can you?"

She lowered her eyelids and then lifted them again and looked directly at him. For the first time Orlando felt he was close to the real Violetta, the woman under the disguises. Despite his anger he still felt the yearning to know more, to get closer. "I may be able to reduce the strain on the marriage. That might be one way to help."

Fury lanced through Orlando, though he wasn't sure if it was the thought of Daniel committing adultery or Violetta making love with anyone but him. His voice rose to an angry roar, the first time he had raised his voice for years. "By encouraging Daniel to commit adultery?"

Violetta shrugged. "Why not? Many people do, and many people are happier for it."

"How dare you?" He took a stride closer to her, and saw her flinch. She recovered her poise almost immediately but he felt a savage satisfaction in producing a response. "You will not do this. I forbid it! I never expected such insensitivity from you, never!"

"Why not?" Her voice rose a little, too, and there was a definite tremor in the last word. "I'm only a whore, after all. He might offer me a better house than you did!"

So that was it. His insensitivity that morning. Not in giving her the house, but in not making clear why he was giving it to her. Still, he could not blame himself for what followed after. She had done that and he would not back down now. Violetta had gone too far with Daniel this afternoon, and he didn't feel like explaining or apologizing to her now. "Perhaps he might. And perhaps, if you had a conscience at all, you might regret forcing a breach between husband and wife!"

"As I understand it, there's a breach already."

"Not as impassable as the one you want to erect."

She shrugged again, an insouciant gesture that infuriated him. "It happens all the time. It is not my fault there is a breach." She lifted her gaze, waiting for him to meet her eyes. He did. What had he to fear? Drowning in a violet deeper than the night? "You made me a certain kind of offer this morning. Unfortunately, I was tempted to accept." She waited, tilted her head slightly to one side. "What? You didn't guess? You could have taken me on the floor and I probably wouldn't have objected. That was why I had to get out." Her voice was louder now, and tears ran down her face unchecked. He was still angry enough to be glad of it, but each word drove through him, past his rage to somewhere deep within. "I had to think. I came to a decision." She stopped.

"Well?" He couldn't believe she had stopped there.

"If I'm to take up my mother's profession, which is whore, whichever way you say it, I will not do it except on my own terms. I will have more than one lover at a time, and I will see them when I wish, not when they command. I will live where I please. I will set the terms, if I am to sell what is dearest to me—my body."

He stared at her in profound silence. He could not think what to say. He had brought her to this? "I never meant that." His voice lowered. His anger was seeping away from him, replaced by sorrow, entering him as swiftly as his anger left.

"You may not have meant it, but it's time I faced reality." She stood, heedless of the book she swept onto the floor and took a few steps away from him. "I wanted an independent life, on my own, but I have to admit a few things to myself."

"You do?" He had to know. He knew—knew they would travel together, but not how far, or for how long. Perhaps their time had already passed, and the weeks just gone were all they would ever have. With a new clarity he realized it had always been up to her. It was her decision. He kept perfectly still.

"I—I want and even need certain things. I don't know if it is better never to know them or to indulge myself now." She turned away from him, lowering her chin. "I don't know."

He moved up behind her and gently, so softly, put his hands on her shoulders, expecting every moment she would shake him off. Under the silky cloth he felt her warmth. It was the most seductive thing he could ever remember. He didn't take his hands away, as he knew he should. This had gone on too long. It had to be resolved before he went mad or he drove her mad.

"Violetta. Turn around."

She froze. For a moment he thought she would throw him out, but then, slowly, she turned so she faced him. It seemed out of time. They stared at each other, each knowing what would come.

With a murmured, "Violetta," he lowered his head and set his lips on hers.

He had kissed her before, but there would be more tonight. Much more. Orlando didn't let himself think about that yet; if he did he might disgrace himself. He wanted her more than he could remember wanting any woman before, so much he felt like a schoolboy again.

But he was not a schoolboy. He vowed to put all the expertise at his command to bring her as much joy as possible, if she let him.

Her lips felt hot beneath his. They met as though they belonged together, and then he felt her hands lightly at his waist. He put his arms around her, gently, and drew her closer, bringing her into his domain.

Although he knew what she said, what she wanted to do and perhaps already had done, Orlando felt Violetta to be the most precious thing he had touched. It was something born of instinct. He kissed her, concentrating on the feeling, the delicious pleasure when her lips opened under his.

She responded, caressing his tongue with hers when he entered her mouth, tasted her. Sweeter every time. He could have kissed her all night, except for the anticipation surging through his body. He allowed himself to savour her, and felt her body against his. So small, so soft.

"Come." He whispered the word, and stepped back, taking her hand in his.

Violetta regarded him carefully. "Yes. Perhaps if we do this I'll find some peace."

"I hope not. At least not for a while." He was pleased to hear his voice was quite firm, though he wasn't quite sure how that had happened.

He drew her out of the room, first making sure no servant lurked in the corridor outside.

"Why do we have to go to your room?" she hissed, sounding like a conspirator more than a lover.

"Perdita will be coming home soon. I don't want to disturb her."

"Oh."

There were no more sounds until they were in his room and the door safely closed behind them. Just to be sure, Orlando turned the key in the lock. Then he leaned against it and carried on where they'd left off in her room, holding her close.

She sank into him so beautifully, felt so good he doubted he would ever tire of her. "I made you a promise." He held her, but didn't attempt to caress her or kiss her. Not yet. "I said I wouldn't seduce you, or take you unwillingly."

"I'm not unwilling."

159

"But you're not sure, are you? I can tell. Will you hate me for this?"

She shook her head. "Never."

"That's enough for me." Unable to wait any longer he bent and kissed her again. He let his hands roam over her back, so slim, so supple. She in turn held him tightly, pressed closer. She gave in. She was his, for tonight at least. Tomorrow could take care of itself.

She leaned into him, stretched to reach him. She flinched and drew back.

"What is it?" His voice had deepened and lowered, intimacy without realizing it.

She gave a shaky laugh. "Your buttons."

His waistcoat buttons were encrusted with brilliants. He chuckled, feeling with the release of his anger and the subsequent rising of passion light-headed. "We can sort that out." He undid all the buttons and removed the garment, tossing it aside as though it hadn't cost a fortune. It didn't matter. It wouldn't have mattered had he been as poor as when his father died. Nothing mattered except Violetta.

She stepped back, regarding him critically. "You're stronger than I thought."

"Not all strong men have muscles like football bladders. I've done my share of heavy lifting. Here, let me show you."

Before she could move he swept her up into his arms and carried her across the room. She mocked him with light laughter. "My, my, what a hero!"

He looked down at her and laughed before he placed her on his bed. She bounced a little. "It always was too big for one," he remarked, looking down at her, a tumble of blue silk. One of her legs was bared, showing delicate silk stockings and matching slippers of blue. Her neat braid was coming loose, fluffing out about her face. He had never seen a woman more desirable, especially with the sweet flush of desire mantling her cheeks. "You look wonderful."

"I'd feel better if you were here instead of there." Her voice, usually low, deepened to an inviting purr. Orlando made haste to loosen the jewelled buckles at his knee, so his breeches hung loose there, and kicked off his evening shoes. His hands went to

160

his neckcloth.

"Come here. Let me do that."

He needed no further invitation. He joined her on the high bed, climbing up the step and settling next to her. While she unfastened his neckcloth, carefully removing the ruby pin he wore and laying it aside, he discovered the front fastening hooks of her gown. It looked good on her, but she would look better without it.

She did. Clad only in shift and stockings Violetta lay in the folds of her opened gown. He pulled his shirt off over his head and felt her touch him. The first time. Was there ever anything so wonderful as the first time? What would happen after tonight was anyone's guess, except it would take a lot longer than one night for him to discover all of her. He would make a good start, bind her to him so securely she wouldn't think of Daniel, or any other man for that matter, ever again.

He freed his head from the shirt and dropped it somewhere, bending over her to kiss her again. He leaned over her, savouring her warmth but holding himself clear, until he curled one arm around her and rolled onto his side, taking her with him, mouths melded in a kiss so devouring it fed his desire like tinder. She participated in the kiss, no supplicant she, following his tongue with hers when he withdrew from her, exploring his mouth as eagerly as he'd explored hers. She tasted delicious.

Violetta surprised herself as much as she surprised him. She was tired of fighting him, tired of fighting herself. She would take a lover, and the only one she wanted was Lord Blyth. Orlando. She had spent weeks too close to him, sharing the occasional kiss, trying to retain control of her wayward emotions but it was no good. She could only hope this madness passed in time. It was like an illness, consuming her, heating her. Perhaps this was the cure.

She rolled over him, leaving her gown behind, then to the other side. It was a large bed indeed. He lifted his hand and cupped her breast through her shift, tracing the shape of it with his fingers until, at last, he touched her nipple. She threw her head back and gasped with shock, and he took advantage of her exposed throat to kiss it, running his tongue down the side in a thrilling sensation of heat and dampness. Her chemise was low cut, the drawstring only loosely tied, and when she felt the tug unfastening the bow, she shrugged, easing the fabric from her shoulders. She wanted to be naked for him, to give him pleasure and permission to do whatever he wanted with her.

He lifted his head and his hands went down to the hem of her shift, rucked up to her thighs. She held her breath, staring at him. He lowered his eyes while he raised the hem, watching her flesh come to glowing life without the veiling of white linen. She sat up so he could lift it over her head. Then it was gone, and except for her stockings she was naked.

He didn't touch her. He sat back, his hands going to his waistband and watched her while he discarded the remaining items of his clothing. She watched him.

Glorious. His skin, glowing with health and heat, gleamed in the light cast from the branch of candles set on the chest of drawers close to the bed. Another branch stood on a small table on the other side, so the bed was illuminated well. When he moved, fine muscles reacted, shifting under his skin, so she longed to touch them and feel the tension. His chest was almost hairless, beautiful, firm with underlying muscle.

She lifted her hand to undo her garter, but he stopped her with a soft movement of his own. "Let me do that."

He took his time, unfastening and unrolling her white stockings, as though this were a wedding night, and they weren't expected to appear again in public for some time, instead of a few stolen hours. They would have to be strangers to each other tomorrow, just as they always pretended to be. This time it would be harder to pretend.

Violetta lay on her back and watched him finish undressing her, then, with a couple of sweeps of one arm, get rid of all their clothing onto the floor. She had time to examine his body, find the small scars from nameless accidents, the length of his well-muscled, long legs, liberally powdered with dark hair, and what lay above. What reared above. He was heavily aroused, and Violetta knew, from experience virgins didn't ordinarily have, that he was magnificent. Conversation in her mother's house had not always been as genteel as it was in the average lady's household. She thought she knew what to expect but she was wrong.

This was him, in all his hot, fleshy reality. Violetta wanted to touch it, but she didn't dare. For all her knowledge, she didn't know what to do next. She lay, vulnerably naked, and waited for him. He put one hand on her ankle. "Beautifully slender," he murmured, and glanced up at her face. He lay next to her, his hand on her ankle, but touching her nowhere else. "I wondered. I knew you would be like this, elegant and graceful. You're so lovely, Violetta, you take my breath."

"I couldn't imagine what you would be like." She reached out and touched his chest, only to draw her hand quickly back.

His chuckle shook the bed under them. "Touch where you like. I hope you'll not mind if I do the same." He raised himself, and without lifting his hand from her body, came up to her. His hand swept the side of her body from ankle to breast, a slow smoothing that made her want to stretch and purr. He lay next to her again, and drew her close.

It was almost too much, this touching. Their bodies came into close contact all the way down. His erection jutted into her stomach, her breasts pressed against his chest. Before she could catch her breath he kissed her, and took it away all over again. He opened her lips with his tongue and thrust inside, sweeping her mouth, stroking her tongue, teasing her, inviting her. She accepted, touching his tongue in return, and when he retreated, supporting her tongue on his, she entered his mouth.

He made a sound, low in his throat, and rolled her on her back, pushing her thighs apart and settling between. His erection now touched her most intimate place, but he didn't enter her. Instead he rubbed her, moving his body against hers in a swirling, deeply intimate way. Violetta was in uncharted country now. She knew what would happen, she had heard the ribald jokes and insinuations, but never had she heard anything like this. To be held, possessed, as though what she felt mattered, as though he wanted her response.

As though she had spoken aloud he broke the kiss and murmured, "I'm a gentleman, Violetta. I'll do my best to ensure your happiness before my own, but I'm not sure how long I can hold out this first time. Forgive me?"

She was wet now, as she knew she should be, a response to the rubbing, caressing motion. He reached a hand down and guided his shaft to her entrance. Then stopped. "Look at me. Please. It's important to me."

Violetta opened her eyes dazedly and stared into his deep

blue ones. He was open to her as never before. There was nothing between them. He watched her as she watched him. She felt him stretch her, and she raised her knees in reaction, cradling his body in hers. He stayed at her entrance, moving slightly until she felt her body soften and ease. Then he plunged inside her.

Violetta came off the bed, but not in ecstasy. He stopped, completely still, deep inside her. His eyes displayed his shock. "Dear God! Violetta, Violetta, why didn't you tell me?"

She gasped, unable to get her breath. He held her close, giving her comfort for what he had just done and waited until she relaxed back onto the bed again. "I'm sorry, sweetheart. I wouldn't have done that if I'd known."

"What made you think I wasn't a virgin?"

He gave a short laugh. She felt it all the way through her. He was still hard inside her. She moved, only for him to follow, not allowing her to escape him. "Wait. Don't move. It's best we're still for a moment." He kissed her forehead, holding her close, his breath hot on her cheek.

He moved gently within her. To her surprise he moved easily. He fit so tightly inside her she thought he might be stuck, but it seemed not. He withdrew a little then pushed gently back in. "What does that feel like?"

"Better." She smiled at him. "Good." She relaxed beneath him, let her legs fall apart.

"Wonderful. It feels wonderful."

He moved a little further out, driving back with a gentle insistence that made her realize he was holding back. "You're made for me."

She let him get away with that remark. She was in no case to argue with him now. He kissed her again, and the intimacy was almost too much. Violetta closed her eyes and felt. Felt his body pressed against hers, all the way down. Felt his body inside hers, above and below, building warmth even deeper inside.

The warmth grew, filling her with a fiery heat, and without thinking she arched her back, pressing her shoulders into the bed and tilting her hips up to take more. His murmured, "Yes, that's it, push," assured and encouraged her. She pushed and held herself steady while his thrusts increased, withdrawing further, thrusting deeper. Eventually their bodies collided with a wet slap of flesh, meeting and separating.

Arms braced either side of her head he arched up, his upper body straining away from her, his every effort to reach further inside her, to build the tension now making Violetta clench her teeth. She heard his exclamation, didn't hear what was said because he took her higher until she spun out of control. Her cry came from somewhere deep inside her, the same place that suddenly seemed to erupt, taking her whole body into a twisting, roaring sheet of flame.

He held her down, gave one last, grunting push and joined her, his voice mingling with hers, then collapsed on her, managing to fall to one side, so he didn't completely squash her. They lay together, panting, getting their breath back until he rolled, his arms around her.

Violetta felt herself drifting, cuddled close to him. "Sleep, love," he murmured. "Rest. I'll wake you in time."

As she fell into a profound slumber she thought she heard something else, but she couldn't be sure and by that time had tumbled over the edge.

Chapter Fourteen

The sound of a door slamming made Violetta sit bolt upright. For a moment she was disorientated, not recognizing her surroundings, then she remembered where she was. The candles were still burning, halfway down to the sockets, so she couldn't have been asleep for too long.

Beside her he stirred and then opened his eyes, staring up at her sleepily. Then he smiled. It was a full, warm smile, and she smiled back. "Come back." He pulled her back down into his arms. She went willingly, turning her face up for his kiss, a gentle, closed mouth salute.

"How long have I been asleep?"

"An hour, perhaps. I lost track of time somewhat."

"What was the noise?"

"Perdita's home. I hope she doesn't decide to check on you, but I don't think she will. She sounded—tired. Her steps weren't entirely steady."

Violetta could imagine. Before she had left, Lady Perdita had been imbibing more wine than she suspected her mistress was used to. "Yes. She'll no doubt go straight to bed."

There was a short pause. "Violetta, I ought to be angry with you, but I'm more angry with myself. I'm sorry I hurt you so. I assumed too much, I thought the losing of your virginity at the house was some kind of public announcement, not a declaration of fact. I was too sunk into my own needs, my own desires."

"You were very angry earlier."

"That was foolish too. And more than half of it was frustration, I think." He kissed her again. "I wanted to persuade you to make love with me when I discovered you were La Perla Perfetta. I thought—" He lifted himself up on one elbow. "How did you stay a virgin in that house?"

"My mother insisted on it. She thinks you deflowered me that night at the house. She wasn't happy about it, but she said it was my decision."

He caressed her cheek. "You should have told me. I assumed too much. I thought, in that house, you must have had an encounter or two. I thought—it doesn't matter now. I've made you what I thought you to be."

"A whore?" Her voice hardened.

"No." His reply was just as firm. "An experienced woman. You're so lovely, I didn't think it was possible for you to live in that house without—shall we say testing the waters?"

She swallowed. "You would take me anyway?"

He smiled, so gently. "Of course. It's you I want, Violetta, and all that goes with you, whatever that is."

"Would you have made love to me, if you'd known?"

"No."

She smiled up at him. "I wanted you to. My virginity isn't as precious as a society lady's, or a respectable maiden's. I'm not respectable."

His fingers stroked her cheek as though she was the most precious thing of all to him. Violetta knew she wasn't, but she allowed herself to enjoy the cherishing touch. "Have you a little more time for me?"

"Yes, I think so."

He bent his head and kissed her, pushing his hand into her hair. Violetta was vaguely surprised to find it was still braided. His had lost his black ribbon sometime, and his dark hair now tumbled about his face. A strand fell over them, binding them in a fragile link, broken as soon as he lifted his head and flicked his hair back. "I took you tonight without any kind of prevention. You could be pregnant."

"I won't be tomorrow."

"What?" He leaned back, startled.

"My mother has given me a potion. She's taken it herself for the last twenty years. It's why she's had no children."

He stared at her. "I didn't know there was any such thing."

"She brought the recipe from Italy."

"What's in it?" He wasn't smiling.

"I don't know. Pennyroyal and some other things."

"Have you taken any so far?"

"Not yet. There's been no need."

He bit his lower lip. "Don't."

"What?" She stared at him incredulously. "If I don't take it, I could—"

"Fall pregnant. Yes, I know. If you take it, it could harm you."

"I told you. My mother's been taking it for twenty years."

He sighed, his hand moving to stroke her hair as though he couldn't help himself. "There's no guarantee it won't stop children permanently, is there?" Dumbly she shook her head, feeling his fingers curl around her skull, almost protectively.

"Please, don't take it. I'll do what I can to minimize the risk, but I don't want you to ruin your chances of conception."

She moved suddenly, jerking her head back. "Why not? How will children fit into my life?"

He reached for her. "You could find someone." Someone? She would never want anyone else. Not like this. "If you take it," he continued, his voice a soft purr. "I'll never make love to you again. That's a promise."

"Really!" It was almost as though he wanted her to bear his child! Although she knew he would not be so selfish, something besides her reasoning saw the hunger in his eyes. "Do you want a child?"

It was his turn to stare at her. "Of course not. No, I couldn't do that to you!" But something lingered in his eyes. "I don't want you to be hurt in any way because of this."

She knew better than to question him further, guessing that he hadn't worked it out himself yet. She wouldn't take the potion. It was true, it had been remarkably effective for her mother. There was no telling but that it had made her sterile, especially considering the frequency she took it.

Violetta had lingering hopes of a child, someone of her own, someone who belonged with her without question. Her mind raced ahead, planning a new disguise. She could pose as a widow instead of a debutante; respectable widows had children. It would just mean the deferment of her original plan for a while, that was all, while the child was born. It would leave her with something of his when he was lost to her. "All right then. I won't take the potion. I promise. I can use a sponge, instead."

"Good. I know a few women who use that." Unaware of his faux pas he reached for her, and his arm was around her when she flinched. He seemed to know what was wrong. "Are you sore?"

She gave him a tremulous smile. "A little."

"Don't worry. It's normal for your first time. Will you let me make you more comfortable?"

"What do you mean?"

For answer he threw back the covers and got out of bed, going over to the washstand. A candle guttered; he leaned over and pinched it out. In a drawer underneath he drew out more candles, and took some time lighting some more to replace the ones that had almost flickered out. Violetta enjoyed watching him, absorbed in what he was doing, his long, lean form reminding her of the pleasure he had just given her.

He busied himself at the washstand on the other side of the room, where the substantial bedposts blocked Violetta's view. "This is a massive bed." Like the rest of the bedroom furniture it was fashioned from glowing walnut, upholstered in dark green.

"Yes. It's from the old house. Too big for this house really, but I couldn't bear to part with it." He walked back to her and she enjoyed the sight of him all over again. His expression was softer than she could ever remember it. He held two damp cloths in his hand. Violetta watched him with misgiving.

Flinging the bedclothes off her he took a moment to study her revealed form. "You're very beautiful." He sat down next to her and applied the cloth.

"Oh! That's cold!"

He chuckled. "It will help, I promise." He cleaned her first, then urged her legs open and placed the other cloth between them, holding it in place. "I hope this will soothe you a little." He looked up at her face, expression sharp and warm. "After all, it's for my own good, too. I hope this won't be the only time you'll allow me into your bed."

"I'm in your bed," she pointed out.

"Take it metaphorically," he suggested. He returned to the washbasin and wrung out the spare cloth, coming back to reapply it. "I hope this makes up a little for my brutality. It's the reason you're hurt so much."

"Am I? It feels much better now." She luxuriated, lying flat, being attended to.

"Good." He glanced at her, swiftly assessing, then removed both cloths and returned them to the washstand, wringing them out first. Very domestic, Violetta thought, and wondered how many domestic tasks an impoverished earl would have taken on for himself.

A thought of him wielding a sweeping brush made her smile. She was still smiling when he came back to bed, sliding in beside her and drawing a sheet over them. "That was very thoughtful of you," she murmured, slipping into his arms as though she belonged there.

He smoothed a strand of hair back from her forehead. "Guilt. I should have known better."

"I'll have to go back to my room, soon."

He sighed. "I know. I want you here all night and every night for the foreseeable future. Will you come away with me?"

"What? How can I?"

His arm tightened around her. "I want some time alone with you. I have a house at Richmond, very private. It's usually rented out but it's vacant at the moment. We could go there."

"Lady Perdita will need me."

He grunted. "Not as much as I do. She won't need you for much longer. You've done miracles there, Violetta. Before you came she was listless, lifeless almost. You deserve a bonus for that."

She had hurt him with her refusal of his gift, she realized that now. Too late to go back. "Then give me a monetary bonus. If you truly think I've done some good there, do it that way. Not too much, or I'll give it back to you."

"I know you will." He turned, and brought his mouth to hers for another kiss. "If you don't go soon I'll be tempted. Think about it. When Perdita goes to Ripley Court, it's likely you can get some time off. We could snatch a week to ourselves and I can join Perdita there later."

"You really want to do that?"

"I really do." His kiss was full of promise.

&

"Are you a complete fool, child?"

La Perla was agitated; even more than when Ripley had told her he would have to go into the country for a while to attend to business and greet his guests. "You refuse his generous offer then go to his bed anyway?" She got to her feet and strode around the room restlessly, her full apple green skirts foaming around her. "What were you thinking of?"

"I wasn't thinking," Violetta confessed.

"I thought you returned to the house to make it clear to him his advances were no longer welcome. You made up your mind, Violetta. What made you change it?"

Violetta told her the only thing she thought might mollify her mama. It was the truth, in any case. "I wanted him. I was tired of resisting him."

"He has pestered you?"

She shook her head. "Not at all. He was perfectly behaved, apart from a kiss or two. I wanted him, mama and I thought this would get it out of my system."

La Perla regarded her daughter shrewdly. Even without powder on her face she was a strikingly lovely woman, one of the youngest looking fifty-year-olds Violetta had ever seen and a walking reproof to the moralists. Not every vice led to eventual degradation and death. "You haven't, have you?"

Violetta shrugged. "No. He wants me to go away with him."

"When? Will Lady Perdita excuse you?"

"She doesn't want me as much as she did. She dismisses

me more. When she goes to stay at Ripley Court she won't need me at all."

La Perla frowned. "Then go with your earl. Spend a week with him. Indulge yourself. Get him out of your system for good, and come home and spend the rest of your life as you wish." In one of those sudden changes of mood that marked her, she swept her skirts aside and knelt at Violetta's feet, taking both her hands, staring up into her daughter's face. "Violetta, I did not do this so you could become what I am. I am despised, hated in some quarters. I do not repine; it was the only way we could survive. If I had done anything else, showed myself under my real name, your father would have come and taken me back."

"I know," Violetta replied, touched by the anxious expression in her mother's face, as she had not been by her reproaches. "I won't, I promise. I will make you proud of me one day."

La Perla sighed heavily. "Because of me, if you find a man to love you will have to lie to him all your days."

Violetta snatched her hands back. "No! If I cannot find a man to love me, and accept you, I will not marry. I will not!"

"You can hardly trumpet me to the world," La Perla said softly. Her Italian accent became more pronounced, less a studied lilt than a flow back into the language of her girlhood. She usually spoke English, for protection and out of habit, but tended to return to her native tongue if upset or agitated. True enough, her next words were Italian. Violetta, almost as fluent in the tongue as her mother, had no difficulty following her. "I am a woman you must be ashamed of."

Violetta took her hands again, feeling the thinness under the rings. "I will never be ashamed of you. You did what you had to, and you were brave. I cannot be ashamed of that. The world does not know what I do. I will always be proud of you."

"Bless you!" Her mother leaned forward and pressed a soft kiss on her daughter's cheek. She stood and shook out her skirts in a brisk motion, returning to English. "So go and spend some time with your lover, but be discreet. Do not allow him to take you out in public, unless you are masked. Foolish to let your guard down now, when we are so close."

Violetta agreed. It would be the height of folly to let

anything slip.

Returning to the Blyth house felt almost like coming home. Lady Perdita greeted her with a casual smile, and returned to her embroidery. Without looking up she said, "I thought I would show Orlando how far I have come at dinner."

"Indeed, my lady. I'm sure he will be delighted when he sees you."

"I do not want to show him any more until I'm perfectly sure I can maintain it."

Violetta stood on one side of Lady Perdita and helped her to her feet, only to be neatly manoeuvred out of the way by the ever-present Lady Judith. Her ladyship took Lady Perdita's free arm. Violetta handed her cane to her, and smiled graciously. "Goodness, what a lot of work we've done to get this far!"

Violetta reflected that she had not seen Lady Judith at one of the morning sessions when Lady Perdita had been massaged and tried, in painful increments, to stand and walk. Lady Perdita's uncertain temper had made each morning a different voyage of discovery, but now they were there, and her ladyship was ready to show her brother.

The door opened and Lord Blyth stood in the entrance, frozen in shock, or delight, or perhaps both.

"Perdita!" Holding both hands out he came forward and embraced her, pressing a kiss to her forehead. "You're standing! Oh how foolish of me, of course you are. It's such a shock, my dear, when I think of the person you were six months ago! I'm so pleased!"

"It took a lot of hard work," Lady Judith pointed out. She moved, causing her skirts to rustle.

Lord Blyth drew back. He had not looked Violetta's way once. "Indeed, it must have done. Such a surprise, my dear!"

"Lady Perdita has been very brave," Lady Judith remarked. "I thought it a good idea for her to try gradually, and then surprise you when she had achieved it."

He frowned. "I think I would rather have helped. However, if that is what you wanted, you have succeeded. May I take you in to dinner?"

"We must invite more people to dinner now I am well," Perdita said.

He looked at Violetta, then. A moment's intimacy. Violetta was afraid Lady Judith would notice, but she didn't seem to. She hardly seemed to notice her at all. Taking her place next to her with reluctance, Lady Judith kept all her attention on Lord Blyth. Violetta guessed she wouldn't be happy at an increase in guests. She'd had Lord Blyth to herself for dinner at least twice a week and she got precisely nowhere with him.

After dinner, blithely ignoring her presence, the ladies discussed strategy. "I'm determined to get you for Orlando," Lady Perdita announced. "What could be more suitable? I know you want him. Do not even attempt to deny it!" Violetta stared at her curiously. Did she think to fob her friend off on her brother? How could she imagine that Lady Judith would be satisfied with that?

"I don't think he's looking for a wife." Lady Judith had allowed all her flirtatiousness to slip now there was no audience for it. She sat in her chair, tracing the pattern from her outspread fan with one finger. "He seems determined to enjoy his bachelorhood a while longer. Why, he as much as told me so last week!"

"Does he indeed?" Lady Perdita tapped her own fan against her lips before spreading it and fanning herself in a graceful motion. "Well, he shall not. He has turned thirty this year, and it's high time he settled down. I don't think he appreciates his good fortune, Judith."

Lady Judith stared at her fan morosely, rosebud mouth turned down at the corners. "You will bring him to the Court? I have to go soon. My mother insists on it. She says I have been spending too much time here and unless my pursuit bears fruit soon she will take matters into her own hands."

"She'll arrange your marriage for you?"

Lady Judith grimaced. "I know who she has in mind. Lord Shapley."

Lady Perdita frowned. "It could be worse."

Lady Judith lifted her head and stared at her friend bitterly. "Would you marry him? He's lost most of his back teeth, his breath is appalling, and I'm sure he's lost most of his hair because no one has ever seen him without his wig! He's thin, weedy, and not even old enough to die off conveniently after a few years." Tears sprang to her eyes. "I wouldn't mind being a rich widow, but he's no older than your brother, and I could be shackled to him until I die!"

"He's very well off," her friend ventured, "and very biddable. He could be trained."

"I don't want a man like him!" Lady Judith cried. "I want someone like Lord Blyth! Handsome, polite and strong." She looked away, straight into Violetta's sceptical gaze. She turned her head so she was back with her friend, in their intimate world. Violetta suspected Lord Blyth wasn't the main reason for Lady Judith's wish to marry him over Lord Shapley. Rather, Perdita was the draw.

"My!" Lady Perdita seemed much struck. "I never thought of him like that, but I suppose he is. He's just been my big brother. He's worked hard to restore the family fortunes."

Lady Judith shrugged, her gold-coloured satin gown moving with her shoulders. The cut was exquisite, Violetta noted, and settled back in place with scarce a wrinkle. The colour, however, was wrong for a golden haired woman, especially one with such sallow skin. She would have put Lady Judith in fresh pinks and greens, not a shade like that.

"A man in love can be foolish. I've been doing my best to make him fall in love with me, but his mind seems to be elsewhere half the time."

Lady Perdita leaned forward and patted Lady Judith's hand in a strangely motherly gesture. "Never mind, dear. Once you get him in the country there are a thousand ways you can compromise him. Lots of open space."

Violetta told Orlando later, after he had crept into her room. It was dark and only two candles lit, but there was enough light for him to see her by.

She was waiting, dressed only in that blue gown he had liked the night before. It was the only gown of any quality she had here, deciding to say it had been given to her by her last employer, if anyone asked. As soon as the door opened she flew into his arms, unable to wait. He embraced her with equal enthusiasm. "I wasn't sure of my welcome," he protested.

"I know I shouldn't but it's all very new to me." She leaned back in his arms, showing him a face shining with happiness.

"Stay like that." His face lost the smile, to be replaced by something else, something deeper. His gaze roamed her face hungrily. "I've never had a welcome like that. I could get used to it." Her laugh was a little shaky. She could get used to it, too. She must not. It was imperative she did not. When he kissed her it was a natural extension of his look. He drew back after a tender touch. "I'm sorry I wasn't here for most of the day. I had things to arrange."

"You must be very busy. You mustn't think I was upset." Or know that she missed him.

"No. Besides, my business today concerned you, indirectly." She arched an eyebrow in query. He laughed. "I've sent Daniel out of your reach."

"I—I wasn't—"

He laid a finger across her lips. "Hush, it doesn't matter. I was foolish and jealous. But something needed to be done about the situation. Daniel and Miranda couldn't continue as they were. That news about Dr. Sewell gave me new hope. I haven't told Daniel my suspicions yet, because Corin and I are not entirely sure ourselves, and we still have some concern about Miranda. She was very ill."

"It was the children, wasn't it?" Violetta had heard something, but only what was general knowledge.

"She nearly died when she gave birth last time, and Dr. Sewell told her she must not have children ever again."

"Ohhhhhhh." That explained a great deal. If Lady Rosington must not have children, the likelihood was they abstained. For any couple who cared about each other that must be unbearable. "How dreadful."

"Hush. It is for them to work out, not us. I've done all I can. If they can't sort out their affairs in the month Corin and I have given them, then we'll have to take more direct methods. Maybe bring my mother into the situation. And this way, I get you with no distractions."

She stared up at him. He was perfectly serious. She could see no guile in his eyes. "So you have me to yourself."

"That was my hope," he confessed. He smiled, gently, intimately. "Have I achieved my aim?"

"For now." She couldn't refuse him. It would be denying herself too much. She deserved this, just a taste, for a little time. Afterwards, her life could begin, settle into the pattern she had planned for herself but this was her own limbo, an island between the two worlds and one she meant to use.

She reached up and pressed her lips to his. He responded gratifyingly, immediately drawing her close and opening his mouth against hers. She drank him in, absorbing him into her, feeling his passion feed hers. He wanted her, still wanted her after last night, and she gloried in it.

He drew away gently, gazing at her. She wore her hair loose tonight, something he seemed to appreciate. He lifted a hand and sifted it through her hair. "It's even better down. Soft, like silk."

"And not a curl in it," she added, wrinkling her nose. She spent hours suffering the ministrations of her maid with curling tongs. She refused to wear rags in her hair overnight because she couldn't sleep that way.

"I like it." His voice was intimately low. "How are you today?"

His deceptively casual tone didn't deceive Violetta. "You mean how do I feel after last night?"

"Yes." His attention went from her hair to her eyes. "Physically."

She smiled. "I had a bath. I feel fine."

He let his breath out in one long sigh. "I'm so glad. I was worried about you."

A thought occurred to her. "Was I your first virgin?"

His smile was broad and lingering. "Yes, as a matter of fact you were. I knew what to expect, but I didn't know how it would affect me."

She leaned back a little against his arm. "How did it affect you?"

His arm tightened around her. "It made me strangely protective. Caring."

"Strangely?" It was surprising to find that she was the

strong one here. She had known what she was doing but it seemed taking him by surprise was the right tactic. Not that she had planned it, of course.

"It's not something I usually feel towards my—" He paused, unable to find the right word.

"Conquests?" she suggested brightly. "Mistresses?"

He frowned. "Neither of those seem right. Lover, perhaps."

She allowed her scepticism to show. "Are you trying to tell me I'm different?"

His frankness disarmed her. "Yes. You're different, Violetta. In what way I'm not yet sure. I'd appreciate a little time to find out."

She stared at him, not knowing what to say. She found him different too. Different from the haughty gentleman she had first thought him. Different from how she imagined a lover would be. "Yes. Just a little time, though."

"We'll see." With her acquiescence, having assured him she was well enough to accept his approaches, he released her, but kept hold of her hand, and drew her across to the bed. "Lie down with me," he suggested.

She lay down, and moved across so he could lie next to her. He leaned up, propped up on one elbow and gazed down at her. "We have all night. I believe Perdita is planning to stay out late tonight."

"Shouldn't you have escorted her?"

"She has Corin. He's promised not to leave her side."

"Ah." She could think of nothing else, nor did she want to. She lay and watched him, tracing the front of her gown with an idle hand, touching her so softly it felt like the touch of a feather. He flicked open the first hook. She smiled. He flicked open the second, exposing a narrow triangle of bare skin. "Your skin seems to invite touch."

"Only from you."

His smile turned wry. "For now. I would like to keep you, you know that."

She shook her head. "I haven't decided what to do yet. I have to make my own way in the world, be on my own, but I'm not as sure as I was a week ago."

"Has what we did last night anything to do with that?" He flicked open another fastening.

"Everything." She curled her arm around his neck and pulled him down to kiss her. It was long, leisurely and deepened very slowly. When Violetta opened her mouth under the pressure of his lips he touched her with his tongue, and then slid slowly inside, caressing her lips, then meeting her tongue in a caress she returned eagerly. He leaned across her and slid his hand inside her gown, around her ribs just below her breast. When he spread his fingers and touched her breast she moved into his hand, revelling in the sensation of being cherished and wanted. He accepted her invitation and moved his hand up to cover and caress her. When he rolled the nipple gently between finger and thumb she moaned into his mouth, feeling the tingle from her nipple right down to her thighs.

He broke the kiss and gazed at her. "We shouldn't be doing this. I decided I wouldn't take advantage of you while you were under my roof. What happened?"

She let him see her reaction to his caresses, her smile softening, arching into his hand. "We happened. I wanted you, too."

"I need to know that. Otherwise I'd be the most selfish beast in nature."

She gazed at him. There were no barriers between them, not at that moment. He had lost the haughty, aristocratic disdain he habitually wore when facing the world, and looked at her with warmth and desire. She could almost feel the heat emanating from him, entering her. She could bask in it for a long time. She moved, flexed her body like a cat and he smiled, enjoying her pleasure. "Perhaps I should minister to you all night. Your personal attendant, here only for your pleasure."

"Don't tempt me. I might take you up on your offer."

His steady caresses continued, not increasing in intensity. "Your pleasure is my pleasure. I please myself while I'm pleasing you."

Abruptly she said, "Is it always like this?"

He didn't pretend to misunderstand. "No." His smile faded, to be replaced by a more intense look. He stared into her eyes and his hand stilled. "We've only made love once, and already I need to see you, be with you. It was like that before but not so concentrated."

"What do we do?"

"I'd like to see where it leads." He resumed his stroking. "I don't want to pressure you. I don't want to make you feel trapped. You don't like that, do you?"

"No." How did he know that? She had thought her disguise as Charlotte Lambert so good, yet he was able to tell a great deal about her. Did everyone see these things? She sincerely hoped not.

The smile returned. "Sufficient unto the day," he quoted, and bent to kiss her.

All the warmth he had been slowly building inside her erupted and she sucked cold air through her nose. If his mouth hadn't been covering hers she would have gasped. It felt as though everything surged up inside her, increasing her need, making all her senses focus on him. Only him.

He lifted his mouth to murmur, "Relax. Let me love you," then he dropped small kisses on her nose, her cheeks, and trailed light caresses down to her throat. His hand continued its magic, and she felt him loosen another hook, and another. He lifted his head and leaned back on his elbow. They watched together as he opened each hook in a steady, relentless passage down to her lower calf, where the gown flowed free. He moved to straddle her body, her legs between his, and opened the robe.

She was laid open for his pleasure, and he took it. He gazed his fill until she flushed, her body suffused with the warmth she still felt inside. "You're truly lovely. Soft, smooth, a joy." He ran his hand down from her breasts to her hips.

Leaning back on his heels he divested himself of the light robe he wore over his shirt and breeches, letting it fall behind him, then his shirt, pulling it over his head. The ribbon came away and he shook his hair free, smiling at her in the intimate way she was coming to know well. She smiled back and curved her body first one way, then the other. His response was a low groan, and he came back over her again, taking her mouth, pushing his hands into her hair on either side of her head.

She wouldn't let him go. Throwing her arms around him, gripping him tightly she returned his kiss, exploring him, feeling him meld her closer. Passion rose inside her to a deep longing. If he left now she would follow him until he gave her what she needed.

He wasn't about to leave. His breeches hid nothing from her, nor did he want to hide, pushing his erection into her stomach in a motion as old as time. She gave him the response, arched her back to push.

He leaned back just long enough to tear the buttons undone at the waistband and kick the last garment down his legs. He came back down on top of her, pushing her legs open and settling between them. He lifted himself up and gasped. "You take me back to boyhood. I seem to have lost all the finesse I took such pains to learn."

"It doesn't matter. I want you. Please."

"One condition."

She couldn't believe it. "Anything!"

"Call me by my name."

Immediately, she cried out. "Orlando!"

Immediately, he responded. He touched her between her legs. "Oh God, Violetta!" He slid down and pushed between her legs, using one hand to guide himself to her. Then he looked up. Meeting her dazed stare with his burning gaze he thrust. They were one.

They cried out, breath meeting and mingling. She arched her back, pushing her shoulders into the mattress beneath her. He kept his thrusts steady, not increasing, building the warmth inside her until she cried out. "Please, please!"

"Please what?" His voice held a teasing note.

"I don't know. I don't know!" She arched her back, tilting her hips to take all of him, feel everything inside her. She felt him push his hand between them and down, and then he touched a place more exquisitely sensitive than she could ever remember it being before. Now she twisted to one side, sure she wouldn't be able to take any more and the movement pushed his hand deeper, harder against her. "Oh, oh, oh!" was all she managed, and she felt him thrust so deeply he touched the centre of passion, something deep inside tore her apart.

Her scream would have brought the servants running had he not kissed her, opening his mouth hotly against hers,

Lynne Connolly

pushing his tongue inside with none of the finesse he had used earlier. She needed this, this roughness, near to violence and he seemed to understand. He gave her everything, prolonging her climax past anything she thought possible until he joined her.

His long, low groan came from somewhere deep inside and she felt him jerk, push and take her over the edge again. Curling her legs around his she pressed her pelvis hard against him, feeling her pubic bone sink into his flesh. He was still pulsing inside her, gasping and burning, until he rested his forehead against hers and groaned long and low.

It sounded better than an oratorio.

Orlando came to lying next to Violetta, his arms holding her tightly. She was asleep. He pressed a tender kiss to her forehead, but she didn't wake, just moved closer to him. Something stirred inside him. It was more than desire, more than the novelty of a new affair. He was terribly afraid it might be love.

He knew her. He liked her. Now he loved her. Orlando wasn't sure what he was to do about it, but he was forced to acknowledge the simple fact. He wanted Violetta, and he couldn't foresee a time when he wouldn't.

He stroked her hair away from her face, enjoying the feel of the strands against his fingers. He needed her in his bed, every night, but he knew it might not be possible. Her breath heated his shoulder, and he felt her sigh. She was awake.

Her smile was warm and deep and heart-full. "You're still here," she said.

She sounded sleepy, vulnerable. He wanted to shelter her, watch over her. "Where else would I be?"

"Did I sleep long?"

"About half an hour. Not long."

"You should go."

"Why? Do you want me to? I locked the door when I came in. No one will come."

She smiled. He felt the movement her cheek made against his shoulder. "What about your room?"

"They'll assume I spent the night elsewhere. It's not

uncommon."

She blinked, came awake. "Am I your only—?" She stopped, blushing.

"Mistress?" He wanted to say something else, but he didn't dare. He didn't want her to look at him with anything but warmth and she was still skittish, still unable to accept any possibility of anything but a temporary relationship. He would have to be careful. If he was too persistent, too needy, he knew she would leave him, push him away. "Yes. I don't make a habit of promiscuity." He pulled her closer. It wasn't cold, they were lying on top of the covers but he wanted to feel her against his body. "I've not been celibate, and I have an undeserved reputation. Strangely, the reputation only dates a few years back, at about the time I restored my fortune." She joined in his laughter. It felt delicious. The feel of her skin against his was addictive, more than anything else he had ever known.

He was sure. This was what he wanted.

Orlando loved her again. Now the explosive desire that had pushed him before had evaporated he could take his time and love her. If he couldn't tell her he loved her, not yet at any rate, he could show her.

He kissed her, long and sweet and felt her response, pushing closer to him, touching her tongue to his. He withdrew a little and played his tongue against her lips, tracing the shape, only to enter again, taking her mouth as thoroughly as he'd taken her body earlier. He pulled back, looking at her face, marvellous eyes heavy-lidded and glowing. "You need a wash." His grin was entirely wicked.

He washed her, spreading kisses over her body. When he reached her breasts he took his time, tasting and circling, until her nipples became hard pinnacles, designed to fit the warmth of his mouth. He cradled them in his hands, drew one deep until he felt the tip touch the roof of his mouth and heard her responsive sound, low in her throat. When she sighed his name he rewarded her and moved lower, circling the delicious indentation of her navel with his tongue and then tracing her stomach down to the nest of black curls covering her most intimate secrets. When he pushed his finger deep into the welcoming wetness he got a startled reaction. "What—what are you doing?"

"I want to taste you." He whispered the words against her stomach, knowing the heat in his breath would have an effect on her. He felt her shudder, and bent his head.

Violetta nearly came off the bed. He put his hands to her hips, steadying her and continued. She tasted bittersweet. Addictive. He tasted her, every fold, every secret, and finally drew the tender pearl into his mouth and caressed, using his tongue to reach all of it.

She gasped and jerked, calling his name. She would be his. He couldn't imagine standing by and allowing another man access to this bounty.

He waited, caressing her until she had subsided before he rose up and sheathed himself inside her body. She reached for him, and he sank down onto her, taking his weight on his elbows, thrusting deep inside.

Her sighs were all the music he needed. He responded, murmuring love words, breathing them to her, wondering if she could hear.

Then he was whirled away to the simmering vortex they created together. Her hands pulled at him, urging him ever closer. He drove hard into her, feeling her take up the rhythm, hearing the sound of flesh coming together. Orlando lost himself in her. When she pulled him down he bent to kiss her, thrusting his tongue into her mouth. Gentleness left behind, they moved together and this time came together. When he felt his body surge and erupt, her hips moved beneath him in an involuntary, urgent drive to open herself to him as fully as she could, take all of him.

At that moment he felt as if she'd succeeded. He collapsed, a sweating, exhausted heap of nothing, over her panting body.

Orlando Garland had lost all the attributes with which he'd carefully endowed the Earl of Blyth. He was nothing but a man, loving the woman he was fast coming to accept was his mate.

He lifted his head. Violetta's wonderful eyes were open wide, strands of black hair straggled across her gleaming, rosy face. She looked alive, and praise be, happy. He hid nothing. It was all there for her to see, if she had a mind to see it.

She said nothing, but stared at him, wide-eyed. He leaned forward and kissed her with all the tenderness he'd forgotten a few minutes before. "I meant it to be gentle and loving," he murmured, his lips still next to hers. He drew back and smiled. "You set me on fire."

"I never imagined it could be like this" She sounded breathless, as well she might.

"I want the privilege of showing you how many different ways there are of making love, of being together. Come away with me, Violetta. We deserve time on our own. You deserve all the attention I can give you. I can't do it here. Come away with me."

She curled her arm around his back. "It sounds wonderful."

"It will be. I promise."

"Then I will, if it's possible."

He closed his eyes briefly. "Thank you." He might be able to persuade her to stay with him longer if she gave him the chance.

He lay next to her and drew her into his arms, smoothing her hair back, enjoying the feel of the silky strands slipping through his fingers. "Sleep now, sweet. I'll watch over you."

"You can't stay."

"I know. I'll go when you're asleep."

She looked up at him, smiling with no guile and no fear. "Kiss me goodnight, then."

He bent his head and kissed her, watching her until her eyes closed. He watched the candles gutter, feeling a tranquillity new to him, his restless mind at rest. No one else had been able to do that, stop his mind racing on its accustomed course for more than the few seconds of an orgasm. Violetta had given him ease and rest. More than that. He felt he had come home, at last.

Chapter Fifteen

Violetta woke to the sound of a door opening. Immediately she realized she was in no state to receive visitors. No wig, no spectacles, stark naked. She thrust her head under the covers, only then coming into contact with a large, warm body. Hell and damnation! He'd promised to leave! *That's what happens when you trust a man*, she thought savagely.

The large, warm body stirred into life and moved over her, throwing the sheet over her head. Violetta lay in the stifling warmth, listening, a faint sense of nausea in her stomach, her heart beating so fast she was sure she would stop breathing any minute.

The exclamation told her the intruder was feminine. At the next sound her worst fears were confirmed.

"Good God! What is this? Miss Lambert? Orlando!" The last word was almost shrieked. By now Orlando lay still, his arm protectively over Violetta. She felt her body shake, and made an effort to control it.

"Orlando what is the meaning of this?" demanded Lady Perdita.

"What does it look like, my dear?" He sounded rested, at ease, damn him!

There was a minute's pulsating silence. "How could you?" She sounded hurt now. "How could you do this to me? To Judith? This is why you haven't looked at her, isn't it? All the time we were trying to fix your interest you were—carrying on! In this house, with my companion!"

Another silence. Violetta tried not to breathe. "Miss Lambert, I expect you to leave this house before noon. I will not furnish you with a character to go to your next employer. I'm truly sorry it should end like this, but you have transgressed beyond what is acceptable. Do I make myself clear?"

Violetta said nothing. Orlando replied for her. "I regret you've been caused this embarrassment, my dear. I'll see you at breakfast."

The door closed. The sheet was withdrawn and she looked up to see Orlando's concerned face. He didn't look as insouciant as he'd sounded a moment ago. "Why didn't you tell me Perdita could walk so easily? If I'd known I would have locked that door, too."

Violetta felt a deep sense of failure. "She wanted to keep it as a surprise for you."

His mouth tightened. "Well it was."

"It's my fault. I should have told you."

"No, it's all *my* fault," he protested. "I broke my promise to you, to leave before dawn. The last one I will ever break."

"Yes," she managed, her voice shaking. "It is. You'd better leave now. If you will, I would appreciate a message sent to my mother's house. I will need the carriage."

"Use mine," he said briefly.

"No."

She threw back the covers and left the bed, ignoring his sharp intake of breath as she revealed her body to him. It was difficult to ignore him, to be as dignified as if she were fully clothed, but she managed it. She found a clean shift in the top drawer of the chest of drawers. She flung it over her head, and turned to see him bearing down on her. Totally, gloriously naked. And aroused. She stared at his face, cheeks aflame.

He put his hands on her arms, pressing them to her sides. When she studied his face she realized it had been an accident. He had fallen asleep despite his good intentions. It was done. She looked down. It was a mistake. She jerked her head back up. His warm smile acknowledged her embarrassment. "I'm sorry, Violetta. Truly."

"It doesn't matter. I'd finished my work here in any case."

She turned around and picked up a pair of stockings from the drawer. Would he stay here and watch her dress? Well, whether he stayed or not she would dress. And leave. She wanted nothing more than to shake the dust off her heels and forget all about this stupidity. It was a mistake ever to come here. She felt his hands on her upper arms, trying to turn her. She shook him off. "Go away. Just go."

"No. You're in no state to be left. Violetta, Violetta, it changes nothing. I still want you, more than I can say, I still— Violetta, I love you."

Panic and bitterness filled her. She didn't know what she should do now and for the first time, her fairytale became hard, bitter reality. She'd slept with a man without marrying him, with no prospect of it, a man she couldn't marry. It was the first step on the road to prostitution. She was ruined.

"Fool!" She spun back to face him, loose hair whipping across her face, fear adding to her anger. "I have a body, a body, that's all! Do you think I inherited nothing from my mother, learned nothing in her house? You want more of me. Well, my lord, since you have started me on this path, you shall pay for anything more!" She saw the hurt in his eyes and felt a primitive triumph. It was his fault, and he should pay, she told herself, though deep down she still didn't believe it. "If you want me, you know where to find me. You can be my first client, my first keeper, my lord. But you won't be the last!"

She hit home, but not in the way she'd wanted. His eyes lit with unmistakable fury. "You will not! This changes nothing. You promised to go away with me last night, and I intend to keep you to it! Don't think you can get away from me, because there is no chance of that."

"Oh yes, I forgot. " Violetta forced herself to icy control. Still shaking under her thin shift she faced him directly. "I may take that house from you after all. I will not be cheap, my lord."

He threw his hands in the air in a gesture of exasperation. "Will you stop this? You weren't meant for that life, you know you weren't."

"You have forced me into it. I've lost my maidenhead now, it's gone. If I am to enter my mother's world, I will be better and more expensive than she ever was. You will not be able to afford me for long, sir. I intend to snare a duke, if not a prince before I'm done!"

"You'll get nothing from them," he snarled, striding to the

door, snatching up the dressing gown he'd carelessly discarded the night before. "And if you persist in this folly, you'll get nothing from me, either."

Thrusting his arms through the sleeves he drew the garment around him and unlocked the door. "My carriage will be at your disposal."

The door slamming drowned her dignified acceptance.

Violetta slumped against the door, despair filling her to overflowing. The tears her anger held back, the reason she allowed her anger full rein, flowed freely now. She had lost everything. Her self-respect had shattered when that door opened, her shame at what she had done overwhelmed her. Physical desire wasn't a good enough reason to do what she had done. She had thrown it all away. She couldn't go back, not to the individual she had been when she'd first walked through the front door of this house, the strong, purposeful person she'd been. And she knew, despite lashing out at Orlando, that it was her fault. He had never forced her into anything. She'd done it herself.

The cold person, the singular person. For two nights she had been one of a couple. It felt right, and she had allowed her guard to slip. Now she was damaged, hurt, and it was as bad as she had always feared.

While she packed she allowed herself to weep. She packed all Miss Lambert's clothes, except the most hideous, dun coloured gown, which had lost its shape from repeated washing. It suited her mood. She put it on, braided her hair and stuffed it under the wig. The spectacles were a defiant addition.

She left the house with her head high, looking neither to right or left. She heard the door of the study open behind her and quickened her pace. The sooner she shook off her experience here and regained her strength the better she would be.

If not happier.

ॐ

There was one person she couldn't hide her emotions from,

and she should never have tried to. Explaining briefly that her employment had come to an end she pleaded a headache and went to her room to rest.

She wasn't to have the rest. After a brief tap on her door, her mother entered her room. Violetta lay on the bed, having stripped away all evidence of Miss Lambert's existence and donned a light wrapper. Her hair was braided down her back. She stared, wide-eyed at the canopy above her head.

"My love, there is something wrong." It was a statement, not a question. "Tell me." Donata Palagio sat on the side of the bed and held out her arms. Violetta gave in to the inevitable and flung herself into the shelter of her mother's comfort. She could only bear to say this once, so she made sure her mother heard. She spoke clearly. "Lady Perdita discovered us in bed together this morning. She told me to leave." She buried her face in the soft comfort of Donata's shoulder, and allowed herself to release all her fears, all her regrets.

Donata held her and stroked her hair, reverting to her native tongue. "You are in the heat of your first love affair. It's not so bad. It will work itself out, one way or another."

Violetta followed her mother's example and answered in Italian. "It was only when we were discovered I realized what I had done. When we were alone it was beautiful, perfect, but when Lady Perdita showed her disgust I was ashamed. It is wrong, Mama. Sordid. I should never have allowed it. Never!" A fresh storm of weeping heralded her distress.

"No, no, never think that. It is not wrong. You love him, do you not?"

Violetta raised a tear stained face. "It was my greatest fear, that he discovered how I felt about him. Then I would have been completely in his power."

Donata answered softly. "Sometimes you have to give yourself completely to gain perfect trust. For you that included giving your body. For me, that was telling my lover why I had run from my husband. I put myself in his power, deliberately."

Violetta swallowed. Her mother had never told her so much before. "Ripley?"

"Yes. I did not leave my husband because of his treatment of me. I did it because he threatened you. He said he would kill you if I did not do what he wanted. I did it, but I knew it would never be enough. You were three years old. Do you remember any of it?"

"Yes," she whispered, childhood returning in force together with the memory that had haunted her dreams for years. Her father ripping her mother's clothes off, then subjecting her to unspeakable things, things she could only be glad happened after he'd slammed the door in her face. Violetta was never sure which was real and which not, and didn't dare ask in case it had all been real.

"I ran. Lodovico, your uncle, helped me to get away but asked me not to tell him where I was going, so he would not have to lie to his family. Lucius was the only person who knew who I was. He could have contacted my husband, but I chose to trust him."

"Why?" Violetta stared at her mother, tears forgotten. "How did you know you could?"

Donata smiled. "I didn't. I loved him, and if we were to have more than that, we had to trust each other implicitly. If not, I would live in fear, always be in danger. I knew he would not allow you to suffer, but I didn't know if his feelings for me would be enough to stop him informing my husband where I was. He is an honourable man."

"When he preferred you to his wife?"

"Yes. You have seen her. He was married to her before he went abroad on the Tour. He tried very hard to make his marriage a success when he returned home. When I fled to England and went to him we did not become lovers. He helped me because he loved me and I him. He tolerated my life because he loved me. He knew I could not depend on him, much as he wanted to take care of me."

"Why not?"

Donata stroked her daughter's hair. "I could not depend on a man ever again. Not after what d'Oro did to me. I needed to be independent in my own right, but if the Contessa d'Oro reappeared in England, her husband would have reclaimed her instantly. I had to be someone else and I had to earn enough to ensure you were brought up properly. There was little choice. I did what I could."

Finally in love, knowing what it meant, Violetta understood some of it. "How did he tolerate it?"

"Lucius? He understood why I did it. He knew he was my love. Anything I gave—sold—to anyone else was worthless in those terms. It was my living, that was all."

Violetta shuddered, and wondered what she would have done in her mother's place, wondered if she could have been as brave. Knowing, finally, what love meant she understood what it must mean to see the loved one turn elsewhere for physical relief. It would hurt. Hurt so much she had no idea how Lord Ripley bore it.

It was clever of her mother to turn the topic to herself, Violetta realized. It made her think beyond her current problems, put her mind to use. It helped. She drew back, drawing her arm over her face in a distinctly childish gesture.

Her mother studied her. Violetta didn't know if she found what she looked for. "He will probably come, you know that. If he does not, you may forget him with a clear conscience. If he comes, we must decide what to do."

"I don't know. I feel so ashamed, mother."

"What are you ashamed of?" Her mother's soft, silken voice seduced Violetta into telling the truth, searching her heart for the real reasons she'd turned on Orlando that morning.

"That someone saw us, that what we had wasn't—right. I attacked him, Mother."

"If it's love, it's right."

"I tried to help Lady Perdita and threw it all away in five minutes."

"Does she walk?"

"Yes." Violetta bit her lip. That was the important thing, what she had set out to achieve. Perhaps she hadn't been such a failure, after all. "She walks."

"You have helped, then. Now you must think of yourself. What do you *want* to do? Why did you attack Lord Blyth?"

She knew the true answer now. "I panicked. This is all new to me, mother. I thought I knew, living in this house, seeing what I have seen—" a smile flickered across her lips when she remembered her mother's efforts to keep her away from extraneous activity, "—a small child can hide in a multitude of small places, Mama."

Her mother stroked her hair. "You were always a secretive child. It was never easy for you to show yourself."

Violetta felt safe here, in the room she had known most of her life, in her mother's arms. She could think once more, with some semblance of clarity. "I panicked. I was afraid of what I'd shown Orlando. In two short nights he discovered more than anyone else about me. He understood me. Perdita's discovery only gave the excuse to push him away."

"Then you have to decide what you want to do now. If you love him, take the chance, give him your trust. Don't push him away, Violetta." Her mother spoke low and soothingly. "When he calls, I will see him. I will tell him of your distress."

"No!"

"*Si.* Listen. I will ask what he intends to do about his contract with you."

Violetta jerked back. "What contract?"

Donata stroked her daughter's hair and pulled her close again. "Do not worry. There is none, but he must be made to understand that we are not merely for the asking. A man must work to gain our favour. Don't make it easy for him, my love. If he loves you truly, he'll come to you, and if he does not, better it ends now than later. Do as I say, and we shall see."

Violetta looked up with a watery sniff, but her eyes were dry now. "You know more than I do about this. I will do it."

Donata chuckled. "You will do it well."

∞

When Lord Blyth called on Violetta he found she was receiving no visitors. He left a note. When Violetta opened it she wept. "I am so sorry," was all it said, and he'd signed it with a flourished "O". No declaration of love could have moved her more.

When he called the second time he only saw her mother, and that for five minutes. He received just enough encouragement to call again. Orlando was not foolish. He knew he was being punished and maybe tested too, but he also knew he deserved it. His sister excoriated him.

"Orlando, how could you do such a thing?" she demanded, at his most vulnerable time. Breakfast. It quite put him off his kippers and eggs. He knew she was planning to speak to him when she dismissed the maid laying out the breakfast things.

"It seemed natural at the time." He saw no reason to explain himself to his sister, but he knew if he didn't listen to her she would never allow him any peace.

"You know Judith wants to attract your interest! Before *she* arrived in the house you were quite interested in her, and we thought it was positively a done thing. Now I understand, it's obvious. Did she make a play for you from the first?"

Orlando gave up. He put down his fork. "No. I made a play for her."

"Did you seduce her?"

"Really, Perdita! What would you know of such things?"

She frowned at him. "What do you think women gossip about? Really, my dear!"

He frowned back. "We had only just become lovers." He tamped down the familiar warm feeling in the vicinity of his groin that he felt whenever he thought of Violetta. Now was definitely not the right time.

"Will you see her again?"

His look became frozen. "I fail to see what concern that is of yours."

She became positively shrewish. "Before her lapse I was becoming quite fond of Miss Lambert. I am not such a fool as to suppose it was entirely her idea. In fact, dear brother, knowing men, I suspect much of it was your fault. You put me in an impossible position. I wanted to reward her for her help, but after that, how could I?"

He relaxed. He would gladly bear all the blame if he could restore her Miss Lambert to his sister's good books. "It was my fault, I fear. I should have shown more restraint, I know. If it helps, I will give her a good character. After all, I employed her. I understand why you cannot, but she performed her duties well while she was here."

Perdita seemed slightly more mollified. "Very well. But I wish to hear nothing of that. I cannot give her a character, you know that."

Orlando got to his feet to help his sister sit. She nodded her thanks. "You are very reprehensible, Orlando, but that only seems to make you more admirable in the eyes of the world. The female world particularly. Word has it you've taken an expensive ladybird into keeping, one Perla Perfetta. Aren't you satisfied with one?"

Orlando sat down again and regarded her with lazy insolence. "My dear, I hope you don't converse like this with your friends. You are supposed to be an innocent virgin, after all." He ignored his sister's snort of derision. "That, if you must know, was in the nature of a wager. A man cannot step down once he has declared himself. Ladybirds, as you quaintly refer to them, are not my style in the general run of things. Until recently I couldn't afford them, and now I can I find I've lost interest in that kind of—" he paused, dabbing his lips with a stiffly starched napkin, "—financial transaction."

Perdita nodded, not as shocked as she should have been, Orlando reflected wryly. "I won't ask anything else, except that you not ruin Miss Lambert. She deserves that, at least. I don't like to think of her fallen from grace."

Orlando kept his expression deliberately grave. Bowed under the weight of the guilt and misery, it wasn't difficult. "I promise I won't ruin Miss Lambert. I won't tell if you don't."

The name "Charlotte Lambert" disappeared from the vocabulary of the house after that discussion. It was as though she had never existed. Orlando had no idea if Perdita told Lady Judith of the reason for her lack of success in fixing Orlando's interest, but it was certain that Lady Judith's visits did not abate, and her interest in Orlando, particularly in private, became more marked instead of less.

He responded politely, but was too sore, too worried to take much notice of her. All his thoughts were of Violetta. Had he lost her? If he couldn't have the reality, she would be in his mind, in his dreams, taunting him, reminding him of what he could have had if it hadn't been for that door opening. And his falling asleep, surrounded by the most profound sense of peace he had ever known.

He presented himself at the house, but despite abasing himself at the feet of La Perla, he wasn't allowed to see La Perla Perfetta. It wasn't her he wanted, the exquisite, accomplished courtesan. It was Violetta, the warm, loving woman with the perfect body, the quick wit and quietly intelligent mind. He was not to see her. He prepared himself for a siege. He would not give up. He *could* not give up.

He had promised to join his sister and Lady Judith at Lord Ripley's house in the country. If he had not won Violetta by then he would take them and come back for her.

He arrived on a Wednesday and was granted an audience alone with La Perla. Aware of the nature of his visit, he arrived in full evening dress, elegant and neat in crimson, the full evening coat echoing his every movement with an expensive rustle. He bowed low to her, and stood. Lord Ripley stood by the chair on which La Perla sat, a consort to her majesty.

"You have seriously distressed my daughter. Your carelessness has cost her a great deal." The statement was irrefutable, as, Orlando was sure, she had meant it to be.

"I apologize profusely for my deep error." How was he to know his sister had the habit of entering her companion's room by the private door? He hadn't even known she could walk. The error was not all his. However, to win her back, he was prepared to grovel. "I only wish to see her in person, to apologize. How may I repair my error?"

Ripley stirred. "The error was in seducing her while she was under your roof."

Orlando couldn't deny that. The only reason, the true reason, was he couldn't wait. It had been the action of a desperate man. "I asked her to come away with me for a time. I should have waited until then."

"Indeed you should." The faint Italian accent gave La Perla a touch of aristocracy. Her small chin was tilted haughtily up. Where had she learned that trick? "My child is distressed."

Orlando bowed.

He heard a slight commotion outside the door to the salon where he had received his audience. The door was flung open, as though it had been forced. "Donata! What is this?"

The newcomer stopped dead, glaring at Orlando. His jaw dropped. "Mother?"

Chapter Sixteen

Lady Taversall glared at her son. "I might have guessed you'd be here!" Ignoring him for the time being she turned to La Perla. "Donata, what has my son done? I have to hear this from a good friend, and that so jumbled I wasn't sure what I was hearing. What is going on?" She turned to Orlando. "What have you done to her?"

Orlando gaped. His air of suave elegance fell away from him, something that had not happened since he was a callow youth. The bottom fell out of his world. "What—?" he managed, before he lapsed into gormless silence.

His mother gave him an irritated frown. "I went to school with Donata," she said, as though that explained everything. How much more did he not know about his mother? Orlando felt adrift, as though nothing was as he had previously supposed it to be.

"Your daughter discovered your son in bed with my daughter," La Perla explained. The Italian accent was still there, but the haughtiness had evaporated. Orlando noted the absence of any honorific. Old friends indeed.

The two ladies stared at each other. Lord Ripley set a chair next to La Perla's as though it was the most natural thing in the world for Lady Taversall to visit the queen of the demi-monde. As, perhaps, it was in this topsy-turvy world.

Orlando watched the two ladies touch cheeks affectionately with a kind of dumb horror. His mother and this lady. The world couldn't stand against them. For them to join forces didn't bear thinking about.

Lady Taversall took her time sitting down and settling her skirts. "Now I see why your man was so keen to keep me out of here. I thought I was going to see something reprehensible, which only made me more eager, but it's not a Thursday. Then I find this." She waved a vague hand in the direction of her son. "He has seduced Violetta, you say? The poor child!" She glared at Orlando. "How could you? I heard of the farce here the other week, thanks to Ripley, but I never dreamed you would act in such an indiscreet manner!"

Orlando gathered his wayward thoughts. "Who told you?"

"About the discovery? No one. I heard about the auction. How could you do such a thing to such a sweet child?"

Sweet child? His mother knew Violetta? Orlando's head spun. "Has the world gone mad?"

"Not in the least." His mother fixed him with a full blown basilisk stare. "I told you. Donata and I have been friends for years. What do you expect, I announce that to the world? However, a friend is a friend, and I could not abandon Donata just because she took a different course to me!" She flicked open her fan, and wafted it before shutting it with a decisive snap. "Donata was not born what she is now. When she came to London she needed my help and I gave it gladly. I do not abandon my friends, and Donata is one of my dearest friends. Do you think women are the defenceless creatures you imagine? Surely not, my son!"

It only deepened the mystery for Orlando. He gathered a few things from the information. La Perla's real name was Donata. She had been born well, but for some reason turned to her current profession. He badly wanted to know more, but he knew better than to ask now. He would have been rebuffed with aplomb. His curiosity must wait. "It was a surprise, ma'am, I must admit this explains some of the mysteries. You are always so well informed. Now I know one of the reasons why."

His mother examined him like some species of beetle under her foot. "You do indeed. If you have harmed one hair of that poor girl's head I shall personally throttle you!" That was better. Once his mother threatened physical damage it was a sign she was beginning to calm down.

Orlando bowed. "I only ask for a private interview with Violetta, so I may apologize to her in person."

"I will see if she will agree to it," La Perla said. "Presently she is prostrate in her bed."

Lady Taversall reached out and covered La Perla's hand with her own in a gesture of sympathy. "I'll see he makes amends," she promised.

It was all Orlando was to receive that night. He left half an hour later, bemused and bewildered by the new turn of events.

He was allowed to see Violetta the following week, but only in company.

La Perla Perfetta appeared in all her pristine perfection at her mother's salon. Her gown was dauntingly formal, a confection of gleaming white satin, held out by a huge hoop. Her mask was made of white peacock feathers, enhanced with a gleaming gloss of some description. Her face was powdered pale, her dark hair covered with a flurry of fine powder. Her full breasts quivered beneath a light veiling of fine Brussels lace. She was, as her name suggested, perfection.

Orlando had dressed to please her in full formal rig, heavy blue coat and delicately embroidered white waistcoat, linen and lace immaculate. He knew everyone present would be watching. Would he claim her? Would she accept him or reject him publicly?

Orlando was at his coolest, his most insouciant. He didn't try to approach her immediately, but paid his respects with a deep bow to the mother, and another for the daughter. Then he turned to speak to an acquaintance. He'd let it be known he would be there tonight, knowing he needed to end this or continue it, one way or the other. He had to leave London soon, to escort his sister to Ripley Court. He needed it settled by then, or it might well kill him.

He thought of drifting across the room to gradually end up by her side, but then thought again. No, he would not make it easy for her. She seemed like a creature from another world, ethereal, as though she could disappear into thin air. Well, as far as he was concerned, she could do just that after tonight. If she said no. If she rebuffed him here, now, he would leave and not look back. Whatever it cost him.

He strode across the room to her. Eyes glittered behind the feathered mask. "Good evening, ma'am."

She inclined her head, unsmiling. "Good evening, my lord."

Back to "my lord" he thought. Not a good sign. "Will you do me the honour of walking with me?"

She laid her hand on his arm in a light, elegant gesture. "Very well."

When she turned her head briefly he saw the ravages the her recent experiences had added to her. A hard line between nose and mouth. The drooping line of her lips. He couldn't see her eyes under the mask, but he would have bet a lot of money that they were shadowed and hollow. She had suffered, then. As he had.

It was as though the whole crowd let out an indrawn breath. An exhalation of tension, released all at once. Murmured conversations returned. "You've not been well," he said, so quietly only she could hear.

"Is it so obvious?"

"Not to anyone else. Only to a fellow sufferer."

She bowed her head, then lifted it with a flurry of feathers. Feathers extended far beyond the edge of her face, brushing other people when they passed. Her chin tilted up. "I am recovering. I'm sure I'll be perfectly well in time."

"I'm not." She shot a startled glance at his face, but continued the stately promenade around the room. That way no one would interrupt them. It was probably best this particular conversation was taking place in public. It was safer. "I'll never get over you, ma'am. I'm not sure I want to."

"It is why I was put on this earth, it seems. To make men happy."

"Then don't defy your fate." They walked for a few steps in taut silence. "All I ask is for a few days. Come away with me, and let us talk this over."

"Just talk?"

He gave her a wry smile. "I can't promise that."

She breathed deeply, her breasts swelling over the tight lacing of the low-cut gown. "I don't know. What makes you think I would ever consent to see you privately again?"

"Only one reason. Everything I said to you I meant. We have unfinished business, my love."

She gasped. "Blandishments."

"Find out. At worst you have a lucrative contract. At best— well, who knows?"

She turned to him, the flash of anger unmistakable under the mask. Her powdered face seemed to grow paler. "Don't taunt me! I know what I am!"

"So do I." He let his words turn into a caress.

She stared at him for a few minutes in silence. He watched the glitter of the diamonds at her throat, and waited for her. "I have to escort my sister to Ripley Court in two weeks. I must know by then."

"For convenience? You like your life set out in neat little pockets, don't you?"

He accepted this. "I used to. No, it's simpler than that. I can't wait any longer. I simply cannot."

"What will you do if I make you wait?"

He kept his face still, so still he feared it might crack. "I will die. Oh, not physically, nothing so dramatic. Only that part of me, the part I've shown only to you will die. I will probably pay court, as the world expects, to Lady Judith and marry her before the summer is out. Then I will no longer allow any softer feeling to enter my life. I have done my duty. I'll continue to do it."

She studied him closely. The little hand on his arm trembled. It was the only sign of the emotion he knew roiled within her. "I can't allow that." They stared at each other in their own island of silence in the middle of a chattering, laughing throng. "I'll come with you."

"Thank you." The words were soft, but charged with meaning. "I will call on you next Wednesday with the carriage. Earlier if I can, but I have an errand to run first." He glanced at her and paused before he continued. "Miranda and Daniel are staying in the country—in Leicestershire, and I need to pay them a visit."

She understood the pause but Rosington's marriage was no longer under threat because of her. "I understand the needs of family."

He stepped back and bowed to her, extremely formally, hand on heart. It was a bow low enough for a princess, and he meant it. He stopped only to thank his hostess for her indulgence at receiving him, then he turned and left. He didn't look back.

ॐ

Violetta stepped out of the carriage with Orlando's help. He had been formally attentive during the short journey, nothing more. Conversation had been general. She wondered if that meant he was as nervous as she was, or if this was normal for him. She wanted to ask him if this was the house he usually brought his mistresses to, but she didn't dare. She didn't really want to know, afraid of what she might hear.

The house was lovely. Built of a soft cream-coloured stone, it was a single fronted house of three bays. A manor house, door in the middle and large windows on both sides. An intimate house. She turned to him. "This is lovely. I wonder you want to live anywhere else."

He smiled at her pleasure. "I'm glad you like it. Come inside." He led her up the steps to the front door, standing open to receive them. Inside only one manservant waited, and he was not in livery. He bowed. "Welcome to Richmond, ma'am."

"Thank you." Violetta looked around her. The floor of the hall was tiled in black and white and a light staircase arched up to the upper floors a few steps away. To the right a door stood open to a large, airy parlour, furnished in light fabrics. The door to the left of her was closed.

"May I show you to your room, ma'am?" Violetta, who had learned to expect a certain superior tone from Orlando's servants, heard no censure in the man's voice, saw nothing in his face except bland acceptance. She followed him upstairs, hearing Orlando's quiet footsteps on the stairs behind her. Looking down she saw a man bringing in their luggage. There wasn't a great deal of it.

Two servants. Orlando followed her glance. "Two menservants, a cook and a chambermaid," he informed her. "There are usually more, but not for this visit."

It was on the tip of her tongue to ask him why so few servants, but she waited. Some discretion should be employed.

The man took them into a room and bowed. Violetta kept her eyes trained on the servant until Orlando dismissed him. Then she turned.

The room was dominated, as a bedroom should be, by the bed. Of light wood, with filmy cream coloured draperies, and a marquetry pattern at its head. The large sash windows were open, and a welcome breeze flowed through the room. Underfoot a large carpet cushioned her feet.

"Well?" His voice, deep and resonant, made her start.

"I'm sorry. I was lost in a dream."

"A good one, I hope." He came forward and took both her hands in his. It was the first time they had touched, skin to skin, all day. "Will you take a bolt back to town? Or will you stay here with me?"

"I made my decision last night. We have this time."

He drew her closer. "Then we must make the most of it." Only in his arms, with his mouth on hers did Violetta feel truly at peace, a strange way to describe the surging excitement she felt. It was the truth. Peace and excitement, at the same time. She gave up wondering and gave herself to his kiss. He broke away and his gaze roamed her face. He cupped her chin in one hand. "I tried to make this as discreet as I could. I knew you'd want it that way."

Overcome at his consideration she lowered her eyelids.

"No," he whispered. "Let me look at you."

"Haven't you seen enough of me?"

His smile caught at her heart. "Never. When I saw you during daylight it was with that dreadful wig, and those spectacles that dimmed the beauty of your eyes. Were they tinted?"

"A little." She looked up with a smile and received a gentle kiss for her reward.

"Thank you for coming. I have to be in town next Wednesday for the journey to Ripley Court."

"Then that is all the time we have."

"No!" His denial was violent. "Please Violetta, please don't put a limit on our relationship. I don't know what is to come and neither do you."

She accepted that. The shadow in her mind receded. For the present. Here, in this sun-filled room it seemed impossible to think of sad things. Gladly Violetta leaned forward into his arms and gave him the full, open-mouthed kiss they both needed. He caressed her inside her mouth with his tongue, outside her body with his hands before pulling back with a gasp. "Very ungentlemanly, to fall on you as soon as the door is closed on us. Would you like some refreshments? To go for a walk, perhaps?"

"Only as far as the bed."

"Oh God, Violetta!" Giving up all pretence at restraint, he led her to the bed and they fell on it together. Her side hoops collapsed underneath her and she felt her skirts rise above her knees. He knelt up, tearing off his coat, pulling at the buttons of his waistcoat. She fumbled with the hooks fastening her gown down the front, but before she could undo more than two or three, he was on her, pushing her skirts away, pulling her on top of him. Their lips met in a long, deep kiss.

Their first mating was undignified, performed as it was in the midst of a pile of discarded clothes, but his deep thrust into her welcoming body was what they needed. Together again, no masks, minds and bodies merged, Violetta at last felt complete again. She felt his frantic need to take her, arched her back and pushed her body up to meet his violent, hard drives deep into the heart of her, crying out when her climax came without worrying about who was listening to them, who might gossip. He stiffened above her and with one final push, released his essence into her, deep inside. Then he fell to one side, bonelessly rolling over her but never letting go.

They couldn't get her hoops off. The tapes had tangled themselves in a knot, so they gave up and when he gave a final sigh and leaned up to view her, the hoops had collapsed either side of her. She giggled. "They'll never be the same again."

"Neither will my breeches." He picked up the offending garment and threw it on the floor. They had torn the breeches at the front flap and at the knee. They laughed together.

Neither was completely naked. Violetta still wore her shift, and her stays hung off her upper body by its loosened tapes. He still wore his shirt. He sat back on his haunches, still panting from his efforts and gazed at her. Violetta stared at him. She had never seen him more open, more—content. She sat up and began on her laces, but he laughed at her. "Completely knotted. Wait." Climbing off the bed he found his discarded coat and rummaged in the pockets. "Ah, here we are." He returned with a small, but wicked looking knife.

"What are you doing with that?"

He hefted the weapon in one hand. "Hold still." She did as she was told and felt the tapes release when he cut them.

"Now how am I to return to London with any semblance of propriety?"

"Perhaps I won't let you return after all. Perhaps I'll keep you here."

She knew he wasn't serious and laughed with him. His face turned grave and he came back down to her, tossing the knife on the floor. It landed with a dull thud. "There's nothing I'd like better." He kissed her, long and slow. She turned to him willingly, disposing of the side hoops with a twist and a shove. The floor must be littered with cast off clothing. Drawing her into his arms he settled them both. There was no need for covers, it was a warm day and they had done a good amount to make it warmer. Violetta felt completely content. "Tell me about your childhood," he asked. "I can't make sense of some of it. Meeting my mother at your house came as a complete shock."

She lifted her chin to meet his eyes. "If you tell me about yours."

He grinned. "You must know most of it. It's been in all the scandal sheets. To be truthful I don't remember much of it. Taversall is, in effect, my father. He brought me up, taught me right from wrong. As well it wasn't my blood father. He was a wastrel, a rake and a gambler. My mother married him after old Rosington died. My brother Daniel's inheritance was carefully secured so Blyth couldn't touch it. When he discovered that, Blyth turned on Mama. She had little of her own. Her portion from Rosington was lost when she remarried, apart from a small annuity." He paused, biting his lip.

Violetta knew hardly anyone had heard the story from him before. The recitation sounded fresh, unrehearsed, and she could see how it affected him to remember. This was something he'd locked away. She became aware of the depth of his feeling for her, that he should choose to tell her. It had to be transient.

This couldn't last, it mustn't. Fear clutched at her heart, but she pushed it away.

"He hurt her," he said. "My father beat my mother."

A bond between their mothers. Both had known what it was to be at the mercy of an abusive man. "How did he die?"

"He was killed in a duel over some woman or other. Not my mother, thank God. At least she was spared that disgrace. It's one of my earliest memories. So clear, it could have been yesterday. I found her. Before he'd left for the duel, he'd beaten her to within an inch of her life. The baby, Perdita, was wailing to be fed, and the sound drew me. She wouldn't have let Perdita go hungry if she could have done anything about it."

"I'm sorry. Don't say any more."

She laid a hand on his chest. He covered it with his own. "I want to tell you. I've never told anyone else. It's time I told someone." He paused, swallowed. "I was five years old. Daniel had been taken away by his guardians and sent to school, but they had no jurisdiction over Perdita and me, much as they would have liked to help. I found the gun case. My father had a pair. I took the one left, primed and loaded it. I had every intention of shooting him when he returned. I fetched help for my mother from a neighbour, and the man came to tell us my father was dead."

"Oh, Orlando, I'm so sorry!"

He turned and forced a smile. "That was the start of the improvement in our lives. To be honest, I remember little of that time, between my father's death and my mother's remarriage. I seem to have blocked that time out. Too painful, I suppose. We managed until Taversall came into our lives. Or rather, returned. He'd been abroad, on diplomatic business. When he heard my mother was a widow he came courting. After that, he took control. He treated Perdita and me as though we were his own. I'll always be grateful to him." He stroked her hand, touching the fingers, each one, with fastidious care.

"Why didn't he give you some money, help you to re-establish your fortune?"

He gave a self-deprecating laugh. "I wouldn't let him. I would have let him help Perdita, but she refused, too. We do it together, she said. Besides, he couldn't give me enough to restore the Blyth estate, only to ensure Perdita and I didn't starve. It wasn't right to remain on his charity once we became adults."

"You developed your fortune into what you have now."

"So I did."

She leaned up on one elbow, shoving the resulting heavy fall of hair back behind her ears. "I think I can add something to that."

He gazed at her. "How?"

"You know my mother knows your mother."

"I wondered about that. How it happened, why they are friends." He lifted a hand and stroked her hair, his eyes the softened blue of the sea on a clear day.

"Are you sure you want me to tell you?"

He lay quietly, gazing at her with a grave expression that told her he understood. He nodded.

"It was when your father died. Your mother was desperate, completely without friends or family and badly injured. She knew my mother from school. I went to the same school, in France, much later. When Blyth died I was the same age as you, but I remember. My mother took your mother in. It's how your mother knows the older servants so well, why she knows the house. She is welcomed there as a member of the family. I call her Aunt Virginia."

His eyes widened. "Why don't I remember any of that?"

"I don't know. You lived with us for a short while, but Mama says you were stunned with shock. Do you remember anything of it?"

"No," he said slowly. "Have I met you before?"

"Yes. Briefly." Her memory of a small, confused weeping boy sometimes filled her dreams. "My mother nursed your mama until Taversall returned from abroad for her." She hesitated, biting her lip. Perhaps she should not tell him everything.

"What is it?" He smoothed her hair. "Tell me. I won't tell anyone else."

"I know. It's something about your mother." She took a sudden decision and hoped it was the right one. "I used to hide and spy on people when I was little. Not a pleasant trait, I know. Your mother said she wanted to enter my mother's profession. My mother dissuaded her. Your mother was tired of marriage, tired of being dependent on others and penniless. Blyth had spent all her inheritance. My mother reminded her she had two sons, and their good name would depend on hers."

"Then why did your mother do what she did?"

"She had no choice. No money, no—family and her only friends in England were in no case to help her. She had me to care for, and no way of earning, but she did her best to disguise me so no one would recognize me in public. She wouldn't take money from Lord Ripley. She borrowed from him and paid it all back. Every penny."

That startled him. "Good Lord! I thought—I thought—"

"You thought he was her keeper since she arrived in England." Her lips firmed. "Everyone does. He is not, nor has he ever been. She has always been financially independent of him, even his loan was notarised. She loved him too much ever to take money from him. Other men, yes, that was a business arrangement, but not Ripley, never Ripley."

"Forgive me." He bent and kissed her lips, lingering a little as he withdrew. "I begin to understand."

It was worth it, after all. "Then you see why I can't take money from you? Or expensive gifts?"

"I think so." His look sharpened. "But that only applies if—" He stopped, stilled his gentle caresses and waited for her.

The very breeze seemed to stop. It was time. To refuse this would be to declare herself an emotional coward, afraid to take the final step into intimacy, give herself to him in every way that mattered. But she was afraid of tearing down her masks, revealing herself completely to him. "Yes. I love you, Orlando. I could never accept money from the man I love."

"Oh, love!" He drew her close and gave up all attempt at tenderness, kissing her with a passion and urgency that took all her breath. His mouth still on hers he rolled her over and entered her with one sure thrust, and only then did he release her lips. "I love you too. I told you at the worst time, but I meant it."

Violetta bent her knees to aid his penetration. Feeling him

probe deep within her, she knew this was right, felt it deep in her bones. He gasped, and stilled within her. "Are you all right?"

"Yes." She opened her eyes and gazed up at him. His eyes were filled with a blazing intensity, an affirmation of his words. "It was why I was reluctant. I couldn't bear to be just another of your—conquests!"

She broke off with a cry as he pushed deep, so deep she felt him throb, deep in his groin where they pressed closely to each other. A single throb, before he pushed again. "Sweetheart, it's enough. You've conquered me just as I conquered you. Together now."

"Oh yes!" Her agreement was more than encouragement. It was affirmation, and joyous acceptance.

Together they strove; together they clung until the glorious swell within her made her release everything else. She lost her breath when it surged hotly, making her one with him, one with the universe. Just for a brief moment, but it was enough. She subsided onto the rumpled sheets and opened her eyes.

Orlando watched her with love, passion still driving him to strive, push inside her to achieve his release. She did all she could to help, feeling her wetness ease his passage, to find another unexpected surge. This time he cried out, and she felt that pulse, several deep throbs low on her groin until he jerked within her and fell across her glowing body.

She held him, panting for breath, but unwilling to let him go. With a small sound he rolled, but kept her with him, his body still locked with hers. He opened his eyes.

Violetta looked back. He hid nothing. No one had looked at her in that way, a mixture of love and passion, protection and desire. She blinked slowly, but when she opened her eyes he was still gazing at her in the same way.

She lifted a hand to his cheek to have it clasped in his. "So we're in love," he murmured. "I knew it wasn't all on my side."

"I tried not to. I don't seem to be able to help myself. It's not the end of the world," she added, trying for consolation. For she knew this was hopeless.

"It's the beginning, not the end," he murmured. His eyes closed, and he drew her close. Violetta was content. She fell asleep while she was trying to memorize the feeling, to revisit in the lonelier times ahead.

℣

The following day, they got up for long enough to eat. Violetta felt odd in a gown without a supporting hoop, but Orlando said he liked it. The meal was simple, none of the elaborate courses usually served in great houses, and they sat next to each other at the small table in the elegant dining room and served themselves.

Violetta wanted it never to end, but at the back of her mind, however hard she tried, she knew it must. She strove to remember every moment, to relive in her mind when she was once more alone. She would not waste this time.

On the following Monday they went for a walk. The countryside around Richmond was lush and green, small brooks wending their way across the fields. Walking hand in hand with him made Violetta wish it could always be like this. Then he articulated it too. "Shall we stay here? Never, ever go back?"

"What a thought!" she exclaimed, but she could not keep the yearning from her eyes. She looked away. "It would be pleasant."

"Pleasant!" He sounded amused. She looked back to see the breathtaking smile she was reluctantly becoming accustomed to. "It's what I want more than anything else. This year seems to be a momentous one for me."

From his tone she realized he meant more than this. "How so?"

He swung her hand. "I've made enough capital to achieve my true aim. I've decided to put the land back into full use. That's the heart of it all, Violetta. It's all been for that. I had to restore the house in the country and in town, to maintain the façade of respectability when I was restoring the fortune. Nothing scares investors off like indications of poverty and scandal. Now I can restore the estate to what it was in my grandfather's time. Or better. It means spending less time in London, although I'll have to oversee the investments there and attend Parliament from time to time."

"You'll be what you should have been all along." In his country clothes, his dark hair tied back simply in a queue, he looked the part. Violetta swallowed. She would have no part in his life. He needed to marry and beget heirs. She knew she couldn't do that. Although she no longer regretted losing her maidenhead to him, she could see no way of their ever being together as she wished.

He turned to her, a question in his eyes. "Will you stay with me?"

She forced herself to shake her head. "No." The longer she stayed with him, the harder it would be to part. "You know that's impossible." He'd helped her make a decision she'd been putting off for some time.

He drew her to him for a gentle kiss. "It's not." He didn't persist, but turned and carried on walking. Violetta went with him, her heart heavy with foreboding. They would have to part. This was all she could allow herself. Any more and she might break.

The next morning she woke up in his arms, and thought it might just be perfect before she remembered it was Tuesday. They would have to return to London tomorrow or later today. She saw the same recognition in his eyes when he opened them. Before he could speak she leaned over and kissed him, but he drew away after a gentle salute. "Good morning, sweetheart. Violetta, my only love, will you marry me?"

She sat bolt upright, tears starting to her eyes. She wanted to pretend she hadn't heard, but she had. "You know I can't!"

"Why not?"

"Fool!" She wiped the tears away. "You would be ruined, all your investments destroyed, and Lady Perdita too. You might drag the rest of your family with you." He pulled on her arm to draw her back but she would not go. "I can't marry you, Orlando." More tears came, and she didn't seem to be able to wipe them away fast enough. She sank her head onto her knees, trying to control her emotions. Why did he have to do this?

"I want you to. I've been lying here, thinking, and I can't see any other way. I want more of you than a casual affair. I need it, Violetta. I need you, I want you fully in my life. Come with me to my estates, help me to restore the land. We need never go near

London again, except to visit your mother."

She gave a short, derisory laugh that shook into silence. "But they would know. Everyone would know. You can't marry a whore's daughter."

She might be able to consider life as a respectable female in Italy but not here, not with her mother on the other part of the divide. Her choice was clear. A life in Italy as a member of the respected Palagio family, or a life as La Perla Perfetta, under her mother's roof. These few days with Orlando had taught her that she was not made for a courtesan's life. There was only one man for her, and he belonged here, in England. She did not. Perhaps, in time, she could join with another man in partnership and friendship, but never again in love. And not in England.

The words didn't stop him, as she had wanted them to. He sat up, reached for her. "I don't want to marry anyone else."

She leaned against his bare shoulder, knowing it was for the last time. She couldn't allow herself any more time. Today must be the first day of learning to live without him. But if she told him her reasons, he'd reject them. He'd accept ruin for her, negate all he'd worked so hard for and drag the rest of his family into disgrace. She would not accept that. She had to push him away, any way she could. "We can't marry. You know that, you have to know that. Marry Lady Judith, give her children. You need heirs."

"Then at least stay with me. Do that much."

She was gaining ground. He was listening to her. He must know, deep down, that it was a dream, impossible to achieve. His arms around her felt warm, comforting, but she couldn't stay there. "I can't. I can't share you. I'm sorry. If I did that I'd be condemning your marriage to failure from the first. Three people would be unhappy, instead of just one."

"Two. Two, Violetta. I can't be entirely happy without you. I love you. It isn't some juvenile fantasy. I wanted you from the first, thought I was running mad to fancy a plump, bespectacled, dowdy spinster, but my body sensed what my eyes couldn't see. Before I loved your body I loved your mind, your loyalty to my sister, your cleverness, and your sense of fun, which you only showed occasionally, but it enchanted me. The feeling has only grown. I tried to deny it, truly I did, but I cannot. I want you more than I want anything else." He kissed her shoulder, moved to her throat, to the place he knew by now drove her wild. She scrunched up so he couldn't reach it. He sighed and kissed her jaw. "Violetta. My own love, look at me."

She lifted her head, not trying to hide her distress. His own face reflected her anguish, not in tears but in terrible pain. His eyes held it, contained it. "We can go abroad, live quietly. Anything, but don't say no."

"No!" she cried, the reiteration strengthening her resolve. "It's impossible. It would ruin you to marry me. You know that as well as I do. And I can't share you. Don't ask me, I just can't."

He held her while she wept, as though he wouldn't let her go when the time came. Her body, his, melded in anguish as they had melded many times in the last few days in love. Violetta didn't allow herself the indulgence of weeping past her ability to control it. She lifted her head again, faced him. "We must go back. It's hard now, but it will get easier. It will, Orlando. But we must not meet again. Not for a long, long time."

Mutely he shook his head, refusing to accept her denial. "There must be a way."

"There isn't. I'm La Perla Perfetta, the daughter of the most expensive whore in London. I tried to get away, but that's what I'll always be. My little dreams were just that. Dreams. I will go back and face my fate." Arrange to leave for Italy. It was what her mother always wanted for her, the reason she'd insisted Violetta remain behind her mask, but until now she hadn't been able to bear the thought of separation. But this way, she might be able to anger Orlando enough to drive him from her. "I will return to London and remove my mask in public." Then society would know what she looked like. Then there would be no going back. He need never know she didn't intend to do that, that she would leave England's shores for good.

"You'll whore?"

She swallowed. "If I have to."

"Then whore for me!"

With a convulsive shove he urged her back onto the bed and, giving her no time to escape, pushed his body into hers.

Violetta had never been taken in anger and despair before, and she hoped never to have that fate forced on her again. It was terrible at first, but the familiar warmth hovered, ready to take control. However he wanted her she would give herself, until the door of this house was closed behind her. He needed it, as did she. Arching her back she responded, pushed until he held her shoulders, pushing and grinding against her. "You want another man to do this to you? With you? Can you simulate the passion you've shown for me? Can you, Violetta?"

She turned her head from side to side on the pillow, her hair tangled and thrashing wildly. "No! That is yours, always!"

He sat up, pulled her upright to him, still sunk deep inside her, his mouth next to hers so she could feel his words as well as hear them. "Whenever you take a man, think of this. Think of me. Whenever you service a customer, remember what love feels like. Remember, for I will never forget!"

With a despairing cry he put his hands on her backside, pulled her closer and cried out. It sounded like pain. His seed filled her for the last time.

Violetta felt a pang of sorrow pierce her climax. She had been meticulous using the sponge. She would not even have the consolation of his child. She allowed herself to hold him close, feel his muscles hard against her breasts, then pushed away and climbed out of the bed.

There was a door leading to a small dressing room. She went there and turned the key in the lock. He could enter through the corridor, but she knew he would not.

Violetta found hot water there. She washed every trace of her lover away, carefully wiping everywhere he had kissed her, everywhere he had touched her. This was the end. It had to be, or she might die a lingering, languishing death. Dying by degrees. She would rather make it swift.

Dressing without a maid engaged all her concentration for the next twenty minutes. She engineered a repair to the mutilated panniers, tying a stay lace to the severed tapes, finding the structure relatively undamaged.

When she opened the bedroom door she found he had dressed in his town clothes. He didn't move to her but held her eyes, waiting for her to speak. "We must go back."

"Yes."

He seemed to have accepted her refusal. She didn't touch him again. A footman helped her into the carriage after a light breakfast during which they didn't sit together, but at opposite ends of the table. She didn't look back when the carriage rolled away. Dry eyed she watched the countryside pass the window on the way back to town. Dry eyed she bade him a brief farewell at her mother's door. The last time.

As she descended to the street and walked towards the front door she heard his voice, softly murmuring words she would never forget. "I love you. I'll never stop loving you."

It was the same for her. Perhaps, one day, far into the future, she would write to him and tell him so.

Chapter Seventeen

Orlando took Perdita to Ripley Court. The marquess and marchioness received them graciously, to all eyes the perfect couple. Their family was prolific, their estate prosperous. But most of society knew the truth behind this. The estate had always been prosperous, and the excellent land steward the marquess employed ensured it continued that way. The marquess and marchioness, while often residing under the same roof, led entirely separate lives these days.

Lady Judith received the guests with great pleasure and bore Perdita off to her room, to show her some new gowns she had ordered specially for the country. And, no doubt, to discuss their plans to ensnare Orlando.

He didn't care. If he couldn't have Violetta, it didn't matter who he married. Judith was eager, comely and eligible. He should be glad. Of course he was not.

He let her draw him in over the next week, not caring what people thought or were saying. He'd locked his emotions away, kept them back. He daren't feel, daren't think. Daren't believe Violetta was lost to him.

But she was. He knew as well as she did what marriage to La Perla Perfetta would mean. He received word she'd removed her mask on the Thursday after they returned to London, but he wasn't there to see it. It would have killed him. He adored her still, but if he married her now, he'd lose everything else. Not that he cared, but it would bring the same ruin to his family. Marriage to Violetta meant the loss of many of his business contacts, the loss of his social life, and possibly self-imposed exile.

The most he could hope for now was an illicit relationship with her, like the one Ripley had with La Perla. To meet her in odd moments, to live separate lives, only to come together for hasty loving when they could. If that was all he could have, then he would have that. Otherwise, he wasn't sure he wanted to carry on. In those circumstances he could think of marrying another woman and coupling with her enough times to make an heir before leaving her to her own devices. Hypocritically, society would accept that and he'd live, much as Ripley did, as the devoted admirer of a woman forever beyond his reach.

Orlando became an icicle, deliberately hiding any emotion, responding as expected to advances, to enquiries, joining in a shooting expedition, killing his fair share of feathered game. With each dull thump of heavy, dead feathers on grass he tried to kill the terrible yearning he felt. When a new guest arrived he looked at her, hoping to find something, anything that reminded him of his love. His lost love.

The numbness merely locked his agony away inside him. Perdita, now fully ambulatory, a light cane the only reminder of her debilitating illness, watched him sometimes, her eyes narrowed. If she suspected, she never said anything. Once or twice he caught Ripley with that same look, speculative and concerned. He hated it. He would have preferred to lock himself away somewhere, and give way to his agony but that would have been self-pitying and pitiful. No, he wouldn't do that. He would do what was expected of him, what he had to do if his work was to continue. Love was closed to him. Very well then, he would make something of his life. He would marry and make heirs for the estate he'd so painstakingly re-created. Perhaps, in time, it wouldn't hurt quite so much to think of what he had lost. Perhaps Violetta would accept him as a lover, since she wouldn't have him as a husband. He wasn't proud, not any more. He'd take anything of her he could get.

Accordingly, three weeks after his arrival, when his sister informed him that "everybody" was expecting an imminent announcement and he needed to make up his mind about Judith, he sought an interview with Lord Ripley.

He found Ripley in his study, an intimate room near the library, impersonal and neatly arranged, the ledgers on the shelves carefully ordered, the desk clear of clutter. Lord Ripley put aside the small stack of documents he was signing and laid his pen in the standish.

"We have something to discuss?" He motioned to the seat in front of the desk. Orlando sat down, then shook his head when the hand motioned to the decanters in the tantalus on a side table. Ripley leaned back with a creak of leather, rested his elbows on the arms of the chair, steepled his fingers and gave Orlando a questioning look.

Orlando sighed, then sat up straight, the epitome of the haughty nobleman. "I would like your permission to pay my addresses to your daughter, Lady Judith."

"Why?"

That was not the response Orlando expected. Immediately, all the reasons for his request came to mind, together, unbidden, with the reasons why not. "I've kept her waiting too long."

The marquess frowned. "While you dallied with Violetta Palagio?"

Orlando felt the heat rush to his face. "That, my lord, is surely my concern."

Lord Ripley slowly shook his head. "Not so. I consider Violetta as much my daughter as Judith. More so, perhaps."

A suspicion took hold of Orlando's mind. Was he proposing to marry one sister and take the other into keeping? No. Rather than that he would give up any idea of marriage to Judith. Lord Ripley saw his alarm. "No, there are no blood ties between Violetta and Judith. Her father is not Violetta's father."

Orlando relaxed in relief, then wondered at the phrasing. "Who is Violetta's father?"

Ripley paused before he replied. "Not me. I have loved Donata for most of my life, but we only consummated our relationship after she came to England. Violetta was three years old, then. I would prefer it to be otherwise. I am very proud of Violetta, more than I ever was of Judith." He sighed. "You might ask yourself who Lady Judith's father is."

Orlando's eyes widened in surprise.

Ripley smiled, but there was no humour in it. "My wife began to stray many years ago. My first two children, my sons, are mine. Now they are older there can be no doubt, for both have a look of me about them. After that she went her own way." Who can blame her, Orlando thought, with a feeling of sympathy for the cold, hard woman he knew. He had no liking for Lady Ripley, but her husband had been lost to her from the start.

"I only tell you because you propose to marry Judith. It must go no further than this room." Orlando nodded his assent. "No one knows for sure, but I tell you plainly now that Judith and her younger siblings are none of my get." Orlando swallowed. Lord Ripley studied him. "That, sir, is what you have in store for you. I know you have feelings for Violetta. You love her, perhaps as much as I love her mother, but Donata writes me that she has refused you. Madness, to propose to her, but in the same situation, I would have done the same thing." He grimaced. "I did."

"Indeed, sir?" Ripley knew far more than Orlando was comfortable with about the situation. He should have realized La Perla would communicate what information she had to her long time lover.

"I think it would be best if we were frank. To that end I would ask that nothing goes outside this room. What we say to each other now must remain completely private."

"That seems fair."

"I don't know about you, but early in the day though it is, I need a drink." Ripley got to his feet and strode to the tantalus, finding a couple of glasses. He poured a generous quantity of brandy into each and brought them back to the table.

Orlando didn't refuse the drink. "Then, I should tell you that the offer I made to Violetta was respectable. I meant it. She refused me because of who she is and who her mother is."

"Will you give up?"

"I can't. Not won't but can't."

Ripley took a deep swallow of the fiery liquid. "I know. I can't leave Donata alone, and I don't intend to. Not any more. Perhaps if I tell you something of my story you can understand a bit more."

Orlando picked up his glass and prepared to listen, but Ripley didn't need many words. He sat down in the chair opposite his instead of at his desk, and turned the glass around in his hands, staring at it while he spoke. "I was married off by my family before I left for the Grand Tour. My father didn't want to risk my being snared by some scheming Frenchwoman, he said. It's not unusual, and being young I didn't understand the full implications of what I was doing. I was a young fool. When I reached Italy I met and fell in love with Donata. She was already married." He paused and turned around to put his empty glass down on the desk behind him. When he turned back he stared past Orlando to a spot that wasn't there, but had been once. Back into the past, into what was his personal tragedy. "Her husband was a brute, more than a brute, but she refused to leave him. I could offer her nothing, so I couldn't insist in it, but it nearly killed me to leave her in his abusive hands. I spoke to her brother, the present conte, and he swore he would do all he could to protect her. I had no right to do anything else. I returned to England, determined to forget her. I made heirs with my wife and tried to make my marriage a success." He looked at Orlando now, and all he could see was bitterness and regret. "I swear to you I entered the business whole-heartedly, determined to find some happiness somewhere. I had seen marriages without love but with a deep degree of companionship and partnership. Perhaps, I thought, I could have that. My wife had no such intention. As soon as the succession was secured she was off."

He smoothed his thumb over the glass, repeating the gesture over and over. Orlando watched it and listened. "One man after another, so many that in time I became wary of claiming my husbandly rights. She took many lovers indiscriminately, from footmen to actors, from earls to a prince. Even she doesn't know who is the father of some of our children. Four children after the first two, the ones I believe are my own. When she came to me and told me she was pregnant with the third child, the one who turned out to be Judith, I hadn't slept with her for six months and after that I never shared her bed again. I didn't disown her or the children. What would be the point?"

He paused and glanced at the decanter, but didn't get to his feet. He faced Orlando who silently listened, sipping his brandy slowly. "Then Donata arrived in London with Violetta. Her husband had nearly killed her, and she had been forced to leave. Lodovico, her husband's brother, had given them a little money, but she was determined to take nothing else from the family. I looked after them, and then it became an *on-dit* that I had finally taken a mistress. At that point I had not, not until my wife expressed her delight that I wouldn't be pestering her any more. Not that I had done much pestering, but it flattered her vanity to think I had. After that Donata and I became lovers. We had played the game straight before, been faithful to our spouses, but by then there seemed little point in continuing in our unhappiness. We snatched some heaven for ourselves. That's why I'm sure I'm not Violetta's father, although I would have been proud of her was she mine."

He bit his lip, and glanced away again. "Do you know how hard it is?" he asked the decanters. "To watch the woman you love earning her living on her back? I offered to look after her, give her everything she needed, but by that stage she refused to allow any man jurisdiction over her life ever again. So I had to share her." He turned back to Orlando, his eyes glistening with the suspicion of tears. "I had no choice. I couldn't leave her. I had to watch her make her damned contracts, even coming to me for advice, and smile and help her all I could. She knew. We never spoke of it, still don't speak of it. Suffice it to say that the last five years, when she finally knew she didn't have to sleep with other men again, have been the happiest I've ever known."

Orlando stared, dumbfounded. He knew the story, but to hear such confessions from a man old enough to be his father astounded him. To spend one's whole life with the wrong woman. It put all his plans into confusion. "So you intend to continue in the same way?"

The marquess grimaced. "One of the reasons I've agreed to stay here for a while is because I want to think. I don't know, and I don't care any more what society thinks of me, but I'm tired of Donata's humiliation. She's been spat on in the street, you know. I've seen it." He paused and stood up to replenish his glass. Orlando had never seen Ripley the worse for drink, nor seen him take more than a social glass or two. It was a measure of his distress that he sought the solace of brandy now. Orlando covered his now empty glass with his hand in a gesture of refusal. Ripley shrugged and poured himself another generous glassful. He sat down. "My wife has undoubtedly taken more lovers than Donata, but it is Donata who is despised. I'm tired of it. I don't know what I shall do, because I need Donata's agreement, but I want to take her away."

"Live quietly in the country?"

"Not this country." Together with Violetta, Orlando thought grimly. No doubt the peasants or merchants who had fathered La Perla thought themselves far superior when they were sitting over their supper of black bread and rough wine. "Perhaps France or Spain, if she'll agree. No one knows us there. So far she has refused, but I live in hope." He lifted his gaze to Orlando's face. "If Violetta was cared for, perhaps Donata might agree. Do you plan to see her again?"

Orlando owed it to Ripley to be as frank as he had just been. "Yes. I love her truly. If she'll have me."

"And live as I have lived? Think carefully, Blyth. You won't gain true happiness like that. She plans to take up her mother's profession, you know. After years of resisting it, of careful anonymity, she has unmasked in her mother's salon. She will reveal her face, and her figure, to whomever can afford it."

Orlando caught his breath on a gasp. The pain was so sudden, so sharp it took him by surprise. Physical pain from heartache? He would never have believed it. He gave himself a moment to regulate his breathing, to control his reaction. His first instinct was to hit out, to damage anyone who dared lay a finger on her, but if she consented, he had no right. However badly he wanted that right, he could not.

He could not. "Then I should go back to London and be the man who can afford her. No one else shall have her."

"You can't stop it. She's as determined as her mother was, but with less reason."

Then Orlando's course was set. It didn't matter who he married, since he couldn't have her as his wife, but he'd have her. He'd marry Judith, give her an heir, then go back to London and take Violetta away, somewhere abroad where they could be together. And never come back.

"Then may I repeat the request I put to you earlier? Will you give me permission to pay my addresses to Lady Judith sometime this summer?"

Ripley sighed heavily. "Will you promise not to hurt her, to tell her the truth? She may not be my flesh and blood, but she is under my protection."

"I can promise that. I will make it clear to her what my

plans are."

"If she's anything like her mother she won't give a damn," Ripley observed dryly. "From what I've seen it's the title and prestige she wants, not a loving bedmate. Go to the devil then, Blyth, but do it your own way."

Orlando got to his feet and bowed.

"I won't give you my blessing," the marquess's quiet voice followed Orlando to the door, "But I give you my reluctant permission."

Orlando went to find Lady Judith.

୫

London was quiet at this time of year. Just as well, Donata thought. She had enough to cope with at home. She looked up from her book in surprise when she heard the voice of her dearest friend. "Why, Virginia! What are you doing here? Aren't you supposed to be with your family in the country?"

Lady Taversall entered the room in a rush and paused before the open window. "How do you bear London in July, Donata? I can hardly catch my breath for the heat!"

"Well, I was planning to repair to the country next week," La Perla said mildly. She closed her book, inserting a leather bookmark to keep her place. "Ripley plans to join me there in a week or two. If you dislike London in the summer so much what are you doing here?"

Lady Taversall turned in a swirl of pink silk. "I couldn't bear to watch any more." She walked more slowly over to the chair where Donata sat and settled herself in the matching chair opposite. She kicked her skirts out of the way in a gesture reminiscent of the schoolroom. "My son is courting Judith Ripley, but in such a melancholy way. I have never seen an icier courtship. I came back to town to see if you could cast any light on the business."

"You know I can." Donata picked up a blue glass jug from the table at her side. She poured two goblets of cold lemonade, ice chinking in the glass. Ice was an expensive commodity in London at this time of year, but worth every penny. She handed a glass to Lady Taversall who sat, nursing it in both hands. "Violetta has been as unresponsive as a stone since she returned from Richmond. I had hoped they would have their fill of each other. It is why I allowed it." She sipped from the glass. "She will not talk to me, Virginia. She never refused to talk to me in the past."

"I found out what happened," Virginia replied. Her carefully powdered face creased for a moment, as though in pain, but she soon regained her careful composure. "Blyth asked her to marry him. She refused." She clicked her tongue. "The boy's run mad!"

"Not such a boy." Donata sipped. "A grown man. As my child is a woman grown. We must remember that, Virginia. They have to make their own decisions."

"Even if the decision is a wrong one?" Virginia frowned. "No, I can't abandon them. There must be something we can do." She gulped her drink and choked on a piece of ice. Donata obligingly thumped her on the back and put her glass down for her.

"Better?" Virginia, eyes watering, nodded. "I do not see what we can do, Virginia. The children fell in love, but they cannot marry. You know that as well as I do. I am what I am. If I had known what Violetta would come to I would have held out for longer."

"How dare you blame yourself! How could you?" Virginia's eyes, now clear and blazing, challenged her friend. "You came here to escape a husband insane enough to kill you and your daughter. You wouldn't take charity, any more than I would have done. I was in no case to help you. You wouldn't take anything from Lord Ripley except moral support. Quite right, too, in my opinion. You couldn't let people know your real name in case your husband reclaimed you so what else could you do? Beg? Steal?" Virginia leaned over to grip Donata's hand. "You did what you could to keep a roof over your head and to keep away from that monster you married. You did well."

"How well?" Donata's stared at her friend, her face troubled. "When I see her in my salon like a block of ice I don't know what to do. I can't talk to her, she won't let me near her! She is in such pain." Tears glistened in her lovely eyes, but they didn't fall. "At least I prevented her from showing her face when she threatened to do so."

Virginia gazed at her in astonishment. "You did? I heard she'd revealed her face?"

"It was someone else. I dressed another woman in her clothes and had her unmask before Violetta could do so. I want to give her time to think, not do this as a gesture of defiance, or even loyalty to me. Not after all my hard work to keep her identity private."

After a short silence she looked up. Virginia was staring into space, a look of wonderment on her features. When Donata would have spoken Virginia held up a hand. "Wait. Let me think." When she turned back to Donata her eyes were suffused with purpose. "I have an idea."

℘

Violetta came in late, having taken a detour to avoid the street with the house Orlando had once offered her. After weeks of agony she knew it would take a long time before she could wake up not thinking of him, not wondering how he was faring, if he was as hurt as she was. It felt like physical pain sometimes. The best she could do was try to block it out.

She knew she had made the right decision, to cut the affair off. It could have gone on for years. She would have been hurt far worse, have destroyed her chances of finding someone of her own. It had been some consolation, that somewhere, probably in Italy, there might be someone who might not be destroyed by associating with her, someone of less exalted status, someone who could please himself in the matter of finding a mate. After a while she might be able to put her past behind her enough to start again. By then Orlando would be married, the father of a hopeful brood. Perhaps he would be able to find solace in his children. Violetta didn't insult him by thinking he might not be feeling this. She knew he was feeling the same despair, the same numbness as she was, that he might reach for her in the night, as she so often reached for him.

It was early days yet. Give it time, she told herself. Time did heal, didn't it?

In the first days after her return she thought of taking

other lovers, quickly, to try to put a distance between what she had shared with Orlando and ordinary, everyday mundanity. Her mother's preemptive move to foil her unmasking gave her time to think, and on reflection, it probably was for the best. She'd declared her intention when she was still heartsick from her visit to Richmond, a gesture of defiance and finality, but it wasn't to be. If she knew London's gossip-network, the news would have reached Orlando by now.

A footman clearing his throat to attract her attention called her from her thoughts. "Your lady mother asks for your presence in the salon, ma'am," he informed her.

"Does she have company?" Violetta was dressed as La Perla Perfetta, in white with a simple street mask.

"Lady Taversall is with her."

Violetta felt a sense of foreboding. What could Orlando's mother want with her? Perhaps to castigate her for her treatment of her son. Yes, that was probably it. She removed her hat and mask and handed them to the footman, lifting her skirts to hurry upstairs and get it over with.

She paused briefly before the door to check her hair was in place, and deliberately paused to perfect the expression of bland hauteur she had adopted for the last two weeks. It had become easier to assume a mask under the silk masks she wore when her mother had company. Now she had a mask of her own, one she had fashioned inside herself these last weeks and she had enough honesty to admit she preferred hiding behind one to revealing herself to all.

Head high Violetta stepped into the salon and made her curtseys. The ladies sat very close together, and try though she might, she could not see any condemnation on Lady Taversall's solemn features. "Sit down, Violetta. Would you like some lemonade?"

Violetta nodded her thanks and took the goblet her mother offered, its gilt rim catching the sun when she sat. She arched her fingers over the glass in a deliberately elegant gesture. She had spent some time studying gestures and movements in the mirror, determined to show as little of herself as possible, keep the frightened, unhappy child buried deep inside.

"You've been to see Cerisot?"

"Yes, Mama. I have ordered several new gowns. If I'm to dress as La Perla Perfetta all day, I fear it is necessary."

"It might not be." La Perla exchanged a meaningful look with Lady Taversall. Violetta became alert. What had these two plotted now?

"I fail to see—" she began, but paused and shrugged. Let them speak.

"We have come up with a plan," La Perla said, with every sign of satisfaction in her loving expression. A smile curved her lips. "We need to talk frankly, my dear. You need to be honest with us, so we know what is best for us to do."

Violetta's stomach tensed. She didn't want to talk about her feelings. If she talked about them, or even thought about it, the unhappiness became too much to hide. Several times in the last three weeks she had to hurry to her room, only to dissolve in floods of self-pitying tears. Now she had begun to repair the damage, she didn't want it torn open again.

However, this was her mother. She could not deny her. She steeled herself to talk without dwelling on the meaning, to answer without giving too much away. Lady Taversall's next question alarmed her.

"Do you love my son?" Violetta stared. Lady Taversall made an exasperated sound. "Well? If you don't tell us we can't help you."

"Yes." She stated it abruptly. "Yes I love him."

"Donata tells me he asked you to marry him. Did he?"

"Yes." Violetta's mouth closed like a trap on the word. "I refused. I can't do that to your family." She ignored the slight sound of distress her mother made.

Lady Taversall shook her head slightly. "Violetta, I would be honoured to have you for my daughter-in-law. Your manners are impeccable, you are beautiful enough to make men stare, and your character is excellent."

"But I am La Perla's daughter."

"Ha!" To Violetta's surprise Lady Taversall clapped her hands and grinned. "Now we come to it. Yes, you are La Perla's daughter. But you are also the daughter of the Conte d'Oro."

Violetta felt dizzy. Yes, it would be best. Italy, now. But

Lady Taversall was still talking. "Your father is dead. There is no longer any reason for you to hide your name anywhere. From talking to Donata that fact seems to have escaped you both."

Oh God. Dare she hope?

No, she dared not. "He won't want me. I've refused him. And the truth is bound to come out. What my mother has done. What I'm about to do."

Lady Taversall sucked in a breath. "Don't you dare!" She held up a hand, forestalling any argument. "This is what you're going to do, my dear. You're going to go back to Cerisot and change your order. No more white. Only colours. In fact, I would suggest you avoid white altogether. It's not your colour, dear, it washes out that lovely complexion. Tell Cerisot there'll be a bonus for a swift delivery. In a week I'll return to Ripley Court. With the daughter of an old friend, newly arrived from Italy."

La Perla smiled benevolently on her daughter. "You will be launched, my love. I will write to your uncle in Italy and tell him what we are about. He will be delighted you are away from my pernicious influence."

"Will I be allowed to speak English?" She didn't know where that had come from, the words coming out as if someone else spoke them. This was impossible, surely?

"Put a slight lilt in it," Lady Taversall advised. "You have a chance, Violetta, if you're brave. You can take your rightful place in society. Even if you don't succeed with my son, you can find someone else and start a new life."

Violetta couldn't believe it. "It's impossible. I'll go to Italy, come back only to see my mother. It's what I planned to do." Deep down she acknowledged her fear of appearing as herself. La Perla Perfetta and Charlotte Lambert were roles she played. Being herself, revealing her true face in public, terrified her. "I've never been Violetta in public. I'm not sure I know how to be her."

Lady Taversall gave a most unladylike snort. "I thought you had some backbone! We'll bluff, my dear. Show these men we can play the game of life better than they can play cards! If anyone sees a resemblance, let them prove it, let them show us. When the impostor unmasked in your place, she took suspicion away from you, at least for now. Your mother has agreed to present her as you, and to undertake contracts on her behalf. She will take the name Isabella." She leaned forward, grasped Violetta's hand. "It's the last hand, Violetta. Double or quits. What do you say?"

Violetta was shocked to hear herself say, "Very well. I'll do it."

Chapter Eighteen

Buoyed up by the enthusiasm and commitment her mother and Aunt Virginia lent to the scheme, Violetta allowed herself to enter fully in their plans for her. Only when the austere front of Ripley Court hove into view through the windows of Aunt Virginia's travelling carriage did she have misgivings. They let Lord Taversall into the plot. It was a surprise to discover he knew all his wife's activities, but when Violetta moved into the Taversall town house, in the guise of Violetta Palagio newly arriving from Italy, she witnessed true devotion and love. Aunt Virginia could have no more hidden her life from her husband than she could have flown.

His lordship accepted the scheme with his usual good humour, saying it was about time his stepson considered settling down, and he couldn't think of a better candidate than Violetta. It was more than reassuring that he knew her past and still accepted her. They kept nothing from him. Violetta had not expected that. Their eldest son, Corin, Lord Elston, was accompanying them briefly to Ripley Court, then going on to what he referred to as "a snug little bachelor party". He accepted Violetta without question, although something sparked in the depths of his deceptively sleepy but surprisingly alert eyes that he didn't divulge to anyone. He spoke to her briefly in excellent Italian and engaged in a little harmless flirting that she enjoyed very much. Usually, when a man flirted with La Perla Perfetta it was with one purpose. Now La Perla Perfetta's gowns and elaborate masks were left behind, perhaps for good and the flirting was lighter, more playful. Violetta began to believe what Lady Taversall constantly said to her. "There is life beyond Orlando, my dear. You will find someone, if it does become impossible between you, you will find a place. I'm sure of it."

When the coach rounded the gentle curve at the top of the drive, the double doors at the top of the shallow flight of stairs were flung open, and a livery clad servant stood impassively in the light of day. Violetta allowed Elston to hand her down and place her hand on his sleeve. He waited for his mother and father, and then they followed them inside.

Ripley waited in the hall, his wife by his side. While they were greeting Lord and Lady Taversall, Violetta studied Lady Ripley, who she had only seen before at a distance.

The lady was aging. Her hair, a natural light blonde, was streaked with silver, the sunlight from the great windows at the front of the house catching it when she moved. The light powder dusting her face did not disguise the fine lines at the corners of her eyes and between her nose and mouth. When she looked up in Violetta's direction her eyes were cold and dead.

Violetta knew of the utter failure of Lord Ripley's marriage, but she hadn't fully understood it until that moment, when she saw the dead eyes light with speculation for a brief moment before the flame flickered and died. She sank into a curtsey before her hostess and felt a warm hand lift her to her feet. "Miss Palagio," said Lord Ripley warmly. "Welcome to Ripley Court. Lady Taversall wrote to us of your arrival. It is our pleasure to welcome you here." He meant it. Violetta smiled back, glad to be with him here. He was the only father she had ever known. She would be proud if he were really her father, but had never dared ask—in case the answer was no.

Now she must use all her acting skills to...be herself. Even if Orlando didn't want her, her course was now set. Lady Taversall would use all her skills to ensure Violetta's success in society. It was a future she was only beginning to come to terms with. She had her dowry, the one her family had restored, plus the sum her mother had added, and an extra sum from her uncle so she was a substantial heiress. She would be sought after, if Orlando decided not to have her. She didn't let her mind dwell on the possibility for long, determinedly facing her new life with all the courage she'd used to face the old one.

Violetta was used to hiding her nervousness. In her new travelling gown, with her new wardrobe in the lumbering travelling coach sent a day ahead, with her French maid Lisette, she looked at her best. Inside she was a quivering ball of jelly. Outside she did her best to appear cool and cordial.

It seemed she succeeded. Lord Ripley took her hand and placed it on his arm. "Allow me to show you around, my dear. Unless you're tired and you wish to rest?"

Violetta gave a small laugh. "It takes more than a small journey in a comfortable carriage to make me tired, sir!" Careful to maintain the slight lilt in her voice, the one she'd had when she returned from her visit to Italy, she allowed him to draw her away.

They exchanged civilities within the hearing of the servants, but half way down the Long Gallery at the top of the house, out of earshot of anyone, Ripley stopped strolling and took her into his arms, giving her a hug before he released her. "I thought La Perla Perfetta was the most exquisite creature I had ever seen, next to her mother. I find I was wrong. Violetta Palagio is lovelier than La Perla Perfetta."

She laughed. "I'm not sure why I'm doing this now. Aunt Virginia and Mama didn't give me a moment to think."

"Since we heard of your unmasking. Was it true what Virginia wrote me? Was it not you?"

Smiling, she shook her head. "Mama had someone else do it, a bare hour before I planned to. After that, it would have appeared foolish for me to do so. I stayed in my room."

"I have to tell you something." He paused, his gentle smile fading in his severe face. "Blyth has asked for my permission to address Lady Judith. I think he's quite given you up."

Her face fell. "Does he love her?"

He made a rough sound of rejection. "No, of course not! I wanted to tell him you were arriving, but Donata told me not to. I've been playing gooseberry. I've done my best, but he's taken her walking in the park today and we might be too late."

Tears sprang to her eyes but she blinked them back. "It doesn't matter. If it's not meant to be, then it will not be. This is my life now, sir. Mama and Aunt Virginia are determined on it. I could have assumed my real identity in Italy, but I'm taking this chance. It could ruin everything, but Aunt Virginia is sure I can succeed."

"Will you turn your back on your mother?"

"Of course not!" She was shocked he would even consider it. "We both know we have to face reality, but I can manage, visiting her clandestinely in London." That had been the hardest part, but her mother gave her no choice, saying she'd cast her out if Violetta didn't take the opportunity Aunt Virginia presented her with.

He took her hands and squeezed them. "I know you are strong, Violetta. You're not without friends, either."

"If this doesn't...work, Aunt Virginia will introduce me to the ton in the autumn, formally." She chuckled. "She's even threatened to present me at court!" Though privately, she determined to travel to her family in Italy long before then, if Orlando wouldn't have her. The news Lord Ripley had just given her came as a blow, but she still had a fighting chance.

"Good." He released her hands. "Don't give up, Violetta. It's not hopeless." He turned, and placed her hand on his arm again. "It's good to have you here. I get lonely without you or your mama."

"She misses you too."

"Hmm." They walked in companionable silence to the end of the gallery, and turned to the stairs. "I'll take you to the drawing room. They'll be serving tea soon. Give him a run for his money, Violetta."

"What?" Violetta had not expected this.

"Make it hard for him. If he's committed himself to Judith, then so be it, but if he's still free to woo you—" he paused and lowered his head, so his eyes were on a level with hers, "—make him woo!"

Her laughter echoed down the long gallery.

Orlando felt heavy hearted. A dozen times this last week he'd screwed himself to the sticking point, and a dozen times he'd failed. Lady Judith expected him to declare himself, but once he'd turned and faced her he found himself making an inane comment about the trees, or the lake, or the maze. In a way, if she entrapped him it would be a relief, but she'd given that up, confident of success.

There was nothing else. At least he could make Perdita

happy by marrying her friend. He turned to Judith, took her hand in his. She watched him expectantly, her large eyes wide.

"Lady Judith would you do me the honour—the great honour—of becoming my wife?"

There! He had said it. There was no going back.

"Why, Lord Blyth!" *Don't say it*, he begged her mentally, *don't say it's an unexpected surprise.*

She didn't. "I would be delighted to accept your offer." She stared up at him once more and then turned, placing her hand on his arm. Orlando nearly collapsed in relief. He'd thought he would have to kiss her. Not yet, not while Violetta's scent and flavour lingered with him. Just a little while longer and he would give it all up for good, lock it in his mind to be brought out only when he was strong enough to remember without heartbreak. If that time ever came. "It will be just the thing, you know," she continued, as though he had asked her to accompany him on a picnic or something as trivial. "I can look after Perdita, and care for you." It sounded as though she was taking on burdens, Orlando thought. He was regretting his decision already, but what choice had he got?

Now it was time he took her back for tea. Before they went back inside he took her aside, in the shelter of a shrubbery. He steeled himself and held her firmly by the shoulders, lowering his mouth to hers, determined to lose Violetta's kiss in Judith's. She opened her mouth under his, but the moment she did, he withdrew. It wasn't right. He supposed he would get used to it in time, but not now. Not today.

He knew he was showing more cowardice at this than he had ever shown before and he knew why. He sighed. Walking in this park which was as near to pictorial Paradise as he had ever got he felt like hell.

Lady Judith chattered by his side. "Dear Perdita is going on so well, isn't she? I did my best, but she has surpassed everyone's expectations!"

"Miss Lambert had a lot to do with her recovery."

Her face twisted, and he knew Perdita had told him something of why Miss Lambert had left so suddenly. She looked disgusted. "That hussy! I cannot blame you, she was after you from the start! I trust you have cut off all communication with her?"

Mildly surprised at her vehemence he nodded an affirmative. "What did Perdita tell you?"

"That her importunate behaviour became too much. It does not surprise me, I always thought she was a forward creature!"

Perdita had shown some discretion, then.

They passed into the house. It was suddenly cool after the heat of full summer outside. He glanced at Judith. Sweat beaded on her nose and there were small, damp patches under the arms of the tight sleeves of her yellow gown. Yellow was not her colour, especially rich butter yellow. It warred with the pale gold of her hair and made her flushed complexion even ruddier. Violetta would have looked glorious in it.

At least she wouldn't remind him of the woman he'd lost. Judith was as unlike Violetta as she could be. And with any luck, if Violetta would take him as a protector, he wouldn't be with Judith for long. He would tell her before they married. It wouldn't be fair to do anything else, but he wanted more time than he had today. She could cry off without scandal, but he could not.

A musical peal of laughter echoed around the walls as they approached the blue drawing room, where tea was customarily served in the afternoons. Feminine, sweet. For the first time in weeks Orlando felt alive.

What was this? Who was this?

He saw a swathe of black hair, coiled around the head of a woman sitting with her back to the door. Lord Ripley, at ease, sat next to the newcomer, holding a dish of tea for her. There were other people in the room. Lord and Lady Taversall, returned from town, several of the other guests, but the younger lady attracted all the attention.

Lord Ripley saw him. "Ah, Blyth, have some tea and meet our charming visitor."

Numbly, Orlando stepped around to the front of the couch. The lady looked up at him, her violet eyes piercing straight through to his soul. "Miss Palagio, this is Orlando, Lord Blyth. Blyth, this is Violetta Palagio, the daughter of the late Conte d'Oro, and Lady Taversall's goddaughter."

Orlando bowed.

The world stopped. This was madness. Was this Violetta, notorious as La Perla Perfetta, sitting in a fashionable drawing room, surrounded by the cream of the ton, or was it her twin sister? With an effort he schooled his face to hide his shock before he rose from his bow.

Violetta smiled politely at him, her eyes twin pools of— friendliness. She was a better actress than he was an actor. He had completely forgotten Judith until she spoke. "Good day, Miss Palagio, it's a pleasure to meet you. Father, we have some news. May we speak, Orlando dear?"

That last endearment broke the news better than he could have done. He saw the flash of reality in Violetta's eyes—pain, hurt—before she regained her society mask. With an effort he lifted his gaze to confront Lord Ripley. Had he known? Ripley gave him a small shrug and a shake of his head. He had not known. Judith's father forced a smile. "Congratulations, both of you! My wife has been expecting your news for some time, you know." He didn't sound happy. The company came forward and congratulated them both, all except for Violetta. He knew she would not. He handed Judith to a chair, but didn't hover over her as a newly affianced man might be expected to. He went back to the sofa and sat down next to Violetta, accepting the dish of tea Ripley had been holding for her.

What did he say? Daughter of the Conte d'Oro?

He handed her the dish, careful not to allow their fingers to touch. To his vague amazement he found himself saying, "Have you come far?"

"Today? No, only from London. It was very kind of Lord and Lady Ripley to receive me." There was a charming lilt to her voice he couldn't remember hearing before. Another masquerade for Violetta. He knew her well enough to know she felt happier behind disguises, masks and masquerades. But he knew the passionate, loving woman beneath. At least he thought he did.

Was their idyll in the country another pretence, then? Had he ever seen the real Violetta? Slowly, he began to piece things together. Violetta was here, with his mother, engaged on another elaborate masquerade. The last time he'd seen her she refused him, because she was a whore's daughter, she said. Nothing had changed. She was still a whore's daughter, whatever she said, whatever she did.

Anger, fuelled by shock, boiled up. He found his voice, his fury giving it ice. "Have you been in England long?" He wanted her to lie, so he could be sure of the other lies. Even while he was lashing his anger, trying to work himself into a rage, he knew it was useless. Whatever she said, whatever she called herself, she was still Violetta, the woman he loved.

"I have spent some time in this country." True enough. She smiled sweetly. "It is beautiful, is it not? I hope I can see more in my visit."

"Do you plan to return to Italy soon?"

She shrugged. "That depends." He raised an eyebrow. "On a number of things. Lady Ripley has offered to present me at court next season, and I would like that very much."

A ripple of interest filled the room. Orlando felt the hairs on the back of his neck rise, fear replacing his anger. Not what he wanted to feel, but he was confident he was showing little but polite interest. He took in the rest of the occupants of this room and saw his brother, watching him with a cool smile on his lips. Orlando knew that look. Corin was amused, and under that sleepy exterior his mind was working at double time. He leaned back and nodded to Corin. "I take it you had a pleasant journey."

"Certainly. Miss Palagio is an excellent companion."

A spirit of mischief gripped Orlando. "Didn't you say you were the daughter of an Italian count? In that case, shouldn't we address you as Lady Violetta?"

She frowned at him. "In this country I am usually known as Miss Palagio. Technically, I suppose you are right, but in Italy I am Violetta Palagio d'Oro. Miss Palagio will do."

"But Violetta is such a pretty name!" he protested. "Such a shame not to use it!"

Her lips firmed. Her pretty, full lips. He remembered their taste and a bitter pang of regret shot through him. "We are, I think, more formal in Italy."

"Violetta," he said caressingly, fully aware of the effect the word on his lips would have on her. She paled. Only slightly, her creamy skin lightening, but he saw it, and was savagely glad. She remembered, as he did, when he last used her name.

"It sounds better than usual, on your lips." Her voice had lifted slightly. With a prick of amusement he realized she was flirting with him. They had never flirted, not in the innocent, society way. There were so many things they hadn't done. Would never do, now.

"You're too kind, ma'am. Dare I suppose your visit here will be of a reasonable duration?"

She glanced at Lady Taversall. He saw a spark of uncertainty. "It depends on my godmother's plans."

"We have no definite plans," Orlando's mother said smoothly. "We are delighted Violetta has decided to stay with us for a while, and we mean to make the most of her."

He shot Lady Taversall a baleful glance. She smiled blandly back. "I must try to help," he said, in a desperate attempt to return to his own body. He felt totally exposed here, as though everyone knew what he had meant to her and she to him.

Judith interrupted and he almost leapt in shock. He had completely forgotten her presence. "When Orlando and I are married we will be pleased to receive you."

Violetta smiled sweetly at her. "You are most kind, my lady."

What was wrong with him? Orlando prided himself on his discretion and his sang-froid. It was all leaving him. He wanted to take back the past hour, come to Violetta and court her. He had to think.

Before it disappeared completely he rose and sketched a bow to the company. "Pray excuse me. We'll be expected in the drawing room for dinner in an hour, and I mean to do my dinner justice. The countryside is so stimulating to the appetite, is it not?" With that final parting shot, aimed specifically at Violetta, he left.

&

In her room Violetta gave way to her fears. Long used to covering her face and emotions with a carefully constructed mask, now she was desperate. It would be the ultimate test of her acting abilities. To conceal her longing for him, to enchant him and make him woo her. If he did not, she would still have something, still have a life. Not one she wanted, but one she would do her best to make tolerable. It was the end now. She had been too late, and he was promised to Lady Judith. Violetta knew Judith wouldn't let him go now.

A knock came at the door. Violetta's French maid, busy laying out the gown Violetta was to wear for dinner, went to answer it.

She closed the door quietly and turned to Violetta. *"C'est un homme, mademoiselle."*

Violetta knew who it was, but she asked, for form's sake. *"Qui-est il?"*

The door softly opened and closed. "Lord Blyth, mademoiselle."

"Que veut-il?"

"Pour vous porter vers le bas au dîner."

She didn't want to be alone with him. Not yet, not until she had regained her equilibrium. *"Non."*

The door opened, soft words were exchanged, and then it closed again.

Violetta stood and allowed the maid to dress her, arranging the elaborate, delicate cream silk around her as though she was a doll. Her hair was dressed, but when Lisette would have draped the powdering gown around her and led her to the powdering closet, Violetta shook her head. She would keep her dark hair, let people get accustomed to seeing it, before she powdered.

She clasped a double row of pearls around her throat and a matching set around her wrist, below the triple fall of Méchlin lace. Her fingers were clear of all rings, their long, perfectly manicured elegance decoration in themselves. So unlike the short-nailed practicality of the hands Charlotte Lambert had shown to the world.

Violetta allowed a footman to lead her downstairs to the drawing room, unwilling to allow Lord Blyth close to her. He was not waiting. She saw him as soon as she entered the room and hastily looked elsewhere. At Lord Ripley, coming forward to draw her into the room.

He made sure Orlando didn't take her in to dinner, but she

felt, actually *felt*, his burning gaze on her throughout the meal. He wasn't doing as well at hiding his emotions as Violetta, but then, she was more practised at the skill. She laughed, responded to the quips and compliments, remembered not to overdo it, to display the nervousness she felt inside. She even managed to eat something.

All the while she was conscious of the steady presence of her godmother and her husband, calming her, reassuring her. Lord Ripley was there, and she knew she could go to him, if things became too hard. He would never turn away from her. This was the role she would keep, the one she would have for the rest of her life, if all went well.

If not, there was always Italy.

Chapter Nineteen

Orlando watched the lovely, charming woman and cursed himself for letting her go. He should have persisted at Richmond. He should have insisted. Now his future was set and he didn't feel the peace he had hoped for but turmoil, and a sickening feeling that he'd made the worst mistake of his life.

He had no chance to get anywhere near Violetta until the next day. It was fine, but not too hot, so most of the guests were to be found outdoors. No specific activity was planned for the day except for an al fresco meal instead of the usual large country house breakfast. He found Violetta surrounded by beaux, including his own brother. He told himself to be cool, as cool as she appeared in fine, ice-blue silk, a simple straw bergère hat tied at a becoming angle over her shining hair. He remembered the feel of that hair in his fingers and experienced something akin to physical pain.

Putting on his smoothest smile, his charming face, he stepped forward, straight through the crowd surrounding her. Judith was absent, as was Perdita, but he only noticed in passing. "Miss Palagio, good morning."

She turned to him, her face expressionless. "Good morning Lord...Blyth." The slight hesitation was to demonstrate that she had to search her memory for his name. A clever touch, he acknowledged wryly.

"Would you do me the great honour of strolling in the rose garden with me? I swear, we won't go out of sight of your assiduous duenna." He grimaced in the direction of his mother, seated comfortably beneath the shade of a large oak tree. That raised a slight laugh from the assembled company.

To his astonishment she stood and laid her hand on his arm. "I would be delighted, sir." He'd expected more resistance than that. Last night she'd definitely been avoiding him, avoided being alone with him.

He waited until they were out of earshot of everyone. The fragrance of the roses swirled about them, heady and seductive. He ignored it. "What are you doing here, Violetta?"

"Entering society."

A wry smile quirked one corner of his mouth. "I would say that one part of society has already entered you, if I didn't think you knew it already."

A fiery blush coloured her delicate features. "It isn't kind of you to remind me."

"I rarely think of anything else, these days. That, and how to get you back where you belong. In my bed."

She said nothing. No confirmation, no rejection. She didn't look at him. "I was a fool to let you go, and more of a fool to rush my fences. Whether you accept me or not, Violetta, I am yours. At your feet, or anywhere else you want me. You know that, don't you?"

"No," she whispered. "I couldn't do that to you. So I've done this."

Violetta did look at him then. Now completely in control of herself again, she stared up at him and he felt the familiar sensation of drowning. "I know gentlemen get over their emotions very quickly." He opened his mouth to protest but she didn't let him interrupt. "Don't try to tell me otherwise. I've seen it. I'm giving you a chance, Orlando, a fair chance. My mother and Aunt Virginia have given me an opportunity of my own, one I intend to take. You've committed yourself now, and you can't draw back. She won't let you. Please consider it carefully. Please."

"Why do you doubt me?" he hissed. "Why do you say these things?"

She smiled gently. "Because, unlike most society maidens, I've seen it. Whores aren't heartless, you know, although gentlemen like to think it. Sometimes, when their lovers drop them, they suffer more than you know. Sometimes they don't." She shrugged, her gown slipping over her shoulders, over that fair skin he loved to touch. "Whichever it is, it isn't good business to show it. I've seen men go from one mistress to another in the course of a year, though in the circle I move in it is more usual for it to be longer. I've seen lifelong devotion."

"Ripley and your mother?"

"Yes." The word was cut off sharply.

"Then I'll prove I can be as constant as your mother's lover."

"I've always been known as a Palagio."

"That," he said firmly, "is something else I wanted to talk to you about." He held out his arm for her to take. She laid her hand on the dark red cloth, and they continued their stroll. "The family is a great and famous one. How could your mother turn from one extreme to the other?"

She shot a look at him. "Do you know anything of our history?"

"Yes, some of it. Your mother was the Contessa d'Oro?"

"She still is, but the only way she could escape my father was to leave the name behind."

"I see." She wondered if he did. Just for a moment she saw the anguish, the agony she had locked away deep inside her. "Violetta, I'm going to talk to Judith later today. I'm going to ask her to release me."

She felt her face go cold, despite the heat of the sun. "You can't. She won't let you."

"Yes, I can." His lips firmed. "I wanted you when I only knew you as Violetta. I want you in every way possible."

"That's why I refused you. I couldn't drag your family into that particular mire. You know I won't let you do that."

"Nevertheless, I will."

"Why?"

His eyes opened wide and he met her gaze with no subterfuge, no polite mask. He couldn't hide anything from her. "You know why."

They stared at each other in a moment separated from ordinary time.

"Goodness! You look as if you've seen a ghost!"

The sharp trill of Lady Judith's voice broke the dream, returned them to reality with a desperate plunge. She smiled brightly and came up on Orlando's other side, to take his arm in a proprietorial gesture it would have been hard to miss. "Miss Palagio, you've put us all in the shade. How is it we've never heard of you before?"

Violetta smiled sweetly at Lady Judith, but Orlando saw the spark of alarm in her eyes. She had avoided being so close to the lady. There was a good chance the perceptive Lady Judith might recognize her as the dowdy Miss Charlotte Lambert. "I have lived in Italy with my family, Lady Judith, except for a time at school. Have you been to Italy?"

"No. Should I?"

"Yes." Violetta lifted her head to one side, angling her hat so it shaded half her face. "It is a lovely country. The Palagios live mainly in Tuscany, near Florence, but we have relations in Rome."

"Is it true that one of your relations is a cardinal? Lady Taversall mentioned it last night."

Orlando tensed. Violetta answered. "My uncle is a cardinal in Rome, yes. The Palagios have had family in the Church for generations."

"Then you're a Catholic?"

There was a pause. Orlando frowned. He hadn't thought about that.

Violetta turned coolly to Lady Judith, entirely ignoring his body between them. "Shall I trust you, I wonder? Yes, you have a trustworthy face." Orlando bit back a laugh. "I was raised a Catholic because I was in Italy, but my family are not particularly religious. If I married a Catholic gentleman, I would retain my faith, but if I find a husband in this beautiful country, well then—" She shrugged, that gesture she made look so elegant. "I will abide by his religion. I believe that God is God, however you choose to worship Him. My uncle would be scandalized, but to be a cardinal in Italy is as much political as it is religious." She stood back. "You are not shocked?"

"N-no."

Orlando let out a breath he was not aware he'd been holding. Then smiled coolly at Lady Judith, who had already unsheathed her claws. She wouldn't give him up without a fight. If it were not that he knew she held not one iota of special feeling for him he would feel sorry for her. Judith wanted to be close to Perdita, not him, she wanted wealth and position, not Orlando Garland. He would not break her heart. However he owed it to her to be kind in his separation from her. If he could manage it. She had remained close to Perdita when many others had abandoned her, and he held no grudge against her, although he still suspected she thought more of Perdita than she did of him.

"You are remarkably tolerant, for an Italian," Lady Judith remarked.

"Yes, I am. I have travelled. I think it is wise to remember the customs of the country one is visiting. Perhaps, Lady Judith, you can help me accustom myself to this one."

"It would be my pleasure."

Violetta had accepted the gauntlet, then. Orlando prepared to watch the spectacle and step in if it got too bloody. It could be worse than a duel to the death between two strong men. Women were so much more vicious.

Later that day Orlando requested a private interview with Lady Judith. He took her to a small parlour on the ground floor. "Please sit down." He didn't want to risk her falling down.

Orlando walked to the window and stared out at the gardens, then turned and walked back to Judith, stopping in front of the chair where she was seated. "Judith, I want to ask you to release me from our agreement."

She looked up at him, head tilted on one side, a small smile lifting the corners of her mouth. "I noticed you were much taken with Miss Palagio. Don't worry. I won't interfere with your dalliances."

He tried again. "I want a partnership when I marry, Judith. I want someone I can trust, someone I can share with. You are an admirable woman, one I am sure will make a man a good wife one day. Just not me."

"Why not?"

"My situation has changed. I have fallen deeply in love with Violetta Palagio."

"In a day?"

He swallowed his response, that one minute with Violetta next to Judith would have been enough. "I made her acquaintance before. But she was unavailable then, and I tried to give her up. Today I saw how useless my efforts are."

"How unfortunate!"

"I wish to ask her to marry me. I will ask her family for their help, if I have to."

She humphed. "They can do nothing. They're Italian. My claim on you will prevail." She threw him a baleful glance. "I will give you five more minutes, sir. I thought we had an understanding. Will you turn that all upside down for this fleeting emotion? Love?" She spat the word.

Orlando couldn't quite believe what he was hearing. "You don't know who the Palagios are?"

The smile lost its edge. "No, should I?"

He ticked off the attributes "Bankers, vineyard merchants and thus wine merchants, financiers and old nobility." He lifted his head and stared at her. "They have fingers in every pie."

Judith made a sound of exasperation. "Trade!"

He stared at her. "Judith, you are demonstrating why we are not a good match. *I* am in trade. It's how I restored my fortune, and how I want to continue making a profit. You will have to entertain City merchants if you marry me, you will have to learn how not to deliver crassly ignorant comments such as the one you have just made." She blenched, but he ignored it. He needed to make her understand. Even without Violetta's presence, this would be a misalliance.

"I daresay I could manage that. If I felt like it." He opened his mouth to reply but she forestalled him. "I have accepted your offer. We have announced it. It suits me, Orlando. I'm too old to go hunting for a husband, I can't compete against the sweet young things launched in society each year, and I must be married. I won't withdraw. If you wish, you must do it." Orlando understood. He wouldn't be able to dissuade her. "On the other hand," she continued, examining her highly polished nails, "I won't object to any liaisons you may wish to conduct. I won't demand your presence day and night, and I won't pester you for attention." She looked back at him. "So you can have your Palagios and your opera dancers. I won't mind."

"All you would ever have of me, Judith, is my name and my status. Enough couplings to start a child. When I have the son I need to ensure the title, that will be the end of it and I'll leave. Perdita won't stay with me forever. She will marry, leave home and then you'll be completely alone." He tried to make her see how hateful such a loveless union would be for both of them.

She stood up and walked to the window in a gentle shush of silk. It was the only sound in the room. He listened, but heard nothing. No sobs, no sighs, not even laughter. Then she spoke. "No she won't. Perdita's too old, and her legs are ugly. No one will have her now. I will have her, Orlando, I'll have her as my own, to control and to use as I want to. I'll say this. Indulge yourself. Take the Palagio as a lover, if you wish. I'll tolerate that. God knows, my mother has tolerated much more!"

"Your mother began the separation between your father and herself," he pointed out acidly.

"She never cared for him," she admitted. "But their marriage has been a success in all but a personal way."

The most important way of all. "Would you settle for that?"

"I've been brought up to it."

He stood perfectly still. "It's not the kind of marriage I want." A thought occurred to him, one that might persuade her to release him honourably. "If you think I'd condone your infidelities, you can think again. If I ever found you with another man, I'd take him to court."

Her smile broadened again. "I thought you knew. You won't find me in another man's arms. I can promise you that. I might have close friendships with other women, but men are not to my taste."

He turned and strode to the door, tired of the conversation, tired of the antipathy that bristled in the room like a third person. Anger grew, that she would try to keep him despite what both of them wanted, merely for the sake of society. "Then, madam, I would keep you in my bed, force you to perform the act you find most distasteful. As I've heard you observe, all a man needs is another woman. I can promise you I would keep you busy, too busy for your female friendships." He hoped that would bring Judith to her senses and spare Violetta some of the scandal that would occur when he broke their arrangement.

Without waiting for an answer he left, closing the door behind him with great care. He heard her chuckle just before the door closed.

Outside the room he heard a swirl of silk but he saw no one. Whoever had been listening had left a fragrance behind, one he knew well. The one his mother and his sister used.

Orlando loved Violetta beyond thought, beyond reason. Watching her, unable to touch her, he thought he might lose his mind if he couldn't have her. There must be a way to placate Judith and prevent scandal that could open up Violetta's relationship to La Perla and his mother's friendship with the woman, there had to be.

Orlando went to his room, disinclined to engage in social activities and pleaded a headache. He had to think things through and he couldn't bear to see Violetta at dinner, flirting and laughing with the others. It was too much today.

The raw interview with Lady Judith brought home exactly how serious his mistake had been, to think he could have found something with her. Anything at all.

His pretended indisposition brought Violetta hurrying to his side.

Orlando had sent his valet away, and was trying to concentrate on some business letters, newly arrived from London. His headache was imaginary. His dilemma was not.

The door opened. He didn't look up, expecting his valet to take the untouched tray of food away. Something alerted him. The scent perhaps, a light floral fragrance any valet would despise. He got to his feet, the light chair he was using clattering to the floor behind him. "Violetta!"

Forgetting everything else he went to her, folded his arms about her and sought her mouth like a drowning man seeking air. She asked nothing, said nothing, but joined with him, her arms going around his back, her face tilted up for his kiss.

He sank into her. He needed her, more than his title, the lands he'd fought so hard for, his respectability. His life. She gave him what he needed. He would never let her go. Never.

He lifted his head, brought up his hand to cup the back of her head. "I'm only complete when we're like this. You're my other half, my love, my life."

She gave a shaky laugh that seemed to degenerate into a sob. "I only came because you were ill. Was this to draw me to you?"

"No, love, but I can't be sorry you came. I had matters to think over." He pressed another kiss to her lips, briefly this time. "Now I'm in turmoil again. Come and sit down."

He released her only long enough to help her to the sofa by the window, before he sat down and settled her in his arms once more. It was only then he noticed she was dressed for bed, in a loose, frothy gown of clear ivory and who knew what underneath. Her hair was braided. He lifted it, to feel the fine, silky strands. She chuckled. "I claimed a headache, too. Lisette got me ready for bed and left me with a book. I don't doubt she'll return before long, and raise merry hell if she finds me missing, so I haven't long."

Forgetting everything but her presence he murmured, "Can you come back later? Can I come to you?"

"Maybe." She breathed the words when his tongue caressed the delicate skin behind her ear. "I'm supposed to keep you at arm's length."

"Why?"

"Because you're betrothed."

"Oh God!" He stared at her, recalled to the present. Her eyes opened wide at his expression of horror and she drew back. He pulled her back where she belonged; into his arms. He nuzzled her hair with his lips. "I have to discuss that with you, love. I'd rather talk it over with you like an adult than leave you with no explanation at all."

She lifted her head. "What do you mean?"

"I asked Judith to release me today. She would not." He swallowed, but even this didn't seem as bad when Violetta was here.

She reached up to caress his face.

He kissed her fingers. "She confirmed what you once suspected. She wants women. I told her I wouldn't countenance infidelity and she laughed at me, said I needn't worry about that. I thought you were seeing things, imagining things that weren't there, but you weren't."

"Will she release you? Can you use it to persuade her?"

He shook his head. "No. There's no law against it. I can make things difficult, but—oh, Violetta, I've been such an idiot!"

She moved closer, smoothed her hand over his jaw. "No, no you haven't. You tried to make the best of things, that's all. You thought I'd revealed my face in my mother's salon, but I did not. Another woman did that, not me, with my mother's connivance. I didn't know I was definitely coming here until a few days ago. It would have been too late then."

He grimaced, then lifted his hand to cover hers, to prevent her taking it away. "He's been playing gooseberry for days. We only eluded him for the first time that morning."

"If we'd been earlier—"

He interrupted her with a gentle two fingers placed over her lips. "If Ripley hadn't been so assiduous I could have been tied hand and foot by now. So far the contract's only verbal. I still have a chance to escape from it honourably, but I need to think. That's why I'm really alone tonight."

She kissed his fingers and he smiled, before dropping his hand to hold her waist. "What can you do?"

"Ripley's agreed to delay the contract to give me a chance." His control wavered, but he continued. "I'll talk to Perdita tomorrow. Perhaps she might be able to help in some way. So far I've hardly had any private meetings with her. Judith's always been there."

"Oh, poor Orlando!" The cry came from her heart, and it broke him.

He pulled her close, as close as he could, feeling her warmth, her comfort. His breath came shakily. "I don't care any more. You could be the daughter of the pope and I'd still want you. I love you, Violetta, and I want you more than I've wanted anything in my life, but I won't ruin this chance for you if you wish to take it."

She gave him a watery smile. "You may have already done that."

He stroked his hand over her hair, bound up in its nighttime braids. He began to fiddle with the end of one of the braids, unravelling its tight neatness. "I know. But, Violetta, I can't be sorry." He glanced up at her face. "Besides, if you're a Palagio, your rich suitors might be persuaded to overlook a discretion." He paused, concentrating on his task, letting the silky fine hair slip through his fingers, slowly working his way up to the top. "Your father was rich and powerful." He looked up. "Why didn't you tell me?"

"Would it have made a difference?"

He smiled and shook his head. "Not to the way I feel about you."

She swallowed. "My father is dead now. He can't come back to claim me."

He saw the echo of fear in her eyes. "What happened?"

She didn't pretend to misunderstand him. "I was three when my mother ran away. It was all she could do. It was only when he turned on me she took me away. He wanted to—he said if she didn't do what he told her he would give me to his friends. It was vile, Orlando!"

Bitter tears fell from her eyes, and he dropped the braid and pulled her close, stroking her back and hair, numbly listening. "He forced her to do things she's never told me about, but I've spent plenty of time thinking. She did it all, to save me, to stop him hurting me. Papa was a powerful man and there was no one to gainsay him, not for many years. He hated Mama because she didn't give him a son. His mistress gave him two."

Confusion warred with the shock. He put two fingers under her chin and pushed her head up so he could see her face. Her tears poured down unchecked, tears he wanted to kiss away, to help her forget what she had seen, what she knew. He pulled her close again and let her sob. His mind whirled. How could a woman like that be satisfied with her lot as a London courtesan? La Perla must have been powerful, important once, more than most women in England, yet she had suffered abuse here, been reviled. His reluctant admiration for her went up a notch.

There was still a chance of Violetta being found out as La Perla Perfetta. He would protect her with everything he possessed, even if it meant his own downfall, the collapse of everything he'd worked for. Nothing else mattered now. Only protecting Violetta from further hurt, caring for her as she deserved.

"Where are your brothers and sisters?" he asked gently. It was something that had been taxing him for some time.

"Gabriella's children? My father's mistress?" She lifted her head presenting a face that was more child than woman. Distress had scoured all her sophistication away, leaving her open and vulnerable. She sniffed. "She took them to Rome, to my uncle. He protected her from my father, and after a few years she moved on to a nobleman in Naples. I suppose they must be there. Mama and I thought it best to leave them alone."

The world rocked under his feet. "You're the daughter of the Conte d'Oro." It was a statement, not a question, an effort to understand.

She stared at him, her beautiful eyes wide. No tears now. "I always thought I was Ripley's daughter. I couldn't bear to think of anything else."

"I know." He kissed her gently on her lips. "I thought so too. I spoke to Ripley. He says he didn't become your mother's lover until she came to England with you, when you were three years old.

"So I would end up with my own Lady Ripley if I married Judith." He leaned forward, hands on his knees and bowed his head.

She stayed silent, sitting so still and quiet he had to look to make sure she was still there. "Judith has laid determined siege to me, with the encouragement of my sister, but she has no sensuality, no desire for me, only for the title." He took her hand, caressed her fingers. "One night. Give me one more night, Violetta. One night of dreams, of love. Then we'll decide what to do."

The burning look she gave him was pure desire. "How can any woman not want you?"

His spirits soared. Despite everything he had someone, someone wholly his. "Come here my love. Let me show you how much I want you."

She went willingly, with the generosity and wholeheartedness he adored about her. Once Violetta had given herself, she continued to give, and wouldn't hold back. He understood now what she had tried to tell him after Richmond.

It was all or nothing.

He gave himself without stint. Lifting her in his arms he crossed the short distance to the bed and laid her down on the turned back sheets. Her hands went to her head and she busied herself undoing the remaining braid while he loosened her gown. It fell away from her with a sensuous slide of rich silk, the lace flounces catching on the clean white linen. He swept it up from under her and dropped it in the general direction of the sofa. Then he crossed the room and locked the door. He turned back. He could see her body, glimmering past the bedhangings, past the mahogany bedposts. She waited, and he looked and finally made up his mind. He wasn't going back. "I'm not letting you return to your room tonight. I want you all night, to love and to sleep in my arms. Let this be a pact, Violetta. I'll not let you go. Not now, not ever."

Throwing his banyan on top of her gown, he began on the buttons of his shirt, pulling it over his head and dropping it to the floor. Violetta raised herself up on her elbows. He made a sound deep in his throat, almost a growl. She watched intently as he shed the rest of his clothes. Breeches, stockings and shoes went in an untidy pile on the floor, with his undergarments.

Before he went to her he locked the connecting door, the one to his dressing room. He doubted anyone would try the jib door, the one leading to the servants' quarters, but he was past caring about that.

He joined her, climbing onto the bed and stretching out beside her, without touching her. Violetta reached out for him. He dragged her close, sealing their bodies all the way down, feeling a surge of sensation as all senses were assaulted by her closeness, by her presence.

Nothing more than this would serve. No one other than she. He lowered his mouth to hers and counted himself lost.

Violetta was no passive partner. She went to him and when he drew her close moved to push him on his back, rolling over him, giving him delightful access to her back and her bottom. He couldn't bear his lips to leave hers, taking her with a determined onslaught, giving her his tongue, taking hers, caressing her in smooth strokes of his hands down her delectable body.

Desperation lent them a passion they had not been aware of before, fuelled by their separation. She sat up. He watched her take his shaft in her hands and guide him to her entrance. He watched her take him. Then he looked up and their eyes met.

"This is how it should be." The words, breathed in a low, sighing breath stirred her, stirred him. He lifted his hands to her breasts, and watched her arch back, pushing them into his hands, inviting his touch, his caress. The nipples were hard buttons against his hands. He lifted his knees and she leaned against them.

The sight filled his eyes. He breathed deep, savouring the heady scent of their lovemaking. Together. When she gasped and sat up, alarm in her face he stilled, but couldn't dispel the clouds of sensuality surrounding them. "What—what is it?"

"Oh Orlando, I haven't—I didn't—I thought you were ill. I didn't come to seduce you and I didn't—"

After their recent conversation it was ironic that this was only their second experience of unprotected sex. He knew he should stop, but he could not. Orlando had always been in control, always been able to bring his willpower to bear, but it was beyond him now. "No matter," he gasped. "We'll have to leave it to God. I can't, Violetta, I can't stop now."

"Neither can I." The confession was made on an outbreath as she leaned back against him.

It would have to serve. They would cope. Somewhere deep inside, where Orlando couldn't usually reach, a primitive instinct growled its satisfaction. To give her a child. The knowledge, dangerous though it was, flashed through his mind and he knew, whatever the risks, he would welcome any child she gave him, be it idiot or genius, athlete or invalid. And it would give him more leverage to persuade her to stay with him. The businessman in Orlando purred in triumph. He always liked to have the better hand in any deal and this meant more to him than any other. "Give me your hands."

"What?" Wholly lost in him, Violetta lifted her head. They looked at each other, smiled.

"Your hands." She lifted her hands from their resting place on the bed and slipped them into his outstretched ones. It made the intimate act deeper. Sunk within her, the act of trust and love gave him pause, made him lift his head. "Look at us. Look at where we join, my love."

She looked. Her hair slid over one white shoulder. She stared, fascinated at the point where they became one, then lifted her chin and met his gaze once more. "It's beautiful."

"Yes, it is." His voice had softened and lowered. He gripped her hands. "Now pull hard."

She pulled on his hands, as he'd asked and shattered. It gave him the purchase he needed to thrust deep inside her, deeper than he'd ever been before. He felt the pulsations, gripped, pulled and thrust. Watched her cry out, arch so that the only part of her body touching his legs was the back of her shoulders, pressed against his knees. He planted his feet firmly on the bed, gripped her hands and pushed, kept on pushing, lost in her. "Dear God!"

It was his turn. The bed canopy seemed to spin as his world shifted. He heard her cry out once more as he erupted inside her, felt his whole being drive into hers. For that moment, that untimeable moment, they were truly one. One feeling, one need, one love.

As the tremors died away he pulled her up into his arms. "Sweetheart, love, dear heart, how can I live without you, without this?"

All she could say was a breathless, "*Ti amo, ti amo*," repeated sotto voce until her voice died away. She snuggled close. She slept. Orlando watched over his lady, held her and thought.

He was not altogether surprised when someone tried the door and relieved when they went away. It must have been his valet or a footman, collecting his dinner tray. The light outside began to soften and fade. Orlando lay still, holding his sleeping princess, willing the night to go on forever. Perhaps Violetta's maid would find her missing. If so that would expedite his desire to marry her. He wasn't about to wake Violetta, to avoid that fate. Eventually he, too, slept, exhausted by thinking to no end. Comforted by her presence he slept better than he had in a long time.

Chapter Twenty

"Goodness!"

Violetta sat bolt upright in bed, only to feel her lover's arms pull her back down into the warm nest they'd created together. "I didn't expect to stay here all night."

"I said I wanted you all night." His voice was a sleepy murmur. He tried to settle her for more sleep. "The doors are locked. Nobody can come in."

"Lisette will know I wasn't in my room last night. She'll tell Aunt Virginia and she—"

"She will make me offer for you, something I intend to do in any case. Be quiet and go back to sleep."

It was too late. Violetta was awake. The dream had gone. Last night she had decided what they must do, and she was determined they would do it. "No. I'm going back to my room. But before I do I have to tell you something."

He opened his eyes, meeting hers in a caress as intimate as a touch. "Good morning, my love."

"Good morning." She leaned forward and pressed a gentle kiss on his lips but drew back before he could seize her and deepen the embrace. She didn't want her senses completely befuddled by desire. Or rather, she did, but she couldn't afford them to be. She leaned up on one elbow. He smiled up at her, so Violetta couldn't help but think how wonderful he looked newly woken from sleep, hair in his eyes, the scent of their lovemaking about them. "I won't marry you, Orlando."

His eyes snapped open. "Yes, you will. We'll find a way."

"No. Think, Orlando. There's more at stake than two people's happiness. You have tenants, employees, business partners, all of whom depend on your good name for their prosperity. We can't ignore them, can we?"

He sighed. "No."

"If we create a scandal all those people will suffer. You'll lose your good name, and a lot of business."

His soft, slow smile found its way through to her heart. "After last night, it's possible you're pregnant. I'll insist on marriage then." He stretched and folded his arms behind his head. His naked arms.

"I want you to talk to Lady Judith again. Tell her the real situation."

"About Miss Lambert, La Perla Perfetta?"

She nodded. "If you have to."

"That won't persuade her. It will merely give her ammunition."

"Tell her. Or I'll go to Italy and you'll never see me again."

She flung back the covers and got out of bed, taking her time finding her wrapper. She slid her arms into the sleeves and drew the garment around her, hearing his reluctant sigh of regret. "Do it for me. Do it for us."

She left him.

Violetta found him later in the day in the garden. He was sitting in a small summerhouse, his hands clasped loosely before him, staring at a bird on the lawn beyond. "Well?" She stood in front of him. He saw her and she saw his face lighten, his expression change to something softer, more loving.

"She said no. Again."

"I thought she would." Violetta walked to the end of the pavilion and looked back. Now it came to it she was filled with profound sadness. This would be the end of her hopes for respectability, for someone, something of her own. "Did you tell her the whole?"

"No. She would have told everyone and ruined everything for you. I told her I love you, told her I would not marry her. She threatened to cause a scandal and destroy everything I've worked for." He didn't sound as if he cared. Well she did, and she would refuse him rather than see him destroy his and Perdita's future.

She must make the best of what she had. She walked back to him, sat next to him. Immediately he reached out and clasped her hand in his, but he didn't look at her. "I can't live without you."

"You may have to." She turned to him, her eyes burning into his. "Lady Judith can cause such scandal that you and your family will be ruined all over again. Marry her, Orlando. I won't stay and see that. I can't, please understand me, I can't. I might go away to my family in Italy for a year."

His hold tightened on her hand. He caught her attention, held her gaze, his eyes blazing. "No! Marry me and we'll face them all down. There must be a way."

"I can't be the cause of so much unhappiness." She stared at him, her eyes brimming with unshed tears. She couldn't lift her hand to wipe them away. "I might lose you everything you've fought for so long. You spent your life repairing your father's mistakes. A scandal like this could cost you everything. Lady Judith won't be silent, you know she won't."

He leaned forward and kissed her lips so softly, so tenderly it did nothing to help her distress. "No. I can't do it, Violetta, I can't marry her. I won't give you up, and I won't dishonour you."

"It's the only way!" she cried out. Tears flowed down her face unchecked. He drew her into his arms and after an attempt at resistance she sank thankfully into them. He held her and rocked her, as he might have done with a child.

"No, sweetheart, no it's not. I've been thinking, wondering what to do."

She sighed. "I won't. I can't."

"Will you promise me something?" He spoke in a gentle coaxing tone.

She lifted her head and he groped in his pocket, bringing out a handkerchief. He busied himself drying her face. "Will you promise not to look back, not to repine? I won't give you up. But if Judith exposes you as the cause for our broken engagement, you will find it uncomfortable in England. We'll go away somewhere. Perhaps to Italy, or somewhere else if you'd prefer. I can arrange for my estates to be cared for in my absence and without my obnoxious presence my mother can undo some of the harm Judith will wreak. Don't fight it, Violetta. I'm not going anywhere without you."

"Oh, Orlando!" She couldn't fight any more. Waking up that morning in his arms, remembering the love they shared, she couldn't walk away from that. He was right. They had done all they could to avert the scandal that threatened to ruin him. "Very well. I love you, Orlando. If you're sure, I'll marry you and damn the consequences."

"Oh, my love!" There were no words after that as he took her mouth in a searing kiss.

By mutual agreement they said nothing to anyone that day. Violetta wanted to write to her mother and speak to Lord Ripley before she told anyone else and he had left for the day. As Lord Lieutenant of the county he'd promised to attend the local assizes, and would be away for a couple of days. Neither was in a hurry, now they had made their minds up, now their course was set.

They tried not to be too particular during dinner, but Violetta kept glancing at him, to find his regard on her. Once she saw Aunt Virginia watching her, and she smiled. Lady Judith shot her a particularly venomous glance and then looked away.

After dinner, when the ladies went to the drawing room, Violetta found a book from a side table and sat a little apart but she wasn't to be left alone for long. She felt the sofa cushions plump beside her and too late she realized she should have chosen a chair to sit in.

"Miss Palagio, how nice! You enjoy reading?"

"Yes, on occasion." She looked up and smiled at Lady Judith. She watched narrowly as Lady Perdita levered herself into a wide chair set close to the sofa with the aid of a slim cane. Violetta found herself smiling at Perdita. At least she'd done something right. She laid the book in her lap.

"My brother seems very taken with you," Lady Perdita said. She subjected Violetta to a close scrutiny. Violetta raised her chin. What had she heard? What did she know?

"Did you know he spoke to me today?" Lady Judith sounded hard, accusatory.

"I asked him to."

"You should know I have no intention of leaving the field for you," Lady Judith said. She smiled and nodded at someone across the room. "Once I am married to him I will take him away from you. I'll have the field and I will take every advantage of it. Love is a fickle thing and won't last long. Mark my words, he'll have forgotten you in a year."

To all eyes it would seem they were engaged in normal social intercourse, but they'd headed her off and now Violetta had to stand her ground and respond. She put herself on guard. She was already feeling fragile after her emotional experience with Orlando earlier in the day, but that must be put aside for now.

"We will see," she said mildly. She would not be provoked into saying more than she should. She was sure Lady Judith was trying to provoke her into making a scene, making her more determined not to do so.

The door was wrenched open and the gentlemen surged noisily into the room. Violetta turned eagerly to the gentlemen and the sight of Orlando crossing the room to her side.

He stood behind her chair and placed his hand briefly on her shoulder. She felt his touch through her body, but kept still. His hand didn't linger, but she knew he needed the brief contact as much as she did. He moved to one side, next to Lady Judith, who took this as a mark of favour. She reached her hand up to him. He gave her a glacial smile but made no move to take her hand.

Violetta didn't care. The conversation turned general and she excused herself early.

Only when she'd had Lisette array her in her prettiest, laciest wrapper over a fine gown of silk did she wonder if he would come to her tonight. She wanted him to take away all her fears, all her worries. To stop her thinking.

She wanted her mother, but she was out of reach. She'd spent all afternoon composing a letter, telling her mother of her hopes and fears, trying to ensure her mother did not take any of the blame.

The doorknob turned. Violetta turned to the door with a welcoming smile.

It wasn't Orlando. It was Lady Perdita.

Chapter Twenty-One

Her ladyship closed the door and crossed the room, raking Violetta's attire with a raised eyebrow. Without being invited, she sat down.

"I know you, don't I?"

"We were introduced," Violetta replied guardedly.

Lady Perdita waved her hand carelessly. "Not that. I told Judith I knew you, and she said you looked familiar, too. She came up with an entirely preposterous name."

"Who?"

"It's of no matter. A notorious woman." Violetta's blood ran cold. If Lady Judith had recognized her as La Perla Perfetta the game could well be up. *Courage, Violetta.*

Lady Perdita didn't notice Violetta's shock. "Then I realized who you were. Or are. A wig and thick spectacles can't hide everything, Charlotte."

Violetta sighed in relief. She knew she had to confess sooner or later to Lady Perdita, about this at least. She could not become family without setting at least some things straight. So she didn't deny the accusation, but nodded. "You are right. I did spend some time as your companion."

Lady Perdita stared at her. "Why?"

Violetta shrugged. "I wanted to help you. Your mama is my godmother, and I heard of your plight from her. I knew what was wrong, why you weren't recovering as you should have been. They were spoiling you when you needed a firm hand to get you back on your feet."

Lady Perdita shrugged, clearly sceptical. "Is this a masquerade? It's obvious Blyth knows who you are, who you were. Is he helping you to do this? I won't see my friends deceived if you are really someone else. You have done enough, I think."

Violetta took a deep breath and tried to explain. "Charlotte Lambert was the masquerade. I am who you see before you, Violetta Palagio of the house of d'Oro. When I arrived in England, your mother told me of your plight and I decided to help you. I went to the agency in my disguise and applied for the job as your companion." She grinned. "You must not think your mother helped me. She was furious when she realized where I had gone."

Lady Perdita raised an eyebrow. "You didn't do all that to trap my brother?"

Violetta shook her head, smiling a little. "I knew of him, but I heard he was cold and rarely at home. Not the kind of man to attract me, I thought."

"You ensnared him."

"No. He ensnared me."

Lady Perdita shot her a sudden grin, her whole manner more confiding, more relaxed. "I can well believe that. I've seen him do it before. He trades on that cold reputation he has. Did he know who you were from the beginning?"

"No. I knew what you needed, and I knew I could help you. Later, I wished I could go back, enter your house as Violetta Palagio, but it was too late." She looked away, biting her lip and then back, forcing a confession she had never admitted before, even to herself. "I like masquerades. I enjoy pretending to be someone else. It is part of my nature, I think."

"You did it very well." Perdita regarded Violetta through narrowed eyes in the assessing way Violetta had come to know well. "It seems I owe you a debt of gratitude. I'm glad I paid you for your services, or I would feel worse." She leaned back in the chair. "Do you mean to take him away from Judith?"

"It was not my original intention. I was to come here to begin my entrance into English society, that was all, but I decided to help you first. Then I met your brother, and fell in love with him."

Perdita stared at her. "Thank God for that!" She let her breath out in a great sigh of relief. "It would never have done. Judith is entirely wrong for him. You must know that."

"Madness," Violetta agreed, and the very word reminded her of her reasons. "She won't let go of him now. He is determined to have me, but there might be a great deal of scandal when she tells her friends what he did to her."

"I know." Perdita frowned. "I owe you much, for what you did for me. Leave it with me. I'll come up with something."

They exchanged a conspiratorial grin.

"Thank you," Violetta said. "It was unintentional, I didn't know I would fall in love with him."

"We all come to it, or so I understand." Perdita stood up, leaning only slightly on her cane. "You're expecting him tonight, aren't you?" Her gaze took in Violetta's pretty, provocative wrap, the obvious bareness of her legs, revealed by the open front.

There was no point denying it. "Yes."

Perdita raised her brows. "Then I'd better go." She turned for the door, but turned back. "I liked you as Charlotte Lambert. I hope I like you as Violetta Palagio. And Violetta Garland."

She left.

ॐ

At breakfast the following morning Orlando greeted Violetta by getting to his feet and drawing a chair back for her, ignoring the quizzical glances of his mother and stepfather. He attended to her needs, making it obvious to all where his interests lay. Other guests, not party to any of this, were definitely intrigued. There was a new proprietorial air about him that no one present had ever seen Orlando use outside members of his family. The murmurs were all about Orlando and Violetta, and how the absent Lady Judith Wayland would feel about the developments. Violetta ignored them all. Warmed by his love, her course was set. She had ignored scandal before. All she could hope for was that Orlando could weather the course.

"Mama, would it be convenient for you and Father to see

me after breakfast?" he asked, once he had seen to Violetta's needs.

"I think that would be a good idea," Lord Taversall said. When he winked at his stepson, the whole of the present company saw it.

"Perhaps Lord Ripley could attend, too," Orlando suggested.

"Wouldn't miss it for the world, dear boy," the marquess, back from his stint as Lord Lieutenant, replied promptly. "I'll inform her la'ship." Violetta sighed. It wouldn't be pleasant, with the Marchioness of Ripley present. Lady Ripley had virtually ignored Violetta while she had been here, not to the point of rudeness, but when Orlando hadn't troubled to hide his interest in her, she turned decidedly cold.

Lady Judith was not at breakfast but Orlando had promised to send a note to her room, requesting her presence. Best to get it over with, Violetta decided. She eyed her plate, piled high, her appetite gone.

The room filled with gentle chatter. Breakfast at Ripley Court was a decidedly informal affair, where guests were encouraged to serve themselves from the buffet on one side of the room, which groaned with dishes of eggs, ham, chops and toast.

Violetta picked up her fork, only to drop it with a clatter when a sound ripped through the tranquillity of the dining room. A scream. Very loud, very urgent.

Orlando was at the door closely followed by his stepfather before most of the others had time to move. Violetta followed as soon as she heard Orlando's cry of "Perdita!"

Had Lady Perdita fallen downstairs, had she met with an accident? Violetta prayed as she followed Aunt Virginia down the corridor to the source of the sounds. They had not stopped. Another scream rent the air, not as urgent as the first, more of an outraged and angry sound.

Orlando flung open a door, and the company crowded in as fast as they could reach the room. It was one of the smaller parlours, set out as a print room. The yellow walls and black and white prints provided an aptly stark frame for the scandal that waited inside.

Lady Perdita lay on the floor, her cane by the door, her

skirts up around her knees. The bodice of her morning gown was in scandalous disarray, unhooked down the front exposing the pink tip of one breast and riding low on the other side. On her knees, her dress in similar disarray in front of Lady Perdita, was Lady Judith.

"Dear God!" Aunt Virginia whirled around to slam the door, but she was too late. Curious guests and two maidservants jostled for a better look. Lady Taversall went to her daughter, now panting and sobbing in distress, pulling up the bodice. Violetta knew what Perdita would rather not show to the public and dropped to her knees to pull down the skirt, covering the scars left by the accident.

Safe in her mother's arms, Perdita was sobbing her story. Lady Judith got to her feet and stood silently watching, her face closed of expression. It was apparent to all that Orlando wasn't going to her support. He stood aside and watched, his face clear of expression.

"She—she tried to rape me!" Perdita cried between gusts of sobbing breaths. "She asked me to come in here and said awful things, awful! Mama, don't let her, please don't let her!"

Perdita seemed inconsolable. Her mother gathered her into her arms, both of them sitting on the floor, skirts blending together. Violetta stared at Lady Perdita.

Under the cover of her mother's arm, Perdita winked at her.

Violetta blinked in shock, but she couldn't mistake the sly gesture. Without losing a beat Perdita continued her complaints, sobbing out the whole sordid story to her mother, who unsuccessfully tried to soothe her. It wasn't until Perdita had made quite clear that Lady Judith had initiated the encounter, that it was blatantly sexual, that it was none of her making and she had fought tooth and nail to prevent it, that she allowed herself to be soothed. Her stepfather picked her up and carried her away, closely followed by Lady Taversall. The other guests murmured and began to move away, no doubt to gossip about this latest, juicy scandal. Letters would be written and dispatched before the end of the day. Violetta had no doubt that Lord Ripley would offer to frank them for his guests. After all, it was the polite thing to do.

Orlando and Violetta remained, with Lord Ripley. By this time Lady Ripley had arrived, in some dishabille, obviously not yet prepared for the day. Her hair straggled down past her shoulders, her gown pulled roughly over her body.

"Close the door." It was the first time Lord Ripley had spoken.

Violetta knew she had no cause to be here, but she would not leave. She crossed the room and closed the door, but stayed inside. She alone had seen the wink, and was probably the only person who guessed what Lady Perdita had been about.

Lord Ripley took his time, lifting his gaze from his daughter to look around the room. He stopped when he got to his wife. "I think I'm finished here," he said. The words were so final, so complete. Violetta stood perfectly still.

"Judith, you have disgraced yourself and the family name. Your brothers are due home from their house party in a few days. I will leave you to their mercies. Needless to say, I cannot countenance giving my permission to a match with Lord Blyth." Violetta took a deep breath to stop her cry of delight. "You are presently not fit to marry any decent man." Judith stood, ramrod straight, gazing at her mother as though she could save her.

All Lady Ripley said was, "For heaven's sake, Judith, why did you not lock the door?" in terms of general exasperation.

Judith began to wail, in a high-pitched keening voice. "She wanted me to, Mama, she welcomed me, she said she wanted it! I thought—I thought it was something I could do to keep her!" She turned to her mother, but Lady Ripley held up her hands, fending off her daughter, a disquieting contrast to the way Lady Taversall had immediately gone to her daughter a short time before. Judith started back, tears running down her face.

Lady Judith had no one. Perdita had been the only person to care about her and now even she was lost. Her mother ignored her, her father was never at home, and her other siblings were either away from home or in the nursery. Violetta felt deeply sorry for the woman, but she was wise enough to realize she could do nothing for her.

"That's beside the point now, isn't it?" Lady Ripley answered, showing nothing but irritation. "Lady Taversall is hardly likely to allow you anywhere near her daughter again." She rounded on Orlando. "Did you know of this? Did you put Perdita up to it? I wouldn't put it past you. I've been watching you, you and that Italian whore!"

Orlando immediately put himself between Lady Ripley and Violetta. "You do not speak of Violetta like that," he said.

"Indeed, ma'am." Lord Ripley was almost a stranger, looking as he did. His face was harsh, stern, his eyes not the dark soft pools of affection she was used to seeing but hard and flinty. "Judith, go and pack."

"What?" The single syllable hung in the air.

"You heard me. You will pack, ready to leave this house. Do not assume you will be coming back while I am here."

He turned his back on his daughter. Violetta stood aside and watched Lady Judith leave. Their eyes met just before she opened the door. Violetta kept her expression carefully blank, knowing that her pity was the last thing Lady Judith would want. Lady Judith glared at Violetta, open hatred in her gaze, but Violetta didn't respond.

Immediately Orlando came over to Violetta and took her hand, studying her face, showing openly all the love he felt for her. Before he could speak a knock fell on the door. On being bidden to enter, Lord and Lady Taversall came in. "I've left Perdita to be put to bed by her maid," her ladyship said. "She's bearing up very well. I haven't long, I promised her I'd come back." She turned immediately to Orlando. "You wanted to see us, my son?"

Orlando's mouth curved up at one corner. "Yes, Mama. Matters have changed a little since breakfast. I would greatly appreciate permission to address Violetta's guardians in respect of her marriage."

"She's over age," her ladyship commented. "She makes her own decisions." She smiled broadly at Violetta. "Have you made your decision?"

Violetta smiled, happier than she'd been for a very long time. "Yes. I would like to accept his offer."

"Really!" The exclamation came from Lady Ripley. "Barely a week since he proposed to my daughter!" She turned to Orlando, ignoring everyone else. "I'm sure this is an aberration on her part. We can sort things out."

Orlando slowly shook his head. "I'm sorry, ma'am. It was borne in on us that we had made a mistake before this—

unfortunate episode. Now it is impossible. I have privately addressed Violetta, and now she has done me the honour of accepting me."

"Well, I'm delighted," Lord Taversall stated. He came forward and kissed Violetta on both cheeks, drawing back to give her his broad smile. "Welcome to the family, my dear."

Violetta blushed, but smiled. Orlando, who had kept hold of her hand all this while drew her closer. For a moment she thought he was going to kiss her, but he wasn't completely lost to all sense of propriety. "She's made me the happiest man alive."

Only Violetta noticed Lady Ripley stalking out of the room in high dudgeon.

∞

Coming out of the parlour with Violetta resting one hand on his arm, Orlando heard a commotion from the main hall.

Entering, Orlando saw it full of trunks and boxes. Another new arrival, perhaps more than one. Violetta froze when she saw the man at the front door.

"Uncle Lodovico!" She raced forward, in a flurry of light skirts and lace. "Oh, Uncle Lodovico!"

Much to the surprise of the onlookers she flung herself at the dark man who had just entered. Even more to their surprise he opened his arms wide and lost all the saturnine grimness, instead showing a smile a mile wide. "Violetta!"

The embrace was noisy, voluble, and in Italian. Recovering first, Orlando stepped over a large hat box and went to join his beloved. She leaned back in the man's arms. "How did you come here?"

"I received a letter from Lady Taversall and I set out immediately." His voice rumbled.

"Oh, Uncle Lodovico, you shouldn't have!" She gave him a hug and stepped back unsuspectingly into Orlando's arms.

He steadied her and met the man's regard with an assessing one of his own.

"I am the head of the family. It is only right I should come." He didn't take his regard from Orlando. Two fighters, ready to square up to each other if necessary.

Orlando bowed as gracefully as he could, with all the impediments scattered in his way. "Lord Blyth, sir."

He straightened and not much to his surprise received the information, from Lady Taversall, now next to them, that he was facing the present Conte d'Oro.

"I would request an immediate interview," demanded the conte. His English, while good, was heavily accented, and Orlando had to ponder the final word before he realized what the conte was saying. He led the way to the study at Lord Ripley's small nod of permission and prepared himself for an inquisition. Although Violetta had tried to enter, the conte bent his dark gaze on her and said, "*Vedrò questo uomo da solo.*" Orlando was only mildly surprise to see her bow her head and leave the room. This man was used to command. His presence was powerful; he brought an air of authority with him.

The conte turned to Orlando and ran his gaze over him. "You are the man who will marry our little Violetta."

"I hope to do so. I love your niece, sir, and I intend to take the greatest care of her."

After an intense meeting, discussing family affairs and discussing the terms of the marriage contract, Orlando emerged slightly stunned. He agreed to the terms of the contract, admiring the conte's business acumen, his attention to detail, but burning to go and find Violetta.

 relaxed

Violetta crept into Perdita's bedroom later that afternoon, when she should have been dressing for dinner. She found her sitting up in bed in a pretty negligée, none the worse for her ordeal. The paltry remains of a tray of food lay on the bed next to her. Violetta lifted it before she thought properly. "There's still a little bit of Charlotte left, then," Perdita observed.

Violetta grinned ruefully. "There must be." She put the tray down and returned to the bed. When Perdita patted the covers, she sat down on the bed, just as she had when she had been Charlotte, before a morning session. "Now we're equal. All debts paid."

"Agreed." The ladies shook hands, grinning. Violetta felt a new friendship beginning, and the thought warmed her. She'd had friends before, but had been forced to leave them behind. She counted some of the ladies who visited her mother's salon as friends, but she would be unable to visit them any longer. "Why did you do it? If it had gone wrong it could have been you involved in the scandal. It might still be you."

"No, it won't." Perdita seemed in her element. "Mama won't let it."

"What about Lady Ripley?"

"She's tainted her own reputation by all the lovers she's taken. She's not at all discreet, you know." Perdita leaned back, the frothy lace of the little caraco jacket she wore spilling over the fine skin of her arms. "My mama says Lady Ripley has decided to go with Judith. They're to live in another house."

Violetta toyed with the soft quilt. "I feel guilty."

Perdita leaned forward and patted her hand. There were none of the overtones Lady Judith always put into such a gesture. Just simple friendship. "Don't. Judith finally told me today that she loves me. I was appalled at her lack of feeling for Orlando, equally appalled that she thought I would enter into her schemes. She would have made Orlando deeply unhappy. I think you are good for him. I've watched you together."

"Thank you. I'll certainly do everything I can to make him happy."

"I know you will." Perdita leaned back against the pillows. "After you marry Orlando I'll go and stay with my mother and stepfather."

"Uncle Lodovico wants us to travel to Italy, to introduce Orlando to the family."

Perdita smiled. "You should go."

∞

It was agreed they should announce the formal betrothal in

the drawing room before dinner. Orlando had no opportunity to talk to Violetta in private. The conte proved a far more effective duenna than Lady Taversall, squiring his niece everywhere once she emerged from Perdita's room, insisting on viewing the gardens, anxious, as he put it, to reacquaint himself with his beautiful niece.

Orlando spent the rest of the day grinding his teeth in frustration and trying to outwit Violetta's keepers. He didn't succeed. He hoped she would be able to receive him that night. He had no intention of spending any more nights alone.

The announcement of the betrothal was greeted with backslapping and so many toasts Orlando feared the evening would never end. What soothed the beast snarling inside him was knowing he wouldn't have to hide any longer, could show his devotion to his love openly. Violetta greeted the congratulations with soft blushes and thanks, the vision of the virgin bride. Only a very select few knew any different.

Orlando couldn't approach Violetta until nearly midnight, and by then she was in bed. He stood over the bed, having negotiated the quiet corridors and his fears her maid might have been stationed in her room. The conte was awake on every suit.

He watched her sleep and was about to turn and leave when she stirred and opened her eyes, gazing up at him as though she expected him to be there. He smiled back and balanced one knee on the bed so he could lean forward to kiss her. She stretched up to embrace him but he drew back. "You're exhausted. Go back to sleep."

"If you join me." Her voice was breathy.

He couldn't resist. He drew back the covers, flung off his robe and slid into bed, drawing her into his arms. "Your uncle will call me out if he knows I'm here."

"I'm sure he knows. He told me he would like to see us marry before he leaves and he can't stay long. My aunt is due to be confined soon."

"He's married? He didn't say. All his conversation was about you and your mother."

"He's been married for fifteen years. He has three sons and two daughters." She yawned, her mouth against his shoulder and took the opportunity to kiss him.

He chuckled and pressed an answering kiss to her forehead. "I was a fool to think I could ever give this up. I want to be with you and watch our children grow." He'd said it on purpose.

Violetta stared at him, her eyes shadowed in the gloom. Orlando had left the single candle he'd brought with him on the nightstand, knowing he might need some light. He was glad now, as he saw the spark of hope dawn in her eyes. It was beautiful, the most beautiful thing he had ever seen. "I'm going to London tomorrow, to get a special license."

"Oh, Orlando!" She flung herself into his arms, tears of joy wetting his shoulder. "I'm only just realizing what all this means!"

Never was a celebration so sweet, so fervent. He loved her, holding nothing back until he was fully sheathed within her. "We have everything. I want you, and I want you quickly. Mine now." His greedy gaze roamed her form, laid out beneath him. "No more nights apart. I'm going to London in the morning and I'll do my damnedest to return by nightfall. We can be married the day after that."

"There'll be gossip."

He laughed. "Not when they know the extent of my devotion to you."

He gave her no more time to demur, but drove hard inside her, revelling in her hot welcome. She opened before him, submitted so he could bring himself to her, his essence. Everything he was, everything he had he bestowed on her.

She accepted it as her due, as a queen should. She took and gave in return, driving him to further efforts. He lost any sense of time passing, lost awareness of everything but her. Nothing else mattered. Only this.

Afterwards, both fell into a profound slumber, locked in each other's arms.

ॐ

Her wedding day. Violetta found it hard to believe, however

much she repeated it. She sat in the chair before her dressing table and watched Lisette arrange her hair into thick coils, nestling close to her head. Orlando had been as good as his word, taking a letter from her to La Perla with him to London when he went for the special license. He'd returned too late for dinner, but early enough to slip into bed by her side and hold her close through the night. He'd refused to make love to her, reminding her with a chuckle that the wait would be worthwhile. Violetta was sure it would be. He'd gone by the time she awoke in the morning.

Not so her maid and Lady Taversall, who bustled in full of excitement. Violetta let them adorn her, let them decorate her, and once she was dressed and ready, they left her.

Violetta didn't know how it happened but suddenly she was alone. Sitting in her glory, completely alone. She appreciated her godmother's sensitivity in giving her a few moments to herself.

The door opened and a solitary figure entered the room. Violetta couldn't believe her eyes, but leapt to her feet. "Mama!"

"Sh!" La Perla cautioned her, closing the door hastily. "You think I would let Blyth come on his own? He brought me back with him yesterday and I slipped away before we reached the house."

Violetta flung herself into her mother's arms, tears blurring her vision. "I'm so glad! Will you be there to see me married?"

"Of course. I will be at the back with the servants."

"You should be at the front, in the place of honour!"

"Hush, my love. That is not possible. It is enough that I am here. I could not be happier. I know Lord Blyth will care for you."

La Perla drew off, held her daughter at arm's length. "You have what I always dreamed of for you. A husband who adores you, a man to care for you. You will be happy, Violetta. We cannot see each other in public again, but we will find a way."

"Yes, Mama. Thank you." Violetta could say no more. She meant every word.

Her wedding passed in a blur. She was in and out of the chapel at Ripley Court before she realized what was going on.

She found herself on the arm of Lord Ripley, going up the aisle and on the arm of Lord Blyth, coming back. Her husband.

He didn't let her away from his side all day.

Chapter Twenty-two

London, Autumn 1754

"Home!"

Without waiting for the steps of the travelling coach to be let down, Orlando leaped down, then lifted his wife into his arms and turned for the house. Italy had been quite an experience, but he was glad to have her back home. They'd set out as soon as they knew she'd fallen pregnant, so she could travel in no danger.

"Soon I'll be too heavy for you to do this." Her face showed only joy, unshadowed by any worry.

He laughed in return and carried her over the threshold of his London house, not setting her down, despite her laughing protests until they were in the hall. "It's tradition," he informed her loftily. He turned to confront the butler, who had cracked his face with a small smile, the first Orlando had ever seen on him. "I've brought my bride home," he told him, setting Violetta carefully down on her feet. "Could you have tea brought up to the small drawing room?"

Taking her hand he led her upstairs. "Your domain, my sweet. Your home."

"So long as you are here."

"Always."

The idyll was not to last as long as they wanted. News travelled fast and the morning brought Lady Taversall and Lady Perdita.

Violetta poured tea and listened to her husband telling his mother of their experiences with her relatives. It had been no surprise that she had been welcomed into the bosom of her family now she could show them her fine, prosperous, respectable husband. She couldn't cavil because it made him happy to see her welcomed, and what made him happy made her happy.

She saw a shadow cross Lady Taversall's face. Trouble. "There's something wrong, isn't there?"

"Yes, my dear, I'm afraid there is."

Lady Taversall could say no more, even though it was clear she was preparing herself to relate unpleasant news. A commotion downstairs made them look around. The door burst open to admit La Perla, finely gowned. She threw back her veil, ignoring Lady Perdita's gasp of recognition.

Violetta got to her feet and threw herself at La Perla. "Mama!"

"So it's true then."

At Lady Perdita's quiet words Violetta drew back. "What is true?"

"You are La Perla Perfetta. Judith was right."

"Not about everything," Lady Taversall said. "Listen this time, Perdita."

She proceeded to tell Perdita all Violetta's story, in admirable economy of detail. The others listened. Orlando put his hand on Violetta's sleeve and led her to a sofa where she sat with her mother. He stood behind her, one hand on her shoulder. She was never so glad of his presence, when her mother's presence filled her with trepidation.

"All you need to remember, Perdita, is that Violetta is a member of our family now. What hurts her hurts the rest of us," Lady Taversall concluded.

The hand on Violetta's shoulder tightened. "What could hurt her?"

Lady Taversall turned a glacial stare onto her son. The ice was not for him. "Lady Ripley is living separately from her husband. The break has become public. She has been spreading the word that Violetta is La Perla Perfetta. She recognized her from a night you spent at the opera. Everyone in London knows."

Violetta clapped a hand over her open mouth. "Oh God!"

"It doesn't matter." Orlando's voice was harder than she'd heard it for months. "We'll weather it. We won't be spending much time in London in any case."

"It will damage your family, your reputation, everything!"

Lady Perdita's blue stare met Violetta's. "If she succeeds, it might have been better if you'd left me in that chair."

"No!" Orlando's hand eased, stroked. Violetta felt herself relax into the caress. "Is there anything that can be done?"

La Perla covered her daughter's hand with her own and squeezed. "I wouldn't be here if the case were impossible. Virginia, unthaw if you please. We have work to do."

Seeing Lady Perdita's appalled gaze, first to her mother, then to La Perla, Lady Taversall snapped, "Oh don't be a fool, Perdita! Violetta only came to you because I confided my worries in her mother. We've known each other for years!"

Perdita subsided. Violetta gave her a small smile. "She really is my godmother. I really am the daughter of the Conte d'Oro. I was also La Perla Perfetta for some years."

Perdita met her gaze. "Yes. Did you have much to say about it?"

Violetta smiled again and shrugged. "We play the cards we are dealt."

For the first time Perdita smiled. "You have the right of that."

They laid their plans carefully.

ॐ

The following evening Lord Blyth and his new countess made their first appearance in society since their marriage in the summer. He took her to the opera. Violetta was exquisite in lavender silk and ivory lace, her dark hair gleaming and unpowdered. Outwardly calm, she was a bundle of nerves inside. Orlando gave her a reassuring smile. "What can go wrong, if those ladies are on to it?"

Lady Taversall and Perdita sat behind, symbols of the

family acceptance. Corin had promised to join them for the next act, when he was clear of an unavoidable engagement.

No one took any notice of the action on the stage. The performers did their best, but there was a far better performance in the Blyth box. Violetta sat proudly, knowing everyone was assessing her, judging her. She would have had a better chance in the courts, except that everything they were thinking was true. She saw Lady Judith and her mother in their box and knew she didn't imagine the malicious smile on their faces. Revenge for mother and daughter.

Violetta knew she would not be able to take much more, but she must. For Orlando's sake, for the sake of her new family, she must go through with this. "After this," she murmured to Orlando, "I want to leave London."

"So do I," he replied, his calm face not revealing the turmoil she knew he felt inside. "Forever, if I had my way."

"Not before you attend our ball next week, after Violetta's presentation," his mother said from behind them. "That will set the seal on it. After that, you may go where you wish."

Orlando heaved a sigh. "I want her cared for, without worry, especially at this time."

"Then be patient, my son. Not a trait you are famous for, but perhaps you can try to develop it now."

A light came on in the box opposite. A footman lit the candles in the sconces. Everyone knew whom that box belonged to, and everybody waited.

Into the box stepped La Perla, Lord Ripley close behind her. Neither gave the Blyth box a glance. After them stepped a masked figure in white. The mask was a confection of white peacock feathers, the gown a froth of white brilliants and shining satin. Behind the younger woman, a male figure entered the box.

"The crafty—!" Orlando exclaimed. Corin, Viscount Elston, entered the box and settled the vision in white. Lady Taversall's rich chuckle could only be heard in the box. "A nice touch," she murmured.

Elston looked straight at Blyth and tipped his hat to him. Blyth, as was only proper, didn't return the salute.

"I thought La Perla Perfetta had unmasked?" he said.

"She may choose only to unmask for her lovers," Violetta said. "It's what I would do. Keep the mystery going as long as I could."

He squeezed her hand. "You do, my love. You don't need a mask for that."

The tenor of the gossip changed, like a tide turning. It was almost tangible. The murmurs almost drowned out the action onstage. The actors raised their voices to compensate, but it was to no avail. Chatter turned to laughter, not orchestrated, as it might have been by a skilled performer, but sporadic, turned onto the Ripley box. Lady Ripley and her daughter sat as though they had pokers strapped to their backs. Red hot ones from the way they were shifting. Suddenly they became interested in the play.

Violetta almost slumped with relief. It had worked, just as Lady Taversall and La Perla had said it would. The simultaneous appearance of La Perla Perfetta and the new Lady Blyth at the same function, one of the few places where they could be seen together, had succeeded. The ton, loath to believe the worst of one of its favourite sons, but thirsty for gossip, had turned its speculation to the Ripleys. It was obvious why they had spread such wicked gossip. It had been well known that Lady Judith had determinedly set her cap at Lord Blyth until he had met, courted and married Violetta Palagio in a breathtakingly short time. Lord Ripley had been devoted to the notorious courtesan La Perla forever. The attempt at gossip was scotched.

❦

The next morning Violetta received an entirely unexpected missive. It was brought up to her where she sat, luxuriating in bed over chocolate and hot buttered toast, morning sickness having never reared its ugly head in her pregnancy.

Orlando found her ten minutes later. Freshly washed and shaved, but not yet dressed, he slipped off his robe and got into bed beside her, after putting aside her tray. He knew, from her expression that she needed him. "What is it, love?"

Wordlessly she handed him the letter. Spreading it out he

began to read.

"My dearest daughter.

"We have not told anyone until now, so you are the first to know. Lord Ripley has persuaded me to retire. He has made preparations carefully, and after our triumph of last night there is nothing more I can do. Nothing more I wish to do.

"We are leaving. We will live in Lombardy, near enough to my family to be able to visit, not close enough to embarrass them. It is too much to hope that we are not recognized but we are together and it is more than either of us needs. You will be safe with Lord Blyth. He loves you dearly and will care for you now.

"The woman Isabella, who appeared as La Perla Perfetta last night, will claim that title permanently. She posed as you earlier in the year as a favour to me, but the lord who had her in his keeping has now passed on to someone else, leaving her with a comfortable annuity to spend. I have sold her the London house, and she may do as she wishes with it. She says she is honoured to be given such an opportunity and will continue as I would wish. I wish her luck. She is a talented woman and will go far.

"I will send you my address when I know it. I trust him, I love him and finally he has me all to himself. He has done enough and so have I. We wish only for peace and each other.

"I may allow myself a small visit to England after your happy event, next spring. Until then, cara, keep safe. I shall write."

She had signed it with a flourish. "Donata Palagio."

No more La Perla.

Orlando put the letter aside safely on the nightstand. He knew she would treasure this note. "At last."

"It's what they wanted. To be alone, together. I could almost feel sorry for Lady Ripley and her daughter."

He covered her hand with his own, brought it up to his mouth for a kiss. "Don't. They'll manage." He didn't say it served them right, although the words hung heavily between them. He moved closer to her, wrapped his arms about her lightly clad body. "No more masks, my love."

"Yes." She could show him everything she was, without

stint and he would still love her. "No more masks."

His smile warmed her heart. "I think you need to rest today. I want to take you to my home soon. My real home in the country."

"Home." She breathed the word. "I've never had one of those before. It sounds good."

He rolled over her and took her mouth in a heated kiss before drawing back. "It is good. It will be better."

About the Author

To learn more about Lynne Connolly, please visit www.lynneconnolly.com. Send an email to Lynne Connolly at lynne_connolly@yahoo.co.uk or join her Yahoo! group to join in the fun with other readers as well as Lynne! http://groups.yahoo.com/group/lynneconnolly

They say that love is blind...too bad it's not, it sure would help.

Lady Strumpet
© *2007 Gia Dawn*

Return again to Westmyre in this second installation of the Demons of Dunmore series.

When the elegant architect Wynn meets Lady Jane Seville—ex-tavern wench and trollop—they clash like the outrageous colors of her clothes, her temper and fiery passion sending him to realms of frustrated arousal he has never known before.

The stakes are high. The king has promised Wynn the position of Lord High Mason...but only if he can marry Jane and gain her newly restored title. Jane, however, is jaded by a lifetime spent on the fringes of society, and is unwilling to reclaim her heritage due to the tragic circumstances of her past.

Wynn has issues of his own. Born albhus, with no pigmentation in his skin or hair, he has spent his entire life climbing the ranks of his profession in order to fit in and be accepted by the upper-class elite. Jane has no such intentions.

Can these two opposites learn to love?

Available now in ebook from Samhain Publishing.

What if you're in love—but you can't make love?

Last Chance, My Love

© 2007 Lynne Connolly

Book One of the Triple Countess series.

Miranda and Daniel, Earl and Countess of Rosington, are in love, but for the past five years their love has been purely platonic. Because if Miranda has another child, she will die.

Daniel resolves to take a mistress, one who will understand the purely physical business arrangement, but when Miranda discovers his plan, she can't bear it. So Daniel's brothers scheme, and Daniel finds himself on the losing end of a wager.

Daniel and Miranda must pose as a simple innkeeper and his wife, forced to work together to save a failing business. Their masquerade brings them into temptation, their searing desire for each other threatening to ruin their good intentions, but it also brings danger, in the presence of the brutal father of a young girl who turns for them for help.

Can Daniel and Miranda save themselves, their protégée and their marriage?

Available now in ebook and print from Samhain Publishing.

GET IT NOW

MyBookStoreAndMore.com
GREAT EBOOKS, GREAT DEALS . . . AND MORE!

Don't wait to run to the bookstore down the street, or
waste time shopping online at one of the "big boys." Now,
all your favorite Samhain authors are all in one place—at
MyBookStoreAndMore.com. Stop by today and discover
great deals on Samhain—and a whole lot more!

GREAT
CHEAP
FUN

Discover eBooks!

THE FASTEST WAY TO GET THE HOTTEST NAMES

Get your favorite authors on your favorite reader, long before they're
out in print! Ebooks from Samhain go wherever you go, and work with
whatever you carry—Palm, PDF, Mobi, and more.

Samhain Publishing Ltd

WWW.SAMHAINPUBLISHING.COM

CPSIA information can be obtained at www.ICGtesting.com
Printed in the USA
238001LV00002B/3/P